Stephen Stromp
In the Graveyard
ANTEMORTEM

stephenstromp.com

W.O.P. Press

In the Graveyard Antemortem

Published by W.O.P. Press

ISBN: 978-0692717899

Cover designed by Damonza

Contents

∞∞∞∞∞∞∞∞∞∞∞∞∞∞∞∞∞∞∞∞∞∞∞∞∞∞∞

Part I

Part II

Part I

Chapter 1

Hollowed Heart

It happened when I was seventeen. It was the beginning of summer in 1985. That morning, I stood clutching my backpack under the service garage awning, waiting for my best friend, Tina, to pick me up for school. A red car with a black stripe down its hood suddenly pulled into the dusty gravel gas station lot. I knew all the cars in Ruthsford. And I hadn't seen that one before. It looked too new, too expensive, for our small town. As the strange car pulled beside me, I wondered just who was behind the wheel. But when the sun struck her teased blonde hair and bright red lipstick, there was no question.

"Killer, huh?" asked Tina as she lowered the passenger-side window, grinning in delight.

"Oh my God! It's so great!" I shouted as I climbed inside. "What kind of car is this?"

"You're kidding, right?" she scoffed. "Lisa! It's a freakin' Mustang!"

"How can you afford a Mustang?"

"Well, it's not like I paid for it myself. My parents got it for me. You know, for my birthday."

"First of all, you are so lucky. And second of all, I am so sorry!" I cringed. "I totally forgot today was your birthday. But I'll make it up to you. I swear."

"No biggie. And don't worry. You'll never forget *this* birthday after the big bash I'm throwin' this weekend."

"Shit. I wish you would've told me sooner. I don't think I can go," I moaned. "I promised my dad I'd help him out with the shifts this weekend."

"C'mon," she scolded. "Don't let this hellhole run your life."

"Don't call it that," I warned as I saw my dad emerge from the garage.

He wore a pristine pair of coveralls, which would no doubt be covered in grease by the middle of the morning. He made his way toward the car, wearing that weird grin he got whenever he was around vehicles that impressed him. "I thought I heard a set of wheels pull up that sounded a bit more Christina's speed," he joked.

"Yup. I'm finally free of the 'Blue Bomb,'" she happily announced, referring to her mom's hand-me-down robin's-egg-blue Buick LeSabre.

"Four- or six-cylinder?" he asked.

Tina shrugged. "Hell if I know." I jabbed her with my elbow.

"May I?" he asked, gesturing to the hood. Tina fumbled for the lever before finally popping it open. "Yup. There they are. Six bangers," he announced before gently dropping the hood back down. "Now, Christina, be sure to drive carefully. Remember, you still only have a learner's permit. And you're carrying precious cargo," he said, turning to me with a wink.

"Don't worry, Mr. Jacobs. I'll get Lisa to school safe. But more importantly—on time!" With that, she sped out of the lot with her foot heavy on the pedal. The tires kicked up gravel, spitting the tiny rocks high into the air. And when the car grabbed the pavement, the tires squealed, creating a small cloud of smoke from the burned rubber.

"Tina!" I shouted. "I can't believe you just did that!"

"Relax. Your dad likes me," she said flippantly as she pushed in the cigarette lighter and then fumbled through her purse for a cigarette.

The strangest thing was that there wasn't anything strange about that day at all. *We never suspected a thing. It was an ordinary day. A day like any other.* Those were the types of things victims' families would say on all those true crime shows when asked to look back to the day of a tragedy. It always seemed like such a cliché. But that day, it truly *was* ordinary.

Tina dropped me off after school. I stopped by the vending machine beside the service garage for a can of orange pop. Nothing seemed out of place as I entered the house and dropped my backpack on the kitchen table. I was hungry. "Dad!" I yelled. He hadn't started dinner, so I wanted to see if I should start something myself. I listened for a moment. He did not answer. The house was silent. So I assumed he was still working in the garage.

I headed across the yard and made my way toward the service station. I knew he was home because his pickup was in the drive. I jerked the side door of the garage open. The lights were off, but I yelled inside anyway. "Dad?" I called, wondering where he could be. Perhaps he was in the backyard? I ran out to the garden. The tall sunflowers bobbed gently in the breeze, their stems barely able to hold up their heavy heads. I cupped my hands around my mouth and called again beyond the garden and into the cornfield, which lined the backyard. Perplexed, but not alarmed, I headed back to the house.

Macaroni and cheese sounded good. So I put a large pot of water on the stove. While waiting for it to boil, the stillness of the house began to frighten me more than I thought it should have. It was strange. I was used to being alone. It was just that I also was used to our afternoon routine. Even if he had a large repair job to finish, he'd always take a break for dinner when I got home from school. And if he was working late, why the heck were the garage lights off?

With that nagging thought, I jolted once more across the yard. I stormed into the service station and flipped on the lights. The overhead fluorescents flickered and popped to life. In the first bay, a red-rusted pickup had been hoisted from the ceiling by a chain. The old truck was from another era. Its large, round, old-fashioned headlights resembled troubled eyes. It seemed sad and lonely strung up by its hindquarters in the dank garage.

"Dad?" I called again as I opened the door to his office. The small desk lamp was on. Keys and invoices were strewn about the desk. But where was he? I noticed his chair was missing. Odd. I rounded the dangling relic of a pickup and stepped into the second bay.

And there, in the middle of the garage floor, my father sat in his office chair. I had told him a hundred times to get a more comfortable chair for his office. But the old wooden chair from his grandmother's farmhouse was as much of a tradition with him as was the old painted sign welcoming the townsfolk to the "Ruthsford Gas & Service Station."

He sat with his back to me, the chair facing the large bay door. His arms hung loose at his sides. It was peculiar, his sitting so still in the garage. "Why are you out here? And why were you sitting in the dark?" I asked, beginning to feel a tinge of trepidation. He did not answer. He did not move. "*Dad?*" I asked, as a seed of fear began to travel up my spine. Slowly, I approached him. "Are you OK?" I asked meekly. His stillness caused me to move forward with apprehension, wanting to delay the moment I would see his face. I struggled to hold onto my mind, which threatened to leave my body and flee to an alternate universe. As I finally rounded the chair, I brought my hand to my mouth. And then I froze. I did not scream. I did not move. I simply recorded what I saw in a numb state of trauma.

His jaw was slack. His mouth wide open. He wore no shirt. His chest and torso—they had been split open. There was a deep vertical cut from the top of his chest all the way down to just above his stomach. And there was a horizontal cut straight across his upper chest. Flaps of skin hung where the cuts intersected.

Even in my state of paralysis, and beyond the fact that it was evident my father had not done this to himself, I realized something else was not right with the scene: there was no blood. The surgical-like incisions were dry. His face and body were so white, there seemed to be no blood in him at all. That is, except for the tiny bit that trickled down his arms from the puncture wounds in the creases of each elbow. The blood dripped down his arms and off his fingertips. It created tiny puddles on the garage floor, where it then streamed into the drain just below the chair.

I wasn't sure how long I stood there locked in that surreal abyss. Unable to move. To feel. To process what I was seeing. I didn't recall moving from the spot. But somehow, I had managed to make my way back to the office. I picked up the phone and dialed the Ruthsford Police Department. The number was by the phone. Not just because it made sense to have it handy, but because the police department was our largest account. "My dad. He's been—come to the gas station," I said simply.

I stared at the phone in a daze until I saw flashing red and blue lights through the windows that lined the top of the bay doors. I emerged from the garage like a zombie, nearly colliding with Sheriff Sternhardt, who stood in my path. Because Ruthsford was such a small town, I had known him all my life. His intimidating presence always made me feel tense, sick to my stomach. Everyone at school agreed that his name, aptly pronounced "Stern Heart," matched his reputation, especially after his notorious locker searches put several small-time high school drug dealers out of business.

Even though our interactions were rare, because of the police department's account with the station I'd see him often. He'd simply refuel without visiting the cashier's window, expecting the unpaid transactions to be recorded and billed monthly to the department. It made it difficult to know if anyone was in fact stealing gas when no one was watching. If someone was, the ironic thing was that it was being paid for by the Ruthsford Police Department.

"Got a call from dispatch," he said. "What's this about, Lisa?"

I didn't hear his words. I could only focus on his thick beard and mustache, which had been half-overtaken by patches of gray. "My dad—" was all I managed as a response.

"I already told your dad he's chargin' too much for his damn gas. I've been talkin' to a station in Sharlaton. They'll give us close to wholesale. Sure, it's a farther drive. But it would still sure as hell beat his prices. We're gettin' gouged!"

My arm felt heavy and weak as I lifted it and pointed to the garage door. "Please," I begged. "My dad. He's in there. He's been—murdered," I said at once, struggling to believe the reality of my own words. And as his jaw became slightly askew with his own measure of disbelief, I immediately turned from him and began my slow shuffle toward the house. At that moment, I didn't worry whether my numbness could be mistaken for calmness.

By that time, the pot of water had turned into a mad boil. I had completely forgotten about the macaroni and cheese and the gas burner. The thought of food itself seemed plainly odd, like it was the least important thing on the planet. I methodically turned the knob and removed the pot from the burner. Then the silence came. It permeated the house like an invisible invader, a quiet stillness that brought with it a perplexing, deafening hum. I gripped the countertop and braced against it as if a strong wave were crashing into me. And then I looked to the yellow phone hanging from the wall near the kitchen table. Its long, tangled cord just about reached the floor. I leaped for it as if I were in deep water and it were a life preserver. Immediately, I dialed Tina.

Typical Tina, she answered after a half ring. Thank God. "Hey, Tina," I said attempting to sound as normal as possible. "What're you up to?"

"Whattaya think, dipshit?" she said followed by a mock snorting laugh. "My party. Now if I make it a pool party, we can see if Mark Kheller's chest is as hairy as everyone says. Will that be enough to get you to ditch that dump on Saturday?"

"My dad is dead," I blurted.

"Whoa. What the hell are you talkin' about?"

"Murdered."

She didn't say anything for the longest while. The silence once again began to creep from the far corners of the house and surround me like an eerie blanket. "Tina! Say something!" I screamed.

"I'm comin' over," she said. "Stay right there."

"No. Don't hang up," I pleaded. "What am I supposed to do?"

"Did you call the police?"

"Yes. Sternhardt's here. In the garage. With my dad."

"OK then. Call Richard. Have you called Richard?"

"No."

"Just call Richard. And I will be there before you know it."

"OK." I took a deep breath. "OK."

Richard. How could Tina have been the one to think of calling Richard and I hadn't? His own sister? I clenched the receiver and dialed, not knowing how I would have the strength to tell him about Dad. He picked up on the fifth ring but did not say a word. "Richard?"

"What is this? I just got to sleep."

"It's Lisa."

"I know who it is."

"Why are you sleeping? It's not even five o'clock."

"I'm tired. That's why. What do you want?" he said, dismissing me as he often did in those days.

"It's Dad. Will you come to the house?"

"Shit, Lisa. I told him I don't have his money yet. I'm working on it, OK? Just tell him to back off for a damn minute."

"He's dead, Richard," I declared.

As soon as I had laid those words on him, the door burst open. My body jolted in shock as Sternhardt rushed into the room, his voice booming at the top of his lungs. "Did I tell you to move from where you were standing, missy! This is an active crime scene! Move back onto the driveway! If you deviate from that spot, I will hold you in my squad car. Do you understand?"

As instructed, I dropped the phone and rushed back to the driveway with Sternhardt close behind. We were met with two more squad cars and an ambulance. Two officers met with Sternhardt, and he directed them to the garage. A man in plainclothes emerged from another squad car and every few steps started taking pictures with a large camera. As he passed me, my limbs trembling, he took a shot of my bewildered face. The giant flash blinded me for several moments. When I regained my vision, Sternhardt's face was inches from mine. As he began to speak, I focused again on the gray and black whiskers that peppered his upper lip.

"Now I need you to retrace your actions, *specifically,* from the moment you got home to the moment you called the police."

As I began to recall my story about being hungry for macaroni and cheese, I saw Tina's blonde hair bobbing toward the station. Immediately, I threw up my hand. "Tina!" I shouted. "Over here!"

"For Christ's sake, Miss Jacobs!" shouted a perturbed Sternhardt. "Is this who you were telephoning?"

"Yes," I answered meekly as Tina gave me a hug.

"I can't believe it. What happened to your dad?" she asked.

Sternhardt cleared his throat, annoyed. "*I'm* the one asking the questions here, young lady. Now go back where you came from. I'm sure Miss Jacobs will call you when it's all over."

Tina folded her arms and defiantly took a step forward. "Sternhardt? Really? They sent you? Finding who did this isn't exactly going to be like finding Quaaludes in a high schooler's locker. Are you sure you're up to it?"

"Tina!" I begged. "Please. I need him to find out what happened." Tina retreated by taking a few steps back but kept her arms crossed and her glare squarely on the sheriff.

Then began the onslaught of questions: "Had your father been acting strangely the last few days? Have there been any changes in his schedule recently? Had anyone strange been hanging around the station? Do you know of anyone who may have wanted to harm him? Did anyone owe him money? Did he owe anyone money?"

But I knew my answers were of no help. I had noticed no strangers lurking about. He hadn't owed anyone money as far as I knew. And the only outstanding debt owed to him, aside from what I guessed was a small amount from Richard, was a few unpaid bills by Ruthsford's very own police department.

Just as he finished his questioning, a stretcher emerged from the garage door. I wanted to avert my eyes but couldn't as it rolled past, my father under the sheet. Tina spun me toward the house. "Oh, Miss Jacobs?" Sternhardt asked. "One more question." I turned back to face him, catching a glimpse of my father being loaded into the ambulance out of the corner of my eye. "What about your brother?"

"What about him?"

"Can you think of any reason he would have to cause harm to your father?" I was startled by the thought, too startled to even answer his question. "I will have to track him down, you understand," he said, tipping the brim of his hat.

"I spoke with him," I offered simply.

"When?"

"Tonight. In the kitchen. After I called Tina."

"So you know his whereabouts?"

"Yes, but I'm sure, after our phone call, he'll be over here soon."

"Excellent, Miss Jacobs, because I'll want to question him, naturally."

"*Naturally*," Tina blurted with sarcasm.

"And then you can ride back with him—to wherever he lives nowadays," he continued.

"Why would I go to his place?" I asked. "I'm fine staying right here."

"Not gonna happen, young lady. This will be a crime scene for quite some time. You can't stay here. Besides, you're under eighteen, are you not?"

"Eighteen at the end of August."

"Well *eighteen at the end of August* means you are still a minor. And that means you cannot legally live on your own. So it's either live with your brother for now. Another relative. Or you can come down to the station and—"

"She's staying with me!" Tina interrupted and grabbed my arm. She began pulling me down the driveway toward her Mustang, parked beyond the cruisers.

"I'll need the address and phone number to where you'll be staying so you can be reached for further questioning. And any temporary guardians will need to fill out the proper forms!" he called after us.

"You know where I live!" Tina shot back. "*Everyone* knows where I live," she muttered under her breath.

Chapter 2

The Grant Mansion

For being best friends, Tina and I surely were different. She had moved to Ruthsford my freshman year. I was amazed how quickly—and boldly—she had asserted herself into the Ruthsford high school scene. She had easily made her way into the most popular group. But she was also indifferent to their acceptance. Case in point, she had chosen *me*, not one of them, to be her best friend. I realized it was pathetic to think I had been *chosen* by Tina, but she really *had* had a choice. She could've had anybody for her best friend. When I asked her why she liked hanging out with me, she quickly explained that it was "because you're not a fake." She appreciated authenticity, no matter how beautiful, mundane, or ugly. She gravitated toward it.

In many ways, Christina, whom I exclusively called *Tina*, was my antithesis. She was blonde. I had shoulder-length, auburn hair.

She was popular. In most situations, I tended to be the wallflower. I didn't consider myself particularly shy, but I didn't exactly blurt out all my inner thoughts and feelings either.

She was pretty and asserted her beauty through her clothes and makeup. I never wore makeup or styled my hair much. Perhaps it was because I had lost my mother at a young age and lived only with guys: my older brother, Richard, and my father. I didn't know the first thing about how to apply makeup without looking like a clown. Luckily, I didn't really have the interest. I told myself my style was *natural*, and that's what I was comfortable with.

I lived in a small cottage house behind my father's gas station, where the awful lime green paint was peeling off the siding. Her family had moved into the old Grant Mansion, which sat atop a hill behind iron gates and down a long, twisting driveway.

If I had been a particularly envious person, I would've been envious of Tina, but not for her grand living. Aside from being the largest, most lavish property in Ruthsford, it also came with a tragic history.

The mansion had been built by Frank and Loretta Grant. They had owned the only upscale restaurant in town, The Silver Dollar. Loretta had managed the staff and had been notorious for firing help on a whim if they had not completed tasks to her satisfaction. She had been particularly obsessed with the wine glasses. The story went that she made the waitstaff wash the wine glasses by hand. She would then personally inspect each by holding it to the light. Sometimes, a single glass was washed and dried a hundred times before she was satisfied.

When Mrs. Grant finally had had enough of the restaurant business, she left the day-to-day management to her more reasonable husband. The staff, and even many a patron, cheered. Yet without Loretta's keen management style, their business began to deteriorate. Still, Mr. Grant worked day and night attempting to keep the doors open. In those years, Loretta became a recluse. And without the sums of money coming in that they used to enjoy, their yard became overgrown—and overrun with cats. The neighborhood children assumed she was a witch, as they'd sometimes catch sight of the old woman on the front porch at dusk, dressed in fancy frocks simply to feed the neighborhood strays. That is, until one day, Loretta Grant was seen no more. The town was shocked to learn she had hanged herself in the mansion.

Frank Grant remained in the mansion alone for the years following his wife's suicide. And after his death, the property stayed on the market for several years—until Tina's family moved to town. During the years when the property sat vacant, there had been rumors of ghosts. Folks claimed they saw lights turning on and off in the empty mansion. And there were even sightings of old Mrs. Grant herself moving by the windows at night.

When I first told her the story of Loretta Grant's suicide and about the rumors of a haunting, Tina was not fazed. "No biggie," she simply replied. "My parents are totally renovating."

As the Mustang's headlights flashed by the iron gates, I began to wonder which was more unsettling—staying in my best friend's haunted mansion or taking my chances at my own house with a killer on the loose. Only so I wouldn't cry, I laughed to myself about those options. Just a bit.

Tina's parents greeted us at the door with an awkward mix of shock and sorrow plastered across their faces. Her mom nervously clenched a can of Diet Coke while her father stood with his arm stretched across her shoulders. They looked like some kind of odd, Day-Glo-clad ambassadors of the Grant Mansion—she in her graffiti top and fluorescent pink shorts, and he, the more conservative of the two, in his turquoise polo and khakis. "We are so sorry, Lisa. Well, I just don't know what to say. Can you believe it, Christina? *Me*, finally speechless," said her mother as Tina rolled her eyes.

"Whatever you need," her father said, taking over, "just let us know. You're like a second daughter to us, Lisa."

"What she *needs* is a place to stay. She can stay as long as she wants, right?" Tina brazenly asked.

"Of course," her mother answered sympathetically. "Of course!" she repeated with added zeal after catching one of Tina's *do-it-or-die* glares.

"As long as she needs," her father affirmed as her mother lightly patted my back.

With their uncomfortable condolences out of the way, we made our way up the winding marble staircase to Tina's palatial room. The marble flooring carried into her room, where sheer drapes gently swayed in the breeze in front of floor-to-ceiling windows. It made me feel as if I were in a Mediterranean castle. As if I'd just have to look out the window, and I'd see a bright sapphire sea. But my fantasy was dashed as a distant flash of lightning easily penetrated the thin drapery. The winds began to pick up and blow cool night air into the room. I peered into the infinite blackness outside. It was dark. And it was terrifying. Even with Tina there, I felt alone.

"Lisa?" Tina's voice called my attention back into the room. She sat at the edge of the bed. She had lit a cigarette, which I was sure wasn't allowed in the house. She motioned for me to join her while blowing smoke over her head, looking like some melodramatic movie star. "Sooo, if you don't wanna talk right now, we don't have to. But I need to know what you're thinkin'. Who the hell do you think did that to your dad? I mean, I'm completely freakin' out. So I can't even imagine what's goin' on with you."

"I honestly don't know who might've done it." Images of his face, his slacked jaw, and sunken eyes flashed through my mind. I began to sob uncontrollably. "And the worst part is, it didn't even look like him. He wasn't even there. Wasn't in his body. He was gone. And I never got to say good-bye."

"I'm so sorry." She gave me a hug. "I shouldn't have brought it up."

"It's OK," I said through the tears. I took a deep breath. "And you're right. I have to start figuring this out. There has to be an explanation. *Someone* did this to him. Someone has to pay!"

"Hell yeah, they do! And listen, you don't have to figure it out alone. I'm gonna help you find the fucker. We'll sure as hell do a lot better than

Deputy Dawg Sternhardt. Speaking of ol' Sternhardt, do ya think he got ahold of Richard?"

"Probably." I shrugged. "Even if he didn't show up at the house, he wouldn't be all that hard to track down."

"Yeah, but we *are* talking about Sternhardt here," she said with a chuckle. "Where's Richard livin' nowadays, anyhow?"

"With a couple roommates in an apartment over near Lanford."

"Do ya think you should try callin' him again? You know, to talk about what happened?"

Guilt seared into my gut in an instant. She was right. Our father had just been murdered, and I hadn't had a proper conversation with my brother about it. He had lost his father as well. He was sure to have been feeling just as alone and frightened as I was. I loved my brother, but we were at a point where even basic communication had deteriorated. I was struck by my own feelings. By my cold attitude toward him. I was afraid what it said about me—that my animosity could not even be broken by a death in our small family. "I will call him," I finally replied. "But I can't, Tina. Not tonight."

"OK now, Lisa. Don't get mad by what I'm about to say. But . . ." She spoke her words so slowly, as if she knew she shouldn't utter them but couldn't help them from escaping her mouth either: "Do. You. Think. Richard . . ."

"Tina! No!" I immediately dismissed her, knowing where the conversation was going.

"Shit! I'm sorry! I'm not sayin' I think he *did it*. I don't know. Maybe he was involved or somethin'. Or has some ideas who might've done it. I'm sorry! I'm just tryin' to think how this could've happened."

"Not a chance!"

"OK. But. He's been violent, Lisa! Hasn't he been violent? Towards you? Towards your dad?"

"That's enough, Tina! It wasn't Richard!"

Chapter 3

Bright as Yellow

Richard was handsome and popular. He had thick, black hair. He was naturally athletic, trim, and muscular. If he had been a year or two younger, I imagined he'd have been the type Tina would've gravitated toward. Like her, he did not bury his thoughts or feelings, even perhaps when he should've from time to time. He kept them on the surface, unhidden. He was who he was. He'd give you an honest answer. And before things started to take a dark turn for Richard, at least you knew you could trust his word. While it was true, I was never one to be very envious of others, I *was* envious of Richard for a couple of reasons.

Being three years older than me, he had an actual memory of our mother. I kept a *feeling* of her presence with me. But I never really understood where that feeling came from. As a feeling instead of a memory, it was not confined to a particular point in time noted in my mind. But rather, a particular essence. This feeling was genuine. But was it true? Did we really have some connection that transcended time and space? That transcended death?

When our cat, Jinx, was sick, I took note of all the times I saw movement out of the corner of my eye, those flashes of something whizzing through the room I swore were really there. I'd stop and tell myself that if I saw those same flashes of movement *after* Jinx died, I wouldn't allow myself to think it was his ghost hanging around the house.

Although the feeling of my mother never left my gut, I sometimes felt the same way about it as I did about the possibility of it really being Jinx, after death, zipping past the corner of my eye: wishful thinking. The idea that this feeling of connectedness was merely manufactured by my brain as a way to cope with her absence tortured me as a child. It was equivalent to an internal struggle of science versus faith. And when my faith was worn down and I began to think of Jinx, to give into my brain's logic, I would find comfort in having Richard recall his more tangible memories of our mother.

"Tell me about her again," I'd ask on more than one occasion.

"It's barely anything," he protested on one particular day as we sat on the porch watching a rainstorm flood the backyard. "It's just a vision, her with me in the yard. I don't even think you were born yet. It's weird. I remember colors more than anything. Green. Everything was green. Dark green grass. And I remember yellow." He motioned over the span of the yard. "Yellow dandelions were scattered all over. And it was sunny. So sunny that everything was blurry, like covered in a yellow haze. I had to squint into the rays of sun as I looked up to her. I don't remember her face. I can't see it anymore. It's fuzzy in my memory. Washed out. But I remember her hair. She had blonde hair, almost yellow. And her dress. She wore a bright yellow dress. That's all I remember."

"What about the necklace?"

"You already know about the damn necklace. Why do I have to repeat it?"

"Just tell me."

He groaned mockingly. "It was a long chain. And at the end of it was a large purple gem. It sparkled in the sun. It gave off purple rays of light," he said flicking his fingertips toward me with a grin. "That's it, Lisa."

"Do you remember when she died?"

Richard was silent for a moment. "I just knew something wasn't right."

"How did you know?"

"I remember seeing the back of her head and wanting her to come to me. She seemed so far away. But when she finally turned toward me, there was blood coming out of her mouth. It was bright red and dripping over her bottom lip and down her chin. That was the last time I saw her, my last memory of her anyway."

"Brain aneurysm." He nodded slowly in confirmation. The knowledge that her brain had simply ruptured without notice, resulting in a massive hemorrhage, had terrified me my entire life. The onset of the slightest headache sent me into an easy panic, as I imagined blood filling up the spaces between my brain and skull.

"I don't know," Richard continued. "Maybe all that blood coming from her mouth, maybe it wasn't real. Maybe it was just a dream. It's hard to tell, ya know?"

"Yeah, I know the feeling. Do you remember her funeral?"

"No. I try to sometimes. But nothing comes."

"I'm going to visit her grave," I said assuredly.

"What? In Florida?"

"One day," I promised. After her funeral, her body was shipped to Florida to be interred in her family's burial plot. I had quietly resented my dad for allowing it to happen. It only worsened the feeling that there was nothing *real* to connect me to her. Not even a grave site.

And the other reason I was envious of Richard while growing up was his relationship with our dad. Richard took an early interest in cars, so naturally he spent many hours helping Dad with the vehicle repair side of the business. It wasn't that I felt stuck in some subservient role. Dad and Richard would cook and clean for themselves; it was just that they were lousy at it. I wasn't much better than them with the cooking. The microwave, McDonald's, and Little Caesars were a few of our closest friends. But at least I knew when it was time to clean a toilet. And when the shower was loaded with soap scum and began to develop that dark brown ring, I was the one who got out the Comet and the rubber gloves. I didn't mind cleaning. At least I always felt like I had accomplished something afterward. There was satisfaction that came with gleaming surfaces and that clean, chemical smell.

But beyond taking it upon myself to make sure the house didn't become a pigsty, I also knew how to switch out pump hoses. And I could run the convenience store. I learned the cash register at an early age. I ordered the inventory, including the candy, which was the best because I'd order all my favorites: Atomic Fireballs, Sprees, and Strawberry Watermelon Hubba Bubba.

No, it wasn't the multiple hats I wore that made me at times resent my situation. It was just that, being the girl in our small family, I was the odd person out. Oftentimes I simply felt—alone.

Although I was not the type to fawn over cute guys in school, there was a particular one who I really wanted to get to know: Greg Michelson. I sat next to him in government class. He was in some alternative band. They called themselves Clam Fungus, of all things. He played the drums. Only he didn't use real drums, just household items like buckets and garbage can lids. I thought he was so cute, especially when he wore his glasses. I would let him cheat by reading my papers before I turned them in. He'd copy whole chunks, and the teacher never even noticed. One day, he gave me a tape of Clam Fungus's songs. They were so awful. Just a bunch of guys making noise and screaming into a microphone. But I treasured the tape as if it were a ring he had given me, knowing how important his music was to him.

When he finally asked me to go out with him, I wanted everything to be perfect. I wanted to be casual, but also differentiate my at-school self from my out-of-school self. And I decided the best way to accomplish this was to wear what I normally would wear so as not to appear as if I was trying too hard to impress, but to add something new to the mix: perfume.

So I headed to the drugstore and bought a large bottle of Exclamation! perfume. Never having worn perfume, I didn't bother to smell it. I figured they all smelled about the same, flowery and feminine. The bottle, with its chic black-and-white exclamation point design, sold me without a whiff. Before going to meet Greg at the Denny's restaurant in Lanford, I generously sprayed the stuff on my wrists and neck. Richard had agreed to drive me there. So as soon as I hopped in his car, I asked, "Do you like my perfume?" I allowed him a good whiff.

"No," he responded immediately, matter-of-factly, as if answering a grocery store clerk's question about "paper or plastic." I was temporarily disabled by his blunt reply. I glared at him dumbfounded. "Well, I don't," he reiterated.

Stunned and angry, I sat in the passenger seat fuming. *How dare he!* It may have just been a simple "paper or plastic" question to him. But he should've known his answer would hurt my feelings. Then again, I *did* ask his opinion. It wasn't his fault I didn't like the answer.

That was the thing about Richard. He was sometimes truthful to the point of not realizing he was being hurtful. At least that's how I described him to myself. And if he really *had* taken pleasure in knowing I would be tortured by his comment, already on edge as I was about to meet Greg outside of school for the very first time, then I would've had a very different opinion of my brother.

On the ride there, I rolled down the windows attempting to air out the perfume smell. And when we got to the parking lot at Denny's, before I dared leave the car, I reached for the beach towel in the backseat. I rubbed as much of the fragrance as I could off my wrists and neck. Damn Richard!

Chapter 4

'Roid Rage

Apparently my bold choice in perfume had not chased Greg off after all. A few months after our date at Denny's, Greg sat in the stands with Dad and me watching Richard wrestle. It meant a lot that he came, especially since I knew he would've rather been out in the parking lot skateboarding with his friends.

Richard had been wrestling since he was a freshman. Physically, he had changed quite a bit since then. He worked out almost every day in the school's weight room. He put on at least thirty pounds of muscle, continually increasing his weight class. In his wrestling singlet, he was quite an imposing figure. And he was quite good. I never paid much attention to his rankings or anything. But judging from his trophies and the number of opponents he had pinned, he was a force of nature.

"Seven wins, four pins, and zero losses," my dad proudly reminded us. At that point in the wrestling season, he was ranked the number one wrestler in his weight class. His opponent that night was Luke Palto, a freshman from Sharlaton. Not that it wasn't warranted with his opponent being younger and less experienced, but Richard's confidence was staggering. He wore it on his face.

As both the physically impressive young men shook hands on the mat, the announcer began, "There's Richard Jacobs, the regional champion last year at his weight class. And there's Luke Palto, a freshman at Sharlaton High. Now I remember when Jacobs was on the other end, a freshman like Palto is now. Back then, he was learning some lessons from more experienced wrestlers. And I have an idea that Palto will learn some lessons here tonight as well. Yes, folks, Jacobs, once a freshman wrestler and now the returning champion, is going up against a freshman. The circle is now complete."

They began to grapple as the announcer continued, "But Palto has been a strong performer, ranked eighth. He just needs a break. And taking down a standing champion would be just that," he said, followed by a boisterous laugh.

The crowd erupted as they tussled further and Richard got Luke in a neck hold, winning some immediate points. This happened several times during the first two periods. But Luke was able to hold steady for the most part against Richard's impressive moves.

Then, in the third period, something unexpected happened. Luke began demonstrating more offensive moves. Much to Richard's surprise, Luke got him caught in an underhook. The crowd stood on its feet and howled. "He's marching him to the edge of the mat!" cried the announcer. "Now this is getting interesting!" Luke's sudden burst of prowess infuriated Richard. Once he was free of the hold, he adjusted his headgear and bent down with his arms open. His face in a snarl of disdain. Determined to finish the fight.

They grabbed hold of one another yet again and were soon locked in another exhaustive dance. And as they were grappling, Richard dropped, for just a brief moment, onto his knees. In that instant, Luke saw an opportunity and tightly wrapped his arm around Richard's right leg and over his right shoulder. The crowd stood in anticipation as the announcer excitedly reported, "Palto's got him in a cradle! And it looks like a tight one!"

The next few moments were tense as Luke attempted to force Richard onto his back. He fought with all his strength as he was raked across the mat. He did a good job of keeping off his back. But Luke did an even better job of driving over Richard's stubborn elbow, which kept his back from touching the mat. And when his elbow finally toppled, so did Richard. "He's pinned!" shouted the announcer with a mix of glee and disbelief. "He drove him over! Stacked him high! And planted him right there! He pinned the regional champion! Must be that Sharlaton magic!"

The crowd cheered uncontrollably. Luke jumped up and down, wildly celebrating, his mouth wide open in his own disbelief. Richard looked like an angry bull watching Luke celebrate. He stood in furious defeat, waiting in humiliation to give Luke the sportsman's handshake. Luke's victory jumps soon had passed Richard's short level of tolerance. And like a coiled snake springing for a strike, he rushed Luke, shoving him with all his might. Luke fell outside the mat and onto the wooden gym floor. His shoulder hit the hard floor with a wince-inducing crack. Richard stood over Luke with his fists ready for battle as Luke clutched his shoulder, struggling to sit upright. A crowd began to quickly rush the floor. Along with the referee, it descended upon Richard.

We began making our way down the bleachers, but with the swarm surrounding Richard, I couldn't see where he was or what was happening. My dad, angry and embarrassed, charged across the gym. Greg and I were barely able to keep up as we snaked our way through the angry crowd. Dad immediately slipped into the car. Not even having a chance to say good-bye, I gave Greg a weak wave as we pulled away from the school. Too angry, Dad didn't say a word the entire ride.

At home, I nervously waited for Richard's arrival, anxious to see how my dad would handle him. It had not been the first time Richard's temper had gotten him in trouble. Just a few months earlier, he had punched a locker, breaking its hinge (and his hand) after arguing with his economics teacher over not accepting a late assignment. My dad was not generally a strict man, but his patience with Richard was being tested. I had the uneasy feeling that the sleeping giant within him was beginning to wake.

Even though the wrestling match was on a school night, Richard did not come home directly after it. Surely, he had punishment doled out to him by the school. But even so, he was not home by nine o'clock. When ten o'clock rolled around, I expected my dad to start calling around for him, but he did not. By eleven o'clock, I went to bed, leaving my dad alone in the living room, halfheartedly reading the newspaper as he waited up for Richard.

Sometime after midnight, I was jolted awake by the doorbell ringing and a loud pounding. I rushed to my bedroom window to see flashing lights in the driveway and Richard's car hoisted upon a tow truck. The front end had been demolished. Even with my door closed, I then heard that unmistakable stern voice that made me sick to my stomach. "I found your boy, Dale. Yup, your genius here drove right into a tree over on Monroe. It's a goddamn wonder this meathead is still alive. And he's lucky he didn't take anybody else out at the speed he was goin'."

As Sternhardt lectured my father, I heard Richard stomp through the house and slam his bedroom door. I crept across the hall and quietly slipped inside. "Richard, what happened?" I whispered.

"I wrecked my fucking car," he said, his voice coming from somewhere within the dark room.

"Are you drunk?" I asked.

"No, I wasn't drinking!" he shouted. "If I was drinking, I'd be in jail." But if he were drinking, I would've understood it. He had a shitty day and wanted to forget about it. He had bad judgment and drove his car. And thank God no one was hurt. But without alcohol? Did he harbor that much uncontrollable rage? That much reckless disregard for his own life, the lives of others, to cause him to speed into a tree? The thought was terrifying. "Just get the hell out of here, Lisa."

Without notice, Richard's door suddenly swung open the rest of the way. My dad flipped on the light, revealing Richard at the edge of his bed with his head in his hands. His lip was bleeding and swollen. My father immediately grabbed his chin, forcing Richard to look up at him. He looked as if he was going to strike him as he yelled, "What the hell is wrong with you! If you want to keep acting like a degenerate, then you are sure as hell going to get treated as one! Any more stunts like this, and I want you out of my house!" Richard shoved away my father's arm and stood defiantly. He stuck out his chest and began to curl his hands into fists.

"Goddamn it, Richard! Stop it!" I found myself shouting. He looked to me as if my voice had temporarily brought him out of his rage. But then he rushed toward me. He shoved me out of his way, and I flew into the hall. My head slammed against the wall. I fell to the floor, the wind knocked out of me. He charged out the front door as I gasped for air, shocked that my brother had actually hurt me, realizing I no longer knew who he was.

Understandably, Richard was kicked off the wrestling team and banned from all school sports. I was sure that not having a sport to concentrate on and to showcase his skills would cause him to spiral out of control. But there was *some* hope. Even though he did not have a sport to train for, he joined a gym. Noticing his dedication, a group of guys talked him into getting involved in bodybuilding. He ate up their reinforcement. And over the next several months, he further transformed himself into a hulking figure that barely looked human to me, more like a comic book muscle-bound superhero. His legs became giant tree trunks. His arms could barely be contained in his shirts. And his chest and neck seemed to bulge unnaturally from his frame.

His dedication even won back my father. We swapped sitting in bleachers at the high school for bleachers at local body-building competitions. He won several trophies, impressive for being so new to the sport. My dad was proud of Richard once more. But it wasn't the same as before. He encouraged Richard, for sure. But he didn't boast the way he used to. It was more of a reserved pride. He held much skepticism.

And as it turned out, his cautiousness was well warranted. Even with his new sport, things with Richard continued to deteriorate. He would come and go in those days. We never knew where he was when he wasn't home. But he was almost an adult then. My father was losing control and giving up hope at the same time. It was late in the school year when the final disappointing blow was dealt, when we received yet another visit from everyone's favorite sheriff.

"I knew he was up to no good. But I finally caught that weasel," Sternhardt boasted.

"What's this about?" my dad asked impatiently.

"Your screw-up of a boy, that's what. I'll tell ya, Dale, if you've got a son at home and he's 180 pounds and three months later he's 210, you've got a problem now, don't ya? What it comes down to is I carried out a locker raid today. And I found the mother lode in your boy's locker. Needles, and what I'm sure will come back positive as steroids. That's right, your boy's facin' possession of drug charges, engaging in a pattern of corrupt activity, and possibly drug trafficking. Now you wanna come down and post bail?"

My dad turned red and brimmed with rage. "Leave 'im in there," he snarled before slamming the door on Sternhardt.

Possession of drugs was ultimately the only charge that stuck. But my dad wanted nothing more to do with him. He had been expelled from high school just shy of completing his senior year, was no longer a competitive body-builder, and did not have any job prospects. My father was incredibly disappointed in the son he used to be so close with. When Richard walked into the house after his release, my dad stood at the door and promptly instructed, "You can grab your things. And then you need to get out."

I was afraid of how Richard would react. He was twice as big and strong as my dad. I could feel the rage rising from within him. It was difficult to tell how much of this rage could actually be attributed to his steroid use and how much just naturally flowed through him. Whatever its source, it was sending him into a tailspin. Without saying a word, he began violently cramming his belongings into garbage sacks. My body jolted with each thud and bang that came from his room. He left without saying a word. It would be a long time before I spoke with Richard again.

While Richard was going through his crisis, I was going through a crisis of my own. At least it felt like a crisis at the time. I had always thought the worst feeling on earth would be finding out someone you cared for felt indifferent about you. And that was the feeling I struggled with as I sat on the curb watching Greg and his friends in the skateboard park.

Beyond that, I resented sitting there like some sort of skateboard groupie with the other girls who had no skateboarding skills or ambition, but instead were interested in one of the guys. It made me feel pathetic. Besides, I didn't fit in with those girls. Not even a bit. I didn't have a skateboarder-girl vibe about me. I didn't get the clothes. Or the music. Or the attitude I was supposed to have. But I endured it because I thought Greg was simply the coolest guy in the world.

So when he fell that night doing a trick move off one of the ramps, I stood up and rushed to him with all the concern of a dedicated girlfriend. I knew it was bad as a large group of skaters, usually unfazed by cuts and gashes, surrounded him. As I rounded the ramp, I found him wincing and holding his leg. "I hit the fucking edge of the ramp," he moaned in agony. Blood began to pool where his elbow had slammed to the cement. I examined his leg. It looked as if his shin bone had snapped and was pressing against his skin.

"Help me!" I pleaded as I cupped my hand under his bloody elbow. One of the skaters helped me bring him to his feet. My hand was covered in his gushing blood.

Frankly, what I did next was shocking. It was humiliating. It was gross. And most of all, it was completely unexpected, even to me. I lifted my hand and began lapping up his blood that had pooled in my palm.

And what was even worse was when I placed my hand under his elbow again for a refill.

That's when I heard someone in the crowd yell, "Hey, what the fuck's she doing?" I honestly didn't know what the fuck I was doing. As bizarre as it was, it had to have been some sort of instinct. Some impulse, I reasoned. It took the heckling of the skateboarders and the on-looking groupies to make me realize what I was doing—and that I was doing it in front of others. Mortifyingly embarrassed, I rushed out of the skate park with my head down. Someone yelled to me, "Hey, come back here, *vampire girl!*" I could hear them laughing and shouting behind me.

But I did not hear Greg's voice. I didn't need to. I knew this meant it was over for us. And not just because I had effectively ostracized myself from the skateboarding crowd. It was because I had his taste on my tongue. Within the metallic, yet sweet, flavor of his blood, I could taste his feelings for me—or lack thereof. I had confirmed, through his blood, my worst fear: he truly felt indifferent about me. He liked me well enough. He thought I was interesting and friendly. But I was not whom he was truly looking for. He wanted someone with a little more excitement about her. Someone a little wilder. And I even knew, from that taste, that he had someone particular in mind. A brunette from another school. She was pretty. Had a cute, messy hairstyle. And wore dark cherry lipstick. She had a sort of crooked smile to match her sarcastic sense of humor.

It was funny how a thought, a truth, could be communicated in a taste. But there it was. It seemed natural, as natural as any of the other senses people experience. It wasn't until the taste abated that the sensation seemed out of the ordinary. But somehow, I still knew what I had learned was the truth. The message was still there. It still hurt. And I was devastated.

Chapter 5

Jar of Emotions

I paced the marble floor while Tina slept in her giant bed. Occasionally, I'd stop and peer out her grand windows to catch the yard and the trees that surrounded it become exposed by giant lightning flashes. Wind whipped through the branches and forced the rain to pelt the windows. I couldn't sleep. I tried, but my dad's face, the life drained completely out of it, was seared into my vision. I saw it every time I closed my eyes. I tried to tell myself that that was *not* my dad. It was just a shell, matter that used to house his spirit. No longer was he inside that tortured corpse. He had escaped, hopefully to a better place. At least wherever he was, he was free of the violence that had caused his demise.

But those thoughts, as comforting as they were, didn't erase the fear and pain he must've experienced. How could I rest when there were so many questions? When the person who mutilated him was still out there? No, I had to refuse peace. There was nothing comforting about his murder. There would be no peace until I knew who did it. And likely not even then.

Questions began swirling in my head. Questions Sternhardt had asked me, questions of my own. *Did I notice anything strange in the days leading up to his murder? Why were there cuts across his chest? Who would want to harm him? Why were there puncture wounds in his arms?* It was agony. How I wished it were morning so I could've been doing something! The night was such wasted time. I needed to talk to Sternhardt to find out where he planned on starting his investigation. What was his plan of action?

I knew where *I* would start. First thing in the morning, I'd speak with the pathologist, who Sternhardt said would perform an autopsy within twenty-four hours. Would Dad's desecrated body hold the clues to finding his murderer?

A bolt of lightning crashed directly above the mansion. My mind was so deeply swimming in questions that I did not even flinch. In fact, it drove me to the window. Perhaps I needed the distraction. I looked out over the backyard as another flash popped. And in that millisecond of light, I saw something unusual—a shadow, stationary in the flash, along the tree line. Sure, it could've been an overhanging branch. Yet between the darkness and the next cascading bolt, the shadow had moved to the edge of the yard. And if there was still doubt that what I saw was not an occurrence of nature, the next blaze of light provided my answer as it revealed the dark figure had moved to the center of the yard. There it stood. Dark. Cloaked. Hooded. Still. As if it could feel me watching it.

"Tina!" I whispered urgently across the room. The figure lifted its head ever so slightly, as if to acknowledge my presence. And then, it moved with swiftness toward the house. I pressed against the window in a panic, watching it head for the pair of cellar doors, which jutted from the cobblestone foundation. It grabbed the handle of each. And with a strength that almost seemed supernatural, it simply raised its arms, and the doors flew open. I ran to the bed and shook Tina awake. "Tina! Someone's in the house!" I shouted, bringing her out of a dead sleep.

She woke in a panic and promptly struck me across the face while letting out an ear-piercing scream. "Jesus Christ!" She sat up, her body shaking in startled confusion as she removed her earplugs.

"Someone just got in the house!"

"What!"

"Through the storm doors! In the basement!"

She paused for a moment, examining the look on my face. And as soon as she detected my level of seriousness, she burst from under the covers. We both ran for the door and promptly crashed into her mom in the hallway. "What the hell is this about, Christina!" her mother shouted, tugging at the strings of her nightgown. Her father, clad only in sweatpants, wobbled sleepily down the hall behind her. "We heard screaming. I thought you two girls were killing each other, for Christ's sake!"

"Lisa," Tina said with a swallow, frightened, "says someone's in the house!"

"Someone got in," I affirmed between heavy breaths, "through your cellar door."

Her father raced back to their bedroom and emerged with a handgun. Her mother let out a gasp. "Jesus, John! Do you even know how to use that thing?"

"I know enough," he said as he started down the winding staircase. "Stay here," he instructed. But Tina's mom being Tina's mom, she kept right behind him. We watched as they descended the staircase, until her nightgown could no longer be seen flowing behind her.

That's when Tina nudged me forward. I dropped onto the first step. "Did ya get a look at him?" she whispered.

She followed close behind as I took another few steps, clearly defying her father's orders. "It was dark. He had on a hood. And a black cape," I said as we began to slowly creep down the stairs.

"*A black cape?* What the hell?"

"A cape. A cloak. I don't know."

"*A cloak?* Who the hell wears a cloak?"

"I don't know! Maybe it was just a long coat?"

Tina grabbed my arm. "Sorry. I'm just scared."

"Me too," I admitted.

After we reached the bottom of the staircase, we kept close to the walls as we snuck through the foyer. The mansion was eerie. At night, the rooms seemed even bigger. Filled with darkness. Filled with the unknown. Each cautious step felt like a risk. Her parents had disappeared into the darkness. We could not hear them ahead of us. When we came to the basement door, an exposed lightbulb above the steps lit the way.

"Mom? Dad?" Tina whispered apprehensively down the stairs. There was no answer. Tina nudged me forward yet again. Perturbed, I jabbed her back with my elbow before reluctantly stepping onto the wooden staircase. The rotting steps creaked loudly beneath our feet.

Considering the top floors of the mansion were so luxurious, the bottom one was simply archaic. Built in a time when basements were not living spaces, the Grant Mansion's lowest level was a dirt floor cellar. I could smell the earth and must. Could feel dampness on my skin. We scurried nervously across the black, dusty floor and toward a half-open door near the back wall. Light poured out from the room. We were afraid to look, but also too afraid not to look. We peered around the door. There stood Tina's parents. Her mom looked on as her dad was atop a short staircase fiddling with the cellar doors.

"So did you find the guy?" asked Tina.

They spun toward us, her mom clutching her chest. "Jesus, Christina! You know your father has a gun on him! It might even be loaded. So cool it with the sneakin' up on us, OK?"

"You listen to me about as well as your mother does," her dad said, shaking his head.

"Well?"

"There's no one in this house," he declared.

I noticed his feet were covered in mud up to his ankles. At the base of the steps, water had mixed with the dirt floor, creating a muddy puddle. "How did all the water get inside?" I asked.

"Doors were open when we got down here. Yup, these old doors need to be replaced. I'll bet they're the originals from when the house was built. Wood is all rotten. Hinges are busted." He smacked one of the metal hinges. It spun around, barely held on by a loose screw.

Tina's mom frowned at him disapprovingly and then placed her arm around me. "Lisa, we've checked the house. No one is here," she assured.

Her father, realizing he was in trouble for revealing they had found the doors open, added with a shrug, "The wind must've gotten a hold of them is all."

"Now I know you've been through a lot," her mother continued. "Far too much for your age. For anybody's age, really. But you are safe here. I promise."

"There's a lot of debris blowing around out there tonight," offered her dad. "That's probably what you saw from upstairs. A branch that snapped off. Or even a garbage can blowing through the yard."

Although I should've found their comments patronizing, I couldn't be angry at Tina's parents. They were kind enough to let me stay. I knew they meant well. And I knew I had to play along. "Must've been," I relented.

"We should all just go back to bed," said Tina's mom, motioning for us to get out of the cellar.

"Do you mind if I stay up awhile and look around for myself? It would make me feel better."

"Sure thing, sweetie. John, let's you and I get back upstairs. And wipe your damn feet before you track that mud all over my new rugs."

"Are you OK?" asked Tina after they left.

"I know what I saw. Do you believe me?"

"Hell yeah, I do. And it scares the shit outta me." I looked to the puddle and then to the broken hinges. "What're you thinking?" she asked. Without answering, I began to examine the dirt floor beyond the puddle. "What is it?"

"I don't know yet. Are there any more lights down here?" Tina managed to find and pull a cord that dangled from the ceiling. The bulb illuminated the other half of the dirt room. I knelt on the floor. "Look at this," I said. "More water. But it's outside the puddle. It's still too dark. Come by me so you're not blocking the light." Tina knelt next to me. "Looks like footprints, doesn't it?"

Tina leaned in for a closer look. "I guess they could be," she said. "But they're probably my dad's. You saw how wet his feet were."

"Right. But your dad was barefoot. These almost look like shoe prints." I followed the watery splotches along the floor. They led to an old wooden shelf filled with tools and gardening supplies. We stood before the shelf.

"What're we lookin' for?" asked Tina.

"I don't know. Anything out of the ordinary."

"It's just a bunch of junk," she said after we studied it a while.

"Yeah," I said, grabbing an old metal bucket off one of the shelves and looking inside. There was a weathered spade and some other rusted gardening tools. I set the bucket to the ground and began pulling off other things after examining them. "C'mon, process of elimination. Help me. Start pulling things down. But only pull down the stuff that looks like it belongs."

"*All* this junk looks like it belongs—and needs to stay—right down here." She held up a dirty porcelain doll with a half-cracked face. "Need I say more?"

I chuckled as I reached for what was in front of my face the whole time. It was a seemingly ordinary, sealed mason jar. Yet when I picked it up, it nearly slipped through my fingers and smashed to the floor. I saved it by quickly gripping its neck. "Whoa, careful," Tina said as she saw me fumbling with the jar. I held it to my face, trying to see its contents in the dim light. "That doesn't look out of the ordinary to me.

None of this stuff does," she said, exasperated. "It's all junk that was never cleared out when we moved in. It creeps me the fuck out."

"Tina, this jar. It's wet." Tina froze. Her eyes widened as she realized what that meant.

We brought it up to her room and took turns holding it up to the light. It was a liquid for sure. It oozed slowly from side to side as the jar was tilted. But it was very dark, almost black. "Why would someone sneak a jar of shit into my basement?"

"I don't know," I replied. "It's not shit, though. But I *do* think I know what it is."

Later that night, I found myself sitting on the cold marble floor of Tina's bathroom. The jar was upon the sink, its black liquid commanding attention due to the sheer contrast it displayed against the sterile, bright room. Tina had finally fallen asleep, but I couldn't. I was exhausted, but my mind would not shut off. Who was the dark figure who had entered the basement? Had the jar really been brought in from the storm? Or had I lost my mind? Had it simply gotten wet from a leaky pipe?

The jar—its dark liquid—called to me. It was the most bizarre sensation. I wanted to touch it, feel it outside of its glass prison. But I protested, hearing in shame the words *vampire girl* repeating over and over. *Maybe I'd be satisfied if I just had a closer look?* I hovered over the jar, letting my hair fall forward and dangle over it.

Yet soon, I found my hand clamping onto the lid like a magnet. The lid was on tight. It took all my strength before it began to slowly give way. Finally, I twisted off the top and turned it over. The liquid had made an impression on the underside of the lid: a black stain with a red hue. I brought the lid to my nose and smelled it. And then I found myself consciously, yet quite involuntarily, pointing my tongue out of my mouth. I licked the underside like one would lick the residue from the underside of a yogurt top.

The taste dissolved onto my tongue. It tasted like the smell that began to waft through the room once the jar had been opened. I experienced a mix of metallic scents and flavors intermingling as one sense. It was like a handful of sweaty coins along with an earthy flavor, like must or mold, combined with the scent of an old forest filled with rotting logs and moss after a rainstorm.

My brief taste, however, was not enough. I craved more. I needed more—information. Without thinking it bizarre or gross at the time, I formed my fingers into a scoop. Like some cartoon bear dipping its claws into a jar of honey, my fingers entered the thick liquid. I reached halfway into the jar before lifting my hand. A trail of stringy strands of blackish-red, nearly coagulated blood began to escape through my fingers. Before the bulk of it oozed back into the jar, I swiftly slurped the clotting blood into my mouth.

As the flavors permeated my tongue, I had to sit on the floor. The emotions were too much for me to take. My entire body shook with an overwhelming sense of sadness, despair.

I knew it was the taste of a man, an older man. I did not see how it happened, but I knew he was dead—not necessarily gone before his time, but struggling with the concept that he would no longer be of the earth. I knew what I was sensing were his final moments. There was such worry and regret, it eclipsed the pain of dying. There was fear that he had not left enough behind, not in wealth or belongings, but in energy, experiences rich enough for him to be remembered. He wondered how soon he would be forgotten after he was gone. Who would remember him? And if he *was* remembered, he fretted over it being only a matter of time before those who remembered also died, effectively erasing his very existence. These thoughts, only apparent as he lay dying, caused great panic instead of peace in his final moments.

I slept on the cool marble floor the rest of the night, unable to stop the feelings I had let enter my body.

Chapter 6

Sold to Grand Hallow

"I don't understand why she needs to identify his body. Didn't she already do that when she found him inside the garage?" Tina protested.

But the coroner needed an official signature on an official form. "It's just a quick look. I promise," he assured apologetically as we stood over my father's body, which was covered by a sheet.

"Christ, this should've been Richard. Not you. You've been through enough. Where the hell is he?"

"We did reach out to Mr. Jacobs," the coroner offered, "but you were the first to respond." He shrugged.

"It's OK," I said. "I want to be here. Actually, I was hoping you would tell me what you know about how he died. You know, based on the condition of his body."

"Oh, Miss Jacobs, I'm not allowed to divulge any information until the final report. And I have only just begun with an initial examination.

Once the autopsy is complete, the report will be turned over to the Sheriff's Department. And after that, you may request a copy."

"How long's that gonna take?" asked Tina.

He shook his head in uncertainty. "Could take a few weeks. I have to be very thorough in this—"

"Weeks! That's bullshit! Are you aware there's a murderer on the loose?"

"Tina!" I pleaded. "It's all right. Let's just get this over with."

He composed himself by straightening his lab jacket. As he pulled back the sheet, I tightly clenched Tina's hand. It was surreal. What lay before me did not seem like my father. It seemed as if it were a head made of wax. His skin was a dull, grayish tone. They had not bothered to align his gaping jaw.

And as I looked upon him, I couldn't help but wonder if he had the same feelings in his final moments as the man whose jar of blood sat in Tina's bathroom. Was he afraid? Sad? Worried he'd be forgotten? And there was another thought I needed to face, one I had been pushing to the back of my mind ever since tasting that blood: Were they one and the same? Did the jar actually contain my *father's* blood? Was I actually sensing *his* thoughts during his demise? Did the murderer leave the jar in Tina's house as some sort of sick symbol? A token of my father's killing?

Finally, I nodded to the coroner. He covered my father's face and handed me a pen and clipboard. Tina gave me a light hug as I signed the death certificate. Immediately, I felt lightheaded. Tina, sensing my uneasiness, kept her arm around me as we began to walk out of the morgue.

Behind us, I heard the coroner clear his throat. "Miss Jacobs?" he called after us, with a hint of trepidation in his voice. "I shouldn't be doing this. And as I've told you, I've only begun an initial examination. And you'll have to wait for the official report—"

"Yeah! Yeah!" Tina interrupted, rushing him to get on with it.

"All I can say is that his body has been—and please excuse my crassness, ladies—I know this must be difficult. But it's been—well, it's been—*hollowed out*."

"*Hollowed out*?" I asked, *my* voice suddenly the one quivering with trepidation.

"Well, you see, his eyes, his tongue were removed."

"Jesus Christ," whispered Tina.

"And his heart?" I asked, visualizing the cuts across his upper chest.

"Yes, and his heart was removed. But so too were his other major internal organs—his lungs, liver, kidneys, intestines. I've never seen anything like it, quite honestly. It's as if someone cut him open and scooped out his insides. I'm so sorry," he paused. "I shouldn't be sharing any of this with you."

"No. I want to hear it," I said, trying to retain my composure.

"And the other thing is, his blood—"

"It was drained, wasn't it?"

"Well, yes. How did you know?"

"I saw it dripping from his arms when I found him."

He nodded sympathetically. "There's hardly any left in his veins."

The door burst open. We each jolted from the sudden interruption. Sheriff Sternhardt's imposing figure stood blocking the exit. "I thought I might find you here," his deep voice boomed.

"Uh, nice sleuthing, Sternhardt. Aren't you the one who told her she had to come down here to sign the death certificate?" asked Tina, followed by her signature eye roll.

Dismissing her, Sternhardt announced, "I'm here to tell you we have officially ruled your father's case a homicide."

"Officially ruled a homicide!" erupted Tina. "Well that's just brilliant! For fuck sake! Whattaya think? He cut out his *own* heart?" The coroner hurriedly put my father's body back in the cooler while Tina chewed her nail, realizing her transgression.

"It *means* we can officially begin our investigation. And you better watch yourself, missy," he said, pointing to Tina. He then turned his accusatory finger to the coroner. "You too, John," he scolded. "We need this done airtight. Dot the i's. Cross the t's. Tie this son of a bitch in a knot!" We attempted to scurry around Sternhardt but were promptly halted. "And one more thing, Miss Jacobs. You've got to get next door to CPS. Now," he commanded.

"CPS?"

"Child Protective Services. There've been some developments in your case."

"Case? What case?" asked Tina. "She's staying with me. Case closed."

"Just get over there," he instructed impatiently. "Ask for Alice Perigord. She's waiting for you."

So I asked for Alice Perigord at the front desk of CPS. We were ushered down a narrow hallway with offices on either side. The receptionist knocked lightly on a closed door at the end of the hall. "Lisa Jacobs is here," she called inside before slowly swinging open the door, revealing a sight that caused me to quietly gasp and take a short step backward.

Even with his back turned to me and his hair a disheveled mess, I knew it was Richard. He turned to face us as we entered. It was the first I had seen him in about a year. His eyes were bloodshot. He had a partial beard. And he wore a black leather jacket over a white T-shirt. My first instinct was to make a joke about him looking like a greaser from *The Outsiders*, but I held my tongue. Knowing Richard, it wouldn't have gone over well. But it was all that came to mind as I stood there with a mix of awkwardness and apprehension.

Tina, on the other hand, did not have the same filtering device. She broke the ice in a way only she could: "Whoa, Richard. You look like complete shit!" she marveled as she stepped past me to get a closer look. "Jesus," she said, fanning her nose. "It's like 10:00 a.m., and you've already hit the brewskis?" He glared at her in annoyance and then ultimately brushed off her insult with a smirk.

"Please. Have a seat, Lisa," offered Alice, a redheaded woman with a warm smile.

I sat next to Richard while Tina took a seat behind us. I found it curious rather than insulting the way he turned his chair slightly away from me. Seeing him up close, I thought he looked tired. Haggard. And as Tina had so eloquently pointed out, he *did* smell of booze. It did not even seem to be coming from his breath, but rather it seemed to emanate from his pores. "How's it going?" he asked, with some measure of sympathy in his voice.

"I'm OK," I lied, conflicted by our reunion. I was happy, I supposed, that we had finally reconnected, especially after Dad's death. But at the same time, I was uneasy sitting next to him. No matter how much I had denied Tina's insinuation that Richard had had something to do with Dad's murder, the possibility weighed heavily in the back of my mind. *And why were we meeting, finally, like this? In a CPS caseworker's office? What was he up to?*

"My sympathies to both of you. I can't imagine your sadness," said Alice. She paused before getting onto her real business. "Now, Lisa, I realize in a few months, when you are eighteen, you will have more options. More choices about where you live. And frankly about what you do with your life. But as you are not eighteen yet, we do have to abide by the laws according to minors. Meaning, you need an appropriate guardian. Now," she smiled, "the good news is, we have found a relative for you to stay with."

I looked to Richard, and I immediately knew then why he was in the room. And my fear and hatred of him dissolved. The past didn't matter. Whatever current problems he was going through didn't matter. What mattered was when I needed him most, he was coming through for me. He was my hero. "Richard," I said relieved, "You're moving back home." It was perfect. He could be my legal guardian, and I could stay in the house that I grew up in.

"Yeah, I'm moving back in," he confirmed. "But . . ."

"But?"

"But *you're* not," he said bluntly.

I felt a sting. My eyes began to tear up with anger and confusion. "What do you mean?"

"Listen, Lisa, I really need a place to stay. I can't afford that apartment, even with three of us there. I don't even have a job. Do you know how I have to make money? I return shit to stores. Shit that's mine. Shit I've stolen. To stores that don't ask for receipts. I need to get away from those guys. I need a new place. A place to start over, to get clean."

"What about me?"

"I can't watch over a kid while I get clean. I need to focus. I can't have any distractions."

"*What about me?*" I repeated, feeling at the same time deceived and panicked. Richard turned farther away from me and sheepishly looked to Alice.

"Well, that's where the good news comes in," Alice interjected. "Since your brother is not . . . well, since he is not *prepared* for guardianship, it just so happens someone got into contact with us who is very eager to take on those responsibilities."

"Who? There *is* no one else. It's always been just me and Dad. And Richard," I added hastily.

"We received a call from your dad's brother, Clayton Jacobs. After checking into it, it does appear he is a relative who is eligible for guardianship. And as I said, he seems very intent on getting to know you and is excited about your living with him."

"*Uncle Clayton!* I don't even know him!" I protested. "All I know is that he and Dad never got along. They never even visited each other. And—" I put my hand to my forehead. "Oh God," I looked to Tina in a panic. "He lives in Grand Hallow. I can't move to Grand Hallow!"

"I know this will take some time to settle in, Lisa. But this really is the best thing," said Alice.

"Richard, I can't believe it! You knew about this, and you didn't do anything? You let it happen," I said, bewildered, betrayed. He had nothing to say. He looked to the floor.

Tina stood swiftly, causing her chair to slide across the back of the small office and slam into the wall. "You son of a bitch!" she shouted, as she towered her small frame over his. "You sold her out—all so you could steal the house from her and turn it into a junkie paradise for you and your loser buds! Well the joke's on you, asshole, because my parents have already agreed to let Lisa stay with us as long as she wants. And that means I'm sure they would be willing to adopt her to keep her from gettin' shipped off to Grand fuckin' Hallow!"

"Christina Cashmere?" asked Alice.

"What?" Tina replied in a huff.

"Actually, I have contacted your parents, as I was informed that's where Lisa was staying currently. And unfortunately, they are not interested in taking on such a responsibility. It was an unusual request, for sure. But it was an avenue I was willing to pursue."

For once, Tina was speechless. "It's OK," I told her. "I never would have expected them to."

"*I* would have," she said, deflated. "I'll never forgive them for this."

"Well." I stood, eager to end the discussion. I felt completely shattered, yet forced a smile. "I can't worry about this now. I have to figure out how to plan a funeral."

Richard cleared his throat. "It's been taken care of," he announced.

"What do you mean *it's been taken care of*? *You* made arrangements for Dad's funeral?"

"I find that hard to believe," Tina quipped.

"No. Uncle Clayton. He said there was nothing we needed to do. He's gonna cover all the costs and handle all the arrangements."

I was shocked. "But how does he know what Dad would've wanted? What *we* want?"

"Lisa, he's springing for the whole thing. Let him plan it. I thought you'd be relieved you wouldn't have to."

"Well, are we at least going to be able to pick out his plot in the Ruthsford Cemetery? I'd like a spot for him in the back, near the river."

"He's not going to *be* buried in the Ruthsford Cemetery. You really don't remember, do you? Uncle Clayton *owns* the Grand Hallow Cemetery. Hell, he owns the entire funeral industry in Grand Hallow, the biggest in the state, in fact, where everyone goes when they die," he chuckled. "That's why he's able to cover everything for us."

No, I didn't remember. "But Dad wouldn't want to be buried there," I continued to protest. "He'd want to be buried right here. In Ruthsford."

"Dad didn't have enough money saved up for a funeral. You know that. Hell, he barely had enough to leave us much of anything at all. Just let this guy do us a favor. Go live with him for a few months. He probably feels real guilty about not getting along with Dad. He'll probably buy you whatever you want. Go get spoiled this summer. And when you come back—when you're eighteen—I promise the shitty little gas station and the shitty little puke-green house behind it will be waiting for you."

Chapter 7

Wrapped Ham

I sat on the curb in front of the service station, my bags sprawled in front of me. I packed light. Aside from my clothes, just a couple of novels and notebooks. And of course, my Walkman. I wondered if I was making a mistake leaving behind my new dual cassette deck stereo as well as the bulk of my tape collection. But I didn't want it to feel as though I was truly moving in with my uncle. It was only for a few months. And a few months, I tried to convince myself, wasn't really all that long. I'd be home before I knew it.

Yet the concept of *home* weighed on me heavily. My father was gone. And without notice, I was being kicked out and shipped off. Richard would be taking over the place where I grew up, the only place I had ever called *home. Where did that leave me? Where did I fit in?* My sense of security was rattled. And if I was being honest with myself, it was at least half the reason I was leaving so many of my things behind. They marked my territory. I didn't want it to be forgotten that there was to be a space reserved for me in that house.

Losing space was one thing. Control was another. With me stuck in Grand Hallow, I would have no say in what Richard did with the house or the gas and service station. I panicked over what would become of my father's pride and joy. A thousand horrible scenarios ran through my head. I wanted to be there to watch over him, to make sure he didn't do anything stupid. This loss of control, this limbo I was thrown into, put me on edge. Damn Richard. It was as if I was powered solely by anxiety in the days that followed our contemptuous reunion.

And that afternoon, my anxiety swelled to new heights. It felt like a thousand butterflies had hatched in my stomach as Tina and I waited. I got quiet when I got nervous. It was my way of hiding, of keeping myself tucked inside myself. My silence drove Tina nuts, so she opted to stand at the end of the driveway, looking back and forth down the road. "Which way do ya think he'll come?" Unsure, yet too sick to speak, I only shrugged. Each time she spotted a car that might've been *the one,* I filled a bit more with dread. I looked to the grass, to the ants. One crawled up an overgrown blade. How I wished I could've shrunk down and joined them, spent the summer with them in the familiar lawn. Yet as my mind desperately searched for a way to escape, I heard Tina shout, "No fuckin' way! You're not gonna believe this!"

I stood at once, my knees wobbling. Tina took several steps back, gaping, before running to my side. Together, we watched as a black hearse emerged from the trees and turned onto the gravel. "Why does it have to be a hearse?" I groaned.

The black car slowly pulled around the circle drive. "Tell me again why I couldn't have driven you? I mean, at least we could've waited till tomorrow and rode with my parents in the morning. Hell, I'd even take a ride from your stupid brother over this," complained Tina, crinkling her nose at the macabre vehicle.

"Uncle Clayton, he insisted on picking me up—tonight."

"That was real sweet of him," she said sarcastically.

"Well at least you're here with me, Tina. Otherwise, no one would believe this."

As the hearse slowly rolled by, we couldn't see the driver behind our reflections casting back from the windows. My hair was a mess, blowing haphazardly in the breeze. And my face looked—and felt—red hot. The vehicle stopped just beyond where we were standing. White curtains were drawn over the rear window, keeping us from viewing into the car. I was nervous to meet him. Nervous to come face-to-face with the person who was strangely willing and strangely eager to become my guardian for the final months before I officially became an adult.

The driver's door slowly creaked open. The car bounced a bit as a man climbed out. The sun reflected off his bald head, making it glow as he made his way around the car. The portly man dabbed his forehead with a handkerchief as he approached. With his eyes frantically darting between Tina and me, he looked just as nervous as I was. He stood before us in a black suit, looking hot and uncomfortable. "Excuse me, ladies . . ." He spoke with a slight southern accent. He stopped to clear his throat before continuing, "But which one of you is Miss Lisa Jacobs?"

"I am." His uneasiness helped make me feel a bit more at ease. I couldn't help but feel empathy for the man who clearly felt as awkward as I did with the situation. "It's nice to meet you, Uncle Clayton," I said and found myself extending my hand.

He took my hand and reciprocated with a weak grasp before exclaiming, "Oh no, no, no, no, Miss Jacobs. I am not your uncle. I am the chief funeral director for Grand Hallow Incorporated. My name is Ned. Ned Cummings. Mr. Jacobs instructed me to come to Ruthsford to pick you up. It is my responsibility to personally deliver you to him."

"*Deliver* her?" Tina questioned with offense as she lit a cigarette. "She's not a wrapped ham!"

"I simply mean, bring her home safely, ma'am. He would like her to become acquainted with her new surroundings before the funeral proceedings tomorrow." Tina exhaled her first puff of smoke in Ned's direction. She eyed him while furrowing her brow, not disguising the fact that she was questioning his character.

"Well, that makes sense," I blurted to ease the tension. "You sure don't sound like you're from Michigan."

"No, ma'am. Not originally. Originally, I'm from Georgia. Well, Miss Jacobs, it'll be dark soon. We best be on our way to Grand Hallow." He opened the door and presented the backseat with his open hand as if I were a celebrity being ushered inside a limousine. I picked up my bags and looked awkwardly inside the hearse. "I'm so sorry, ma'am. Let me help you with those," he said as he grabbed my largest bag and placed it on the seat.

"You don't have to do that," I said, not expecting him to help with my bags. "I was just wondering. Where is Tina going to sit?" I didn't want her to have to sit up front, alone with Ned.

He looked confused. "Well, I only have instructions to retrieve you, Miss Jacobs. There was no mention of a Miss—"

"Cashmere," Tina finished. "Well, you might not have instructions to retrieve me and all. But hey, man, give me a ride. I'm a guest at the funeral for shit sakes."

"And she's my best friend," I pleaded. "Please let her ride with us. I'm sure Uncle Clayton won't mind."

"Oh dear," fretted Ned. "Well, I suppose it won't hurt any, seeing as she'll be at the funeral regardless." He grabbed my bag from the backseat and opened the rear of the hearse. I stood by his side as he pushed the bag into the chamber. That space—it was not lost on me—had likely been host to many final rides. Seeing it, a slight chill came over me. It was like looking behind a forbidden curtain. A glimpse into another world. One that wasn't meant for me, at least for many years I hoped. But one I nevertheless found myself crashing into unwittingly.

"Oh, Miss Cashmere. I'm sorry. But there is no smoking inside the vehicle. Grand Hallow rules," Ned relayed as politely as possible. Tina took one long and final drag before flicking her butt to the gravel. Then we both climbed inside and began our journey. As we pulled away, I looked pensively to the service station and the tiny house. It felt like I was abandoning an old friend.

Part II
Chapter 8
Into the Mouth

Even though the rear of the hearse was spacious, Tina and I sat huddled together. We were well outside Ruthsford when Ned cleared his throat. "You ladies know about Grand Hallow?" Before we had a chance to answer, he began, "Well, it's not *just* a funeral home. And it's not *just* a cemetery. No, it's a holistic operation encompassing funeral services, mortuary sciences, a top crematorium, various interment options, plot maintenance, and even transportation services—all under one roof, so to speak. Yes, it's a one-stop shop for all of your death and dying needs.

"It's actually quite remarkable what your uncle has built, an empire that has become the top funerary destination. He has effectively built a town from scratch. Put it on the map, he did! A town that is the first of its kind. Detroit may be the automobile capital of the world, but Grand Hallow is the death capital. We draw dead from all across the state."

He turned back to face us, assuring we were engaged. His jowls sank into his collar as he nodded before returning his gaze to the road. "Yes, sir. Excuse me. I mean, *ladies*. It's because we're nondenominational, you know. We'll take anyone. Those of any faith. Those of no faith. Those who planned poorly with nothing left for a funeral. Even prisoners.

"You see, your uncle cut a deal with the state prison system to bury those with lifelong sentences. By the time they die, their family has either died out themselves or have forgotten about them. Keeps the prisons from having to bury 'em on prison grounds. They may get the plots out by the marshes, but we'll take 'em. Yes, quite the businessman, he is. Because of your uncle, the ratio of dead to live citizens in Grand Hallow is three thousand five hundred to one!" he said with a chuckle of delight. Tina stuck her finger down her throat in a mock gag.

We drove for at least another half hour through farmland, passing fields of corn and fields of cows before the car finally came to a stop at an intersection. We were surrounded by a corn-processing plant. On either side of the road were several warehouses and clusters of massive steel silos. After passing the plant, the car rocked over a set of railroad tracks. And just beyond the tracks was a small sign that read "Entering Grand Hallow."

The landscape quickly changed from fields to woods. Untrimmed trees touched each other over the road that kept their trunks divided. The arching trees made it seem like we were in a tunnel. Between the thick leaves, bright sparkles popped and flickered across the landscape like giant camera flashes. As the trees thinned a bit, I realized just what the rays of the setting sun were reflecting off to cause those bursts.

Upon the hills and into the distance, gravestones littered the countryside. They filled the empty spaces between the small random groves of trees. Paths wound around the marble and granite markers like a complex labyrinth. There was a randomness to the scene and an order to it all at once. The horizon filled with tombstones gave the landscape uniformity. Yet the monuments themselves were a hodgepodge ranging from the simplistic (traditional crosses and basic stone markers) to the ornate (life-size statuaries, miniature steeples, and above-ground crypts, which dotted the hills looking like fancy outhouses).

"Ladies, welcome to Grand Hallow," Ned announced with pride. It was difficult not to be impressed or amazed by the sight that overwhelmed the hills on either side of the road. "What we're approaching now is what we call *the Mouth*. Coming into the property from Park Drive, the Mouth is the true entrance to Grand Hallow. You're looking at the beginning stretch of over seven hundred thousand graves spread out over 578 acres."

As we made our way over the hill's peak, an unnerving, yet magnificent, sight came into view. Tina pushed me aside, poking her head into the front seat to get a better view. "Holy shit," she whispered.

Sprawled out as far as the eye could see was a valley filled with graves against the crimson backdrop of the setting sun. And in the center of it all was a gigantic complex. The cluster of buildings sprawled out like a college campus. At the heart of it was the largest building, composed of red brick. Many of the buildings were several stories high. And some boasted dramatic peaks and turrets jutting haphazardly into the red sky. The complex was surrounded by a tall iron fence. It stretched what I estimated to be a half mile on either side before disappearing into a line of trees that flanked the massive property.

The road dead-ended right into the complex. It was like reaching the end of an expressway and being dumped off in some town. But this road led to only one place. It truly was the Mouth of Grand Hallow. As we drove up to the open gates, I noticed "Grand" written in cursive metal on the gate to the left and "Hallow" on the right. I grabbed Tina's hand. It felt as if we were about to be swallowed. There was no way out. There was no turning back. As we passed through the tall gates, it truly felt as if we had been sucked into another world.

He drove us around the back of the complex. It looked like the back of some large warehouse store with a line of about twenty bay doors. As we approached, one of the bay doors began to lift. We drove inside the dim building. A clean-cut young man in a suit and tie appeared out of the shadows and approached the driver's door. Ned handed him the keys before helping us unload our luggage. As my eyes adjusted to the light, I realized we stood in a massive garage filled with rows of hearses and limousines. Ned noticed us admiring the impressive fleet. "Quite a significant piece of revenue comes from our chauffeured vehicles for funeral processions. We have quite the variety of Cadillacs and Lincolns too."

"Mercurys and Subaru?" Tina immediately interjected, following with a hearty laugh. Ned looked to her, extremely confused. "Geez. Guess you're not a Blondie fan," she muttered.

He patted the hood of the hearse that had brought us there and continued. "And this Cadillac Victoria. Beautiful hearse, isn't she?" Sensing Tina was about to give her own opinion of the vehicle, I immediately made eye contact with her and shook my head as if I were a parent warning a child she had better keep her mouth shut. And she did. Even though she didn't look happy about it.

"Now follow me, ladies," he said, motioning. We followed Ned through a door and down a long, tunnel-like corridor. At the end was a heavy oak door. He set his shoulder against the door and used his weight to push it open. "This one always sticks," he explained. "It's the humidity. Makes the wood expand."

What we saw on the other side of the door took my breath away. It was as if we stood at the epicenter of a massive and lavish convention center. The arched ceiling was colossal. Three skylight domes were carved into it, spaced evenly down the length of the hall. There were many doors on either side of the wide hallway. On the wall outside each room was a plaque with the room's name. Ned noticed me reading the plaques. "Ah, in this wing, the viewing rooms are all named after Michigan counties."

In the hall outside each room stood a sign with customizable, magnetic lettering. We passed the *Tuscola* viewing room with a sign that read, "Harold Faustine—Viewing 6:00 p.m." The double doors to the room were open. I peered in to see several people gathered near the far side of the room. And there he was: Harold Faustine, on display in his coffin.

Before my father had been murdered, I had never seen a dead body. And casually walking by Harold, made up and displayed to look so peaceful and healthy, only made me more uneasy. It was an eerie thing, seeing the dead. I could not help but stare. It conjured an unnatural feeling, one that could not easily be reconciled by my brain. Even from my distance, he appeared more asleep than dead. It seemed as if at any moment, Harold was sure to wake from his slumber and scare the living shit out of everyone. Especially me.

We continued down the hall. As we passed the rooms, some were empty while some held small gatherings of mourners. Ladies wore dark dresses. Men wore simple suits. There was an unsettling hum that flowed from the rooms into the hall. Barely audible whispers combined to create a low chatter. Perhaps the hushed tones were an attempt not to burst the bizarre illusion everyone seemed to share, which was that commingling with the dead was normal. It was *not* normal. It was surreal.

We rounded the corner and were faced with an identical hallway that extended into infinity in both directions. We then branched off this main artery and entered a sequence of narrower hallways. "This wing houses our smaller viewing rooms and our more modest nondenominational chapels," he explained. When we reached a set of fire doors and branched off yet again down another long and narrow corridor, I knew we were in a maze. And at the mercy of Ned's navigation.

"Didn't know we were supposed to bring breadcrumbs," cracked Tina.

"Oh, I'm afraid it does get a bit tricky. But Miss Jacobs will get the hang of it, eventually. We're just right ahead," he said, breathing heavily, pointing to the door at the end of the hall with a sign that read "Employees Only." He reached deep into his suit pocket and produced a set of jangling keys.

As he rifled through the keys, I checked out one of the chapels across the way. Folding chairs were stacked in the corner. There was a stained glass window behind a barren altar. A bulb shone from behind the mosaic glass, providing mock daylight. It reminded me of a Vegas wedding chapel. Simple. Bright. Cheap. "Now once we pass through this door, we're in the nerve center," Ned announced as he finally found the key he needed.

The carpet in this area was a lush plant design with giant sweeping vines and leaves curling over the top of one another in mints and dark greens. We stepped across a balcony. I gripped the iron railing, unable to resist seeing what was below. At once I could see why Ned called this area the nerve center. A grand staircase covered in the same garden-inspired carpet led to an impressive lobby on the first level. Three of the main hallways intersected here like terminals at an airport. Guests coming through the series of giant glass doors that lined the front of the building would enter this hub before branching off in different directions.

"Just a bit farther," he promised as we followed him down another hallway taking us deeper into the structure. Halfway down the hall, he reached into one of the rooms and hit the light switch. It was a dim office. Unorganized paperwork and stacks of binders were strewn across a large oak desk. "This is my office. If you need anything at all, this is where I can usually be found."

"And what is it exactly you do around here?" asked Tina.

"Ah. A good portion of my day is spent meeting with clients prior to their inevitable demise—to plan and fund their funeral."

"So you're basically a death salesman?" Tina blurted.

Ned sighed and then chuckled a bit. "I'd prefer *end-of-life consultant* if I had to label that part of my job. But as the chief funeral director, I'm also responsible for arranging all the details of the services—meeting with families, staffing, and overseeing services and casket sales. I also make sure all the paperwork is filed properly with the county and other local jurisdictions. You know," he said with a wave of his hand, "legal documents, requesting copies of death certificates, life insurance benefits, closing bank accounts, transferring titles, working with Social Security—the types of rudimentary services one generally does not associate a funeral home with providing. Oh yes, and sometimes I help write and submit obituaries."

"But this place. It's so huge!" I exclaimed. "You have time to meet with every single family?"

"I sure do try, ma'am. What's pretty remarkable about the way your uncle runs Grand Hallow is even though it's a massive operation, we're a small crew. Departments only have a few full-time staff each, if any. Coveted positions these are. But you see, we mostly get by on a steady group of ancillary, part-time staff hired on an as-need basis. Yes, they're the true backbone of Grand Hallow. Yet for day-to-day operations, the entire facility is run by the seven of us."

"Seven of you?"

"Let me see. There's Bruce who runs the transportation department. The head groundskeeper, Henry. Norman, our head mortician. Nathan, in charge of the crematorium. Grave digging, which is overseen by Charlie. Then there's me. And of course your uncle, our founder and chief executive officer," he said with admiration. "Let's move on, shall we?"

We followed Ned down the hall of offices and through another door, after which the tone changed from welcoming to industrial. Gone was the carpeting with the earthy hues. Instead, it was replaced with plain, white tile floors. The hall was as sterile looking as a hospital. Fluorescent lights hummed incessantly overhead. But because they were spaced so far apart, much of the hall remained drenched in shadows.

"I apologize we cannot provide better accommodations, Miss Jacobs. But Mr. Jacobs is presently the only one who lives on the grounds. And his quarters are simply not suitable at the moment for the two of you. However, we have cleared out this storage room for you." He opened the door with some degree of reluctance. "It *does* have a window," he said apologetically. "Oh dear, I hope this will be OK."

"You're bullshitting us, right?" asked Tina as she eyed the small room.

The cinderblock walls were covered in a glossy shade of muted green. The exposed lightbulb amplified the green hue, causing the room to glow eerily. A twin-size bed sat in the middle. It had an arched headboard that had been painted white. Yet the half the paint had peeled away, revealing dark metal beneath. Looking about the room, I tried to come to terms with what would be my home for the summer. "It's fine," I said politely.

"Looks like solitary confinement in an insane asylum," cracked Tina.

"Miss Cashmere, I will be sure to look into sleeping arrangements for you tonight as well," said Ned, ignoring her critique.

"No!" I shouted a bit too fervently. "We'll make do with this room." I was not about to be separated from Tina. As long as she was at Grand Hallow, I wanted her with me. "I sprung Tina on you, so it's not fair to ask for a second room. This'll be great," I said, trying to muster some enthusiasm. Tina groaned before reluctantly throwing her bag into the room like a spoiled child.

I stepped back into the hall, attempting to gather my bearings. I knew which way we had come down the hall, but I wasn't so sure I'd be able to retrace our steps much beyond that. It was then I noticed that in the opposite direction, the other end of the hall opened into a room flanked by two pillars. And though it was dark, I could make out some type of metallic object sitting just beyond the pillars. "What's down there?" I asked curiously as Tina joined my side.

Without saying a word, Ned charged down the hallway. He flipped on the lights and then shoved the metal gurney out of the entryway and deeper into the room. "So sorry, ladies. You shouldn't have to see that," he said, shrugging his shoulders apologetically, yet leaving us utterly perplexed.

Without warning, I felt a hand grasp my shoulder. "It's the morgue," said a deep voice directly behind me. Startled, I spun around to see a man who looked remarkably like my dad. The resemblance took my breath away. He smiled cautiously. It was my dad's smile, the one that formed into a mischievous smirk no matter if any mischief was in fact intended. He had his same soft facial features, his salt-and-pepper hair, and his hazel eyes. It was uncanny. It was as if I were looking at my father all spruced up for a graduation or wedding, wearing a suit and clean-shaven. Only it wasn't him. Just some pieces of his DNA. He held out his hand. And as I shook it, life came back to my stunned lungs. "Hello, Lisa. I'm Clayton." He cleared his throat apprehensively. "Your Uncle Clayton."

"Hello," I replied meekly. "Thank you for all of this. I mean, taking care of my dad's funeral."

"It's the least I could do," he said while wringing his hands.

"You're telling me," snapped Tina. "A room next to the morgue?"

"I do apologize about that. If you and your friend would be more comfortable—"

"It's fine," I assured him. He adjusted his collar and looked down the hall behind him as if someone were watching from the shadows. He was pleasant, yet seemed preoccupied, his eyes shifting every which way. It could've just been his nerves. I imagined he was just as nervous meeting me as I was meeting him. Yet it also could've been because he was simply incredibly busy with the responsibilities that came with running such an enormous and complex place.

"So." Tina couldn't help herself. "Why did you want Lisa here so bad? She was just fine in Ruthsford, ya know."

"Tina!" I protested, secretly wanting to hear his answer.

His face sank a bit. He wiped his brow. "Well, I know it seems a bit selfish. But you see, a couple of years ago there was an accident. I lost my wife and both my daughters. My daughters, they were younger than you are now. I know you're not a child. I know you'll be eighteen soon. You're practically an adult. But it would feel so good to have a daughter again."

"Shit, man. I'm sorry," Tina apologized.

It didn't seem appropriate at the time, so I didn't question the circumstances of their deaths, but rather languished in the emotion.

"And the other reason is," he said, looking sullenly to the floor, "I thought if I could just take care of my brother's daughter when he couldn't, if only for a short while, then perhaps I could start to make things right. In a small way, at least."

How could I not feel for him? Losing his wife? His daughters? And then his estranged brother?

"I realize I'm putting you in an uncomfortable situation. I do apologize. I want to make your stay here as pleasant as possible. But I suppose if you don't want to stay the summer, I'll understand. I won't force you. But I'm hoping that you *do* stay here with us, Lisa."

Chapter 9

The Green Room

"Tina?" I whispered in the dark. "Are you awake?"

She flipped onto her back and groaned. "What the hell do ya think? There's a freakin' morgue outside the door. I shut my eyes, and all I see are dead bodies."

"Yeah. Me too."

"Even worse, your damn elbow keeps pokin' me in the ribs."

"Sorry," I said as I flipped onto my back as well. Together, we gazed into the darkness. "What time do you think it is?"

"I dunno. It's gotta be close to midnight."

"So. What do you think of my uncle?"

"I can't believe how much he looks like your dad. But man, is he a sad case."

"Yeah," I agreed. "But still," I began at the risk of sounding completely insensitive, "he's strange, don't you think?"

"Oh, he's totally fucked up," Tina replied without missing a beat. "Did you see him? He was jittery as hell. But I can see why. His wife and both his kids die. Plus, he works *and lives* in this death factory surrounded by miles of gravestones, which I gotta say has to be even worse than livin' in the spooky old Grant Mansion."

I cracked a half smile. *"Way* worse."

"And it's so weird thinkin' you had an aunt and cousins you didn't even know about."

"I know. They were here all this time. And I never even knew they existed. And now, I'll never have the chance to meet them. It makes me kinda sad, actually. I just can't stop thinking about what could've happened to them. Like, how did they die? What kind of *accident*?"

"Maybe they *accidently* burned to a crisp after he *accidently* shoved them into one of those cremation ovens?"

"Tina! I'm being serious."

"So am I! It's creepy. Like all three of them died? At the same time? Together?"

"OK. So if your mind is going there, then hear me out on where *my* mind is going. I'm just gonna say it. And I need you to be my litmus test, all right? You need to tell me if I'm going crazy. Because I'm honestly starting to wonder."

"Me too," she cracked. "But go ahead anyway."

"I hate to even think this because I just met the guy. He seems nice enough. And I want to believe his story about inviting me here to make it right with my dad and all. But do you think there's a connection between him and my dad's murder?"

"What? Because I basically just accused him of offing his whole family? Because he's jittery and has a pair of crazy, darting eyes? I dunno. Maybe. What other proof do you have?"

"No proof. I know I'm not being fair. But think about it. However it happened, we know his daughters died. Then, he says himself he wants to replace them with another daughter. And here I am. Summoned to Grand Hallow. Against my will. By him. What normal man his age would want a seventeen-year-old living with him for the summer? God, I feel awful for thinking this. But did he kill my dad to get me here? And now that I'm here, what are his plans for me?" I couldn't tell. Were my racing thoughts rational? Or was my mind making connections that simply weren't there?

Tina thought a moment. "I don't think you're crazy. And who says you need to be fair to anybody right now? With the shit you're going through, that's the last thing you need to worry about. The way I see it, until we get more information, everyone is a suspect. And as far as he goes, there're two ways about him. Either he's a sad sack who just feels real guilty about not patchin' things up with your dad—and he really wants to do what he thinks is a good thing. Or he's some sort of jittery, creepy freak lying about why he brought you here. Now we just have to find out which it is."

I playfully smacked her side, impressed by her clear perspective. "And how did you become so levelheaded all of a sudden?"

"See. I can be serious!" she protested. "But to be honest, I'm kinda just pretending like I'm in an episode of *Charlie's Angels* right now." I laughed, picturing Tina as one of the Angels. "Otherwise, I'd be running back through those gates so damn fast you'd see dust."

"But there's nowhere to run," I replied grimly.

"You know what bothers me? Your dad had to have a damn good reason why he cut out his brother. He just iced that fucker out cold! Do you remember anything? Anything at all about why he and your dad never talked? Like what happened? *Something* must've happened!"

"I wish I knew. My dad never spoke about Uncle Clayton. I only knew he existed because Richard told me. It was just one of those things we knew not to bring up with Dad. Damn. I wonder if Richard knows something more."

"Ask him. Tomorrow. After the funeral."

Our conversation was interrupted by a sudden loud rattle from the room down the hall, as if a baking sheet had fallen to the floor. Tina shot upright. "Did you hear that!" she whispered.

"No," I lied. Then I said immediately, "Something must've fallen off a shelf. That's all."

But I was proved wrong as a dim shaft of light appeared from the crack beneath the door. It was quiet for a moment. But soon, the silence was again shattered. This time, by a slow screeeeeech as if metal was being dragged across metal.

"What should we do!" Tina asked.

"I don't know. Just be still."

Then, loud banging began. It sounded as if someone was pounding a drum with a hammer. Boom! Boom! Boom!

"Should we turn on the light?"

"No."

I envisioned myself leaping up and swinging open the door to boldly discover just who—or what—was on the other side. But my body froze. Huddled together with Tina in the darkness, I felt like a coward. I watched, petrified, as the light beneath the door began to shift and become broken up by the movement of a shadow on the other side.

"Someone's comin' down the hall!" panicked Tina.

The shadow crept farther into the room through the crack beneath the door—until whoever it belonged to stood directly outside. It was still for a moment. We could hear heavy breaths. Then, as if suddenly alerted to our presence, the knob swiftly turned with a light squeak.

I remembered seeing a simple hook latch like on the outside of a shed, but I had not secured it. I hoped, prayed, that Tina had had enough sense to lock us in before we climbed into bed. I clutched the bedpost, wringing my hands over its chipped paint, anticipating the moment the shadow figure would burst into the room. When the knob was fully twisted and the figure leaned into the door, it opened only a smidge before being caught by the hook. Thank God for Tina!

The frustrated figure began twisting the knob with fervor. It heaved its weight against the door, attempting to force it open. My heart raced so heavily I could feel the blood coursing through my neck. Discouraged yet persistent, the figure then dropped to the floor. It slid its face against the crack. I didn't want to, but I forced myself to try to make out the face through the sliver of an opening. Yet all I could see was a brief flash of an eyeball scanning the room. With us atop the bed in the dark, I didn't imagine it could see much.

Apparently satisfied, the figure stood and began its way back down the hall toward the morgue. I nervously pinched my bottom lip as a reminder to stay as still and as quiet as possible. We heard more dragging and scraping as the shadowy stranger resumed its mysterious work. Whatever it was heaving had to hold quite a bit of bulk as the noises were often punctuated by loud grunts and groans.

After about twenty minutes, the light beneath the door disappeared. All was quiet again. Yet we stayed as still as cautious deer for what was likely hours. We were completely silent until Tina finally announced, "I gotta pee so fuckin' bad." If it wasn't for the fright that still coursed through my veins, I would've laughed aloud. "Do you think it's safe now?"

"I don't know. But we can't stay locked in here forever."

"OK. I'm gonna open it real quick, like pulling off a Band-Aid," she declared. She lunged for the light switch. The bulb flashed on, jarring the green room into recognition. But she was only on her feet for a moment before promptly falling backward, landing on her back with a wince-inducing slap.

"Oh my God! What happened!" I rushed to join her on the floor. "Did you hit your head?"

"I don't think so. I slipped on something," she said, dazed. I looked to her bare feet. They were covered in red. She sat up, and I noticed the underside of her white nightgown was also covered in red—blood. As she lifted her hands from the floor while attempting to stand, Tina herself noticed the blood. She screamed uncontrollably as it dripped from her palms and down her arms. I wanted to tell her to keep her voice down, but it wouldn't have mattered at that point. Her shriek was loud enough to wake the dead, which literally surrounded us. "Is that my blood!" she cried. "Am I dying!"

"You're not dying," I promised as I helped her off the floor. "And it's not your blood. Look." I pointed beneath the door. From the hall, in surged a slow-moving, yet steady stream of the syrupy liquid. It oozed into the room, painting our gray cement floor a deep shade of crimson. We soon found ourselves crouched back atop the bed as the blood flowed around its legs.

"What the hell is going on!" Tina screamed.

I looked to the window. Although the shade was drawn, there was no light around the edges. *Should we wait until morning?* I wondered. I answered myself with an eye roll before taking a deep breath. I shook off my fear and hopped over the puddle of blood. I grabbed my sneakers. After lacing them up, I stepped squarely into the pool of blood and unhooked the latch. Clenching the knob, I turned to Tina. "We gotta get outta here," I said before swiftly swinging open the door.

Even though Tina had to pee, we did not make our way toward the old locker room we were told to use as our bathroom. Neither did we run toward the lobby looking for an escape. No, without even discussing it, we kept tight along the wall, boldly inching our way toward the morgue. It was dark, but we were determined. I could faintly make out the sluggish river of blood that ran down the center of the floor. As we approached the opening of the room, it smelled strange, but not terrible. Antiseptic. Like a muted mixture of cleaning products with an added hint of peppermint, of all things.

Mysterious structures glistened dimly in the ambient light. I fumbled along the wall until I found the light panel. The room crackled into stark brightness. The cavernous facility was pristine and sterile. The floor and walls were made up of small, white square tiles. It felt like we stood in some massive public shower room. Only, unlike a shower room, about forty slabs jutted from the floor. As we stepped forward cautiously, I took a closer look at one of the slabs. The topside was a shallow porcelain basin the size of a cot. There was a headrest on one end and a large drain on the other. Beneath the drain ran a thick pipe that disappeared beneath the floor.

On the wall deep on the left side of the room were rows of what looked like stainless steel miniature fridge doors. They were stacked five high. I wasn't naive enough to have to guess what they held inside. The rows of drawers continued beyond the curvature of the main room and behind an interior wall, where I imagined they went on into infinity. A series of large sinks and several walk-in coolers like those found in an industrial kitchen took up the majority of the far wall. And strewn about the edges of the room were an assortment of stray metal gurneys.

We followed the stream of blood through the morgue. Although I was consumed with finding what was at the end of the ghoulish trail, I couldn't help catch a few glimpses of Tina. There was blood on her feet. Blood all over her white nightgown. Blood smeared into the mussed hair on the back of her head. She looked like a corpse bride, appropriately lumbering through the morgue. We snaked through the slabs and were led to the back of the room. There, behind the partition, in the corner where the rows of refrigerated drawers began, sat about ten barrels. The large plastic drums were precariously stacked from the floor to the ceiling.

"What are these doing here?" asked Tina.

"And why are they filled with blood?" I wondered as I noticed one of the barrels on the bottom of the stack had ruptured. Blood flowed from the punctured barrel through the morgue, down the hall, and into the green room, where it ultimately pooled.

From the back of the morgue, we heard a door swing open. "Shit! Where should we hide?" Tina panicked. She quickly ducked behind the stack of barrels. But seeing that her bloody footprints led straight to her hiding spot, I figured hiding wasn't the best option. Instead, I stood in the center of the room. Frightened, yet unapologetic, I braced myself to face whatever had entered that morgue. Reluctantly, Tina joined me by my side.

In came the most peculiar-looking man wearing a white lab coat. He was thin. And had to be at least seven feet tall. His face was emaciated—and pale, as if he only came out at night. His cheekbones protruded beneath his bright green eyes. His jet-black hair lay in perfectly straight strands. His bangs were cut with precision halfway down his forehead, framing his face in a symmetrical bob. He eyed us intently. Tina, barefoot in her bloody nightgown. And me, in my nightgown and wearing bloody Nikes. He did not reveal any emotion. Calmly, he looked about the room, to the mess the blood trail and our bloody footprints had made of the floor. "What are you doing in my morgue?" he said finally in a calm and steady tone.

Jarred by his unbreakable, piercing stare, I found myself stammering, "We—we were sleeping down the hall. And we heard a noise—"

"Someone tried to attack us!" Tina shouted.

"Well, we don't know that, actually. Not for sure, anyway. It's just that someone was trying to get in our room—"

"There was blood comin' under the door. And we found these barrels," said Tina, pointing. "What's up with the barrels of blood? It's freakin' disgusting!" The man did not reply. He was as still as the corpses tucked in the drawers, holding his unshakable gaze upon us. Frustrated by not getting a response, Tina blurted, "Well don't you know who this is?" Suddenly, I felt her nudge me forward. "This is Lisa Jacobs! Her uncle owns this place!"

I found myself holding out my hand in an awkward greeting. He looked at it as if it were a gesture from another planet. "*Lisa Jacobs?*" he questioned with some sense of intrigue. "You were not supposed to arrive until this morning," he said, still wary of my open hand.

"Yeah, well she's here now," said Tina.

"Yes. I see," he said, raising an eyebrow.

"Who was rattling our door? Was it *you?*" accused Tina.

Without answering Tina, he stepped forward and reluctantly took my hand. His hand felt cold. And his grip was extremely weak, as if I might've crushed his hand with the slightest bit of force. "Welcome, Miss Jacobs," he said with a painfully forced smile. He retrieved his hand and held it awkwardly away from his body as if it had just been contaminated. "My apologies for your, shall I say, *discomforting* night." With that, his arm outstretched, he headed to one of the large sinks.

"Who is this freak?" Tina whispered to me under her breath as he fervently washed his hands.

Immediately, he turned away from the sink. And with another tortured smile, he responded, "Oh, I am Norman. The head mortician, of course."

"What're you doing here in the middle of the night?" she asked.

"*Middle of the night?*" he questioned, delicately drying his hands on a towel. "It is 6:00 a.m. And if I do not begin preparations soon, things will begin to *stack up,* so to speak."

"What was all that banging we heard?"

"Likely what you heard was nothing more than the refrigeration systems. We have multiple units, you know. Do you have any idea the amount of Freon these coolers use? Constantly turning on and off. Off and on. Yes, I'm afraid it makes the old pipes rattle something dreadful."

"It wasn't pipes! Someone was in here!"

It was clear her persistence irked him. His eyes widened in disapproval, as if Tina were a naughty child swearing in church. "As I have just arrived, I can assure you it was not me," he said tersely. "Re-frig-er-a-tion sys-tems," he repeated slowly, as if saying it again would finally satiate Tina.

"The barrels?" I intervened. "Why are those barrels stacked up in the corner?"

"Ah yes." He motioned to the blood on the floor. "I will have one of my apprentices mop that up. Our drainage system, it's broken. It has been backed up for weeks now. The barrels are simply being used to store the waste for the time being. So you see, the blood in your room was a result of a simple leak and basic gravity.

"Now you two are welcome to stay and continue to ask me questions. But I *do* need to begin my work." He swiftly grabbed one of the gurneys and wheeled it to the wall of refrigerated drawers. He then opened a drawer and slid out a body encased in a black bag. With strength his lanky body did not appear to possess, he efficiently transferred the body to the cart and wheeled it near us. Without warning, he unzipped the bag from the feet up to reveal the blue torso of a fresh male corpse, stopping just above his blue lips. "So much to do," he said, and then cheerfully began gathering equipment about the room while chanting his to-do list: "Disinfect. Thread jaw shut. Arterial embalming. Aspirate the cavity. Restore! Restore! Restore!"

"No. That's OK," I said while slowly pulling Tina out of the room. "We have to get ready for my dad's funeral."

Chapter 10

Good-bye, Dandelion

Whether or not it was Norman who tormented us through the night, I owed him gratitude for making my dad look like my dad again. It clearly was *not* him in the coffin. But at least it was something closer. His jaw had finally been closed and properly aligned. His skin tone was no longer gray, but a warm, pinkish hue. His lips were pursed in a natural, serene smile. In fact, the most unnatural thing about him was the suit he wore. It wouldn't have been my choice for him. But I understood it was more dignified than mechanic's coveralls.

I turned from the coffin to see Ned ushering in guests. I waved to him politely. He had taken it upon himself to oversee the service. Although my dad was a lapsed Catholic, Ned had arranged for a Catholic priest to perform the homily. And he chose what had to be the most beautiful viewing room at Grand Hallow. It was bright with a tall cathedral ceiling. It had real pews instead of folding chairs. And unlike some of the other rooms with faux stained glass panels, this room boasted genuine stained glass windows. They masked the view of the rolling cemetery outside but let in natural light that passed through the panes of color to create a dazzling display throughout the room. Tina aptly described it as being at a "peaceful disco."

The room was too large for our small gathering, but I appreciated the gesture. Tina's parents were there, along with some other folks from Ruthsford who knew my father. I noticed the few Grand Hallow ancillary employees helping Ned. I could tell who they were by their black pants and white polo shirts that had the Grand Hallow logo sewn into the upper left corner: a sketch of a lone tree with lush leaves aboveground and its roots exposed below the surface. The word "Grand" stretched in a downward arc above the top of the tree and "Hallow" in an upward arc below its roots.

Just as the service was about to begin, Richard entered the room. Finally. His hair was stuck up in haphazard tufts. I couldn't tell if it was purposefully gelled that way or if he had simply rolled out of bed and driven straight to Grand Hallow. He *did* wear a button-down shirt and tie. So at least he had put in some amount of effort.

Looking so much like my dad, Uncle Clayton was easily identified by Richard. They made their way toward each other, and the two clasped hands. Uncle Clayton gave him condolences while Richard rudely scanned the room. When he found me, he nodded slightly in my direction. He then took Uncle Clayton's shoulder and ushered him to a corner. It was a bit curious. What could they have possibly been discussing that required their backs to be turned? Their heads bobbed in a quick, yet animated, conversation. Richard then offered him a firm handshake before breaking their private huddle to join Tina and me.

I gently patted his back as we stood before our father's coffin. I expected him to smell like booze again. He did not, although his eyes were bloodshot and glassy. Perhaps he had been crying. Or perhaps it was due to some drug. I didn't care. I was in no mood to judge Richard. I was too busy judging myself over feeling more determination than sadness at my own father's funeral. I couldn't help it. I was on a mission, one I thought I was going to have to put on hold during my summer at Grand Hallow. But as it turned out, Grand Hallow held mysteries of its own, mysteries that seemed as if they just might have a connection to my tragedy in Ruthsford.

We sat in the front row of pews. Richard to my right, Tina to my left. "What do you know about Uncle Clayton and Dad?" I whispered to Richard as we waited for the priest to begin. "Why didn't they get along?"

Richard groaned. "You really need to ask me this *now*? Right before the funeral?"

"Sorry." He was right. What difference did it make? I could talk to him about it after the funeral. I felt like a jerk.

Richard began shaking his head like he knew better, but whispered back to me anyhow. "I've been thinking about it myself too," he confessed. "But my memory of Uncle Clayton is just about as good as my memory of Mom." He turned around to see if anyone was within earshot. "Still." He hesitated. "I do remember one thing. At least I think it's something—"

"What is it?"

"Mom was still alive. I remember sitting in her lap. Out of the blue, Uncle Clayton shows up. I mean, now that I think about it, it *had* to be Uncle Clayton. Right? He looked like Dad, but it wasn't him. Anyway, there was some kind of fight between him and Mom and Dad. Yelling. And then Uncle Clayton starts grabbing at Mom. She was screaming. And then—" Richard paused as the priest took his position at the front of the room.

"And then?"

"He left."

"That's it?"

"He left," Richard continued quietly, "*with Mom.* He took her. All last night I've been thinking about it. And this part keeps replaying in my mind. I keep seeing her being taken away in this long, black car. I remember being so scared I'd never see her again. I don't remember how long she was gone. But when she came back, she wasn't the same. She was sick. And the next memory I have is the one of her bleeding from her mouth before she died." As the priest began, Richard slumped back in the pew, disturbed by his own revelation.

I felt like I had been punched in the gut. Although I wasn't quite sure what it meant, it revealed a dark relationship between Uncle Clayton and my family that heightened my suspicions and made me more uneasy than ever. And my mother. Had Uncle Clayton abducted her? How long was she with him? Was she held captive? At Grand Hallow? Had she finally escaped back home to us only to become sick? Did he somehow, intentionally, make her sick? *You can't give someone a brain aneurysm*, I reasoned. My thoughts swirled throughout the service. Although my body was there, I certainly was not.

Before I knew it, I was standing outside near the front entrance, coming out from my daze. The unfiltered sun brought with it warmth, and just a bit of clarity. It felt freeing to be outside. I received a hug, and Richard got a handshake from each guest from Ruthsford. After that, their cars were delivered to them by the Grand Hallow valet staff. One by one, they drove through the gates and chugged up the steep hill like carts on a roller coaster, escaping Grand Hallow for the normalcy of Ruthsford.

As the last car drove over the hill between the glistening tombstones, I found myself standing alone with Richard. He surprised me with an uncharacteristic hug. I was conflicted. While unexpected, it felt nice. But at the same time, it signaled he was leaving without me. Even though his memory was not a smoking gun indicating Uncle Clayton had inflicted any lasting harm to our family, Richard was willing to leave me behind with the possibility. "Just keep your eye on Uncle Clayton," he warned.

I wanted to scream at him, but did not protest. I had to accept Richard for what he was, and that was a very selfish person. I wouldn't have abandoned him in the same situation. Yet I needed to let it go. He was never going to be the brother I wanted. So I let him off the hook. "Be sure to stock the snacks at the station," I advised. "They've got to be getting low. And we make a good profit off them. The phone numbers for reorders are written on the notepad in the top drawer to the left of the register. And don't forget the Sprees. The kids always buy them out." And with that, he was gone.

I hugged Tina for the longest time as her parents patiently waited to leave. I didn't want to let her go. I was petrified to be left alone. But I also knew I needed Tina back in Ruthsford. In Ruthsford, she could keep an eye on my dad's investigation while I conducted my own investigation at Grand Hallow. "I just hate to leave you here with Creepy Clayton and Norman Bates," she said.

"I'll be OK," I said, trying to mask my panic and focus on what was most important. "You have to promise me to give that jar we found in your basement to Sternhardt, OK? The blood in it, maybe he can test it or something and see who it belongs to?"

"I promise," she said with a nod. "As soon as we get back. And I'll keep an eye on Sternhardt too. Make sure he does his damn job." Tina waved to me out the back window until she too disappeared up and out of the Mouth.

I stood in the shadow of the compound hugging myself. I was alone. Isolated. Trapped. Abandoned. With everyone gone, the air felt different. I suddenly realized the freeness I felt from being outside was an illusion. The grip of the oppressive cluster of buildings behind me hung close like a gravitational force. The back of my neck began tingling as I felt someone approach. "It's sad to see friends and family leave, isn't it?" Uncle Clayton asked rhetorically as he placed his hand on my shoulder.

I stepped out of his grip and faced him. "Yes. But I'm looking forward to my summer here," I lied with a smile. I felt it was important he didn't sense how wary I was of him.

"Good. Good. And how did you sleep last night? I heard there was some sort of—commotion?"

"No commotion," I lied again. "Norman explained to us there was some sort of accident with some storage barrels."

"*Norman*," he laughed a bit under his breath. "Norman's not so good dealing with the living. But he's super at his job. Trust me, he was probably more afraid of you than you were of him."

"I wasn't afraid," I said with a bit too much defiance. I looked beyond him to the grandiose promenade, which led to the giant main doors. I couldn't make myself go back inside. Not at that moment, anyhow. I needed an escape, if only for a bit. "I'm going for a walk," I announced.

He looked perplexed at first. But then opened his palms and gestured over the land. "It's all yours," he proclaimed. "When you get back, we'll have a nice lunch."

I began slowly down the path to the cemetery. "Oh, Lisa," he called after me, "do stay out of the wooded areas, won't you? You will find many small patches of forest. The ground is quite moist among the trees, I'm afraid. It may even be flooded yet from this spring. And the trees can become quite disorienting by the time you come out the other side. Why, we lost an intern who went for a stroll in one of our forests a few years ago. Haven't seen him since." He chuckled and then waved his hand as if to erase the comment. I made my way into the first few rows of headstones, wondering if it truly was only a joke.

Walking through the graveyard was a much different experience than simply driving through it or looking upon it through a window in the complex. Even taking the first few steps felt as if I were being taken in by the current of a deep and vast sea. The ground was uneven. It looked as if the land had been cleared of trees. And without being leveled, it was simply then paved over with meandering paths. It didn't take long to realize I should've changed into more comfortable clothing. I would've killed for jeans instead of my funeral dress, and sneakers instead of black pumps. But I wasn't about to turn back since I felt the eyes of Uncle Clayton—and Grand Hallow—burning into me.

I wound through the monuments of dark granite, white marble, and everything in between. Past crypts. Up hills. Into gullies. In the distance was one of the patches of forest Uncle Clayton had warned about. It looked like a small island surrounded by undulating waves of gravestones. While there was no direct path, I headed in its general direction. The late morning sun felt so good on my skin. The bugs humming in the grass and the occasional chirping bird encouraged me to keep going. Finally, I neared the forest. Just before the tree line, the ground rose in a dramatic hill before plunging into a steep decline.

It was while I was in the gorge that a peculiar uneasiness came over me. It came with the breeze. It came with a slight sound that reached my ear, a voice that I could've sworn called *"Lissssa."* I thought, maybe, I had misinterpreted a cooing bird. But soon, I heard it again. Still soft, yet strikingly distinct. *"Lissssa."* I froze. I tried to remain calm. Rational. I looked back through the sea of headstones to realize it was easily a half-hour brisk walk back to the complex. I took a tepid step forward, and the wind seemed to respond by bringing with it light, playful giggles. The laughing seemed to come from overhead.

I looked to the row of crypts along the crest above. Tiny rocks and pebbles tumbled over the edge and landed at my feet. I used my hand as a visor against the face of the blazing midmorning sun. And there, between two of the crypts, I saw a flash of movement! My heart raced. I took off briskly down the path, as fast as my pumps could carry me, anyway. And when the ridge became level enough with the path, I surprised myself by climbing it. While petrified of what I was to find, the mystery was too intriguing. Once on the path above, I backtracked toward the crypts that lined the ridge. I approached with hesitation. And then, I stopped, stunned, as two figures emerged from their hiding places. The mischievous pair stood blocking the path.

Both girls had shoulder-length red hair. They appeared to be between the ages of ten and twelve. They were dressed similarly, although not identically. One wore a green sundress with white polka dots, which, after closer inspection, were actually the heads of tiny daisies. The other wore a white long-sleeved shirt tucked into a plaid skirt. Both wore knee-high socks with black, polished, dressy-looking sandals.

Although their clothes were not identical, it was clear *they* were. Standing in the open, the twins had obviously wanted me to see them. I greeted them with a simple "hello." One of the twins giggled while covering her mouth. The other simply looked to her shoe while shyly making a circle with her foot on the pavement. "What are you doing way out here?" I asked.

The giggling twin removed her hand from her mouth. "We're sorry about your dad."

I was shocked. "How do you know about my dad? Were you at the funeral? I didn't see you there." They did not answer. "You had better get back," I continued. "All the cars have already left for Ruthsford." This time, both girls giggled, as if it were their way of answering my questions without giving an actual answer: *No, they were not at the funeral. And no, they were not from Ruthsford.* So I tried a different question: "What are your names?"

"I'm Elizabeth," said the twin to my left. She bumped the other twin with her hip and said, "And this is Imogene." Imogene finally stopped looking at her shoe and met my gaze.

"My name's Lisa. But I have a feeling you know that already. Right?" Neither would admit it, so I said, "I heard you calling my name. Will you tell me how you know my name?"

They both shook their heads from side to side. Elizabeth then placed her finger to her lips followed by a coy "shhhhhhh," solidifying her unwillingness to reveal their secrets.

"Will you at least tell me what you're doing out here alone? Are you lost? Where do you live?"

"We live here," Imogene finally piped up. "In the cemetery."

Elizabeth scowled. "We're not supposed to say!" she shouted, stomping her foot and promptly socking Imogene in the arm. "Let's go!"

"Wait!" But the two of them took off running down the hill, dodging headstones. "Wait!" I yelled again as I took off after them, stumbling down the grassy hill.

They headed for the nearby patch of woods, laughing as they ran from me. As they neared the edge of the trees, Elizabeth turned to shout, "Good-bye, Dandelion!"

"Dandelion! Dandelion! Dandelion!" they both chanted and laughed as they disappeared into the trees.

I entered the dark cluster of trees not far behind them. But my eyes did not adjust to the dimness of the forest quickly enough. Immediately, I stumbled over a bevy of fallen branches. Lying in the mud, I looked up to see the twins had disappeared. No longer did I see them ahead of me. Nor did I hear them running through the woods. Perhaps they quietly hid nearby?

I picked myself up. But instead of trudging directly through the trees, I quietly crept along the inside edge of the forest. As I followed the perimeter in a semicircle, I scanned the interior of the woods for any sign of the girls. Nothing. The ground was wet, flooded in the low spots. The tiny pools of stagnant water were swimming with bugs and larvae. Were the twins out there somewhere? In that swamp? Crouched behind trees?

By the time I reached the other side, I had given up. I emerged from the trees only to find myself in a maze of tightly arranged crypts. I zigzagged through the labyrinth of tombs, trying to find my way out. Heat rose off the hot stone walls. I charged through the twists and turns, which only led to more twists and turns. The more I ran, the tighter the crypts seemed to cluster. I felt trapped. Began to panic. Feeling claustrophobic, I picked up my pace. Was there no way out? I wanted to scream but could barely breathe. I felt as if I was about to hyperventilate. And then, finally, I sprinted into the open—only to suddenly crash into a man. Startled, I found my breath and belted out a healthy scream.

The man picked up the rake I had knocked from his hands. He had a thick, gray beard down to his chest. His face was weathered, as if he had been raking in the hot sun for about sixty years. "You scared me!" I told him, trying to justify my hysterical scream. He did not seem surprised. He merely shrugged at the notion and continued raking the stone path as if it were every day some crazy teenager came running from the crypts. "Did you see two girls run by here?" I asked.

"No girls out here," he replied simply, in a gruff voice.

He watched with a raised eyebrow as I took off my shoes. Irritated that my peaceful walk ended up anything but, I took off through the grass, cutting across the paved paths as I headed back to the complex. *Dandelion?* I asked myself. *What was that about?*

Chapter 11

Corpses Don't Bleed

Uncle Clayton and I ate an uncomfortably silent dinner. Most of the staff had left for the evening. So it was just the two of us in the large break room. Each bite I took of the steak, asparagus, and baked potato was excruciatingly awkward. I chewed methodically and forced a fake smile whenever our gazes met.

I wanted to interrogate him. Ask why he and my father had a falling out. Confirm whether or not it was related to Richard's memory—to the fight he had had with my parents, to the abduction of my mother. See if I could ultimately pin him to my dad's murder. But would he tell the truth if I asked outright? Likely not, I figured. Besides, if I started questioning him, he'd know I was onto him. No, I had to play it smart. Nose around first and see what I could find out.

But in the meantime, I needed another topic to squelch the silence. My mind raced. I could've asked who had prepared the meal. But didn't. I could've asked how his family had died. But didn't dare. I had only just met him. And that wouldn't exactly have been casual dinner conversation. I could've told him about the twin girls I had seen. But figured they were likely the daughters of a staff member. I didn't want to get anyone in trouble for bringing their children and letting them play in the cemetery while they worked.

So finally, I settled on, "Do you mind if I use a phone?" At Grand Hallow in 1985, I was effectively cut off from the outside world. I had last seen Tina only that morning. But it felt like days had gone by since the funeral. "I'd like to call my brother and see how things are going at the station. And I'd like to talk to my friend."

He seemed to consider it for a moment but ultimately burst into a laugh. "Now, Lisa, you just saw them this morning. I'm sure everyone is getting along just fine without you."

"Yeah, I'm sure they are too. It's just that, before bed, I'm thinking I'll just be a bit—bored," I gently protested. "I only brought a few books. And the batteries in my Walkman are about dead."

"I'll find you some fresh batteries," he offered. "And I have a small TV that I don't use. I can bring it to your room tomorrow. Will that help?"

"Yes. Thank you. But I'd really like to call my friend if I could."

He suddenly slammed down his fork. My body jolted from the surprise. While his action showed anger, he kept his voice light and friendly. With a smile plastered across his face, he said, "This is a lesson I remember having to teach my daughters. Distractions such as televisions and phones are privileges. Not rights." I squirmed in my chair, not expecting that response. "There will be no use of the phone. Now if you'd like to listen to your music, that's fine. As I have said, I will supply you with fresh batteries. And I will bring a television to your room. But a phone? It's off limits. Do you understand?"

Perplexed by the juxtaposition of such a stern message delivered in such a pleasant tone, I was initially stunned to silence. Yet I had no choice but to agree. "Yes," I replied timidly.

He shook his head, seemingly surprised by his own reaction. He looked to me apologetically. "I *do* want you to enjoy your stay here," he said, reaching his hand halfway across the table. His face was full of regret as he held his hand outstretched for a moment before slowly retracting his arm.

I wondered just what his deal was. I had never seen an outburst turn so tepid so quickly. It was like his emotions were erupting lava abruptly met with ice water. It wasn't difficult to sense some sort of internal struggle, some conflict, raging just beneath the surface.

"Now how about some lemon cream cake?" he asked with a wink and sudden return of his smile.

After dinner, we parted ways quite unceremoniously. I headed to my room and he went to his living quarters, which I knew were somewhere on the grounds. I didn't have a clue where. It was still early. Barely seven o'clock. So I grabbed my Walkman and sat on a stiff, formal chair in the balcony overlooking the main entrance. The only reason I stayed in this area was because it was one of the few places from which I knew how to get back to my room. I was afraid if I went exploring, I'd never find my way back through the network of passageways.

As if not eerie enough already, Grand Hallow was particularly haunting in the stillness of evening. Sitting alone, I found it so quiet. I could feel it, that odd absence of sound that caused my anxiety to rise. The fear was in the anticipation that the silence would end abruptly. That something unknown hid in the stillness, threatening to strike and destroy it at any moment and cause a startling fright.

I allowed my eyes to trace the giant vines in the carpet's pattern. I followed their twists down the stairs and through the lobby to the main doors. Outside the glass doors, against the dimming dusk, the tight clusters of headstones appeared to overlap and begin closing in on the building. And from my high vantage, I could see a bit down each of the main hallways. Why I craned my neck to see down each artery as far as I could, I didn't know. I was terrified, half expecting to see some shadowy figure striding toward the lobby.

Before the maddening silence had the chance to further take over my imagination, which was already primed for the ghoulish, I swiftly strapped on my headphones. Magical music. Amazing how it could chase away demons, even in a place as powerfully creepy as Grand Hallow. The imposing tombstones and the morgue down the hall behind me lost their powers of fright when listening to Prince's *Around the World in a Day*.

I relished the escape, startled only when the player stopped, clicked, and reversed the cassette back to side A. Just those few moments of silence before the album restarted were unnerving. It was like an evil despair oozed from the walls, held at bay only by encasing myself in sounds and harmony. It was unfortunate, then, that I had only made it halfway through "Paisley Park" when the tape stopped, and my protective layer was broken. I pressed the *play* button again. But the moment I feared had come: my batteries were dead. Reluctantly, I removed my headphones and became—exposed.

In an attempt to evade the omniscient spirit of Grand Hallow, I crept ever so quietly down the hall. Tip-toeing, I made my way to Ned's office. Perhaps I would find some batteries. Or even better, use his phone. After Uncle Clayton's bizarre outburst, I was even more suspicious of him. Did he really not want me to use a phone to teach me some lesson in manners? Or was he really just trying to keep me from reaching the world outside Grand Hallow? If only I could've gotten ahold of Tina, her familiar voice on the other end would've been better than music. It would've for sure squelched the evil vibes surrounding me. Desperately, I yanked on Ned's door. It was, however, locked.

Swiftly, I retreated toward my designated room/closet. I made my way down the dim hallway with the barely efficient fluorescents humming overhead. And as I approached my room, that *thing* that hid in the silence only to break it—struck. A loud bang came from the end of the hall. *Not again.* I stood just outside my door straining to see into the morgue. *Just ignore it. Get in your room and lock the door.* But before I could heed my own advice, the lights in the morgue crackled on. And my heart skipped a beat.

Without taking time to think it through, I found myself boldly approaching the lit morgue. I entered cautiously, yet surprised myself as my fear became secondary to my curiosity. Adrenaline kept me alert. Focused. Ready for anything.

The room was empty. And immaculately sterile. There was no trace of the blood trail from that morning. The slabs used for body preparation gleamed under the lights. That is, except for one. In the far corner of the room, on one of the slabs, lay a cadaver. I began to nervously chew on my thumbnail. Although I was not exactly startled to see a corpse in a morgue, why was it out of the cooler? And who had turned on the lights? I approached the dead woman with the wiry gray hair. Had I been in a hospital or anywhere else, I would've assumed she was asleep. However irrational, I was afraid to turn my back to her.

But the color red, it caught my eye. It came from one of the large sinks along the wall. I peered over the edge of the dual basins. Both were filled with several plastic clear sacks the size of pillow cases. The bags were filled with a deep red liquid. Blood, naturally, I assumed. It was strange how I immediately felt compelled to touch them. However gruesome their content, the blood bags seemed invitingly tactile. I ran my hands over the plastic. Each bag was stretched to its limit, bulging at the seams. It was odd to think the thin, transparent membrane was all that kept the blood from gushing free. As I began to use a bit more pressure, I felt solid matter among the dark liquid. I squeezed one of the bags. Doing so, I was able to bring one of the pieces to the surface. What pressed against the clear plastic looked like a chunk of raw meat. Immediately, I brought my hands from the basin. *What the hell?* I wondered as I took a few steps back. I startled myself further by backing right into the slab that held the corpse of the woman.

My brief fright turned to sheer terror when the door to one of the large walk-in coolers suddenly flew open. A pair of feet appeared to float horizontally through the double doors. As the legs covered with purple splotches came into view, it was apparent, without warning, that a body was being rolled my way on a gurney. With nowhere to hide, I simply froze as the body rolled forward.

A young guy pushing the gurney emerged from the cooler. Instead of releasing the gasp that threatened to erupt from my lungs, I simply straightened my back and cleared my throat. "Hello! I'm Lisa Jacobs," I firmly asserted while extending my hand in a formal greeting. The man jumped and let out an immediate scream. The clipboard he held under his arm dropped to the porcelain floor with a crash. "I'm so sorry!" I apologized as he scrambled to retrieve his paperwork.

He gathered himself and then emerged upright with an uneasy smile. "Well at least now I know my scream isn't entirely like a little girl's."

"No. It was a very manly scream," I assured him.

He appeared to be in his early twenties, not much older than me. He had moppy dark hair that would've fallen into his eyes if it hadn't been swept behind his ears. "I'm David," he said, as he held out his slightly trembling hand to accept mine. "I'm still shaking," he acknowledged.

"Well you scared me too! What are you doing here so late?"

"I *work* here. Second shift."

"Really? I didn't know there was a second shift. Hey, were you here last night? Sometime after midnight?" Could he have been the one making all that noise? Attempting to force open the door to the green room?

"No. Second shift ends at eleven. Besides, I only work Mondays, Wednesdays, and Fridays."

"So who worked third shift last night?"

"There is no third shift."

"Hmm." I looked him over as if I had a right to be suspicious. Unlike Norman, who wore a lab coat, David wore a simple white apron as if he were a clerk at a butcher shop. Like Norman, he was tall and thin. "Are you Norman's son?" I asked.

"Um. No," he replied with some offense. "Oh, God. You think I look like Norman? I am *not* related to him!"

"No. No. Not at all. Well, it's just that you're tall. And have black hair. And you're a mortician."

"I'm not a mortician. I'm just one of Norman's apprentices. I started down in the transportation department. Driving hearses. Carrying caskets. But when there was an opening for an apprenticeship in the morgue, I went for it. If I get hired on as a technician, I'll get a nice raise. I could use the extra money. And I'm not squeamish. Although, apparently, I startle easy."

He pushed the fresh corpse he had rolled from the refrigerator and carefully transferred it to the slab next to the dead elderly woman. Then, from the other side of the room, he wheeled forward a machine atop a narrow steel cart. The machine looked like an industrial-size blender or food processor with a cloudy yellow liquid filling the oversize jug. A hose protruded from the base of the machine. The front panel displayed a pressure gauge along with several dials and switches. He strapped on a pair of gloves and then grabbed a scalpel from a tray that slid out from the cart. "*You're* not squeamish, are you?" he asked.

"No," I said confidently, while masking my unease over what exactly he was about to do with that scalpel.

He pulled the sheet back, enough to expose the man's neck and shoulder. Without warning, he made a small incision near the collarbone. Surprisingly, there was no blood. "Corpses don't bleed," he told me, as if he heard my thoughts telepathically. "You need a pumping heart to bleed." He bent down to get a closer look. Using the scalpel and fishing with his fingers, he informed me, "I'm searching for the carotid artery. Ah, there it is." He grabbed the tube from the machine and clamped it into the neck. He then grabbed another short tube. "Now for the internal jugular vein." He fished again with his scalpel and made another internal cut. Satisfied, he affixed one end of the tube to the vein and laid the other on the slab near the drain.

He then moistened a sponge before flipping on the machine. The machine began to whir and gave off a slushing sound. The liquid jostled and bubbled like a water cooler tank being emptied. He adjusted the dials and used the sponge to massage the lower neck and arms in a downward motion.

Watching the grisly procedure did not make me queasy. It was too surreal. In fact, I found I could *not* look away. My only worry was about the visions my mind was recording. When I was alone, would they come back to haunt me?

"The embalming fluid is now being pushed through the arterial system," he announced over the noise of the machine. "If I did it right, the blood will be forced out through the jugular." He pointed to the tube lying on the slab. Sure enough, blood began spurting out into the basin.

But as the gush of blood headed for the drain, I suddenly shouted, "Stop!" He looked to me as if I were insane. "Don't let the blood go down that drain!"

"Why not?"

"It's broken. It's all backed up!"

He immediately shut off the machine. We watched as the blood pooled around the drain—and then swiftly disappeared beneath the grate. "Why would you say that?" he asked, switching the machine back on.

"Because Norman told me the drainage system has been backed up for weeks," I explained, embarrassed.

"No," he shook his head. "That's impossible. I was here Monday. And it was working just fine."

I rushed behind the interior wall and was shocked. "What happened to the barrels?" I yelled across the room.

"Barrels?"

"The barrels that were stacked right here—the blood that was being stored because of the broken drain!"

"I don't know what you're talking about. The drainage system, you can see it's working just fine."

I could feel my frustration—and distrust—escalate simultaneously. "What are those bags in the sink?" I pointed, demanding to know. "Why are they filled with blood? And God knows what else?"

"I don't know," he said, continuing to massage the corpse with the sponge. "I just got the hang of embalming. I have no idea what else Norman does around here. You know, you sure ask a lot of questions."

"Yeah, I do," I agreed, annoyed. "So why haven't you asked *me* any?" I wondered aloud. "It's kind of weird, actually. I barge into your work. You don't know who I am. And you just go about draining a body in front of me?"

"But I *do* know who you are. You're Bette Davis."

"*Bette Davis?* What is that supposed to mean?"

He lowered his voice to just above a whisper and leaned closer to me. "The lady with the veins bulging across her face. That's what we used to call her."

"What *lady with the veins*? Who are you talking about?"

"The one who ran the place. She was small in stature. But man, was she ever in charge. You know, your aunt."

"*My aunt?* Oh. I never met her."

"How is that possible?"

"I never even met my uncle until yesterday. My dad and he were—on bad terms, I guess you could say."

"No kidding? Wow, that is kind of wild. Well, your aunt, if you saw her coming down the hall, you'd better be sure you didn't make eye contact. And you'd better stand aside to let her pass like she was some sort of army general and you were her soldier. She didn't get that nickname because of her eyes, you know."

"So why the hell would you call *me* Bette Davis? You just met me. And I'm nothing like that!"

"Because you're the next female Jacobs in line since they're all dead—your aunt, her daughters. Rumor is you are her replacement, the niece who's coming to take over the place since your uncle is—I know I shouldn't say this—a mess. *You,* Bette Davis, are all everyone is talking about. You're like royalty. An heir. Coming to save Grand Hallow, while at the same time make us all just as miserable as the original Ms. Davis had."

"Well, I can assure you, I'm not next in line for anything."

"Obviously," he said with a chuckle.

"Hey! What's that supposed to mean?"

"To be honest, I pictured you much older. You're like what? Sixteen?"

"I'll be eighteen at the end of August."

"Well, I stand corrected," he said sarcastically. He flipped off the embalming machine and began rubbing the cheeks of the dead man. "See those rosy cheeks? That means he's done." He covered the man back up with the sheet. "Hey, I'm sorry for talking about your family that way. If that bothers you—"

"Don't worry about it. Like I said, I just met my uncle. And I didn't know my aunt or my cousins."

"Actually, I was told not to talk to you *at all*."

"Why?"

"For my own benefit, I guess. And it was probably damn good advice seeing as how I offered up the Bette Davis story without so much as being provoked," he said with a laugh. "And besides, it's best not to give away any of the other secrets Grand Hallow holds," he said with a wry smile that made me wonder about the level of his seriousness. "It's not that I didn't *try* to avoid talking with you. Truthfully, I'm impressed. I was sure the embalming would've scared you off. But there you stayed. What kind of girl sticks around to watch a guy embalm a corpse?"

"What kind of guy likes to embalm corpses in the first place?"

"Never said I liked it. Just said I was here because I could use the money. Why are *you* here?"

"Because I'm trapped, I suppose."

Chapter 12

Marco Polo

Witnessing an embalming apparently did little to traumatize me. Instead of reliving gory images of blood being flushed from a corpse, my mind was instead kept occupied by something else. *"Dandelion? Bette Davis?"* I kept repeating as I lay in bed. How was it that I had managed to procure *two* nicknames in a place I had been for barely twenty-four hours by people I had never met? Diffused light came through the window, reminding me that even the ceiling was green. "And this green room!" I cursed it as my eyes became heavy. I clutched the blanket and turned on my side, miffed I was stuck in that closet of a room. Miffed that Grand Hallow seemed to offer more questions than answers.

Tap! Tap! Tap! My eyes sprang open. Was that David at the door? Had he finished his shift and wanted to tell me something more? Had he simply wanted to say good night before he left? Since I was half asleep, it took me a moment to orient myself to the room. And as I sat upright, I realized the taps had *not* come from the door—but from the other side of the room. I sat still and listened. Maybe whatever it was would go away? Tap! Tap! Tap! No such luck. The polite tapping came from the window. I strained to see. But from the bed, I couldn't see anything out the window besides the pole light along the nearest walking path, which was dimmed by a strangling mist.

I couldn't handle any more unknowns. Brazenly, I tore off the blanket and marched to the window. There I stood, impatiently waiting for an answer. The rolling hills of graves were engulfed in a blanket of fog. The thick mist gave the lamplights twinkling halos. They dotted the landscape, appearing to float above the graves.

And just as I became lost in the ethereal scene, I heard the tapping once more. Yet still, nothing was at the window. Or so I thought. After a moment, I noticed a brief flash of movement near the bottom of the glass. I jolted back to see a hand slowly rise into view and begin gently tapping against the lower portion of the pane. Tap! Tap! Tap! Cautiously, I moved back to the window and placed my forehead flush against the glass.

The massive building accommodated the hills, not the other way around. The main building's facade was grand, with its majestic staircase and multilevel structure. But the rear, where the morgue had been constructed, was atop the hills, effectively making it a ground floor. Yet even from the back of the morgue to my room, there was a dramatic drop in the landscape. And out my window, even one with considerable height couldn't simply tap on the pane without standing on someone's shoulders—or using a ladder.

Yet as I peered below, I saw the top of a head with red hair parted perfectly down the center. The girl dangled from the window sill. How in the world she got up there I didn't know. Was she given a boost? And how did she manage to tap the pane when it would've taken *two* hands to grip the sill without falling?

I tapped back gently, and she immediately gazed up to me. It was Imogene. I could tell because she wore the same white shirt and plaid skirt she had worn earlier that day. Only that night, her long hair was braided into ponytails clasped at the ends with pink marble-size bobbles. She smiled and then began to giggle before dropping to the ground below like a skillful gymnast. As she stepped backward, she motioned for me to join her. From the fog emerged Elizabeth, still in her green sundress with the daisy pattern. As soon as she materialized, they latched together like opposing ends of a magnet.

I unlatched the window and called below. "What're you doing out there?"

"Come play with us," called Elizabeth, her voice echoing in the mist. Imogene waved up to me, keeping her hand at her hip. Elizabeth clasped her other hand and slowly pulled Imogene into the fog. I could barely make out their figures in the haze, but clearly heard them calling, "C'mon Lisa. Come and play."

Hastily, I got dressed and made my way through the dark and empty morgue. I exited through the back service door. And as the door shut behind me, I found myself feeling vulnerable and isolated in the dark and foggy night. The fog was so dense, I couldn't see three rows into the graveyard. I stepped forward onto the walkway and then moved uneasily down the slope. *What am I doing?*

"Dandelion!" I heard one of the girls call from the fog. "Follow my voice."

Against my better judgment, I stepped off the paved path and onto the grass. It was too late to turn back. I couldn't resist the chance to find out why these strange girls had made the cemetery their playground. I passed gravestones as I climbed a hill and made my way down the other side. I tried to stick close to the lamplights. But much like a car's high beams in fog, the light only reflected back on the vapor, causing an even thicker gauzelike veil to cloud my vision.

"Over here!" one of them called again, causing me to speed off in another direction.

"Where are you?" I called into the fog.

"C'mon Lisa. This way!"

I marched forward, following their voices until I was quite sure I had been literally swallowed by the fog and would have no chance finding my way back.

"You're real close," said one of the girls in front of me to my left.

"Almost there," said the other to my right. "Just a few more steps."

"There. Now stop!"

I stood with my arms stretched in front of me feeling the air like a blindfolded child who had just been spun for a round of Pin the Tail on the Donkey.

"Now we can play our game."

"What game? I can't even see you."

"You're not *supposed* to be able to see us, silly."

"Because we're going to play Marco Polo. Do you know how?"

"Yes. But I've only played in a pool. You can't play on land."

"We'll pretend we're swimming—in a sunken graveyard!" said one of the girls excitedly.

"And the fog, it's so thick. Whoever is *it* can even keep their eyes open because it won't matter."

"OK. Let's try," I agreed.

"One, two, three—not it!" screamed one of the girls.

"Not it!" quickly declared the second girl. "You're it, Lisa!"

"Of course I am," I muttered.

"Now see if you can find us!"

I lunged to my left where I distinctly heard one of the voices. But the girl had vanished. I rushed toward the other girl. But she too had disappeared. With no choice, I resorted to shouting, "Marco!"

"Polo!"

The girls' shouting in unison made it difficult to tell their positions apart. Yet I felt good about having isolated one of them in the distance. I trudged forward. Up another hill. Down another gulley. I made my way until I found myself next to a crypt large enough to house a family of five corpses. But without the girls in sight, I was forced to rattle off another "Marco!"

"Polo!"

I couldn't believe how far ahead their voices had moved. How had they traveled such a distance without making a sound? So light-footed they were, moving swiftly without as much as snapping a twig. "This isn't fair!" I protested. "We have to stay in the same area." I followed the giggles ahead.

"Marco!"

"Polo!"

I was gaining on them. I entered a low-lying section of graves. The fog rolled over the graves like clouds wisping over miniature mountains. I crouched down to look for the twins' white stockings beneath the mist.

"Marco!"

"Polo!"

I was practically on top of them. I could hear their breathing. I reached in front of me, grabbing the air. "I'm gonna get you," I teased. I belted out one more "Marco!" to seal the deal. But in return, all I received back were some stifled giggles. "Marco!" I repeated impatiently. I waited in silence, anticipating their voices to finally give them away. Yet the next sound I heard was not from a few feet in front of me. Or even to my side.

"Polo!" one of the girls finally belted out—from above. It took me by surprise. Before I even had a chance to look up, I felt my hair being touched. And then yanked! I let out a scream as I frantically smoothed my hair back to my head.

I wasn't sure what the hell was happening. I began to run. But I didn't make it very far before I felt my hair once again rise from my scalp. "Polo!" the second girl shouted from above as she too yanked my hair.

They giggled with glee as I ran into the fog screaming hysterically. "Stay away from me!" I screeched. I narrowly dodged tombstones as I ran through the morbid obstacle course.

"Lisa!" one of the girls called after me. But I wasn't about to stop. I ran away from their voices, aimlessly through the misty shadows. I ran until I just about crashed into one of the girls standing right before me.

It was Elizabeth. She stood calmly with her hands folded in front of her dress.

"How'd you do that?" I asked, frightened, out of breath.

"I've just been standing here. And this whole time, you've been running in circles," she said with a laugh.

"No. How did you get *above* me! Into the air?"

She answered me only in a giggle as Imogene emerged from the fog and joined her sister's side. She pointed to the sky. "We were up in the tree, silly."

"I told you not to say!" chided Elizabeth.

"You could've won," said Imogene. "If you had yelled 'fish out of water' when we were in the tree, when our feet were off the ground, you would've won. Those are the rules."

I collapsed to the wet ground, exasperated yet relieved. "That was a dirty little trick you two played on me!" The girls gathered around me with giant grins on their faces, accepting my hysterics as kudos. "Oh, Imogene," I suddenly noticed. "You're bleeding." I pointed to her hand. She knelt beside me and held up her arm. The blood trickled slowly down the side of her hand from a cut on her outer pinky.

"I got scraped by a branch when I jumped out of the tree."

"You know what we should do?" Elizabeth said excitedly, eyeing the blood. "We should become blood sisters!"

Imogene too lit up at the notion. "Yes! Can we?"

"*Blood sisters?* But you already *are* sisters. *Real* sisters. And more than that, you're *twins*. You can't get any closer than that. You *already* have each other's blood in your veins."

"But we're not blood sisters with *you*," countered Elizabeth. She fiddled with the lining of her skirt for a moment and then declared, "Look, I can use my skirt pin." She unclasped the pin to show off the sharp needle. She then held out her thumb and was about to stab herself.

"Wait!" I shouted. "What's really going on here? Why are we out here? Why are *you* out here in this cemetery? Where are your parents?"

"We're not supposed to say," said Imogene apologetically.

"We're not allowed," added Elizabeth before casually plunging the needle into her thumb. Blood pooled to the surface before spilling over and running down her hand. "Won't you be our blood sister?" She offered me the pin.

I looked to the pin with much hesitation. Finally, I said, "OK. I'll bargain with you. If I do this, will you tell me where you're from? Will you tell me who your parents are? And why the heck you keep calling me *Dandelion*!" Imogene burst into a laugh at the mention of the name. Elizabeth, however, thought for a moment. She then replied with a simple smile and nod. Reluctantly, I took the pin. And with a brief wince, I pricked my finger.

"How do we do it?" asked Imogene.

"I think we just hold our hands together and let the blood mix," I said. With that, we joined hands, our pinpricks and Imogene's cut. We sat in silence for about a minute.

As I released from the grasp, Imogene shouted, "Now you're my real sister too!" She gave me a hug. I gave her a light hug back. But she wouldn't let go. Her grip became more and more firm. They both laughed joyously as I toppled over. They celebrated our new sisterhood by climbing atop me in a playful wrestling match.

"*Now* you have to tell me why you're out here," I demanded, as I attempted to shove them from me.

"Get her!" Elizabeth shouted with a huge grin, apparently ignoring our deal as she grabbed my arm and sat on my chest. Imogene grabbed my other arm. They pinned me to the ground, laughing. I was laughing too, at first, even as I fought to sit up. Then Elizabeth cried, "Drink our blood!" before jamming her bleeding thumb into my mouth.

"Yeah, drink it!" Imogene followed as she too stuck her bleeding finger in my mouth. They were both on top of me. Holding me down. Their fingers in my mouth. Feeding me their blood. I struggled to break free in a claustrophobic panic. It was then I felt one of their mouths close in around my own bleeding thumb and begin to lightly suck.

While it was happening, all I could see was the delicate mist slowly undulating overhead. And then, it was over. As quickly as they had subdued me, the twins had released their grip and vanished. All that remained for the next moment was their laughter, which faded swiftly into the fog.

I sat up. My head pounded. The taste of their blood was on my tongue. It was just a taste, but the feelings that coursed through me were strong. Raw, as I expected adolescent emotions to be. But the emotions I tasted, they weren't very happy. Jealousy was primary. Then there was anger. Fear. And—something else. Not an emotion, but an *entity* that *conjured* strong emotion. A strong force bound to the twins. However distant and elusive it was to my perceptions, I felt its power, its control. Could it have been me? My *own* blood that I tasted in the mix? No. Sensing such qualities from me wouldn't have been possible.

It was all too much (and at the same time too little) to put my finger on. But it was *something*, I supposed. More than I had known about the twins before wandering into the fog that night, anyhow.

I awoke the next morning unsure of how I had found my way back to my room. The night seemed like a dream, with the wistful fog, the floating haloed lights, and the bizarre girls converging on me like a pair of young lion cubs learning to overwhelm their prey.

Part III
Chapter 13
Expired Jam

I had survived my first few weeks at Grand Hallow. I started getting used to showering and getting ready in the old out-of-use locker room. But after that, I was unsure of what to do with myself. In the summers, I'd typically be up before 6:00 a.m. By 6:30, I'd have the fuel pumps inspected, the daily rates updated on the marquee, and the convenience store open for business.

At Grand Hallow, I had no purpose. In the evenings, I'd walk the monolithic hallways. Each time, I'd dare myself to enter the maze just a bit farther, only to see if I could find my way back. During the day, I'd wander the vast property, even venturing out to some of the isolated patches of woods. In one of my notebooks, I began developing a crude map of the grounds, sketching all the buildings and forests I had found. If I found a new section of graves or cluster of trees, I'd add them to the map. And after thoroughly exploring a sector of the map, I'd shade it in.

I explored and mapped not just out of boredom. I was searching for any evidence to substantiate or refute the twins' claim that they lived somewhere out in the graveyard. I was determined to find exactly where they came from. And whom they belonged to. Yet even after our disturbing game of Marco Polo, I hadn't bothered telling Uncle Clayton about the wayward girls loose in his cemetery. And why would I? It was a little mystery I could ponder. Something to help distract me from feeling I had already hit a brick wall in my ability to pin him to my father's murder.

One morning, before taking off on one of my exploratory strolls, I found myself standing outside Ned's office eavesdropping. "Oh, no, no, no, no, no, Mr. and Mrs. Avery. Take your time with these decisions. I promise, I'm here to help. Not to overwhelm. You needn't worry at all. I'll walk you through the entire process. The important thing is that you're happy with your choices. And that your father is well honored."

"Can we look at the caskets one more time?" asked a distraught Mrs. Avery. "I'm just not sure which is the right one for Dad."

"Or for our pocketbook," joked Mr. Avery.

"Certainly. Yes," replied Ned. "Trouble is, there is a viewing in the east wing in a few moments, and I must oversee the preparations. Oh my. Let me see," he fretted. I could hear him pick up his phone. But then he set the receiver back down. "Oh, Miss Jacobs?" he shouted into the hall. "Ma'am?"

My face became flush with embarrassment. Caught in the act, my only option was to expose myself. I entered the doorway. "Hello," I greeted them with a sheepish smile.

"I'm sorry to ask this of you, Miss Jacobs. But if it's not too much trouble, would you mind escorting Mr. and Mrs. Avery down to the showroom?" From his desk drawer, he produced his comically large set of keys. He rifled through them and isolated one on the ring before carefully handing it over.

"I'd be happy to," I said as I nodded sympathetically to the middle-aged woman with red eyes and her exhausted-looking husband. "Only, I don't think I know where the showroom is."

"Ah, yes. It's down one level. In the lobby, take the hall behind the main staircase. It's the third door on the right."

"Got it," I said as I led the couple out of his office.

"Please return the keys to my desk upon your return. And thank you ever so much, Miss Jacobs." He hurriedly put on his suit jacket as he rushed by us.

Surprisingly, I did not have trouble finding the room. I could see why the Averys had a hard time deciding. The massive showroom housed hundreds of coffin displays from basic mahogany to modern white—even a line infused with real gold. While they browsed, I found a stack of blank order slips upon a desk. After about a half hour, they finally settled on the Lincoln Poplar with Glossy Finish and Cream Interior, model number 8712, for $1,700. Although I had no way of knowing, I told them it was a good choice—perhaps not for Mr. Avery's pocketbook, however. "Thank you, honey," said Mrs. Avery gratefully as I filled in the model on the order form.

I made the trek back up to Ned's office feeling I had actually accomplished something. However small, at least I felt useful. I set the keys on his desk atop the completed order form. I was about to leave his office but found myself staring at his phone. It begged my attention. Before I had a chance to second-guess myself, I quietly swung shut the door and picked up the receiver. I did not hear a dial tone, so I began furiously punching the extra buttons along the side of the keypad. Finally, the hum of the dial tone came to life. I dialed swiftly.

"Tina?"

"It's about damn time," she answered. "I thought you'd never call."

"I've been having problems getting to a phone," I hastily explained. "I don't have a lot of time. What's been going on? Did you get that jar of blood to Sternhardt for evidence?"

"Oh, fuck. I was afraid you were gonna ask that."

"Tina? What happened?"

"Well, when we got back home, I was so tired. I mean, c'mon. We didn't even sleep the night before. So I kinda just forgot about it. But then I went to pee in the middle of the night, and I saw it sitting in the bathroom. I was like 'oh shit!' So I took it down to the fridge. You know, so that it would stay fresh for the analysis or whatever."

"Good idea."

"Yeah, I thought so too. And then, in the morning, I went to grab it and—it was gone."

"*Gone?*"

"Ugh! Well, my mom's an idiot. She thought it was some sort of expired jam. And she dumped it down the garbage disposal."

"Tina, no!" I slapped my palm to my forehead.

"I know! I know! I'm so sorry!"

"It's all right," I said, trying not to let her hear my frustration. "Where's the jar now? Can you get it out of the trash?"

"Well, it's at the dump by now. The garbage guy took the trash yesterday. But there was nothin' left in it anyway. She rinsed it out and everything. Clean as a fuckin' whistle. I checked, Lisa. I swear."

"OK. It's OK," I sighed.

"But get this. I've been buggin' the shit outta Sternhardt. Only he won't tell me a damn thing because I'm not family. So guess what I did?" She began to chomp her gum excitedly. "I tracked the fucker! That's right, *Scarecrow and Mrs. King* style! He's been parkin' his cruiser across the street from the gas station watchin' Richard. So there I am, watchin' Sternhardt watchin' Richard. So Richard comes out in just his underwear. Burpin' and fartin' and scratchin' his ass. Completely oblivious as to why a line of cars filled with pissed-off customers are honkin' their horns on a Saturday morning. Holy shit! Was I laughin' my ass off!"

"Damn it! I knew he was going to ruin the business. I just didn't know it would be so quick."

"So yeah, he's definitely casing Richard. They've searched your house and yard a couple more times. But either they haven't found anything. Or haven't found anything that sticks it to Richard seeing as they're lettin' him live there for now. But I'm tellin' you, he better watch his back because Sternhardt has it out for him either way."

"So that's all he's been doing? Watching Richard? He has no other suspects?"

"Well, I'm just gettin' started, sister. The other day, I followed him all the way out to Shilling."

"*Shilling?* That's halfway to Grand Hallow."

"I know! And it wasn't easy. The whole way, I kept my distance and all—like you're supposed to when you're trackin' somebody. Anyhow, he goes into this neighborhood. A new neighborhood. Not even any trees or anything. It's *that* new. Only it's not finished. Like it's new construction that was started but abandoned or somethin'. There's like nobody in the streets. Big dirt piles everywhere. Houses half built. Anyway, he goes to this one house and busts through the door. Like rams it open with some rammer thing. And then he starts takin' out things like boxes and blankets. Even food. He loads the shit in his car. Then he starts boardin' up the house. He had an electric screwdriver and everything, goin' around to all the doors and windows. You're gonna wanna write this down. Have a pen?"

"Yeah."

"The address is 966 Lindley Street in Shilling. Got it?"

"Yeah. But Tina," I said, appreciative, yet less than impressed, "it sounds like there were just some people squatting in a vacant house. I don't see how this could be related to my dad's murder."

"But why would Sternhardt bother goin' all the way to Shilling to check out some squatters? That's not even his town."

"True," I admitted. "But Shilling's even smaller than Ruthsford. Maybe the towns share police services or something? Still," I said to appease her, "this is great information. I don't know what I'd do without you." Truly, I didn't. She was my eyes and ears in Ruthsford. And however unfocused Tina could be, I was always impressed with her dedication as a friend.

"So what's happening on your end? Interrogate your uncle yet?"

"*Interrogate* is probably not the right word. I've talked to him a bit, I guess. But let's just say he's a little—quiet. Not exactly the best guy to get information out of. I've been trying to play it safe. See what I can find out on my own. But I've been a little—distracted by something else going on."

"*Distracted?* By what?"

"It's not important. What's important is, thanks to you, I now have a new idea to get my investigation on track."

"What do you mean?"

"You've inspired me. I think it's time I go a little *Scarecrow and Mrs. King* myself."

Chapter 14

Emerald Bridge

The small stone cottage looked like something out of a fairytale, with its slanted roof, vine-covered exterior, and stone walkway. I had found it on one of my walks. It was nestled among a grove of mature maples near the crematorium. I approached unannounced with a couple of assumptions. The first was that Uncle Clayton would be preoccupied enough with work that he would not return to his home until later that evening. The second was that he wouldn't bother locking his door.

Bees swarmed the densely planted chrysanthemums on either side of the door. I paused for a moment with my hand on the knob, working up the nerve to cross into *breaking and entering* territory. With a quick twist and a shove, the door opened—sort of. It jammed a quarter of the way, snagging against the stone floor. *Must be the humidity*. I squeezed through the tight opening. And there I was. Inside. Line firmly crossed.

The place smelled of must. From the entryway, I could see a bit into the open kitchen and modest living room. But it was dark. The shades were drawn. And I didn't have a flashlight. Yet even though it was daytime, I knew enough about sleuthing not to be lifting shades or turning lights on and off. So I used what bit of natural light I had to inspect the rooms.

I wasn't quite sure what I was looking for. Anything related to my father. Anything that would lead me to the truth about Clayton Jacobs. The man who, according to Richard, had abducted my mother shortly before her death. The man who had never reached out to be a part of my life until *after* my father had died. The man who was hell bent on keeping me trapped at Grand Hallow without allowing so much as a phone call to the outside world.

In the living room, I focused on a bookshelf. It was filled with books and stacks of magazines with such titles as *Mortuary Management, American Funeral Director,* and *American Cemetery*, all with glossy covers of serene cemetery landscapes and impressive mausoleums. I supposed his reading material was normal enough for a man who had built a funeral and interment empire.

Yet something peculiar *did* draw my attention. The sun coming through the edge of the shade reflected strikingly off something silver. It was tucked behind a tall pile of magazines. I placed the stack on the coffee table, revealing a metal picture frame. And as I grabbed the frame, my heart stopped. It was covered in dust. I blew on it to get a clearer view of the photograph, to see if my eyes were truly seeing what I thought they saw.

It was a photograph of my dad and Uncle Clayton. They stood in front of the very same *Grand Hallow* gates that I had passed through. Yet behind them, headstones dotted only a small portion of the hills. And there was only one small building, not the giant campus that I knew. It was surreal. Obviously, I had never seen them together. It was from a different time. They looked so young. Happy.

It was shocking enough, seeing the brothers standing together in front of what seemed to be an early version of Grand Hallow. But that wasn't what made my heart skip a beat. It was that between them stood—my mother. Despite the colors being washed out, her hair defied the print and shone through as a pretty golden blonde. She wore a wide grin, as if she were caught in the middle of a laugh when the photo was snapped. And to my amazement, on a chain halfway down her chest, was a purple pendant. The necklace was *real*. It wasn't just a figment of Richard's childhood mind. Cut in the shape of a diamond, the gem called attention to itself, glistening even in the faded photograph.

I had seen very few pictures of my mother. There were a few in a scrapbook from when she and my dad were dating. There were a few from their wedding. Those I had seen, I had memorized. And along with Richard's memory of her, they made up the skeletal framework of her story. In a way, seeing the newly discovered photo was like meeting her again—or at least a piece of her that had been missing. I wanted so badly to keep it. My heart ached as I placed it back upon the shelf and carefully hid it once more behind the stack of magazines.

I suspected the feud between my dad and my uncle had been the reason why the photograph had been tucked out of view. Yet as I made my way down the hall and inspected the master bedroom and office, I took note that there were no other photos on display either. None of Uncle Clayton's wife. None of his daughters. It was not exactly suspicious. Just curious.

Having found nothing else remarkable in the tiny bungalow, I approached the last room at the end of the hall. The door to this room was shut—and locked. As an amateur sleuth, this naturally piqued my interest. I couldn't simply break down the door. So I tried the next best thing: I felt above it for a key. My dad would say that sometimes the simplest ideas are the ones most likely to find the solution. And there it was. One of those generic keys that work on most bedroom and bathroom doors.

As soon as I swung open the door, a rush of dust wafted toward me. Immediately, I sneezed. I fished for a light switch. The bulbs were dim in the ceiling fan that slowly began to rotate, dumping more dust into the air as it fell from the blades. It suddenly became apparent I stood in some sort of tomb. And judging from the amount of dust, it hadn't been opened in years.

The carpet was pink. So too were the curtains. And the wallpaper had a pink-and-white striped pattern like a strawberry candy cane. The double closet doors were open, displaying an impressive array of oversize stuffed animals and dolls. Among the stuffed animals were a giant purple gorilla and a life-size python. And the dolls seemed to line the shelves by the hundreds. Many were porcelain, but there was also an entire set of Holly Hobbie rag dolls. Nearby sat a wooden doll house that was surely custom-made. It included all the detail of a real house and was large enough for a whole family of dolls to comfortably call home. Beside the house was a fleet of toy cars, boats, and planes ready to transport the dolls to any desired destination.

There was a vanity covered in a mess of plastic necklaces and brushes, still with strands of hair in the bristles. On the other side of the room was a craft table with opened tubs of Play-Doh. A winter scene made with the long-hardened dough was frozen in time; it had two snowmen covered with sprinkles of silver glitter. The table also held two Easy-Bake Ovens. And in the corner hung two marionette bird puppets covered in colorful feathers. Basically, it was the childhood bedroom of my dreams.

In the center of the room were two twin beds. They were turned down, exposing Strawberry Shortcake sheets. It was a fascinating time capsule, but also sad—and immensely creepy. It gave me chills, standing in what had to be—

"My daughters' bedroom." Uncle Clayton stood in the doorway with a look of anger mixed with anguish.

I was mortified. I couldn't swallow. "How—how did you?"

"The next time you plan to go sneaking through my home, try to remember my office window has a clear line of sight of this house. So I am quite aware of anyone coming or going."

I panicked. "I just came—looking for answers," I said truthfully, spilling my intentions, which, on the surface, were innocent enough.

However, I realized quickly this insinuated I didn't trust him. I didn't. But I didn't need him knowing that. The man wasn't entirely stable. I had to be careful. Handle the situation delicately. But beyond that, I still owed him a better response. Because at my core, I also felt incredibly guilty. It was a sacred place for him, a place of remembrance of his daughters. And there I was, literally trespassing on top of that memory. So I revised my initial response to a grovel: "I am so sorry. I had no idea. I shouldn't be here. Please, take away my Walkman if you'd like. I shouldn't be here," I repeated with remorse.

He entered the room and marveled at it, almost as much as I had. A sudden change came over him once he stepped upon the pink carpeting, something he obviously hadn't done in years. He looked as if he was simply enchanted. "I've kept this room exactly how it was when they were alive," he boasted. "And then one day, I locked it up. It's not that unusual, Lisa. You know, they've done the same thing with Elvis Presley's bedroom. It's exactly the way he left it the day he died. His cologne, his toothpaste. Hell, even his hair dye. They are still sitting on his sink, in the same position he left them that final day. The windows are sealed airtight. It's controlled for RH, that's *relative humidity*, and temperature—or so I hear. I'd imagine it's kept around a constant seventy degrees with an RH of fifty." I stood frozen in the middle of the room, between the beds, as he made his way toward me. "Oh, it's just the type of sordid topic we mortuary types gossip about at conferences."

He was about to sit on one of the beds and then stopped, looking at the preserved crease in the comforter. After appearing to make peace, he gently sat as if he had just entered a warm bath, finally able to relax. He motioned for me to take a seat on the opposite bed. I did so uneasily, feeling as if I had caused a blemish in driven snow. There, we sat face-to-face. He looked to me with that same smile plastered across his face like a slick preacher, the smile he used to hide whatever truly percolated beneath his skin. I kept notice of the door in my peripheral vision. And I kept one foot on the carpet, ready to bolt if need be. "So what kind of answers did you come here looking for?" he asked.

Shit! I contemplated my response for a while and finally went with, "Well what I wanted to know was—what happened between you and my dad? Why didn't you get along? Why haven't I ever met you until now?" I figured it was better than asking, *"Did you murder my father?"*

"You mean he never told you?" I shook my head. "He never told you *anything?*"

"No," I professed. "I knew you existed. But that's about it, to be honest."

"Well, my dear. Grand Hallow, it was your father's idea."

"My *dad's* idea? I find that hard to believe."

"Yes, it's positively true. Oh, he probably never imagined it quite at this scale, but he surely was the impetus for it. You see, he was looking to start a small business. He was tired of working on assembly lines with bosses becoming younger than him. He said he had heard the funeral industry was a good investment. He was my older brother. I trusted him. Believed in him. So when he asked if I wanted to go in with him, make it a family business, I had no reservations.

"He had found this little cemetery out in the middle of nowhere. The owner was looking to sell. It was nothing really. Desolate. Hundred or so graves. We started small with cemetery maintenance and burial services. From the proceeds and our own investments, we built a funeral parlor. Not the one you see now, of course," he softly laughed. "It only had one viewing room. But we managed. We did OK. And then . . . well, then, we found we just weren't able to make it work."

"Well, it seemed to work. I mean, look at this place."

"Oh no, the business grew beautifully. He was right about that. Things just started to—*unravel* between your father and me. A falling out, I suppose you could call it. We just could never get along after we started the business. Just could not make it work. Well, he ended up pulling out. He moved to Ruthsford and started his own business, his service and gas station, of course. And I kept Grand Hallow."

"I guess I should've just asked what happened between you and my dad in the first place instead of snooping around."

"Well, I'm glad you finally did."

"So what was the falling out over?" I asked. "Why exactly did he quit the business?"

"Let's just say some details are best left in the past—to save a bit of embarrassment, for your father, but mostly for myself," he said with a wink. "The short of it is, we were just two stubborn fools who later turned into two *old* stubborn fools. Yes, I suppose the lesson here is you shouldn't go into business with family. Ah well, I guess history is destined to repeat itself."

"What do you mean by that?"

"Oh nothing at all," he said and then cleared his throat. "Your brother. He is now running the family business, no? *Your* business?"

"My *dad's* business. Yes, but that's just temporary."

"It's not my place. But you seem to have a good head on your shoulders, Lisa. Your brother, on the other hand. He seems a bit, well, reckless with his choices."

"Richard's a mess. But he's harmless."

"Is he?" he asked with a raise of his brow. I was stunned. Was he implying Richard was capable of worse than being a deadbeat? Finally, after leaving me to contemplate his insinuation, he continued, "I didn't want to tell you this. But Richard asked me for money at your father's funeral. A great sum in fact. I gave it to him. That's not important," he said, waving his hands. "It just tells me a great deal about his character." So that explained what Richard was doing pulling him aside at the funeral. I should've known.

"But you. You haven't asked for a thing. That tells me a great deal about your character as well. Ned told me you helped with a casket sale? You could be a great asset to the service station business, for sure. But as well you could be a great asset to a place like Grand Hallow."

I didn't know what to say. All I could hear was David calling me *Bette Davis*. I didn't want to insult Uncle Clayton. But the thought of spending another moment longer than I had to at Grand Hallow made my stomach roll. "Thank you," I finally replied, not giving away my thoughts on the idea. My dad always told me to never turn down an opportunity, especially one that paid. But how weird would it have been working at the very business my dad had left because of the rotten feelings in his gut? He likely agonized watching his idea grow beyond his wildest expectations—without him—as he struggled with the service station.

"Well!" Uncle Clayton slapped the palms of his hands against his lap and stood. "If your curiosity is now sufficiently satiated, I best be getting back to work. And I'm sure Ned would appreciate your helping hand. That is, if you're free."

"Sure. No problem. But I *do* have one more question." I couldn't imagine a better opportunity to ask. As awkward as each of my exchanges with Uncle Clayton had been, that afternoon in his daughters' bedroom was off the charts. So I decided to go for it with the assumption it couldn't get any *more* awkward. "I hate to ask since I've invaded so much of your privacy already, but if you don't mind. What happened to your wife? Your daughters? How did they die?"

He turned away from me and caressed his chin for a moment. "Emerald Bridge happened," he finally replied. "Emerald Bridge killed them."

"Emerald Bridge?"

"It was February," he began, gazing off to another time. "She was taking them to a ballet class in Shilling. Now to get to Shilling from Grand Hallow, one must cross the Emerald Street Bridge over the Emerald River. It's an old wooden bridge just outside the Grand Hallow property line. There was heavy freezing rain that night. It coated the bridge in glare ice. She lost control. The car bounced off the loose guardrails like a pinball until a section finally gave way. The car, it slipped over the edge and fell seventy feet, plunging beneath the ice. They were trapped. Didn't stand a chance.

"When they didn't come home, I went out looking for them. When I finally made it to the bridge, I saw the broken guardrail and the break in the ice. I was too late. Several hours had passed by then. There were no emergency vehicles that could get out there in a reasonable timeframe, especially during an ice storm. So I gathered a few staff members. And we brought our own equipment. It was *I* who dragged that car out of the river. It was *I* who took their frozen bodies back to Grand Hallow."

"How horrible," I said. "I'm so sorry."

He sighed deeply as his mind returned to the room. "Truth be told, my wife was the real brains of the operation. After your father left, it was *she* who ran this place. I know enough, I suppose. Can keep it up and running. Maintain the status quo. But it was *she* who made the decisions that mattered. Without her, I'm lost. And the twins . . ." He moved to a covered frame above the dresser. "What happened to them is just too painful. That's why I keep this room closed. That's why I covered this portrait." He yanked off the dust covering in grief.

I began to tremble. The portrait was of red-headed twin girls. They held hands upon a grassy hill with a vast blue sky behind them. "What's going on?" I asked as I stood, my voice shaking. "Those girls. I've seen them. Out in the cemetery. Playing."

Immediately, Uncle Clayton's demeanor changed. His eyes squinted and his lips frowned as if he had just tasted a sour lemon. "Why would you say that, Lisa? That's impossible. Elizabeth and Imogene died— three years ago! Why would you say such a thing?"

"But I—" My knees began to wobble. I was speechless. The girls, Elizabeth and Imogene, stared at me from their portrait. The clothes they wore were different from my encounters with them, Elizabeth in a yellow sundress and Imogene in a green skirt. But it was them, their red hair parted and curled. "What's going on?" I asked again under my breath as I slowly walked backward toward the door. *Was I going crazy?* "I should go," I announced. I just wanted to get out of that room. "I should go. Now."

Uncle Clayton, still looking at me as if I had just stomped all over his rose garden, announced, "Your little walks around the cemetery and up and down the halls are acceptable. But you are not to leave these grounds. Ever. Do you understand?"

"Just to my room," I clarified, clutching my chest as if I had just been shot. "Just going to my room."

Chapter 15

Pork Rinds and Liver Pâté

I hadn't exactly exonerated Uncle Clayton. But at least I felt he was being truthful. The photograph I had found of him with my parents in front of the original cemetery did corroborate his story of attempting a business partnership with my father. And the quarreling Richard had seen as a child — it wasn't unreasonable to think it had been around the time the two were angrily parting ways.

It still didn't explain my mother's supposed abduction. Yet even if he *had* taken her, she *did* return — for a short while before her death anyhow. And something else I needed to take into consideration was just how accurate Richard's childhood mind could've been at recording (and storing) what he had witnessed.

In taking my magnifying glass off Uncle Clayton for the time being, it meant I was back where I started. Yet being stuck at Grand Hallow made it easy to identify my next suspect. I would turn my sights to the one person I knew at Grand Hallow to *not* be truthful. The one I had caught in a verified lie: Norman the mortician.

That's why I didn't feel guilty or think it wrong to be using a hairpin I had found in the morgue's cosmetic supplies to attempt to pick the lock of his office door. Even though I didn't know how to pick a lock, it seemed like a good idea. *How hard could it be?* I figured. I had seen it work on TV a thousand times. Yet despite my extensive background in TV crime drama investigating, the lock wouldn't budge. I was hoping to have it opened and my evidence reviewed before David's shift began. But before I knew it, he came waltzing in, witnessing my frustration. A careless sleuth, I didn't even try to hide.

"What are you doing to Norman's door?" he asked, confused yet interested.

Perturbed, I blew the hair out of my face. "What does it look like? I'm trying to get into his office. And do you want to know why? Because my dad is dead. *That's* why. And *someone* is responsible. And your boss . . . God knows what for . . . he's got blood bags in the sink. And he's lying about drainage systems and barrels and shit. And *I'm* going to get to the bottom of it!"

"OK, settle down, Nancy Drew." He reached into a drawer by the sinks and handed me a key. "Knock yourself out."

I grabbed it from him skeptically. "You won't tell?"

"Why would I? Besides, you're the boss, applesauce."

"I am *not* the boss," I seethed. "I'm just looking for answers!"

"What're you hoping to find?" he asked, looking in with his arms stretched above the door as I sat in Norman's chair.

"Anything suspicious," I said, furiously rifling through the mess of invoices and receipts. I opened the first drawer of his desk. It was filled with bags of pork rinds, some opened. And about a dozen small cans. One of the cans was covered with a resealable plastic lid. I peeled it back for a look. The rancid smell made me gag. "Disgusting. What is this? Cat food?"

"It's liver pâté."

"Gross."

The second drawer was filled with tightly packed jars of Vicks VapoRub. "What's with all the VapoRub?"

"It's to help with the smell of death. You just dab a little under your nose." He produced his own jar from his smock. "Never leave home without it."

"The smell of death is that liver pâté," I said, slamming the drawer shut. I opened the final drawer, which was filled with hanging file folders. Each folder was tagged with a plastic label, including a last name and four-digit ID. "These look like they're all patient files."

"Yes. Well, they're not exactly *patients* anymore."

"You know what I mean."

Most files included a photo of the person when he or she was alive — to aid in preparing the body for viewing, I assumed. It also included a copy of the death certificate and information on next of kin. "I think in that drawer is where he keeps the records of all of our *active* bodies, the ones in the coolers before they go for viewing and burial." I flipped through the files but didn't notice anything unusual. I reclined back in the chair with my hands over my face and groaned. "You seem totally overwhelmed. What's wrong? You know, aside from the fact that you actually *live* in a mortuary?"

"Can I ask you something?"

"Shoot."

"Have you ever seen a ghost?"

"No," he answered without hesitation.

"Well, I'm clearly going crazy because, since I've been here, I've been seeing ghosts," I confessed.

"You have? Where?"

"Out in the cemetery. And they're just not *any* ghosts. They're the ghosts of my cousins. You know, the ones I had never met. Before they died, at least."

"Bette Davis's girls? Elizabeth and Imogene?"

"Yes," I sighed, with a mix of embarrassment and exasperation.

"Oh, you mean *those* ghosts."

"What do you mean by that?" I swiveled the chair to face him. "If you've seen them too, you better tell me right now!" I demanded through clenched teeth.

"No, no," he clasped his hands and gave an apologetic smile. "I haven't seen them. Not after they were pulled out of that river, anyway. Never seen a ghost in my life, in fact. Don't believe in them. Don't get me wrong. I'm open to the idea. I'd just need to see one with my own two eyes.

"But the ghosts you've seen, Elizabeth and Imogene. Well, I guess I kind of take those ghosts for granted. You have to realize, the people here work around dead bodies and caskets and graves all day. They're bound to see all kinds of strange things. Your mind can play tricks on you out here at Grand Hallow, you know. Us guys down in transportation, after we'd fix a vehicle, we'd test-drive it around the cemetery. All the time guys would come back saying they'd seen those red-headed girls running around out there. And when they'd get close, they'd disappear behind headstones. Never paid much attention to it. Like I said, I'd need to see it with my own eyes."

"Well, when I saw them, they were *not* mind tricks. They couldn't have been. Could they? No!" I answered myself resoundingly. "I never even knew what they looked like before I saw their ghosts. But now I do. And it was them. Only they didn't seem like ghosts. I mean, they weren't apparitions. They were solid. They touched me. Pulled my hair. Held me to the ground. Although they *did* seem to be able to appear and disappear pretty easily."

"So if you've never seen a ghost until now, how do you know what they're supposed to look like? Maybe that's how it is then. Maybe half the people we see out on the street are ghosts. They look normal. Just like us. Only we don't know they're dead."

"Maybe. Wait a minute. Are you being facetious?"

"What does that even mean?"

"Patronizing me?"

"Of course not! It's just a theory."

I slouched farther in the chair until my head lay against the middle of the backrest. I shut my eyes, trying to calm my agitation. When I opened them, I gazed down the inside of the elongated file drawer, beyond the pink, yellow, and blue tabs—to the very last folder. It had no plastic tab. It was just an unmarked manila folder. On a whim, I stretched forward and dug out the file.

Inside was a typed-out list of addresses. I flipped through the four stapled pages. Many of the addresses had been crossed out with large Xs. The Xs had been bored into the paper over and over with quite some ferocity. It didn't seem like anything of relevance. Yet when my eyes came to one of only four addresses that had yet to be crossed out, my heart began to race. "There's a copy machine in the break room, right?"

"Yeah. Why?"

"We need to get a photocopy of this document. Right away."

"Yeah. Sure. But what're you thinking? Why do you have that look on your face?"

"I'm thinking I want to ask for your help. But I'm deciding whether or not I trust you."

"Oh? You're deciding that *now*? *After* I helped you break into my boss's office? *After* you asked me to photocopy a document stolen from his drawer? Not to mention the part where you made fun of his snacks."

"Yeah, that might've been a lapse in judgment," I admitted. "But now I have to decide if I still involve you before things get a little bit more—nuts."

"*More* nuts? OK, now you have me intrigued."

"So you worked in the transportation department. Do you think you could get me a car?"

His eyes became wide, and a wry smile curled upon his lips. "Are you shitting me?" When it became apparent to him that my look of determination likely meant I was in fact *not* shitting him, he said, "*Maybe* I could? I don't know. Yes? Wait. Where do you think you're going?"

I pointed to the unmarked address and declared, "966 Lindley Street."

Chapter 16

The Great Escape

I worked a full day for Ned. I sold three caskets totaling just over $8,000. And I helped set up and usher three funerals, which included checking coats in the lobby (old people are always cold, I discovered, even in the summer), helping guests find the correct viewing room in the labyrinth of halls, and constantly reminding guests to sign the guestbook. At the end of the day, I stood at Ned's door exhausted, yet feeling accomplished. "I finished stacking the chairs and cleaning up the Cheboygan room," I reported.

"Well, I just don't know what I'd do without you, Miss Jacobs."

"You can call me *Lisa*," I offered.

"Yes, ma'am. Now be sure to keep track of your hours, won't you? And I'll have your uncle add you to the payroll. Although I must warn you, it won't be much, I'm afraid," he said with a frown.

"Oh that's not necessary." The acknowledgment from Ned was enough. He seemed genuinely thankful to have some extra help.

"Now don't be silly. Work is work. And you've got to get paid. Good evening now, ma'am." I stood at his door for another few moments, smiling like a dolt. "Is everything all right, hon? Can I help you with something?"

"Oh no. I'm fine."

What Ned didn't know—or what at least I had *hoped* he wasn't realizing while I stood before him, turned slightly sideways—was that I was enacting the first sequence of my breakout plan.

I had seen it on an episode of *Different Strokes*. It was the one where the Drummonds wake up Christmas morning to find all their gifts have been stolen. Turned out the thief was a street corner Santa invited earlier into the Drummond house as a guest. As he left, he stuck putty over the door latch, which enabled him to gain entry later that evening.

I didn't have any putty. So I stood at Ned's door hiding my hand behind my back, trying to cram an eraser into the latch. Earlier, I had modified the eraser by cutting it to size. I didn't want him noticing it while sitting at his desk, so I colored the eraser with a black marker and waited until he was about to leave for the evening before jamming it in the door.

Finally, after I felt it was secure, I scurried around the corner to wait. *What if he sees it? What if it falls out? What if he tugs on the door after shutting it and realizes it hasn't latched shut?* I couldn't not watch. With much anxiety, I peeked around the corner.

When he finally emerged, he had on a brown fedora and was carrying a stack of papers under each arm. With his hands full, he grabbed the handle with his pinky finger and swung the door his way. I cringed, worrying that without anything for the door to latch onto, it would simply bounce back open. If that happened, my goose would certainly be cooked. The door, however, miraculously stayed shut. And Ned, none the wiser, made his way down the hall softly whistling a tune. I was ecstatic. But to be safe, I waited several minutes after he rounded the corner before I crept back.

The latch had stuck a bit into the eraser, but I was able to force open the door. I grabbed the giant key ring he kept in his top drawer and dropped it in my bag. Then I dialed Tina.

"You're not going to believe this! That address you gave me? I found it on some sort of list in the mortician's office. So there is definitely a connection between him and whatever Sternhardt was looking into."

"Oh my God! Told ya! And I'm not surprised it involves that freakazoid mortician. Do ya think he wears a wig? It's gotta be a wig, right?"

"Listen, we need to go check it out. And we need to go tonight. Can you meet me there in about forty-five minutes?"

"Jesus, Lisa. You could give me a little more notice. Where am I supposed to tell my parents I'm going this late?"

"You'll figure something out. You always do."

"True. This sorta thing is kinda my specialty. But how are you gonna get there with no car?"

"I've got it taken care of."

"Listen to you. You've *got it taken care of?* Like when did you turn so freakin' cool?"

"Tina, I wasn't going to tell you this. But in case I can't get there tonight. Or if I can't make it to the phone again, you need to know this."

"Oh God. What is it?"

"Your house, it was also on the mortician's list of addresses."

She was silent for a moment. "Seriously?" she finally asked. "Shit! What does that even mean?"

"I don't know yet. I'm hoping we'll know more after tonight."

"Son of a bitch. See you there."

Carefully, I shut the door behind me, leaving the eraser securely in place. I then briskly made my way down the winding stairs and into the maze, where I had memorized the path. Enter the east wing. Right down the main hallway. Another right. Left past Washtenaw, Shiawassee, and Ogemaw. Right. Left. And finally toward the sealed door at the end of the hall, behind which was one of several service passageways leading to the main garage.

There, as planned, I found David waiting. He stood with his hands in the pockets of his morgue-issued apron. As I approached, he nervously tucked his hair behind his ears. I held up the key ring. "Which one?"

He grabbed the ring and began rifling through the keys. "Hell if I know. When I worked down here, I was only given a set of three keys. Ned must have an all-access pass. Let me start with the ones that are *this* size," he said holding up a key. "If I remember right, it's got to be one of these."

I kept watch down the hall. It was after normal hours, but there was still activity going on. There were several scheduled pickups for burials and drop-offs for body prep. And there were plenty of late viewings arranged by Ned but run by the part-time staff. In fact, as David tried the keys, a casket came partially into view at the end of the hall. "We've got company," I whispered.

David spun around and hid the key ring behind his back in a panic. "I could get fired for this, you know!"

"It's OK. Just keep trying. I'll go check it out."

As I rounded the corner, I expected to see a part-time staffer in a Grand Hallow polo attending the casket. But there was no one there. It was as if someone had just rolled the casket down the desolate hallway and then abandoned it. The smaller rooms down that particular corridor, named after Michigan rivers, were intended for more intimate or cost-effective viewings. I looked into the nearby Pine, Tahquamenon, and Rogue River rooms, but their lights were all off. I began to make my way back to David when I heard a woman's voice say, "Bring him to me."

Startled, I rushed back to the casket. "Hello? Is anyone there?" I called down the hall.

"Bring him to me," the voice repeated.

The voice sounded as if it had come from the Tahquamenon Room. I flipped on the light. At the front of the room sat a woman. She was dressed in black, complete with a veiled black hat. "Are you OK?" I asked. "Why were you sitting here in the dark?"

"I'm fine, dear. Just bring him to me." As she instructed, I grabbed the handles of the gurney and pushed the casket into the room and down the aisle. As I neared the front, she said, "Right there is fine, dear." I stopped the casket just far enough forward to catch a glimpse of her pale cheek.

"I don't believe this room is reserved," I informed her. "Do you need some help finding where you're supposed to be?"

"You've helped enough," she said as she adjusted her black lace gloves. "I am where I'm supposed to be. Now leave us." After leaving the room, I turned back for a final look. The woman had stood but still faced the front of the room. It was odd, for sure. But I wasn't going to let it interfere with my escape.

I started back to David, only to see he had disappeared. When I came to the door, I found it slightly ajar. He had gotten in! I rushed down the narrow passage to a second door, which he had also left unlocked behind him. I snuck into the near-dark cavernous garage. It was smart of David not to turn on the overhead lights. I wasn't sure where he was until I saw him lifting one of the bay doors manually. "If I use the opener, the motor might attract attention," he said as I approached.

"Good idea."

"And here's your car," he said, tapping the hood of the hearse, which was already positioned in front of the bay door.

"It had to be a hearse, huh?"

"The keys to the limousines and town cars are kept in a locked box. And I don't have access to that anymore. It's the best I could do."

"No, it's great," I said appreciatively. In fact, I wanted to kiss him. Or at least give him a hug for his help. Yet instead, I found myself dispensing instructions: "As soon as I leave, be sure to put those keys back in Ned's drawer. And dig out the eraser. And don't forget to jam open the doors to the garage so you can get back down here later."

"Anything else?" he grinned, holding up the two blocks of wood he intended to use as door props.

"No. I guess I'm ready," I said as I sat behind the wheel.

"I don't understand why you won't let me go with you."

"Because I don't trust you," I joked.

"Very funny."

"It's too risky. You have to be in the morgue tonight. It would look suspicious if your cadavers backed up. Or if you're not there if someone comes looking for you."

"But if you just wait until tomorrow, I'll drive you myself."

"I can't wait another day. Besides, I don't want to drag you any further into this than I already have. I have no idea what I'm going to find when I get there."

"Exactly. I could protect you."

"I don't need protection. I've got Tina."

"*Tina?*"

"My best friend. She'll be there. Trust me. She's protection enough. Just be back down here by midnight to let me back in, OK?" I asked as I started the engine.

"You got it. Good luck. And listen, keep your headlights off until you get beyond the main gate," he advised.

"Thanks for everything, David. See you at midnight."

"Midnight," he called after me, holding his thumb in the air as I slowly pulled out of the garage.

In my rearview mirror, I watched him pull down the bay door. I drove carefully through the dark cemetery. Without headlights, it was difficult. I could've easily drifted off the narrow, winding road and crashed into a tombstone, effectively ending my great escape. Yet with my slow maneuvering, I made it unscathed to the main road. I flipped on the lights as I passed the gate. It was soon in my rearview mirror. And as I headed straight up the hill and out of the Mouth of the mighty Grand Hallow, so too were the dark buildings and tombs in the valley below. I breathed a sigh of relief, yet also tingled with excitement and a sense of freedom. I felt alive! *How dare Uncle Clayton tell me I couldn't leave Grand Hallow's grounds!*

From my bag, I grabbed my directions to the Shilling neighborhood, where I would meet Tina. When I came upon the Emerald Bridge, I drove slowly over its old wooden frame. I tried not to look to the river below. But couldn't help noticing the mangled guardrails. As soon as I had made it safely to the other side, I floored it, driving the speeding hearse into the night.

Chapter 17

The Offering

Tina's red Mustang stuck out as if it were the only colorized object in a black-and-white world. She smartly parked down the block and around the corner from the house. I pulled up behind her. "I can't believe you showed up in a freakin' hearse!" she marveled as I stepped out.

"I know it's not as cool as your Mustang. But it's the best I could do on short notice."

We crept toward the house. As Tina had described, the neighborhood was dark and desolate. The streetlights were out. Or had never been wired. There were no lawns. Just dirt and mud landscapes. Large mounds of bulldozed dirt sat in backyards and in empty lots. Rainwater pooled into pits that had never been filled.

Many houses were half built—driveways missing, wind blowing through their skeletal frames. Other houses were complete, but stood empty—their windows broken or boarded up, garage doors dented. It was an odd ghost of a place. To be called *abandoned*, I figured someone had to have lived there in the first place. Instead, it was a decaying neighborhood that never even had a chance.

We were wise enough not to attempt busting through the front door. We'd have surely risked calling attention to ourselves on the porch should anyone have happened to drive by. Besides, trying to get through a layer of nailed boards and a deadbolt would've been more work than we had time for. So we set our sights on a side window. It was eerily quiet as we began prying off the boards. Tina had thoughtfully brought a pair of hammers, but it was still difficult. Due to the height of the window, most of the boards were over our heads. "If we can just take out these three lower ones, we should be able to fit through," I said.

Tina was uncharacteristically silent and focused. She worked diligently. Yet she surprised herself with a loud grunt as she worked to pry off the corner of the final board. She followed with a much-restrained chuckle at her own expense.

Thankfully, the window was already broken. Jagged pieces of glass hung from the casing. Tina grabbed a small flashlight from her pocket and knocked out the remaining pieces with the blunt end. She then bent over and locked her arms together. "Here, I'll give you a boost inside." I grabbed her shoulders and tried balancing in her arms before reaching for the windowsill. In an instant, we both toppled to the ground.

I got up to see Tina back in position, ready to try again. And that's when I lost it. I began laughing uncontrollably. Seeing Tina in that ridiculous position—and just the absurdity of our attempting to break into a vacant house to look for clues made it seem as if we were in some *Laverne and Shirley* slapstick routine. Tina took one look at me and busted out laughing herself. "Jesus! The look on your face!" she laughed.

"What are you? A Weeble?" I asked in a fit of giggles.

She performed a silly dance while singing, *"Weebles wobble, but they don't fall down!"* She then got on all fours, which made me laugh even harder. "Now stop it!" she cried. "And get the hell in there!" she motioned toward the window with her thumb. I couldn't breathe as I stepped onto her back, wobbling as I hooked my arms inside the window. I dangled for a few moments before I felt her push on my butt. With her help, I slid through the window. I then grabbed her hand, pulling her up as she climbed the siding. After she tumbled over the edge, we both lay collapsed on the floor cackling.

As we slowly got up and realized our surroundings, the house instantly sucked the humor out of us. We found ourselves in an empty dining room with black stains on the walls. Inside, the atmosphere was different. There was a heavy tone. The air was stagnant and smelled of mold. Tina handed me my own flashlight. We huddled together as we made our way to the kitchen. It had a sink and a stove, but there were empty spaces where the refrigerator and dishwasher were to go. We canvased the room with our lights, which both settled on the stovetop. Over one of the burners sat an old-fashioned tea kettle. It was black with a coiled metal handle. "Must've been left from the squatters," I reasoned.

We made our way down the hall and entered an empty bedroom. The carpet was spongy. It squished under our shoes. I noticed a small hole in the corner of the ceiling where water dripped down the wall. Beneath the leak, the carpet had turned black and the floor had bowed, creating a saturated depression.

The second bedroom was in much better shape. The room was dry and clean. A ripped sheet covered the window. And there was a card table pushed against the wall. Tina checked the closets while I stood in the middle of the room and shone my light around the perimeter. Something in the carpet reflected back. I bent down and picked up the pair of rainbow-striped plastic hair bobbles.

"Weird," said Tina from over my shoulder. "Bibble-bobbles. That's what I used to call them when I was a kid. What's it doing here?"

"I don't know," I said with an uneasy feeling in my stomach. I dropped it back to the floor.

"Maybe I was wrong," whispered Tina as we took the steps down to the lower level. "I mean, I just don't get how this house could be connected. We both know Sternhardt is a clown. Do we really think he could solve your dad's murder? Maybe it's just a coincidence. Like you said, maybe Sternhardt just came here to barricade out some squatters. And your buddy, Mort the mortician, just also happened to have this address on his list?"

"Could be," I admitted. "It could've just been a list of addresses where police found unidentified bodies."

"Yeah. Maybe it was on his list because some junkie squatter OD'd on angel dust or something here and this was the only address they had for 'im?"

"It's not that far-fetched, I guess."

"Wait a minute. That doesn't explain why *my* house was on the list."

"The Grant Mansion was vacant for years, just like this place, before your family moved in. Who knows how many people had broken in and used it for God knows what? The sad fact is, sooner or later, most of the people in this part of the state are going to wind up in Norman's morgue."

"Wow. Thanks for the rainbow and sunshine thoughts," said Tina with a sigh.

"Sorry." I smirked. "Believe me, I'm not any happier about it than you. But look on the bright side; we'll at least be dead when it happens."

"Har. Har."

The walls and ceiling in the basement were black and crumbling. It was mostly unfinished, open space. Yet two rooms were crudely sectioned off by water-damaged drywall. There was a room with a closed door near the bottom of the steps and another at the other end of the basement with its door open. As I opened the door nearest us, I immediately buried my nose in my sleeve. "What the hell is that smell?" cried Tina. "It smells like—"

"Death," I finished. The overwhelming smell of decay made me gag and wish I had thrown one of those jars of VapoRub in my bag. Our flashlights revealed that the carpet in this small windowless room was drenched in a thick pool of dark liquid. But unlike the water pooling upstairs, the dried carpet around the edges was stained red. "Blood," I announced. There was so much blood that it had actually risen above the carpet, reflecting back our flashlight beams.

"What the hell happened in there?" asked Tina. "Did someone skin an animal? Did your mortician do that!"

"I don't know," I said under my breath. "Let's just finish looking around and get the hell out of here." I began to tremble. My face broke out in a sudden sweat as I slowly shut the door, sealing the horror back up inside.

As we approached the room at the other end of the basement, I felt a much-needed cool breeze. It refreshed my face and brushed the hair aside that had been stuck to my cheek. We entered the potential rec room. It had a sliding glass door leading to a patio. The glass door had been shattered almost completely. In its place was a tattered black tarp rumpling back and forth as the room breathed in and breathed out. "Sternhardt must've not boarded up the back," Tina observed. "Christ! We could've just waltzed right in!"

I traced my beam over the cement floor, where shards of broken glass had fallen, and once again over the undulating tarp. As my light reached the corner, I noticed that a piece of tarp protruded farther into the room. What's more, it did not sway with the breeze. It looked as if it was covering something solid. Tina too noticed the anomaly. And with our combined lights, it became apparent that the dark material was not part of the tarp at all.

A low groan suddenly came from the hunched figure that stood in the corner drenched in black. And then, it jolted forward. We both screamed, yet amazingly, held our positions. It stood in the center of the room, halfway between us and what was left of the sliding glass door. It was the same figure I had seen creep across Tina's yard. It wore a cloak, its hood keeping its face in the shadows. I pointed my beam of light at the figure like a weapon. But Tina immediately dropped her flashlight. And out of nowhere, she produced a pistol.

"Norman, is that you?" I asked timidly.

At first, the figure only gurgled, but then it let out a deep moan. It began swaying back and forth. It coughed and spit up blood that splashed onto the concrete floor. I raised my light, shining it directly in its face. But its face simply squelched the light. The bulb dimmed, effectively keeping its features masked in darkness. Yet when I moved my beam away from its face, the bulb inexplicably sparked back to life.

Beside me, I heard the unmistakable sound of Tina cocking her gun. Was the thing that stood before us responsible for my father's murder? If so, I supposed I wanted it dead. But I didn't want it dead without knowing for sure. And without knowing *why*. And however willing Tina was, I didn't want her to have to bear that burden. "Wait!" I pleaded. She didn't pull the trigger. But she also didn't take her aim off the cloaked figure.

Without warning, it dropped to its knees. It did not gently kneel down. It literally dropped, with a thud on the cement floor, onto its knees. It knelt before us as if asking for mercy, moaning and gurgling at our feet. It worked for a moment to clear the blood, which was apparently still gorged in its throat, before bowing its head. Then, from the inner folds of its cloak, its hands emerged. They clasped something I could only attribute to being what it must've considered some sort of offering: a sealed glass jar filled with dark, red blood. Its thin arms, wrapped tightly in strands of black material, slowly extended the jar toward me.

I took a hesitant step forward. "What the hell are you doing?" Tina whispered in horror. Carefully, I wrapped my hands around the jar. And as soon as my grip was firm, it released its grip and slowly retracted its arms back beneath its cloak.

And then, as quickly as it had knelt, it jolted upright and swiveled away from us. In an instant, it crashed through the tarp, leaving me standing with the jar of blood. Tina chased after it, her pistol firmly gripped. I pushed the tarp aside to see the figure climb the huge mound of bulldozed clay and dirt that filled the backyard. It sprung up the hill in two giant leaps. I followed behind Tina as she climbed after it.

Together, we stood atop the mound, looking over the sea of lifeless homes. "Where is it?" I asked, out of breath.

"Gone. You shoulda let me . . . shoot the fucker . . . while I had . . . the chance," heaved Tina, also out of breath.

"Where'd you get that gun anyway?"

"Took it from my dad. Thought we might need it."

"You're full of surprises."

"So are you," she said, gesturing to the jar I clutched.

"Now we know there's no coincidence," I affirmed. "There's definitely a connection between the houses on that list and that—*phantom*. Right after my dad's death, I see it at your house. And now, we find it here."

"Passing out another party favor," finished Tina. "That jar of blood, it was handing it *to you*. And when it came to my house, I think it came to leave that other jar of blood for you too. So the question is, why's that monster givin' you jars of blood, Lisa?"

"I don't know," I replied as a wave of terror shot through my body. I couldn't say what I was thinking aloud. I couldn't let Tina know. How in the world could I have explained it? By giving me jars of blood, it was blatantly sending a message that it knew my secret. Whoever—or whatever—was beneath that cloak *knew* of my ability to taste a person through his or her blood and my ability to glimpse into that person's thoughts, feelings, and emotions. But how could it have known, when I had never told a soul? And what did it want with me?

"Was it the mortician?" Tina asked point-blank.

I still hadn't positively linked the two in my mind. Before that moment, I had still preferred to think of it as a faceless entity. A phantom. A monster. Because that's what it was. But Tina forced me to be honest with myself. "Yes," I declared. "Has to be."

"Do ya think he killed your dad?"

"Yes. I do."

"So *why* didn't you let me put a bullet in his ass?"

"Because it can't be that way. Because I need proof. Because I want to hear him say it."

She nodded, understanding. "Well, one thing's for sure," she smirked as we began to climb down from the hill. "That was no cape. It was totally a cloak."

Chapter 18

Prisoners in the Bog

The jar jutted from my bag in the passenger seat. Tina could've relinquished it to Sternhardt for analysis. But I decided to keep it myself. When it came to that particular piece of evidence, I figured perhaps *I* was the best investigator after all. I had a unique advantage, a unique skill Sternhardt did not have at his disposal.

I stayed focused on the road even though the jar's red hue was calling my attention. It was already past eleven. I needed to keep my promise of meeting David back at the garage by midnight. I rushed over the Emerald Bridge. And by the time I cut the lights and flew through the gate, I had only moments to spare.

I waited outside the bay doors, filled with anxiety. But also with exhilaration. Yes, I was terrified of what we had discovered at 966 Lindley. But finally, a piece of the puzzle had locked into place. While I didn't get all the answers I needed, at least I knew my next steps: prove Norman was my father's killer and find out why.

As the door slowly rolled open, my exhilaration drained. Freaked, I even contemplated throwing the hearse in reverse and driving far, far away. David was there, as he had promised. But on either side of him so too were Uncle Clayton and Ned. David sheepishly kept his gaze to the ground. Did he get caught? Or had he ratted me out? Either way, I was furious. As soon as I stepped out of the hearse, Uncle Clayton grabbed my wrist and began marching me through the garage. "Oh my, my, my, my, my," worried Ned as he followed not far behind, wringing his hands.

"Let go of me!" I demanded as I was dragged down the passageway and into the main facility. The jar in my bag repeatedly slammed against my hip as I was yanked through the halls.

"You have broken my trust, young lady," he scolded. "I warned you not to leave Grand Hallow. And you disobeyed me by seducing this mortuary apprentice and convincing him to help you steal one of our hearses."

"*Seduce him*!" I growled. "That's complete bullshit!"

"Oh yes, that's how it always starts. The simple tricks of a temptress."

I couldn't believe what I was hearing. I shouted to David, who followed reluctantly behind Ned. "Tell him he's full of it!" But David dared not speak.

"Hell of a pit viper, this one. Just like her mother."

I boiled with anger. "What the hell is that supposed to mean? *You* of all people are not allowed to talk about my mother!" I attempted to jerk my arm away, but he tightened his grip.

"Oh dear. Ma'am, just mind your uncle now. It will all be all right," advised Ned as he anxiously tried to temper my struggle.

"Stop calling me *ma'am*! And stop calling me *Miss Jacobs*, Ned! You know my name! Why are you even here?"

"Ned was preparing to go searching for you," answered Uncle Clayton. "And *this* is how you repay him for getting you on the payroll?

It's a shame I had to disturb him, especially at this hour. But once I learned of your escape, I had no choice."

"My *escape?* So it's true! I *am* being held here against my will!"

"*Against your will?*" he scoffed. "You have no will. You are still a minor. Do not forget, *I* am responsible for you."

"Don't *you* forget. It's only till the end of summer. And then I am gone!"

"My. My. You have proven yourself to be quite ungracious. A disobedient and delinquent pit viper indeed."

My prisoner's march halted outside the green room, my cell. I finally made eye contact with David as he passed on his way to the morgue. Had he lost his job? Because of me? I really hoped he hadn't. But his face was not forthcoming. He looked strangely unemotional. I couldn't tell if he felt sorry for me. Was angry at me. Or if he was glad I got what came. With his poker face, I wasn't sure whether I wanted to apologize to him or sock him in the gut real hard.

Uncle Clayton released me into the room. "I was wrong about you. You are more like your brother than I realized," he said before angrily slamming the door. Before I heard their footsteps head down the hall, I heard a click. *That wasn't a lock, was it? Could he really have locked me in? No.* I grabbed the handle and pulled. The door was locked from the outside. I couldn't believe it! I literally was a prisoner at Grand Hallow.

I pounded on the door. *Was David still out there? Would he help me out one more time?* I began to pace, seething with anger, wondering if I was reliving my mother's fate. Trapped inside Grand Hallow. Kidnapped. Kept away from my friends and family in Ruthsford. Would I finally escape, like her, only to come out a changed person? Sick and dying? And although I was convinced Norman was my father's killer, was Uncle Clayton really innocent? Was Ned? No, I couldn't trust anyone at Grand Hallow.

I paced until it became apparent there would be no rescue. Finally, I retreated to the bed. The cheap coils squeaked as I lay down. With the door locked and the green walls closing in, the only way to avoid the claustrophobia driving me mad was to shut my eyes. Although it felt as if I possessed the pent up energy of a caged tiger, my body was truly beat from that day. Soon, it began to tire. It was a miracle my brain finally gave in as well. And the moment it did, I fell instantly into a deep sleep.

I awoke to the sound of the door clicking shut. Thinking I had been released, I jolted out of bed and tried the knob. But I remained an inmate. As I stood at the door, a throbbing pain on my side suddenly became apparent. I checked to discover a large bruise had developed where the jar had been banging against my hip.

The jar of blood! I had been so angry the night before that I hadn't even thought about the gift I had received. I quickly swiped under the bed for my bag. Immediately, I knew something was wrong. My bag, it was too light. The jar was gone. It took me all of fifteen seconds to search the tiny room. It was not there. It wasn't difficult putting two and two together. Waking to the door being shut, I was certain someone had crept in while I slept and stolen it.

My ears picked up muffled laughter from the other side of the window. It was just before dawn. The sun had not yet risen, but a few weak rays had begun to penetrate the misty horizon. And there, skipping up the hill of headstones, were the twins. Since both were dressed in long white nightgowns, it wasn't difficult to catch glimpses of the deep red jar one of them held in her hand as they playfully made their way through the graves.

I pushed open the window and looked below. The drop wasn't all that far. About ten feet. Still, examining the distance, I thought about Imogene tapping on the window, dangling from the sill. *Ghosts. Floating up to my window.* I wanted to roll my eyes at the notion. But there they were. The pair of mischievous devils getting away with my jar. Desperate, I crawled out the window. I dangled from the sill as Imogene had. Extending my arms as far as I could, I attempted to close as much distance as possible between the pavement below and myself. And then,

I dropped. The balls of my bare feet seared with a flash of pain as they struck the cement.

I scrambled up the hill after the twins. As I gained on them, I was careful to keep my distance. I didn't want them to know I was following them. I wanted to track them. Surprise them. Take back what they had stolen. Was it possible to hide from a ghost? I wasn't sure. But I tried my best. I crouched behind headstones and used the hilly landscape to my advantage. I'd let them get to the crest of the hill ahead before climbing it myself.

Following them took me out farther than I had ever gone. Beyond the familiar paths and groupings of trees. Beyond the mausoleums. And beyond the acres of crypts, which I had nicknamed *Skeleton City* after what Ned had told me: that corpses in aboveground crypts turn to skeletons fastest since the crypts basically act as ovens efficient at baking flesh off of bone in the summer heat.

On my map, I had sketched the far-off woods we approached, but I had yet to make it to them. It remained one of only three forests I knew of but hadn't explored.

Something curious happened just before the girls were to enter the trees. They stopped. Frozen like deer sensing danger, they began scanning the area ahead. There were only a few rows of cemetery left between them and the woods, and only a few rows left between them and me. I managed to duck behind a large family headstone. There, I spied as best I could. Ultimately, they decided not to enter the woods. Instead, they began walking through the open field beside it. As they headed farther into the field, I had no choice but to give up my cover and follow them into the open.

The field was filled with tall plants and weeds. Instead of tombstones, dead tree trunks were scattered throughout the landscape along with small groupings of windblown pine trees. Hues of browns and greens and splotches of crimson colored the landscape in delicate wisps. Without actually moving, the ground seemed to undulate like waves due to the multitude of tiny hills. It was like walking into an impressionistic painting of a lush wasteland.

The girls playfully hopped from one mound to the next. I followed their path. The ground was odd. It reminded me of shag carpeting—if it were to cover a lumpy floor. It was then the smell of decomposing plants and animals hit me. It was putrid. If I hadn't been so determined, I would've turned around. But I kept on with barely a gag.

The twins had settled on a fallen log. Sitting side-by-side, it appeared as if they had planned to watch the sunrise together. The image would've been sweet and charming—had they not placed the jar of blood between them. I kept somewhat of a careful distance. That is, until one of the twins began to slowly unscrew the lid.

My feet left the mound on which I stood as I attempted to rush toward them to claim what was mine. Yet as I stepped forward, I felt a strange sensation in the ground beneath my feet. It felt soft and spongy. And then, without warning, it broke apart. The ground gave way. And instantly, I was submerged in water. Panicked and struggling, I reached for roots and plants, attempting to hoist myself back to solid ground. A large, black snake raced in front of my face, scared away by the commotion. My head bobbed among moss and weeds as I waded, grasping for anything I could use to pull myself up. As I struggled, I heard their unmistakable laughter overhead.

"We're in the bog, silly. You can't just walk where you want."

"I told you she'd fall in."

"Help me!" I pleaded. I looked up to see the twins towering over me against the backdrop of the rising sun. Elizabeth held the opened jar in her hands. She laughed at me as she licked her red-stained lips. Imogene licked blood from her fingers before pointing to the clump of ferns she stood upon. I worked my way toward them until I finally clutched the solid mound of plant roots beneath their feet.

"Oh look!" Elizabeth shouted excitedly as she pointed behind me. "You've stirred up the prisoners!"

Still grasping the ferns as I caught my breath, I looked behind me to see the large swath I had cut through the mire. The moss had been like a net holding them beneath the surface. Yet once it had been ripped open, up popped a group of skeletons and badly decomposed bodies. Something slimy touched my leg before I felt it move up the side of my body. I didn't want to look, but it was too hard to avoid confronting the head that had emerged beside mine. Its face was bloated. Its eyes were white, bulging from its skull. Its rotten tongue extended halfway down its chin.

I scrambled up the mound screaming. The only thing that halted my screams was when I felt I was going to be sick. The waterlogged corpses and their stench were just too much. I vomited back into the bog and over the corpses that crowded the surface. When I finished heaving, I sat next to Elizabeth and Imogene, who howled over another example of my Grand Hallow naïveté. When they finally regained their composure, Imogene aptly stated, "You smell like a dead frog."

"You wouldn't smell so good either, covered in swamp juice and dead-body slime. Why *are* there bodies out here anyhow?"

"It's where they dump the prisoners," Elizabeth explained. I then remembered Ned had told of Uncle Clayton's contracts with the state prisons. He had said prisoners without family were buried out near some marshes. I assumed he meant buried in graves, not just dumped in a crude wasteland.

Elizabeth had set the jar down beside her. I reached for it, but she quickly grabbed it before I could and screwed tight the lid. "That's my jar," I told her squarely. "Give it back."

"Where'd you get it? Who gave it to you?" she asked.

"It was a gift," I answered simply.

"Well, it's ours now," she said. She held it in front of my face, taunting me before hiding it behind her back with a laugh. "I bet you want a taste? Huh, *vampire girl?*"

I was stunned. Always with the nicknames. But *vampire girl* was one for which I understood the reference all too well. I had only been called that once. A painful memory of isolation. Rejection. I hadn't told anyone. Or so I thought. On the contrary, I *had* told the twins, unwittingly, through my blood. I should've known that night in the fog after we played Marco Polo that they had tasted as much of me as I had of them. I had given them information. Had made myself vulnerable. However possible, perhaps genetically since they were my cousins, it had to be true. Alive or dead, they possessed the same abilities as me.

Not wanting to be one-upped, I decided to reveal my own cards. "I know who you are," I boasted. Imogene's eyes widened with curiosity while Elizabeth folded her arms in skepticism. "Imogene said you lived in the cemetery. At first, I thought that meant you literally *lived* in the cemetery. I was looking for some sort of camp or house hidden in the woods. But now I know exactly where you live. It was right in front of me the whole time. I've been inside your house. I've even been in your room."

"Impossible!" challenged Elizabeth. "There's no way you'd be able to get in."

"Well I have. I found the key." Both girls looked utterly shocked. "I saw the pink carpet and the Strawberry Shortcake sheets. I saw all your toys: the purple gorilla, the bird string puppets, and all those dolls. I even saw your portrait. So you don't have to pretend anymore. I know your dad is my uncle. I know you are my cousins. I know you died when the car your mom was driving fell off the Emerald Bridge. I bet you still go to that sad, lonely room when you're not wandering the cemetery. But maybe you don't have to anymore. Maybe it's time to leave this place. Maybe it's time to go find your mom. Leave Grand Hallow and be with her."

The twins were silent. They looked to each other for a moment. And then Imogene finally said, "We don't live in that house anymore, silly."

Elizabeth was a bit crasser in her response: she burst into a laugh. "We would never live in that awful house next to the crematorium again. Not with our dad there. He's weak! And so are those stupid doll houses and all that little kid stuff."

"We like it out here," affirmed Imogene. "Where we're free!" She lifted her arms over her head as if attempting to touch the horizon.

"You don't know so much," said Elizabeth, unimpressed. She grabbed Imogene by her outstretched arm, pulling her up. "Now let's play a game."

"C'mon, Lisa." Imogene tugged on my shoulder. "Elizabeth always has good games." Stubborn and pouting like a girl younger than they were, I wouldn't budge.

"Imogene and I are going to run to the other side of the bog," explained Elizabeth. "If you can make it to the other side without falling in, I'll give you your jar back. You know what? I'll make it even easier. Even if you *do* fall in, if Imogene or I fall in too, I'll give you your jar back. But if you fall in and we don't, it's ours." I stood unenthusiastically, my wet, rancid clothes clinging to my skin.

"Watch out for the dead deer," advised Imogene. "He fell in and couldn't get out. Don't trip on his antlers."

"Ready? Set? Go!"

I watched them take off briskly, Elizabeth holding my jar. Each took a different path through the bog. Expertly, they stepped only in spots they had memorized and knew to be safe, like some kind of ancient warriors skilled at silently stepping through a forest so as to not make a sound. They skipped across the bog with ease as the morning sun began to blind my eyes. It was no use. Carefully, I made my way out of the bog the same way I came in, humiliated once more by my dead, red-headed twin cousins.

Chapter 19

Edge of the Map

Those cunning girls! As I began my long, defeated trek back to the facility, I finally figured it out. The twins were about to go into the forest but changed their course and led me to the bog instead. They *knew* I had been following them. It was a simple misdirection. They had originally intended to take my jar with them into that woods, which begged the question: *What was in those woods?* I turned course and marched straight for them. Barefoot. Bugs swarming me, attracted to my bog stench.

It was primarily a pine forest. A thick canopy of branches blocked out the majority of sunlight. I slowly made my way through it, trying to look for anything unusual. My feet did not hurt so much since the floor of the forest was mostly covered in a soft carpet of dried pine needles.

I passed a fallen log covered in bright orange mushrooms with black dots. Upon closer inspection, I discovered the dots were in fact thousands of crawling black bugs. I itched my ankles and swatted the mosquito buzzing near my ear. As in most of Grand Hallow's forests, there were depressions filled with stagnant water. I passed one of the small ponds and was startled as two ducks, alerted to my presence, lifted themselves out of the water, quacking as they flew out of the forest.

As I approached the center of the forest, I noticed morning light pouring in. Like an eye of a hurricane, there was an opening in the canopy. I wasn't sure if it constituted being unusual, but inside this clearing, the ground was elevated in a robust mound. I climbed the hill and looked to the open sky. It was strikingly blue with no clouds. The air was fresh; the pines effectively filtered out the smells of the nearby bog. From my high vantage, I scanned the forest. Nothing else besides the knoll I stood upon seemed out of the ordinary. That is, except for one thing.

Beside me, a large pipe jutted from the ground. It was rusted brown and curved at the end like a periscope. And then I noticed on the other end of the mound was an identical pipe. *What was beneath this hill?* I wondered. I stomped my bare foot. It felt like earth, solid. I held my ear to one of the pipes' openings and listened for a few minutes as muffled air swirled below.

I then took a few steps forward and discovered the other side of the hill was cut off abruptly in a steep, almost vertical ridge. The ridge was covered in a patch of dandelions. Some had bloomed into yellow flowers while others were covered in their cottonlike parachute seeds. I jumped off the ridge, clipping several of their heads on my descent. After I landed, I watched the seeds I had released float majestically throughout the forest.

At the bottom of the ridge, parked against a cluster of large boulders, was an old wheelbarrow. It was filled with fresh lumber. And beside it was a bucket of tools. Perplexed, I looked to the ground to give me an idea of the activity that went on there. Yet the dense carpet of pine needles effectively prevented the formation of tracks. I peered through the mesh of trees and began following a tight path I imagined could've reasonably been used to push a wheelbarrow in and out of the woods.

The path eventually led me out of the forest and dumped me into an empty plot of cleared land. There were no graves. Just paved walking paths circling an overgrown field. Since it was clearly a place designated for future expansion, it appeared I had reached the very edge of Grand Hallow.

Back at the facility, tired, pissed, and stinking to high heaven, I swung open the back door to the morgue. I stomped my way across the floor, not caring that I was leaving muddy footprints in my wake. Norman immediately dropped his scalpel and rushed to me. Appalled, he blocked my path to the hall. With a plastic splatter mask covering his face and his gloved, bloody hands clasped firmly before him, he bowed toward me. "Miss Jacobs, I'm sure you can appreciate how me-tic-u-lous I am about keeping my morgue an-ti-sep-tic and free of such—filth," he said, examining me from my mud-filled toes up to my swamp scum-infused hair.

"If you were so worried about being *an-ti-sep-tic*, you wouldn't have let your secret blood barrels leak all over the floor. And you would've cleaned up after the mess you made at the house in Shilling." With that, I shoved the creep aside. He was seemingly less offended that I had pushed him than that I had touched his lab coat with my germ-ridden hand. He looked to the spot of concern and recoiled as if I had thrown a steaming pot of coffee over his head.

Having gotten by Norman, I rushed to my little green room and unlocked the door from the outside. After ripping the map out from my notebook, I charged to Ned's office. Barging in, I slapped the map down on his desk. Startled by my rude entrance, he shot back in his chair. "Oh my, Miss Jacobs," he said before promptly correcting himself. "Excuse me, *Miss Lisa*. I'm so happy to see you've been released from your— punishment."

"I was *not* released," I snarled. "I climbed out my window."

He began to play with the end of his tie. "Oh dear," he said nervously. "Are you all right? That is quite a drop."

"I survived," I stated simply and then pointed to the corner of my crude map, to the pine forest on the edge of the property.

"What have we here?" he asked, putting on his glasses.

"What's out there?" I asked impatiently.

"If I'm understanding this map correctly, there shouldn't be *anything* out that far. Just a pine forest if I recall."

"What's in the *middle* of the pine forest?"

"I'm not sure I'm following you, ma'am. Oh there I go again. Pardon me, *Miss Lisa*. Perhaps your uncle could help."

"We both know he's not going to tell me a thing. There's a hill out there with pipes sticking out of it. I'm asking *you*. What is it?"

"Ah yes," he said, raising his index finger. "I believe that would be an old root cellar. Many years ago, there used to be a farm on the neighboring side of that forest. I wouldn't be surprised if there are more just like it throughout the woods of Grand Hallow. Originally, that's why this land was cleared, you know. For farming."

"A root cellar? I didn't see a door."

"Oh, heavens no. The door would've been boarded up years ago. And now, it is likely covered in years and years of soil. In fact, the cellar itself was probably filled in so as not to create a haven for rodents and such. But I'm afraid the exact history of such buildings on the property predates my tenure."

"There was a wheelbarrow with lumber in it out there. And tools."

"The grounds staff certainly does stay quite busy around here. Routinely, they have a multitude of projects all throughout the property. Now I'm not sure why they would be out working in that particular forest. But I can ask Henry if you'd like."

"Yes. Ask Henry," I instructed as I stepped into the hall, not bothering to take my map with me. "And Ned," I called from the doorway, "I'm taking the day off."

Exiting as abruptly as I had entered, I left a bewildered Ned and headed to the door on the other side of the balcony. I had yet to go inside this particular unmarked door. I wasn't invited. Nor, I presumed, was I welcome. Yet I had an important message to deliver. I took a deep breath and grabbed the handle. To my surprise, I was faced with a steep and narrow stairway. I moved up the flight of stairs, cringing at the sound of each squeaky step, much preferring to arrive unannounced. A second door at the top of the stairs was open, so I let myself in.

The office was easily the size of the entire main floor of my house in Ruthsford. Yet unlike my house, it was minimalist and sterile. The ceilings were fifteen feet tall. And the walls were made of glass on three sides of the room, providing a panoramic view of the campus and surrounding cemetery. There he stood, taking it all in. Even though he had to sense my presence, he kept his back to me and his arms folded like some maniacal dictator looking out over the land he ruled. As I stepped farther inside, I realized he was right; the stone cottage came into a perfect birds-eye view.

"I wasn't aware you had been let out for breakfast yet," he said, still without facing me.

"I just came to tell you I was out to the edge of the property this morning. I saw the prisoners. You know, the bodies you've been dumping in the marshes. I could be wrong, but I'm pretty sure it's illegal to dump bodies in a mass grave—even if they *are* the bodies of prisoners. So unless you think you can clean them out before I can report you, you better keep my bedroom door unlocked from here on out." He turned to me with a raised eyebrow. "And something tells me even if you *wanted* to clean up that bog, it would take you at least until the middle of fall to fish out all those corpses."

"But my dear, you don't have access to a phone. Or a car for that matter, rest assured, after your little stint. How on earth would you ever report this alleged mass grave?"

"I have my ways," I warned him. "Remember. I'm a delinquent, just like my brother. And a pit viper, just like my mother."

Part IV
Chapter 20
Body Factory

Boom! Boom! Boom! I came to understand that being awakened in a startling panic was quite customary with life at Grand Hallow. Predictable even, on any given night. It was the same loud banging Tina and I had heard that first night in the green room, like someone striking a large bass drum. The noise reverberated from the morgue and down the hall. It was then followed by those same scraping noises, as if someone were dragging a heavy filing cabinet across a gravel road.

Yet unlike the first time Tina and I had heard the unexpected noises in the dead of night, I decided then and there I was not going to cower like a frightened rabbit. This time, I'd find out exactly what was going on. And who was responsible. Swiftly, I crept from beneath the covers and grasped the doorknob with a prayer that my bargaining chip with Uncle Clayton had worked. I twisted the knob. And much to my relief, I was free. I pulled open the door, just a bit, and peered down the hall.

With the coast clear, I cautiously tiptoed toward the morgue. As I got closer, I noticed only the lights along the back wall were lit. Suddenly, a figure stepped before the lights. I couldn't make out its detail, but it cast a long, slender shadow. The shadow stretched down the hallway and intersected with my own. I was quick to slip into the darkness along the edge of the hall, watching the figure as it moved chaotically like some marionette being tossed to and fro by a frantic puppeteer. In the frenzy, dropped trays and fumbled instruments crashed onto the porcelain tiles. Undeterred, I scurried forward until I finally made it to the morgue's entrance. There, I peered from behind one of the pillars. The slender figure had abruptly disappeared, leaving the morgue in disarray.

Three fresh corpses occupied the slabs at the far end of the room. I knew they were fresh because they had not been prepped in the least. Their mouths were agape. And the smell that carried into the hall told me they had not yet seen the inside of a cooler, much less been embalmed.

The doors to two of the walk-in coolers were wide open. Clustered around them were four cadavers upon gurneys. Two were zipped in body bags while the other two were fully exposed. About half a dozen of the singular cooler drawers also were open along the wall. It looked as if someone had haphazardly opened the drawers of a giant card catalog and then abruptly walked away without finding the needed book.

Yet among all the chaos, most conspicuous was the reappearance of the objects of much contention during the first night Tina and I had stayed at Grand Hallow: the collection of plastic barrels. Instead of being discreetly stacked in the back of the morgue, they were chaotically placed throughout the room. Some were sealed. Yet several others were empty with their lids tossed aside.

From the short hallway that led out the back of the facility, the figure once again entered the morgue. I pulled tighter behind the pillar but caught a clear enough look to know that it was in fact Norman causing the middle-of-the-night ruckus. Perhaps since it was his morgue, his working there during the middle of the night might not have been considered far from ordinary. Yet his behavior surely was. He was clearly manic, darting from one body to the next. "No! No! *You* go whole," he said to a corpse in a body bag, wheeling it toward the back door. "*You're* a barrel," he pointed to another on a slab. "And *you* . . ." He thought for a moment with his finger on his chin before pointing to an exposed corpse on a gurney. "*You're* a puree!"

He strapped on a pair of surgical gloves and grabbed his scalpel before approaching the male corpse on the slab designated a *barrel*. He began by making a cut from the top of the corpse's chest down to its navel. Then, using forceps in one hand, he began to peel back the skin while at the same time cutting the connective tissue with his scalpel in the other hand. With the corpse's chest and torso effectively skinned, he severed the flaps from the body. He held up the large swaths of flesh and admired his work for a moment before throwing them into a nearby medical waste bag.

He then pulled his splatter mask over his face before reaching for a miniature handheld circular saw. But just before switching it on, he suddenly set it down. "Lisa, Lisa, Lisa," he repeated as he began searching for something else. "Locked away. Locked away. But mustn't wake her. No. Ah, there it is." From the counter, he brought back a stainless steel mallet. With precise blows, he began breaking apart the sternum and rib cage as blood sprayed over his mask and apron.

Satisfied, he dragged over one of the plastic tubs. I chewed on my thumb, horrified, as he used various instruments to dislodge the organs. Once loosened, he at first used his hands and then a large spoonlike tool to scoop out the organs from the abdominal cavity before tossing them in the barrel.

He had trouble dislodging the heart, so he grabbed an apparatus that looked like a pair of calipers I had used in science class to measure rocks. Except this tool also had a large crank. He jammed the jaws of the device between the cracked ribcage and then turned the crank to spread the bones apart. He then was able to grab hold of the heart. And with a few good yanks, he finally had it removed. He held it in his hands, marveling at the organ for a moment before carelessly tossing it into the barrel with the rest of the corpse's innards. He then disconnected the flexible tubing beneath the slab and inserted it into the barrel to catch the gruesome runoff.

Next, he manically pranced to one of the sinks. From it, he produced a blood bag like the ones I had seen in the sink the night I met David. He awkwardly hugged the oversize bag as he carried it to the barrel. "Now for the gravy," he said with a devilish grin. With his scalpel, he sliced open the bag and let the contents of blood and what I assumed to be chunks of flesh and mashed organs splash into the barrel. He licked his lips as he watched the barrel fill with the marinade. Happy with his concoction, he used a rubber mallet to pound the lid on tight. Boom! Boom! Boom! He then dragged the heavy barrel down the back hallway and out of the morgue.

When he returned, he took the corpse designated a *puree* and wheeled it over to the sinks. He rolled the entire body into one of the basins. Its torso landed with a thud. Yet it did not fit properly. An arm and leg stuck awkwardly into the air. So he began hacking at the cadaver's limbs with a large cleaver of a knife.

I really didn't want to learn how Norman went about making a *puree*. Luckily, I didn't have to. He was unfocused. Rushed and frazzled. Distracted by his own mind. Like tending a stove with too many boiling pots, he couldn't keep up. He soon abandoned the body in the sink. Instead, he grabbed the gurney he had wheeled to the back door and mumbled incomprehensible phrases as he pushed it outside.

I used the opportunity to jolt down the hall. In the green room, I quickly pushed open the window and craned my neck out as far as I could. There was a white van parked at the edge of the building. The Grand Hallow logo was painted on its side in a serene shade of green. I watched as Norman lifted the body bag off the gurney and placed it in the back of the van.

Seeing him in action, it was clear to me that it had in fact been Norman attempting to force his way into the green room the night Tina and I had come to Grand Hallow, no doubt trying to assure the coast was clear before carrying out his wretched deeds.

Instantly, I knew what I had to do. If I could catch him bringing his mutilated corpses off Grand Hallow property, it'd be a chance to expose him as a monster. A criminal. I'd prove he was the phantom offering me the jars of blood. I'd prove he was the one responsible for the blood-soaked room at the house in Shilling. And most importantly, with his skilled work at slicing up cadavers and removing their organs, it wouldn't be hard to link him to my dad's murder. But it wasn't *me* who needed convincing. And especially while he was in his cloaked and hooded disguise, it wasn't enough that Tina and I had already been witnesses. No, if I was to accomplish outing him as the corpse-stealing psychopath and murderous butcher he was, I was going to need a witness of some authority.

I didn't have much time. I needed to think quickly. I grabbed my photocopy of the addresses stolen from Norman's office. And on a whim, I dug through my purse and also grabbed my Video Tyme rental card. I rushed to Ned's office. Without the warning time I would've needed to set up my eraser trick, I grabbed the knob and slid the plastic card between the door and the jamb. It took some wiggling while forcing the knob to turn. But soon the latch sprang free, and the door swung open. *Damn, I should've tried that the first time.*

After swiftly shutting the door behind me, I grabbed the phone. I needed Sternhardt. It was his case. I'd have the best chance convincing him to investigate what Norman was up to. But I didn't have the direct number to the Ruthsford Police Department, not that I would've gotten ahold of him in the middle of the night anyhow. And I didn't want to dial 9-1-1 and talk to some random operator. How in the world could I have explained the situation so it would've made sense? *Hello. I want to report a crime that hasn't taken place yet. No, I'm not entirely sure where it's going to take place. And the victims, they're already dead.* No, I didn't have time for that. So I dialed—who else—but Tina.

"Hello?" Tina's mom answered after nearly five rings. She sounded too groggy to be pissed off.

"Hi, Mrs. Cashmere. I need to talk to Tina."

"Lisa? It's nearly 3:00 a.m.," she said, quickly sounding more pissed off than groggy. "Christina's asleep. What's this about?"

"I'm not asleep, Mom," Tina piped up from her extension. "Now hang up the phone and cut her some slack, OK? She's living in a funeral home for Christ sake."

"Not again at these hours, girls," warned Mrs. Cashmere.

"Sorry, Mrs. Cashmere. Never again," I promised.

"Oh, don't worry about her," Tina blurted as soon as her mother clicked the receiver. "She's got me under house arrest ever since she caught me pullin' up the drive after our trip to Shilling. And she's *still* got a stick up her ass about it. But oh—my—God! She's not the only one pissed at me. Sternhardt is too! I told him we went to that house. And he's like all offended and shit! Can you believe it? 'Interfering in my investigation' is what he said. 'Tampering with a crime scene.' He didn't even seem to care when I said we ran into a guy. In a cloak. Handing you a jar of blood like it was a bouquet of fuckin' flowers. He told me that you and I need to stay away from there. That the neighborhood is dangerous. I mean, it's like he thinks it was some random bum dressed up for early Halloween. My God. What an idiot!"

"Tina!" I begged to interject, but she could not be stopped.

"But listen to this! After buggin' the shit outta him, he tells me there've been all these unsolved squatter cases goin' back for years, before I even moved to Ruthsford. Same thing we saw. All these abandoned houses with blood all over and shit. Cops are thinkin' it's like satanic rituals or animal sacrifices going on. And guess the fuck what? You're not gonna believe this! They knew it was goin' on at the Grant Mansion before we moved in. They *knew* a satanist or whatever had taken it over for a while when it was vacant.

"You know all those rumors you told me about my house being haunted? Ghosts walkin' by the windows at night? Well, the police knew about that too. Only they knew the *truth*. It wasn't the ghost of old lady Grant who hung herself. Or even her dead husband. It was someone actually living here! Of course, Sternhardt takes his sweet-ass time investigating because he figures it's just kids makin' up haunted house stories. So by the time he goes to check it out, the whole basement is covered in a pool of blood. And the little devil has disappeared. It had to be all cleaned up before we moved in. Makes sense how my dad got this mansion so easy. I mean, first an old hag hangs herself. And then pools of blood in the basement? Shit!

"So anyway, for years they've been tryin' to track down who's been moving from house to vacant fuckin' house from here all the way to Grand Hallow doin' all this witchy stuff. But the Satan Squatter, he's staying one step ahead."

"Well, the *Satan Squatter* is on the move again," I said. "Listen, Tina. Right now, Norman's loading a van with corpses and barrels of blood. We can catch him in the act. I just need you to write down three addresses for me. And then call the Ruthsford Police."

"Holy shit!" shouted Tina. "Why didn't you say so? Let me get some paper." I heard her stomping about her room. "You've got me shakin'. OK. Go ahead."

"OK. The first is 3 West End Avenue in Shilling. The next is 1428 Birch Street in Sharlaton. And 4267 Roxbury in Ruthsford. Now call and tell them to wake Sternhardt right away. Make sure they tell him that the person who killed my dad is going to be at one of these addresses, along with plenty of evidence to link him to his murder—as well as solve Sternhardt's satanic squatter mystery."

"Got it. Wait. How do you know he's goin' to one of those addresses?"

"After the house in Shilling, those are the last addresses on Norman's list that haven't been scratched off. He *has* to be going to one of those. I just don't know which."

"So how is Sternhardt gonna be in three places at once? I mean, the Ruthsford fuzz is not exactly the most willing—or able—police department in the state. I'd be surprised if he got to *one*, in time at least."

"That's why I'm going to track Norman myself."

"Now that just sounds batshit crazy! How you gonna follow him? You're not gonna steal a hearse again, are you?"

"You don't even want to know."

"Lisa—don't! If he sees *you* seeing *him* without that hood on at one of those houses, you're in trouble. You're freakin' toast! Stay right where you're at! How about I'll get a hold of Sternhardt and have him come straight there to arrest the bastard?"

"Because then there's no proof! No one's going to care about a mortician carving up bodies in a morgue. He needs to be caught in the act—away from Grand Hallow. It's the only way. Look, just give me the Ruthsford Police number. Even if no one comes, I could find a phone. I could go to a next-door neighbor. I'll do what I have to. I'll hold him down myself until the cops show up if it comes to that. I just need to pin the squatter thing to him. If I can do that, then I'm betting it won't be too hard convincing Sternhardt to also charge him with murder."

Each time he left the room to load another gory thing, I moved a bit closer. First, I crouched in the alcove in front of his office door. Then, I snuck behind the interior wall in front of the refrigerated drawers. Finally, I tucked myself behind the back door, which he had propped open. I watched from the gap as he passed mere inches from me back into the morgue, lecturing himself, something on the importance of timeliness. And as soon as he turned the corner, I slipped outside. My heart beating a million times a minute, I climbed into the back of the van.

The floor was crowded with barrels. Shelves lining both sides were stacked with corpses in body bags. I climbed atop the barrels and squeezed behind the shelving on the left side of the van. The floor beneath the bottom shelf was packed with blood bags. I squatted next to the bags before quickly working to wedge myself between them. Once I was pressed between the bags of warm blood and pulverized organs, a layer below and several layers above, I let my body recline and tucked my arms inside. I had to adjust my head just right to find an air pocket. And when I did, I barely breathed the whole time Norman finished loading the van.

Chapter 21

House of Blood and Bones

I was a stowaway in his van of carnage for at least an hour by the time the vehicle pulled off the pavement and onto rough terrain. Gravel churned under the tires. The van swayed and bounced. Blood and guts sloshed in the barrels. We hit a series of chatter bumps that violently rattled the frame. A body bag and the corpse within dislodged from the top shelf and fell atop the barrels.

But worst of all was what happened after one of the tires smashed into what had to be the world's largest pothole: the blood bag beneath me ruptured. At first, I felt a warm sensation across my back. And then, as the bag leaked and began to deflate, I was slowly lowered to the van's floor while at the same time submerged in the grisly liquid. The runoff flowed through the van. Chunks of mashed organs rode the wave and became lodged between the barrels. I winced in pain as my back was pressed into the corrugated floor by the weight of the heavy bags on top of me. Yet even when the van finally stopped, I resisted the urge to claw my way out of my uncomfortably blood-soaked and pinned position.

Instead, when he opened the rear doors, I was as still as one of his corpses.

He yanked down the corpse that had fallen onto the barrels and tossed it to the ground. After that, it didn't take him long to notice one of the bags had burst. "No! No! No!" he sniveled. "This is un-ac-cep-ta-ble!" Frantically, he began gathering the spilled chunks of flesh. He stuffed what he could find into the pockets of his lab coat. The whole time, he whimpered as if he had been physically hurt by the accidental rupture. His white, pristine jacket quickly developed splotches of red. His hand reached between the barrels for the source, the deflated bag beneath me. I was afraid at any moment his exploring fingers would latch onto my exposed shoulder. Panicked, but as slowly as possible, I tucked myself farther beneath the bags until I was crammed against the side of the van.

Likely realizing it would be easier to find the leak without the barrels in the way, he heaved the first one out the back. I expected him to grab a second barrel, yet he did not immediately reenter the van. Squished between plastic, it was difficult to hear. So I popped my head out from between the bags and cocked it like a dog concentrating on a far-off noise. I didn't hear a thing for minute. But then I heard his grunts, followed by the crackle and pops of what had to be the barrel being dragged across gravel. As the scraping echoed farther and farther away, I wondered if it was time to make my escape. But if I was to use that moment, I knew I couldn't hesitate. He'd no doubt be back at any moment for the next barrel.

In a flash, I squeezed from beneath the bags. My cramped back spasmed as I stood. But I ignored the pain and climbed atop the remaining barrels on all fours. When I reached the edge of the open doors, I peered out, cautiously, with just one eye.

The night was black. There were no stars. The only light came from the front of the house. A yellow porch light was on. So was an inside light illuminating a small mudroom. It was a two-story farmhouse with a wraparound porch. A soft wind blew through the trees, crowding the aged home. I did not see Norman. But he had left the door to the mudroom open, making the home appear deceivingly inviting. I peeked out to gather intel on the surrounding neighborhood. Nothing. Just more trees. "Perfect," I sighed. *Stuck with a nutcase at a farmhouse down an isolated dirt road.* The number on the house was 4267, so at least I knew I was at the Ruthsford address.

Norman's figure suddenly appeared in the mudroom. I jumped from the back of the van. Hunching over, I sprinted across the yard as he stepped from the porch. I hid in the dark behind the side of the house, watching as he grabbed the next barrel and dragged it across the drive.

There was no sign of even a random car coming down the dark road, much less Sternhardt or some backup unit headed my way. So I decided to investigate alone. Sure, I could've stayed safely put in the shadows, hoping for the police to show. But if I could find a phone inside, I could call and let them know exactly where to find Norman.

Yet beyond that very practical reason of getting to a phone, I had to be honest with myself; I was also driven by something else. I needed to see exactly what he was up to with my own two eyes. Why was he bringing fresh and mutilated corpses to vacant houses? What did it all mean? And if I found out the answer to that, I was hoping perhaps it would lead to the reason why he had killed my father. I didn't feel as if I really had a choice in the matter. I was compelled to creep around the back of that dilapidated farmhouse. For my dad. And for my own curiosity that would not be silenced.

A white picket fence enclosed a small portion of the yard directly behind the house. I unlatched the fence and entered what was likely at one time a thriving garden. In the center was a large trellis. The trellis created a tunnel entrance to the back of the house. I could faintly see a door on the other end. But the path was unkempt and overgrown with grape vines and crawling ivy reaching in all directions. Using the path would be a challenge. Yet cutting through the overgrown vines seemed like a better choice than facing Norman unloading his treasured handiwork.

I ducked into the tunnel. Almost immediately, I realized something else besides overgrown vines obstructed my path. Spooked, I jumped as I brushed against what I first thought was a dried branch. But this branch, it ended in very humanlike fingers, which limply stroked my neck. I turned to see an almost fleshless limb, reaching out, woven into the tapestry of vines.

It was then I realized that intertwined with the foliage were dozens of badly decomposed corpses. They were stitched into the sides and ceiling of the trellis. It seemed as though the ivy had come to life as a group of unsuspecting souls had passed through, ensnaring them in a tragic fate. Some still had a layer of brown, leathery flesh while others were no more than skeletons, their skulls and limbs trapped in the mesh of plant life.

As I passed, they reached for me. I could feel their stares. Their pleas for help. These bodies, these people, it was almost like they had been strung up as a grim warning that was telling me to turn back before it was too late. I struggled to move. But I pushed forward, apologetically breaking their brittle arms and legs when needed in order to make it to the end of the tunnel. And when I finally did, I clutched the handle on the chipped, blue door. I still had my Video Tyme card in my pocket. But the door opened with a robust yank.

I was faced with a short set of steps descending into the basement. "Not the basement," I groaned. *Why the basement?* But perhaps it was a better mode of entrance for staying unnoticed. I grabbed ahold of the cord dangling above the steps. But the bulb was dead. Of course it was. Quietly, I sealed the door behind me and began my descent into complete darkness.

In junior high, our science class went on a trip to an out-of-commission gypsum mine. When the guide took us down the elevator and into its bowels, he shut off the lights. *That* was total darkness. No moonlight or stars to find your way. A strange sensation it is to open your eyes as wide as they will go and still see nothing except the darkest black.

That's what it was like to be in that basement. As pitch black as a gypsum mine. Hanging onto the railing, I was able to make it safely to the bottom of the stairs.

From there, I shuffled. Not wanting to trip, I didn't lift my feet. And I kept my hands in front of me hoping to find a wall that could guide me to a door that would lead me to a staircase. The wall nearest me was filled with what felt like gardening tools. Rakes. Hoes. I came upon a shelf where I felt a spade with dried specks of dirt as well as the sharp points of a handheld gardening claw. I grabbed the gardening claw, taking it with me as I shuffled forward.

The smell of the basement was earthy and musty, like an antique shop filled with old books and furniture. Yet as I rounded the corner into the next room, the putrid smell of death overpowered the quaint smells of old things. That indistinguishable smell of rotting corpses caused me to pull my shirt over my nose and clench the handle of my gardening claw just a bit tighter. With my free hand, I gently dragged my fingertips along the wall. I shuffled for a while this way as I listened to the floorboards creak above, to Norman madly tending to his house of blood and bones.

And then I abruptly halted as I bumped into something solid at the hip. I felt the corner of what had to be a wooden table or workbench. I tucked the garden tool in my back pocket and used the long, rectangular edge as a guide to the other side of the room.

Yet as I made my passage, I kept brushing up against cold flesh. I wasn't sure what compelled me to, but I reached onto the table. My hand landed on a clump of thick, matted hair. And when I moved my hand forward, I felt lips and teeth as my fingers involuntarily slipped into an open mouth. I quickly retracted. Yet after that, it was strangely more frightening *not* to know what dreadful thing was right next to me in the dark. So as if to face the nightmare head-on, I ran my hands over the top of the entire table, discovering the full collection of corpses that had been piled there. The clammy flesh. The mangled limbs. The frozen faces.

When I reached the end of the table, I was without the guide of walls or furniture. I reached blindly into the empty darkness. Lost in the sea of infinite blackness, I panicked. While quickly trying to find direction, I made the mistake of taking full, brisk steps instead of my careful shuffle. Inevitably, I tripped and fell—planting myself atop a bevy of cadavers. Frantically, I began crawling over the rotten bodies, through the tangled mess of limbs and torsos, hoping I might find a way out of the basement if only I could make it to the other side of the pile.

It was then that light burst from above. It illuminated a staircase, which, of course, was just mere feet from where I swam with the corpses. Norman trudged down the steps, dragging a body bag behind him. Hurriedly, I pulled as many of the stinking body parts on top of me as I could. And then I tried to remain as still as them. When he reached the bottom of the stairs, he unzipped the bag and threw the fresh corpse onto the pile. Even though the weight was crushing me, I didn't move—not until he flipped off the light and shut the door at the top of the stairs.

I was in the darkness once again but finally knew my path. I clawed my way out from the pile and felt my way up the stairs. Gently, I cracked open the door. The house was drenched in shadows. But with no immediate sight of Norman, I snuck out of the basement and found myself standing in a hall. In front of me was a large, open staircase with an ornate wooden railing. The stairway seemed to be the centerpiece of the house, dividing it in half. To my left was a formal foyer. And to my right was the kitchen. In the kitchen, I spotted a phone on the wall. But I couldn't risk it. At least not at that moment. Not when I didn't know where Norman was.

Sounds of movement, brisk footsteps, came from elsewhere in the house. Exposed in the hall, I moved in tightly to the staircase. I peeked over the steps to see Norman moving about frenetically in a room on the other side. When he left my view to go deeper into the room, I quickly scurried halfway up the stairs. While the open stairway did not offer much coverage for hiding, I was high enough that I was mostly concealed by the first floor ceiling.

I peered below to see Norman arranging his goods in some sort of parlor or sitting room. A bag of blood sat atop an old liquor cabinet. There were bodies piled on the floor. Bodies piled across the sofa. There was even one on a piano bench with its head resting against the keys. He seemed particularly preoccupied with one cadaver propped into a reclining position in a lounge chair. He kept rearranging the arms of the dead man from his side to his lap and back again. "No, this is how we like it," he said, seemingly satisfied with the man's arms folded loosely before him. He then spun in the center of the room like a little boy, delighted by his work. "Ready and displayed to appealing perfection!" he cheered and then clasped his hands. "But I mustn't forget! No, never," he said before leaving the room and charging to the bottom of the staircase.

Shit! I quickly scrambled up the rest of the stairs and rushed down the hallway. I yanked the handle of the first door, but it was locked. So too was the second. Freaking out, I pulled out my video rental card as I approached the third door. My hands were shaking as I slipped the card into the door jamb. But as hard as I turned the knob, the damn thing wouldn't budge.

Knowing it was only a matter of moments before he reached the top of the stairs, I grabbed the gardening claw out of my back pocket. And when I saw him emerge in that hallway, something primal kicked in. It surged through my veins. Fear. Preservation. I wasn't sure where it came from. All I knew was that I was screaming at the top of my lungs as I took off running toward him, clutching my weapon overhead.

It was a surprising revelation that I, Lisa Jacobs, could cause fear in another human being, especially one as monstrous as Norman. But I did. I knew because his face was stunned with it. He was screaming just as loud as I was as I ambushed him, plunging the metal claws deep into the side of his ugly face. I yanked hard to remove the curved claws. And when they came out, they brought with them chunks of his ripped flesh. Blood gushed down his face as he screeched in agony.

I raised my arm to strike again. But this time, he was ready. He shoved me. Pushed my shoulders with all his might, and I tumbled backward down the stairs.

I wasn't sure how long I had been knocked out. I wasn't sure how he had gotten me back up the stairs. But when I woke, there I was. In an upstairs room. Overlooking the front yard of the old farmhouse. Tied to a chair. And there were skeletons. Lots of skeletons. As my vision came out of the fog, I realized the room was essentially storage for those corpses whose flesh had rotted clean away. Bones were piled in the corner. Bones covered an old bed. Skulls lined a hanging shelf. At least skeletons didn't smell.

Norman stood before me, apparently waiting for me to wake. He had affixed a dish cloth to the wound on his face. It was held in place by clear packing tape, which wrapped his head several times over. "Thankfully, I always carry antiseptic salve," he said, gently caressing the blood-soaked cloth.

He produced a scalpel from his lab coat. Even though my head was pounding, I knew what it meant. That scalpel, it could've been the very one that had dissected my father. And like him, tied to a chair, I too would be filleted. I would be bled out until I lost consciousness. He'd collect my blood and pour it into his little jars to pass out to future unsuspecting victims. After I was drained, one-by-one he'd remove my organs. My heart, liver, stomach, spleen—even my tongue and eyes. Pieces of me would be harvested—for God knows what—dumped and sealed in a barrel like canned meat or pureed and poured into plastic bags.

But in what I was sure were my final moments, I was most upset that I still didn't know why. Why did he do this to my father? Why was he about to do this to me? With his firmly clenched scalpel just inches from my body, I shouted, "Why the fuck are you doing this!" I winced, anticipating the first slice. I figured it'd hurt the most.

But instead, he used the blade to cut one of my wrists loose from the thick plastic rope holding it to the chair. Once he had sliced free my other arm, he jumped away from me. He held his hands up defensively, as if he were cautiously letting loose a wild animal from a cage. "Haven't you figured it out yet, Miss Jacobs?"

"Figure *what* out?" I attempted to stand, but my throbbing head forced me back to the chair.

"Is it that you don't understand? Or is it that you are just that un-grate-ful?" he asked, seething with frustration. He took a deep breath and clasped his hands together as he tried to calm himself. He then turned over his hands, offering me his open palms in a welcoming gesture. "It's for you," he said. He closed his eyes and spun around as he had in the parlor, reaching out to the skeletons. "It's all for you." As he spun with a crooked smile, red and blue lights began flashing on his face. Sensing the lights, he opened his eyes in a disoriented panic. "What is happening?"

"The police are here."

"*The police?* But why!"

"I called them. It's OK. They just want to talk to you. All you have to do is tell them what you did and make them understand. All right? They want to hear everything you have to say."

"What have you done!" he wailed dramatically while clutching the ends of his hair. He looked out the window as Sternhardt and his men approached the house. He then brought his face directly before mine. "You are a stupid, stupid witch." With that, he took his scalpel and plunged it firmly into his neck. He stabbed himself swiftly and repeatedly. Over and over, he sliced into his neck, successfully puncturing his jugular vein on several attempts. As his blood sprayed out across the room, he eventually fell to his knees. His arm went limp. He dropped the scalpel. Finally, he collapsed, his body twitching in a pool of blood.

I just stood there. Frozen. Covering my mouth in horror. My brain had trouble processing. I couldn't believe what I had just witnessed. It happened so fast. There was no time to reason with him. No time to stop him. I finally stumbled out of the room in a daze. My legs felt like rubber as I made my way down the stairs. I was in shock. I didn't feel what my body knew—that, after my fall, it still suffered the equivalent of being hit by a truck. And so it was a surprise to me when I collapsed on the lawn at Sternhardt's feet.

Chapter 22

Bottom of the Jar

The two days I spent in the hospital were my first taste in a long time of a normal world, a world without corpses and caskets and strange ghostly girls hovering in trees—not to mention suicidal cadaver-obsessed psychopaths. Yet even there, I could not escape. The local media got ahold of the story. And from my hospital bed, I watched as the reports came in.

"A house of horrors has been discovered in the small community of Ruthsford as bodies are found piled up both inside and outside a rural home," reported the Channel 13 anchorwoman. "Citizens are in shock tonight as the gruesome discovery was made early this morning at an abandoned home on the outskirts of Ruthsford. Investigators are saying that so many corpses have been discovered at the home on Roxbury Street that a federal disaster team is being brought to the area. A portable morgue is on its way to help identify the remains, which is proving to be difficult due to the various stages of decomposition present.

"Investigators are saying there is a possible linkage between this house on Roxbury and the human remains found within to Grand Hallow Funeral and Mortuary Services, which, incidentally, is so large it was granted its own zip code in 1978. There is speculation that lawsuits will soon be underway, brought forth by family members who thought their loved ones had been interred at the facility only to learn their bodies were being ghoulishly displayed at this residence.

"We now go live to the scene at 4267 Roxbury, where local police and investigators are trying to make sense of this tragic discovery."

And there he was in all his glory: Sternhardt. Right there on camera in front of the farmhouse. For the interview, he was sure to put on his sheriff's hat. "I'm here with Sheriff Sternhardt of the Ruthsford Police Department. Can you tell us how you discovered that this residence was housing all these remains? And judging from the state of decay many of these bodies are in, why it took so long to discover?" asked the fresh-faced reporter.

"To be frank, I can now reveal there have been isolated cases at other abandoned residences throughout the region. My deputies and I have been tracking this type of activity for some time before making this discovery. But never have we found intact cadavers as we have here. This abandoned residence was so remote, it took some time to discover. It appears the suspect had been using it for quite some time as a type of base in addition to the isolated secondary cases I mentioned."

"You mentioned a suspect. So you have a suspect? In custody?"

"We do, in fact, have the person we believe to be responsible. However, I can report at this time that the suspect involved is now deceased."

"And what can you tell me about the owners of this house?"

"The last known resident was a widow who died several years ago. Our preliminary investigation has uncovered that ownership of the house shortly after her death was illegally transferred to the suspect through means of deed and title forgery."

"Can you tell us if it is true there is a link between what has happened here and the mortuary industry in Grand Hallow? And if so, how did you determine that link?"

"All I'm willing to release about that at this time is that the deceased suspect *was* an employee of Grand Hallow. We were made aware of the linkage to Grand Hallow through an insider tip."

"That's you!" Tina shouted from the visitor's chair beside the bed. *"You're* the insider! They should be interviewing you. Not damn Inspector Gadget. There he is all actin' like he discovered the house and solved the damn case when you handed it to him on a silver platter. What a poser!"

"No thanks," I said to the idea of local fame. "Let him have his day in the spotlight. I don't care. I just want it to be over. I'm glad it's finally over."

"Back to you, Deborah," said the reporter.

"So many questions yet to be answered in this case, Steve. We will surely bring you more on this disturbing story as it develops."

"So why didn't Sternhardt say that in addition to having a corpse fetish, the creep was also a bona fide murderer?" wondered Tina.

"He just must not be ready to release that information to the public," I speculated.

After my hospital stay, I was sent back to Grand Hallow to finish out the remainder of my sentence. Thankfully, it was finally nearing the end of summer. There was only one week left before my birthday. Yet the idea of even a brief return made me uneasy. And as it turned out, for good reason.

Walking the halls for the first time after the scandal, I could feel an anxious energy. Staff huddled in groups, whispering. They stared at me as I walked by, gawking as if I had forgotten to wear clothes or something. My discovery had obviously struck a nerve. I could've stayed quarantined in the green room for the week. Hid out there and avoided their stares. But I decided not to. Instead, I was determined to stay occupied that final week. Keep active so the days would go by as quickly as possible. So naturally, first thing on my day back, I reported to Ned's office for my daily assignments.

"Oh dear. Miss Lisa," he stood as I entered. He came to the other side of the desk and gave me the most awkward hug ever. "I am so sorry for what happened. Yet I am so pleased you are well enough to come back. How are you feeling?"

"I'm doing OK," I said as I reciprocated his weak hug by gently patting the back of his shoulder. "Do you have the list ready?" I asked, eager to get busy. "I can get started on the viewing room placards."

"Oh, that won't be necessary. This is most unfortunate. But I've just received word from your uncle that operations are being shut down." That explained the gawks I had been getting. I couldn't help but feel bad. Guilty even. I never meant to jeopardize the livelihoods of anyone working at Grand Hallow. Ned, reading the concern on my face, immediately added, "Oh, it will just be temporary, I'm sure. Just a precaution—what with all these news stories floating around. And as you know, we no longer have a head mortician."

"Yes, thank you. I'm aware of that, Ned," I shot back scathingly. "He only killed himself in front of me after I caught him mutilating and transporting stolen bodies."

"Oh, I'm sorry. I shouldn't have . . . I didn't mean . . . It's just that I meant we'll need time to figure out a contingency for morgue operations is all."

"It's OK," I said, instantly regretting snapping at him. "So where is my uncle, anyway?"

"Up in his office handling the police and press inquiries." I realized then the magnitude of the situation was greater than Ned had let on. I had brought unwanted publicity to the entire operation, possibly threatening its future. Ned, once again responding to my angst-ridden face, added, "Now you mustn't worry about that. It'll all work itself out. You did Grand Hallow a great favor—in the long run, at least. Now why don't you go for a nice walk? It's a beautiful day. Things will get sorted out around here. You'll see. We just need to regroup a bit. That's all it'll take."

Ned was right. I couldn't dwell on the short-term consequences. What was most important to me was that Norman had been stopped. And he was right about another thing. It *was* a beautiful late-summer day.

On his suggestion, I began climbing the hilly paths, hoping the exercise would tame the part of my mind that kept replaying Norman's death by self-stabbing. I had to let that go too. Yes, it would've been better if he had been taken alive. Then I might've had the chance to dig a bit deeper inside his twisted mind. But I had the feeling I never would've been able to understand exactly what made him do the things he did, what made him tick, anyhow.

I meandered through the paths on the east side of the property. The late morning sun bathed the cemetery in a yellow hue. The dew, still clinging to the blades of grass, sparkled like mini twinkling lights. As I made my way up a small slope, I saw a glimmer of red in the distance like a pulsating light. I lost sight of it when heading downhill. But there it was again, visible for a second time when I was on higher ground—a bright jewel in the distance. It wasn't a bouquet of flowers. And it didn't look like a balloon, which visitors sometimes left. It was something that trapped the light and reflected it back in cherry tones. It called my attention, a beacon of sparkling red in a sea of green grass and granite stones. Curious, I began making my way in its direction. Trying to keep the strange object in sight while heading across the vast east lawns was a bit like walking toward a desert mirage or paddling after a bottle floating in a sea. Yet after some time, I eventually got closer. And when the bright object came into clear view, I became a bit afraid.

I stood back a good ten feet from the jar of blood, assessing my surroundings. I was on a hill along a narrow loose-stone path among a cluster of tightly packed graves. The bad news was that I was alone—far, far away from the complex. But being out in the open, at least I couldn't be cornered. Given my experience at Grand Hallow, I couldn't blame myself for wondering if it was a trap. Were the twins nearby, ready to play one of their morbid little games?

As I contemplated whether or not I dared step forward, I heard a click, followed by strange hissing sounds coming from just below the ground. My body tensed up, preparing for battle. And then, sprinkler heads popped up from the ground all around me. I breathed a sigh of relief. The hissing noises of water being pressurized continued until steady streams began shooting from the nozzles. I sidestepped a forceful plume as it passed. But it didn't matter. Soon all would be wet, including me, as the sprinklers canvased the lawn.

The jar sat in front of a gravestone. Exactly in the center, as if it were an offering for the soul buried beneath. Of course, it was Norman who produced the jars of blood. But had he placed it there? If so, it would've had to have been before his fateful late-night delivery to a certain isolated farmhouse in Ruthsford.

I took a few steps closer and noticed the jar was only half full. That's when it hit me. I might've not been able to prove it. But I had a hunch it was the same mason jar Norman gifted to me at the house in Shilling. The same one the twins had stolen from me the next morning. The one they had opened and slurped nearly half the blood out of while out in the bog. But what was it doing in the cemetery? On that grave? Did they mean for me to find it? Were they returning it as some sort of peace offering?

The deep red blood collecting and reflecting the sun's rays was enticing. Giving in, I took the few remaining steps and knelt before the jar's warm glow. I wrapped my hands around it. The glass was wet and slippery from the sprinklers. But it was also warm and inviting, like a mug of hot cocoa. I clutched it to my chest. I was about to stand and leave with the gift that was rightfully mine. But instead, I found myself held to the ground as if by a powerful magnet. I had finally noticed the grave's inscription. And once I had seen it, I couldn't stand. I became dizzy with shock and confusion.

The grave had my mother's name on it: *Lynn Jacobs*. My mother's grave was in Florida. I never had the chance to visit it. But seeing a grave with her name etched into stone shook me to my core, as if she had just died again in that moment. It was permanent. Final. I realized in a cemetery the size of Grand Hallow, there were likely more than several Lynn Jacobses buried throughout the grounds. It was a common enough name. But why was the jar of blood placed on *this* grave? Who was the Lynn Jacobs buried before me? Who was this woman who shared my mother's name?

The year of birth was 1935. It was odd. Both women had been born around the same time. Shared the same name. And both had died too young—my mom at age thirty-eight in 1973 and the Lynn Jacobs in the grave at age forty-seven in 1982.

As if to release me from the powerful grip the grave site held over me, an even more powerful spray of cold water smacked me in the face. Clutching the jar, I jolted up and stumbled backward as the sprinkler rotated by.

I rushed back to the facility and snuck the jar into my private locker room. I set it on the sink, mystified, trying to decode the message the twins were sending. What was it about Lynn Jacobs, my mother—or the Lynn Jacobs in the grave—they wanted me to know? I looked at the blood on the other side of the glass. I wondered if perhaps it held any answers. But how could the blood from one of Norman's mutilated corpses tell me anything other than the thoughts of a poor, dying soul? Suddenly, what had seemed so alluring out in the cemetery repulsed me. I found myself wanting nothing to do with it. Even if the twins had intended to return the jar to me, it felt like a posthumous gift from Norman, the exposed phantom who took my father.

I unscrewed the lid and began dumping the blood into the sink. Yet instead of liquid, the stale blood had coagulated. It plopped into the sink in jellylike blobs. Slowly, the dark red blobs slid toward the drain. I shook the jar angrily, and the clotted blood splattered into the basin.

With each shake, I felt as if I were exorcising Norman, regurgitating him out of my existence.

And on my final shake, when I thought no more was left, a piece of hard material that had been trapped in the congealed blood at the bottom of the jar shook loose. It dropped into the basin with a clink. It was a stone attached to a long chain. Along with the clots that surrounded it, it slid down the drain. I grabbed the chain just in time before it too disappeared beneath the surface.

I held the necklace covered in sticky blood in my palm. As I began washing its stone under the faucet with my thumb, I realized it was a gem. A purple gem. An amethyst. I couldn't believe it! It had to be—my mother's. It was the necklace Richard had remembered. The one I had confirmed actually existed after seeing her wear it in the photograph tucked within Uncle Clayton's bookshelf.

Once the blood had been cleaned off, I let the chain drop to full length. I held it in front of me while looking in the mirror. It was like holding a mythical artifact, a relic from the past. Touching the gem was in a way like touching hands with my mother through space and time. The grooves in the gemstone that my fingers caressed were the same grooves felt by her in a different time. I was compelled to put the chain around my neck. I admired it in the mirror for a moment while at the same time realizing what I had to do before I left Grand Hallow for good: confront Uncle Clayton about my mother.

Chapter 23

1982

I knew it was presumptuous, but I did it anyway. Uninvited, I walked straight in and took a seat on the other side of his desk. As he spoke on the phone, his eyes immediately became transfixed by the purple stone. The blood drained from his face, as if he too had begun seeing ghosts. "I'm going to have to call you back. Yes. Yes, I will. You can come take a look for yourself whenever you would like. Of course. No problem, sir."

He hung up and began anxiously shuffling papers. "Lisa, you will have to excuse me. I am quite busy, as you can see. I've been taking calls all day from reporters and detectives. The sheriff wants our intake records going back several years. That will take a few days to prepare, at a minimum. At police request, I also need to instruct Ned to seal off the morgue at once. And a federal unit will be here soon in need of a facility tour."

But I wasn't interested in his plight about intake records or the trouble he faced with reporters and police. If he had kept a good eye on his own business, he would've known about the missing corpses. He would've found out for himself about the extracurricular activities of his head mortician. The troubles he faced were all avoidable—as was my father's death.

"Don't worry. When they get here, I won't tell them about the prisoners in the bog," I promised. "A deal's a deal," I said with a wink.

He gritted his teeth and clenched the arms of his chair, trying to remain composed as his world caved in around him. Lucky for him, I wasn't out to make his life any worse. I figured he had done a good enough job of that on his own. No, at that moment, all I wanted from him was some answers. Fiddling with the gemstone that dangled from my neck, I asked, "Recognize my necklace?"

"Where did you get that?" he asked with a tinge of dread in his voice.

"Found it. In the cemetery. In a jar of blood."

"*Norman*," he groaned.

"That'd be my answer too. But where would Norman have gotten my *mother's* necklace? And why did I find it on top of a grave marked with my *mother's* name?"

He slumped back in his chair. "I was wondering when this day would come," he sighed. "I was hoping I would never have to do this. I was hoping your father would've told you by now. But now that he's gone, well—"

"Hoping he would've told me *what?*"

"What I told you before, it was true. Your dad and I had planned to be partners in the great funeral industry," he said with a light chuckle. "Well, as you know, we ended up going our separate ways. But what I avoided telling you was *why*." He ran his hand over his face in trepidation.

"Go on," I probed him.

He abruptly stood and peered down the staircase a moment. He then shut the door to be sure our conversation was secure. "Your mother. She was very—persistent," he said as he returned to his chair, trying to choose his words carefully. "You see, the reason your father and I stopped talking. The reason he quit the business—was because your mother and I . . . we were in love. And she left your father to come live with me here, at Grand Hallow."

"That's not true!" I burst out. "You're a liar! Richard saw you take her away. But she came back. She got away from you! She came back. And then she died. She would've never wanted to live with you at Grand Hallow!"

"But there's more to the story," he protested. "And this is the most difficult part. The hardest part to imagine. No, poor dear, you were told a lie by your father. Yes, she *did* come back to you. But only to say good-bye. She did not die. Your mother, she started a family here with me. We had two children. Our twins, Elizabeth and Imogene. The lie was your father's idea. Out of his deep hatred for me and your mother over what we had done, he wanted you and your brother to believe she was dead rather than have you know the truth—that she had left your family to start a new one here with me." He shook his head in remorse. "I couldn't blame him. I credited his resolve and accepted the consequences. They were certainly deserved."

I wanted to refute him, to deny the horrible thing he was saying about my mother. But at the same time, my mind flashed through the inconsistencies surrounding her death. And his story, as heart-wrenchingly outlandish as it was, *did* answer some peculiar questions.

It explained why Richard, who would've been old enough at the time, didn't remember attending her funeral. It explained the weak reasoning we were given for why her body had been buried in Florida instead of Michigan. And why, as a family, we had never even attempted to visit her supposed grave there. It also finally gave a compelling enough reason why we had never visited Uncle Clayton or his family even though we had lived relatively close.

And ultimately, it explained the existence of the grave far back on the east lawn. The one marked with her name and date of birth—but with an extended date of death. "So it was my *mom*, not my aunt, who died in the Emerald River?" I asked, tears welling up in my eyes.

"Yes. In 1982."

My heart sank. At that moment I had never felt so betrayed. So unloved. "I thought about her every day," I said with a lump in my throat. "I tried so hard to feel her essence, her spirit. Sometimes I even thought I had. And now you're telling me this whole time—this whole time—she only lived an hour away? For the nine years after she left, from 1973 until she truly died in 1982, she never once came to see us? She never once tried to contact us?"

Even if my dad had wanted so badly for us to believe she was dead, she obviously was willing to go along with it. She didn't fight for her children. She just let us go. It was clear once she had decided to move on, she wanted nothing more to do with us. We were truly unwanted. Abandoned.

Uncle Clayton looked genuinely troubled on my behalf. "You're wrong to assume she had never visited you. She *had* visited you and your brother. On occasion. From afar. She was there when you had your tonsils out. She was there, watching, when you went on your first date. She did want to connect with you. She just didn't know how. Didn't know it was a possibility. I imagine somewhere inside of her, she carried some of the same guilt that I too carry. God knows I'm the last person you want to hear this from, but please do not take what she has done to you to heart. The decision to stay out of your life was not based on anything you or your brother did. Or who you are. Please know that. It's just that she was a very sick woman."

"*Sick?* I assume she didn't really have a brain aneurysm?"

"No. No aneurysm. What I mean by that is, once we were married, she started to—change."

"Change how?" I asked, grabbing a tissue from his desk and dabbing my eyes. That was one thing you could always count on around Grand Hallow, a never-ending supply of tissues.

"When I first met your mother, I just couldn't resist. Lynn was, dare I say, very attractive. And she made me feel as if I were the only man on earth. Clever. Important. Powerful. All the things I wanted to be for her.

But there was also something else. Something I couldn't put my finger on. While I knew what we were committing was utterly reprehensible, it was intoxicating. I was like a bug attracted to light. I couldn't help myself, even though the whole while I knew I was heading straight for the flames. Your mother, I now know, she was quite simply, a *temptress*."

I was in no mood to defend my mother. But his claim was preposterous. "Last I checked, it takes two to have an affair," I snapped.

"Yes. Yes. That's true," he said, shaking his head as if I had misinterpreted him. "I'm not saying I wasn't to blame. I was. It was wrong. But I couldn't stop feeling as if I had been ensnared. Deceived. Tricked into believing her love for me was genuine. You see, once she had come to Grand Hallow to live with me, she became—cold. Distant. Instantly, it turned into a loveless marriage. She was emotionless. That is, unless she wanted something from me or from someone else. And then, she'd become demanding. Spiteful. Ruthless. I just couldn't shake the notion that she had gotten what she wanted in Grand Hallow, this dreadful place of all things. And once she had her hands on that, she wanted nothing more to do with me. I was only in her way.

"She didn't like the way I was running the business. So she took it over. That's why I'm at a loss here now. She ran the operations for so long, I barely remember how to keep it all afloat. And she ran things *her way*. She cut corners.

"Those bodies in the marshes, the prisoners. That was her idea. She wanted to keep the grave sites designated for the prisoner contracts available for higher-paying customers instead. So the funds from the state were pocketed while their bodies were dumped. She'd say, 'No one is ever going to travel all the way out to Grand Hallow to visit the graves of forgotten prisoners.' She was actually right about that. But that didn't make it the right thing to do."

"That's awful."

"And then, I'm afraid to say, she got to Norman," he declared.

"What do you mean, *got* to him?"

"The same way she had gotten to me. She charmed him. And he was absolutely smitten. It was this relationship, I believe, that ultimately led to your father's demise. You see, Lynn took a great interest in the mortuary side of the business. She worked with Norman implementing several of her cost-cutting initiatives. Cutting corners on cadaver preparations. Stockpiling corpses before sending them to the crematorium. She only wanted to blast the furnaces about once every other week. After all, she'd say, 'A box of dust is a box of dust.' She figured it didn't matter whose ashes were buried in which plot or returned to which family. And Norman was all too happy to obey."

"But none of this explains why he killed my dad."

"Doesn't it? I think the key is right around your neck."

I held the amethyst in my palm. *"Her necklace?"*

"She was supposed to be buried in it. But he must've taken it. I'm afraid Norman became more than a touch obsessed with her. And when she died. Well, it only got worse. He was lost without her. But he knew of *you*."

"How?"

"Because of her. She did not keep you a secret. Not from him, anyway."

"So you think Norman killed my dad to get me here as a replacement for my mother?"

"It's hard to know what went on in Norman's head. But judging by his gift to you, it makes the most sense. Does it not?"

"Wait a minute! How do I know you're not lying?" I charged. "Norman and my mother aren't around to tell their side of the story. For all I know, *you* could've had Norman kill my dad. Or maybe you killed him yourself? And if you were so miserable with my mother, how do I know you didn't just kill her too?"

At first, he looked shocked by my accusations. But then he sighed. "I suppose there is no way for you to know. I suppose you'll just have to trust me."

His blunt reply didn't give me any more faith in him. But ultimately, he was right. I had no other evidence to refute him. I thought for a moment about the likelihood of the scenarios. And then, finally, I ripped off the necklace and jammed it tightly in my fist. In a matter of a day, it had turned from a symbol of an idyllic version of my mother to one of rejection—and then murder.

"Dear Lisa," he continued, seeing my despair, "I must apologize to you, about a great many things. But one thing most of all." His voice began to quiver. "You must understand, I had resented your mother for so long. I resented her for taking over the business and running it the way she did. I resented her for destroying the relationship between your father and me. Yes, as you rightfully pointed out, I realize I was just as much at fault for these failures. Yet try as I may, I could never temper my hatred toward her. Even after her death, and the death of our daughters, the pain of being isolated here, alone, without any family because of what we had done, was unbearable.

"Having you here gave me hope. Hope that I could salvage at least a part of the family I had lost. But you look so much like your mother when I had met her. And when you left the facility with the help of that mortuary apprentice, I took all the anger I had pent up for her out on you. It wasn't fair. I know. And I'm sorry."

"That's OK," I said automatically, even though I didn't really want to forgive him for locking me in a fucking room like a prisoner. Not to mention the only reason I was there in the first place was because his mortician killed my father, giving him custodial rights. Elizabeth was right. He *was* weak. Yet even though I didn't have much respect for his laissez-faire approach to dealing with his relationships as well as his business, we did have one thing in common: our lives had both been shattered by Lynn Jacobs.

Part V

Chapter 24

Sorry, We're Closed

My bones rattled after I was literally shaken out of a dead sleep. Even during my final week, Grand Hallow did not disappoint in its ability to dole out the rudest awakenings. "What is it!" I screeched as I shaded my eyes from the bare lightbulb.

"Lisa. It's time to go," Uncle Clayton stated firmly.

"What time is it?" I asked, still partly between worlds.

"Almost five."

"In the morning, right?"

"Yes. Now you must pack your things. You're going home now. Think of it as an early birthday present," he said with an uneasy smile.

God knew I appreciated the gesture. But I was confused by the urgency. "What's with the rush?"

"You've been through a lot here at Grand Hallow. I can't even begin to imagine everything you've had to process. You deserve to go home.

To be with your brother and your friends. And under the circumstances, it's probably best if you leave sooner rather than later."

Under the circumstances? The phrase made me nervous. "What's going on?"

"Just a precaution," he promised. "The scandal with Norman. The staff layoffs. Morale certainly has taken its toll on the remaining employees."

"And you're worried they'd actually take it out on *me*? Like physically?" I was shocked. "Wow. It is really that serious? Don't they realize it's not *my* fault for Grand Hallow's bad reputation? They should be blaming Norman. Not me!"

"Like I said. Just a precaution."

I didn't like the look in his eyes. He was nervous. His pupils darted about the room. Twitchy, like when I had first met him at the beginning of summer. Even though he had opened up to me, finally telling me the truth about my mother. And even though I had some level of sympathy for him over how horrible he had been treated by her, it wasn't as if we had bonded in some My Life Was Ruined by Lynn Jacobs Club. Perhaps we had developed some camaraderie after we both nearly busted out crying in his office. But it didn't make me any more trusting of him.

Sure, the stares and whispers made me embarrassed. But was there really something truly malevolent behind them? Did I actually have a target on my back? I was skeptical. And curious. What was really up? Why was I being shipped off so briskly? I had never imagined myself requesting an extended stay at Grand Hallow. Yet there I was, about to ask for one. "Can I at least stay until tonight? I'd like to say good-bye to David before I leave. To be honest, and no offense, something tells me I won't be coming back to Grand Hallow for a visit. So tonight will be my only chance to say good-bye."

"All nonessential staff have been laid off. Effective immediately. David will not return until we are able to reopen the morgue."

"I don't have a ride," I countered.

"Ned is ready to take you now." On command, Ned appeared from the hall. He greeted me in a stilted wave.

"Geez. I guess this is good-bye then," I conceded. They both watched as I gathered my things from the green room. They then followed me into the locker room as I packed my bathroom supplies. It made me feel uneasy, as if I were being fired and they wanted to make sure I didn't steal anything belonging to Grand Hallow on my way out. *As if I really wanted a souvenir.* I rolled my eyes at the thought.

The three of us walked together down the hall, Ned holding two of my bags. Before we turned the corner to head to the main lobby, I took one final look back. I wouldn't miss it. But I knew I was leaving as a different person. I had accomplished what I had set out to do: discover my dad's murderer. But along the way, I had learned of his deep heartache—and anger.

And I also had discovered my mother. New pieces that forever altered the version of her I held inside of me. She sat in my stomach like an undigested pit. Her revelation was a thing I didn't even know how to begin to process. It was something I imagined I'd have to cope with, struggle to come to terms with, for the rest of my life. I left Grand Hallow with deep scars. But one thing was for certain: I was a hell of a lot tougher than I had been before I arrived.

We stood at the top of the grand staircase a moment before Ned and I would begin the long trek through the hallways and corridors to the garage. Uncle Clayton looked as though he were about to lean in and give me a hug. Instead, in the final moment, he extended his hand. "Don't make too much of this, dear. I assure you, you will be safe. Believe me, I'm far less popular than you at the moment," he added with an uneasy laugh. "Yes, I suppose if I could leave now too, I would. But my fate, it belongs to Grand Hallow. Although I do believe," he sighed, "my days here are numbered."

"Don't worry, Uncle Clayton," I said as I politely accepted his hand. "They can't fire the boss." Behind his plastic smile, he looked genuinely worried. I almost felt sorry for leaving him behind.

As much as I should've been happy to leave, *and I was*, I was also apprehensive about going home. Richard had had the run of the place for nearly three months. And with my father gone, I wondered just what I was returning to. Would it be a place I'd still want to call *home*? As the town car pulled in the drive, I instantly realized my worst fear had come true. There were no cars. No customers. The station, on an early Monday during the morning rush, was closed. More than closed for the day, the cashier's window and the front door were boarded up. Boarded up! In less than three months under Richard's management, we were out of business.

I angrily slammed the car door and marched up the drive. Ned followed, carrying my bags. "Oh dear," he said as we passed the station. "This doesn't look good. No, not at all."

"It'll be fine," I said, masking my anger. I opened the side door to be sure I wasn't locked out. But then stood with my back to it, blocking Ned's view of what was sure to be an embarrassing state of affairs inside. "Would you like something to drink? Or a snack for the ride back?" I offered.

"No, no, Miss Lisa. That is quite all right. I am a bit concerned about your predicament here, however. Is there anything I can do to help? Perhaps I could alert your uncle of the situation? Perhaps he could provide some assistance?"

"No. Please don't say anything to him," I said, attempting to hide the fact that I felt utterly overwhelmed. "If I can handle Grand Hallow, I can handle this."

"Well, I will agree with you on that one," he said with a wink. "I will surely miss your help—and your company around the facility."

"Thanks, Ned. I'll miss you too. And hey, sorry for breaking into your office. And using your phone. And stealing your keys."

"You did what you had to do. And no one should blame you for that."

I gave him a light hug, which wasn't so awkward the second time. I had grown fond of Ned over the summer. I appreciated his kindness and respected his work ethic. If only I could've gotten Ned to manage the station. I would've swapped him for Richard any day.

Beer bottles. Pizza boxes. The sink overflowing with dirty dishes. Rancid smells coming from full bags of garbage that hadn't been taken to the curb. Food stuck to the countertops. Unfortunately, judging by what I had seen on the outside, the inside was about what I had expected.

And there he was. Lying in his underwear. Snoring on the couch with the TV on as if he had been tranquilized. I wanted to kick him awake. Scream at him. I needed to talk to him. He needed to hear about our mother and her connection to our father's killer. But I was so disgusted with him in that moment, I stomped to my room instead. I slammed the door behind me, hoping it'd jar him awake. But I was doubtful even that would've done the trick.

I collapsed onto the bed. But looking around, it didn't take me long to realize something wasn't right. My room was different. I looked to my dresser. My jewelry box. My new dual cassette stereo. My collection of tapes I had left behind. They were all gone. Red hot with anger, I rushed back to the living room and gave Richard an awakening that was equally as rude as the one I had experienced myself earlier that morning. "Where is my stereo!" I demanded in a bellow.

Groggily, he came to life. "Whoa. What're you doing here?"

"I'm back. Summer's over."

"But your birthday's not till this weekend, right?"

"Richard, where are the things you took out of my room? My stereo? My jewelry box?"

"Oh. I sold them," he said matter-of-factly. He sat up and shrugged. "Stop looking at me like that. I needed cash. What else was I supposed to do?"

"You were *supposed* to run the gas station!" I shouted. "That's where our cash was *supposed* to come from! Why is the store boarded up?"

"Because I busted the lock on the door. So I had to break the glass to get in. And then kids kept breaking in and stealing all the candy. Little shits. Lucky I didn't catch 'em."

"No. Why did you close down the store in the *first place*?"

"I don't know anything about running the store. You know that. That was your thing."

"All you had to do was follow my instructions on the notepads!"

"You and your damn notepads. Christ! Back off. I'm doing things. I'm running the garage."

"What do you know about running the garage?"

"I used to help Dad with the car repairs, remember? He taught me. I know some things."

"OK. So how many cars are in the garage right now? If I go and look, how many bays will be occupied?"

"Well. None right now. But I talked to Joe Larson earlier this week. And he's going to have me switch out his brake pads."

"*Joe Larson?* Isn't he one of your old roommates?"

"Yeah. What difference does that make?"

If I had to explain it to him, it was useless. I'd never get through. His mess became my mess. And it was obvious I'd have to clean it up myself. I dug deep into my pocket and produced the amethyst necklace. I tossed it on the coffee table. *That*, I did not have to explain to him. Yes, it was cruel to introduce it that way. But he had shut down the business Dad had worked most of his years to achieve. He had sold my things! I was frustrated. Hurt. And in the moment, I wanted to throw a bit of hurt his way.

"Holy shit. That's it. That's Mom's necklace! Where'd you get it?"

"At Grand Hallow," I began. I told him what I had discovered from Uncle Clayton. I told him the story of our mother, how she had abandoned and betrayed us to start a secret family with our uncle. I told him about our two cousins, or half sisters, who were conceived and died before we even knew of their existence. I told him how Norman had become obsessed with our mother and murdered our father.

The whole time he listened, he looked down, cradling his head between the palms of his hands. "Richard, are you all right?" I finally asked when I was finished. Without looking up, he rocked back and forth for a moment. Then, he grabbed the necklace off the table and threw it across the room. The purple stone bounced off the wall and spun across the hardwood floor. He abruptly stood and then charged through the house and out the door. I followed him halfway to the garage but ultimately decided to leave him be. On my way back, I heard the sounds of tools ricocheting off the cement walls.

Naturally, I called Tina to let her know I had come home early. "Since we didn't get to celebrate my birthday at the beginning of summer, I'm gonna throw the bash of the century for your party this weekend," she promised.

"Tina, I can't," I apologized. "If I don't get this place back in business by this weekend, I'm going to end up homeless."

"What'd I tell ya about letting that hellhole ruin your life? I'll tell ya what. Why don't I come over and help you clean up that disaster area Richard left you with. If we can get it up and running by Saturday, we're having that party. Deal?"

"Deal," I agreed. "You're a lifesaver. And God, when you get here, do I have something to tell you about what I found out from my uncle."

"Sounds juicy. You know me. When it comes to telling tales out of school, you don't have to ask twice. Me and my ears are on our way."

The store was a mess. The kids had swiped most of the candy. And the rest of the food and drinks were rotten and expired. While Tina threw out the bad food, cleaned, and swept, I was on the phone with vendors ordering all the essentials, including fresh candy, snacks, windshield wiper fluid, quarts of oil, picnic supplies, travel-size toothpaste, antacids, and, of course, cigarettes.

"Any Sprees left?" I asked. "I could use some Sprees right now."

"No. Brats cleaned you out," Tina reported. "Just order a shit-ton."

With Tina's help, by Friday we had the pumps operational again and had cleaned up enough to at least sell gas. But the convenience store, with its shattered door and lack of inventory, would have to stay boarded up until at least the first shipment arrived.

On Saturday, as Tina darted all over the house and backyard setting up for the party, I attended the cashier's window during our joke of a grand reopening. We didn't exactly have a marketing budget. So it wasn't as if anyone in town even knew we had reopened.

I wasn't sure just what Tina was up to. She told me she would take care of setting up the entire thing. I had no idea who or how many people she had invited. My worries over attempting to revive the station didn't exactly put me in the partying mood. And the truth was, I just liked hanging out with Tina. I didn't need a party. In fact, the idea of a party with lots of people typically would've filled me with anxiety. It'd mean I'd have to make small talk, which I found to be as awkward as it was boring. Yet strangely, before this party, I had no anxiety. Having lived through that summer, I felt impervious to such trivial fears.

I was more worried about what it meant that I was sitting in the cashier's window on a Saturday morning watching the occasional car roll by. I had wanted so badly to get back home. But would this be my life? Stuck in Ruthsford? Co-owner of a failing gas station? Barely getting by? Constantly chasing after Richard to help out? Cleaning up his messes? Would I ever be able to leave? Go to college?

The gas station. After his attempt at running Grand Hallow, it was my father's dream. It was never *my* dream. But did I owe it to him to continue anyway? Maybe it was time to let it go and be free—like happy-go-lucky Tina, whom I watched blissfully unloading a cooler and bags of chips from her Mustang. *What would happen if I left Ruthsford and started my life anew?* I may have felt a newfound boldness. But did I actually have it in me to take such a drastic step?

I wasn't sure if I was supposed to take what happened next as a sign of renewal—or a very bad omen. I leaned heavily toward *bad omen* by the time the hearse rounded the circle drive and parked near the cashier's window. I had been home from Grand Hallow for less than a week, and already I was seeing a hearse pull into the drive? Was it some sort of post-traumatic stress-induced mirage? No. It was just Ned. He stepped out carrying a pink cardboard box. Spotting me, he approached the window to show off the sheet cake with orange, blue, and green balloons made of frosting. "Well, happy birthday, Miss Lisa!"

While I was not exactly disappointed to see Ned, I found his visit rather—odd. Then I figured Tina had invited him on one of her whacky larks. "Hi, Ned. Thanks!"

"Why you certainly turned this place around in a jiffy."

"I had some help," I said, nodding to Tina as she made her way to the front yard.

Tina took one look at the hearse and then to Ned and exclaimed, "Well no shit! If it isn't Ned, our chauffeur to the dead! What're you doin' here?" She took one look at his cake. Without letting him answer, she tugged on his sleeve and led him behind the house.

I didn't dare leave Ned alone with Tina, so I quickly locked up the store. I figured it wouldn't make a difference anyhow, seeing as there were no customers in sight. As I headed to the backyard, Tina rushed back my way. "So you didn't invite him?" I asked.

"Hell no. I thought you did."

"What's he doing here then?" I wondered.

"I don't know. But I sat him down at the picnic table with his giant balloon cake," she said, unable to control her snickering. "Do ya think he's gonna put on face paint and a rubber nose? 'Cuz he'd make a great fat clown for the party," she howled.

"Tina!" I scolded. "It was kind of sweet of him to come. I just don't know what to do with him."

I rounded the back of the house to attend to Ned but was instantly blown away by Tina's work. She had transformed the backyard into a miniature tropical paradise, albeit a faux neon one. "Surprise!" she shouted.

Yellow, pink, and teal plastic neon blow-up palm trees sprouted unnaturally throughout the yard. Super excited, she took me down a path lined by tiki torches on either side. It led to a kiddie pool filled with cans of pop and beer. "I'll put the ice in when it gets later," she said, before rushing me down another path that led to another kiddie pool. This one was filled with floating rubber ducks. "So this is a game. You pull out a duck and see what's written on the bottom. And then you have to do what it says. Look," she said, pulling a duck out of the water, "this one says 'double shot.' But others are like 'do a cartwheel' or 'spell your name backwards.' It's going to be so much fun!" Somehow, she even had Richard bringing in loads of sand from the back of the yard in a wheelbarrow. "And that's going to be the dance floor," she said, pointing to where he dumped the sand.

"This is so awesome, Tina! I'm so totally impressed right now."

She clapped excitedly, beaming with pride. "Oh. I almost forgot," she said, spinning toward the patio. "My dad's letting me borrow his stereo and speakers, so we'll have some serious tunes. And this'll be the food and gift table," she said pointing to the picnic table where Ned sat.

There he was, in his full suit and tie in front of his balloon cake surrounded by a mountain of chip bags. The excitement drained from Tina's face as she looked upon him. She sauntered up to him and asked, "Ned, are you staying for the party tonight?" She was not trying very hard to mask the fact that he wasn't exactly included in her plans.

"Oh heavens no," he threw up his hands. "I just came to drop off this cake and wish Miss Lisa a happy birthday."

"Great!" she said as she grabbed a few paper plates and plopped them down next to the cake. "There's a knife next to you, Ned. Why don't you cut a couple pieces? That way, you and Lisa can try some of your cake before you leave."

"Oh, that would be wonderful."

Ned carefully cut the cake and served us both generous pieces. We ate awkwardly while Tina watched us, impatient, with one foot leaning on the bench. "This is really good, Ned. Marble cake is my favorite." He smiled back appreciatively, trying to keep his full mouth closed.

I could feel the heat of Tina's stare as we ate. I could tell by the squinting of her eyes and pursing of her lips that her head was percolating something her mouth had no chance at stopping. And then, it came. "Something else is goin' on here," she blurted. "You didn't come all the way here just to give Lisa that balloon cake, did you?"

"No, ma'am. I did not," Ned revealed, followed by a sigh of relief, glad he no longer had to hold in his secret.

"So why *did* you come here, Ned?" I asked.

"Well, Miss Lisa, to wish you a happy birthday, certainly. But also—" he paused. "You might want to call your brother over before you hear what I have to tell you."

Tina yelled for Richard as butterflies began to hatch in my stomach and flutter about. *Oh God. What now?* Richard grabbed a beer from the kiddie pool and joined us at the table. "Richard, you remember Ned from the funeral home?"

"Not really."

"I worked with him this summer. He drove all this way to give me this birthday cake."

"Really? Why?"

"Well, not just that. I guess he also has something he wants to tell the both of us."

"Yes. I'm so sorry to bother you at your home. But I wanted to tell you this in person," he said, pushing his cake aside with a look on his face as if he couldn't bear to take another bite.

"What is it, Ned?"

"There's no easy way to say this. It's your Uncle Clayton. He's dead."

Chapter 25

Happy Birthday

Tina was never going to forgive me. Another of her parties ruined by a death in my family. I felt super guilty. But I knew I had to leave with Ned right then and there. I felt an overwhelming need to return to Grand Hallow as soon as possible. While I wasn't all that close with Uncle Clayton, I needed to know exactly what happened. I couldn't wait for the funeral.

In many ways, Uncle Clayton was an enigma. His temperament ranged from calm and cool to cruel and overbearing—all the way to extremely vulnerable. His rage toward my mother, blaming her for his lonely entrapment at Grand Hallow, boiled just below the surface. But it was his nervous twitches I could never figure out. It was the looks over his shoulder, his jittery worriedness, that perplexed me most. Just what was he afraid of?

There was something in that final morning I had seen in him. Something in his eyes that haunted me. He had said his "days were numbered." Was it just a figure of speech? A legitimate worry about how long he could run such a large operation in the midst of a scandal? Or perhaps he was hiding something more ominous. Perhaps he was correctly prophesying what was to happen to him.

"How did he die?" I asked Ned. This time, I sat next to him in the front of the hearse on our way back to Grand Hallow.

"It was his heart. I hadn't seen him all day. And when I finally went up to his office to obtain his signature on an invoice for caskets coming due, there he was. Slumped over in his chair."

"When did it happen?"

"Sometime Wednesday. I'm not sure the exact time. I had seen him that morning. But I had been busy all day. You see, after the investigators left on Tuesday, Clayton gave the go-ahead to resume operations on a limited basis. We haven't yet been cleared for intakes. But by Wednesday, we had begun fulfilling the funerals for those still on our roster. There was rescheduling of dates. Switching around viewing rooms. Calling back selected staff to work on a partial schedule. Oh, it was all too much to handle at once. A hectic day—especially without your assistance, I might add. I'm afraid by the time I found him, I was too late to be of any help."

"Is his body still at the hospital?" I asked as we walked the hall to Ned's office.

"No. It's here. At Grand Hallow."

"I'd like to see it. Is it in the morgue?"

"By this time I do believe he has been prepped and delivered to his viewing room. He should be in the Cathedral Room, the same room where your father's funeral was held."

I didn't know what I expected to find by going to see his body. But I marched down the halls, determined and angry. *Determined* to confirm whether his heart truly had given out—or if something more insidious was at play. And *angry* at Grand Hallow for summoning me back. *What a tricky, tricky place.*

No one was in the grandiose room. The sun filtering through the stained glass windows lit the stark walls in a brilliant kaleidoscope of primary colors. The room was so bright and clean. As I made my way between the pews to the coffin, it felt as if I were disturbing some pristine place. Like I was walking on freshly fallen snow. The slight pressure of my shoes clicking on the hardwood floor echoed overhead.

For the owner of Grand Hallow, his coffin was modest. Even with the lid closed, I knew the model. I had them memorized. It was the Solid Poplar Wood Casket with White Velvet Interior, model number 8687, for $850. Good lord. I knew too much about caskets.

I grabbed hold of the lid and took a deep breath to relax myself before quickly lifting it open. But nothing could've prepared me for what happened next. Out from the coffin sailed a bouquet of helium-filled balloons. I took a bewildered step back as the orange, blue, and green balloons floated several feet into the air—until they were abruptly restrained by their strings. Calling upon my determination, I forced myself to look inside. The balloons were loosely tethered to Uncle Clayton. The strings wrapped around his neck and then disappeared, tucked into his collar.

Beneath his shirt, I could see the faint outline of some rectangular object. Grimacing, I reach my hand under his loose collar. What I fished out was a note card. The ends of the strings were tied through a hole punched in the corner. As I unraveled the strings, a message on the card was revealed. The handwritten note simply read, "Happy Birthday, Lisa." Stunned and horrified, I immediately let go of the card. The balloon bouquet sank for a moment. Then it rose, hovering ominously just over my head before floating down the center of the room, wavering between the lower and upper atmosphere of the towering ceiling.

Instead of letting the morbid birthday offering faze me, I was emboldened. I grasped the rim of the lower portion of the coffin and brazenly heaved it open. Without giving myself time to process what I was about to do, I ripped opened Uncle Clayton's suit jacket. With my hands shaking, I began furiously unbuttoning his white dress shirt. And as I peeled it away from his skin, I was aghast by my discovery.

Down the center of his body was a deep gash. He had been split open and then crudely sewn back together with thick, black stitching. No attempt had been made to be sure his skin actually came together naturally. Instead, there were grisly open gaps in some places along the incision and overlapping flaps of excess skin in others. But even more shocking, his body—from beneath his upper chest to the bottom of his torso, was concaved. He looked as if he had been deflated. It was a startling sight. There was nothing to him. All that rested above the lining of the coffin was about an inch of hollowed out flesh.

I had seen enough. I had seen it before. Uncle Clayton had been killed the same as my father. But how could it have happened again—when Norman was dead? Was he not my father's killer? Had I served up the wrong suspect to Sternhardt? And if so, where was I to turn? The only other suspect I had in mind was the mutilated man I stood before. But then, something clicked inside my head as I looked to the hovering balloon bouquet. I snatched it as I charged out of the Cathedral Room.

"Is this some sort of sick joke?" I asked as I flung the balloons into Ned's office.

Startled, he rose from his desk. "What do you have here?" he asked as he examined the balloons. "And whatever do you mean?"

"Real demented, Ned. Did you really think I wouldn't be able to piece together your little clues? Your balloon birthday cake—and the birthday balloons you put in his coffin? My God Ned, they're even the same colors. Orange! Blue! And green!" Ned slowly shut the office door to muffle my accusations. "Oh, and I know for a fact he did *not* have a heart attack. He was murdered. His organs were removed. Just like my father's. Explain that, Ned! Because I thought for sure I watched as the only organ-removing killer I knew stabbed himself to death!"

Ned grabbed the card that dangled in midair before him. "Oh my," he said as he read the birthday wish.

"Don't play games with me," I warned. "You better start spilling the truth, because without Norman around here hacking up bodies, *you* are now my main suspect. Jesus, Ned, I thought you were my friend."

"Miss Lisa, I can assure you I am your friend. Those balloons on your cake, they were just balloons. Nothing more. I didn't choose those colors. The cake was frosted just that way before I picked it out at the bakery."

My head spun. Was I really pinning a murder on Ned over cake frosting? Had my time at Grand Hallow successfully rotted my brain to the point I could no longer see things clearly? Had it been primed to jump to conclusions? To look for connections, however loose, so that, with some degree of resolve, I could holler something as drastic as *murder*? I didn't want to live like that. I didn't want that to be the lens I'd have of the world for the rest of my life.

But the trouble was, I just couldn't help myself. "Hold on," I said, trying to follow my own flight of ideas, "So you were his second in command. Without my uncle, you stand to run the entire operation yourself. Is that what you're after? Grand Hallow itself? Is that why you killed him?"

"As far as who inherits your uncle's funeral empire, I can assure you, it's not me," he replied with uncharacteristic sternness. "And let me tell you about your uncle. I was an out-of-work former funeral director of a small Georgia funeral home that had gone out of business. I answered an ad in the back of *Mortuary Management*, not thinking anything would come of it. He didn't know me. He didn't owe me a favor in the world. But your uncle, he was kind enough to give me a chance. He hired me on the spot, after a phone interview of all things. As soon as I hung up, I was headed to Michigan. He even paid my way. He explained he had created the position I have now because his wife had passed, and he was in need of the funerary expertise I could provide.

"Now, I didn't know until he had confided to me earlier this week, just before his death, that the wife he spoke of was also your mother. He told me with great anguish and regret. And I can't imagine how disturbing that must've been for you to discover.

"But *me* murder Clayton? No. I would've never harmed him. Despite the pain he had caused your family, I must say, he was a good man to me. And I owe him great gratitude."

He opened his desk drawer and produced a stack of papers. "Now, I wasn't going to tell you this until after the funeral so as not to overwhelm you. But I can see under the circumstances, it's probably best you see this now." He turned the papers to face me. "This is Clayton's trust. Basically, these papers state the succession plan for Grand Hallow. There are instructions for the new chain of command in the event of his death. Once you sign this, and we call our lawyers, have it notarized, etcetera, etcetera, *you,* Miss Lisa, will essentially be my new boss. Grand Hallow, it will be yours. So you see, no one stands to benefit from your uncle's death—except for you."

My legs were weak. I slipped into the chair and flipped through the papers until I saw my name. There it was. Feeling as if I had been blown over by gale force winds, I had to applaud Grand Hallow. What an encore. I sat speechless for a moment. But my tenacity was still intact. "Well, then," I said finally, "in that case, I'm going to need the name of the person who prepped him in the morgue as well as the names of all the visiting room attendants. I want to know of all staff who had access to his body."

"Yes, Miss Lisa. I can provide the names of the attendants for you. But as far as who exactly prepped his body, you will have to contact the morgue. I don't have that specific information. Yet before you attempt to pursue a second murderer, there's something you need to know. Your uncle, he was an organ donor. And I was told the condition of his body was due to the fact that they harvested much of his internal tissue and many of his organs. Now, I was surprised myself by how much they had removed, seeing as his body had been left expired for some time. But the medical field is vastly advancing their technologies every year, you know."

Touché.

For being mayor of his very own City of the Dead, the turnout was sadly low. "It's all *white shirts*," Tina whispered the next day at the funeral. I didn't know what she meant until I noticed the dozen or so attendees in their black pants and white Grand Hallow polo shirts. At least members of the Ruthsford community had thought enough of my dad to make the drive to attend his funeral. It was evident that outside of his life at Grand Hallow, Uncle Clayton truly had no one.

Afterward, I invited Tina and Richard up to Uncle Clayton's secret office overlooking the grounds. Richard headed to the windows while Tina spotted the mirror beside the door. From her purse, she produced a can of Aqua Net. She teased her hair while spraying generously to add some lost volume.

"So I have a decision to make. And I need input from the both of you," I announced.

"What's up?" asked Tina.

"As part of Uncle Clayton's trust, I've been offered his position as CEO of Grand Hallow. It covers all of the businesses under Grand Hallow Incorporated—like mortuary services, funerals, burial services, the fleet of cars. All of it."

"No way!" Tina gasped, turning her attention away from the mirror. "You inherited a company? And you're like the president? That's like winning the freakin' lotto! OK, a morbid freakin' lotto. But still!"

"Well, what am I supposed to do? I mean, I don't *have* to sign it. I'm only eighteen. I have no idea how to run a company. And if I stayed here, what about my senior year? I can't just drop out. And I sure as hell couldn't run a company while going to school."

"Screw school," advised Tina. "You're super smart. You could test out of senior year no prob. Get a GED or whatever. Who needs school when you could own a huge company? Think of all the money you'll be making!" She took that thought and then looked out over the cemetery. Suddenly, she crinkled her nose as if smelling something rancid. "But the bummer is—it *is* Grand Hallow. If you had to pick the lamest company to own, this would be it. Think about it. Stuck out here all day long with all the dead bodies. And the white shirts. And the creeps and crazies. Kinda a double-edged sword you got here."

Richard, clearly not as engaged as Tina, had yet to break his own gaze out the window. "What do you think, Richard?" I asked in an attempt to bring his thoughts back to the room.

He clenched his jaw a moment before spinning around. "Well, it clearly doesn't matter what I think since I get screwed out of everything. *I* am the oldest! How is this fair? It should be *me* running the company! *Not* you!" he spewed.

"Richard! I didn't ask for this, believe me. I still can't believe it myself," I said, avoiding the list of the dozen reasons why he as the head of any company would've been nothing short of a disaster.

"Yeah, I believe that," he said sarcastically. "Cozying up to Uncle Clayton all summer long. Getting him to hand over the keys to the kingdom. Like I said, real fair."

Steamed, I shot back, "Do you want to know what killed your chances of getting your name in that trust? I'll tell you! For starters, next time you're at a funeral, try not hitting up the brother of the guy in the casket for money."

"Oh, I'm sorry if I needed money and had to beg for it. You think I wanted to? No, you have no idea what it's like to have to ask for money. Remember, I didn't have all of Dad's gas station money to spend like you had these last few years. So the least you could do now, your highness, is give me a job. Or do I have to beg for that too?" he asked, antagonizing me. He got on his knees and clasped his hands together in a mock grovel. "Will you at least give me a job at your company, Miss Big CEO?"

"Get up, asshole," Tina demanded. "Now is the time to put on your man pants and stop embarrassing yourself with your little tantrums."

"Yeah, I'll give you a job," I snapped angrily. "Because I just decided to take the position," I said with defiance.

"Hell yeah!" Tina shouted, enthusiastically giving her seal of approval.

In that moment, Richard's chiding may have pushed me. But it wasn't the only reason I decided to take on the position. I had an idea. A plan. By taking on the role, I could stay and investigate as an insider. And not just any insider. One with an all-access pass to Grand Hallow. First, I'd need to determine if I bought Ned's organ donor explanation as the reason for Uncle Clayton's body being dissected. If I found his organs had, in fact, been stolen, it would mean I was probably wrong about Norman. It would mean someone else was likely responsible for my uncle's death—and my father's.

And then there was the matter of the balloon bouquet. My uncle's body was obviously intended to symbolize some sort of sick birthday gift to me. And that meant whoever wrapped those balloons around his neck knew I stood to benefit from his death. I needed to find out who else knew of his plans for Grand Hallow. And what they stood to gain from my taking his place.

Chapter 26

Bette Davis

Sadly, officially closing the Ruthsford Gas & Service Station was easier than I had thought it would be. Richard had virtually shut it down himself over the course of the summer. All that was left was to disable the pumps and cancel the tanker deliveries and vendor orders I had placed. Despite having to continue to pay on the mortgage, we would keep the house. We would need a place to return when our business with Grand Hallow was over.

We crammed our belongings into Richard's car. And as we pulled away from the station and the small green house behind it, I vowed it would only be temporary. That I'd leave Grand Hallow for good as soon as all my questions had been answered.

I didn't want to share a space with Richard. He and I needed to distance ourselves from each other. Not only because it made sense if I was to be his boss. But also because it made sense for my own sanity. Cleaning up after him and getting into constant arguments were things

I needed to avoid if I was to focus on my investigation. So I moved into Clayton's stone house. And I made Richard move into the green room.

Honestly, it felt good showing it to him. "Welcome to my world," I told him as I opened the door. He didn't dare protest, yet I could tell what he thought of it by the sour look upon his face. I reveled in the moment, perhaps a bit too much. For right or wrong, I did feel some sense of payback for his selling me out to Grand Hallow in the first place. And as if I didn't get enough of a kick out of showing him that his lodging was virtually a tiny green cell, I sure as heck did when I showed him the morgue down the hall.

My only questions were these: How long would Richard put up with an actual job? When would the fact that there was an empty house he could crash at for free back in Ruthsford outweigh the joys of an actual paycheck?

My first order of business in the stone house was to heave a dresser in front of the twins' bedroom door. Thinking about the ghostly chamber/time capsule on the other side of that door gave me the creeps. I wanted to forget it was there. I could've cleared out all their belongings, ripped out the pink carpeting and painted the room a bright, cleansing white. But I wasn't sure it was worth the effort. I didn't know how long I'd actually be living in the house amid the grove of maples with the crematorium on the other side.

On my first official day as CEO, I stood in front of the bathroom mirror nervously playing with my sleeves. *Is this how business clothes are supposed to fit?* Nothing felt right. The sleeves were too short. The shoes too narrow. In the dark suit with my hair pulled back in a ponytail, I looked like a different person. Yet instead of empowering me, the suit felt like a costume. A farce. I looked ridiculous. *Who am I trying to kid? No one who sees me is going to believe for a second I know anything about how to run an organization.* I felt sick to my stomach. I wanted to stay hidden in the house.

In the middle of my panic, I noticed that in the bottom of my clear plastic toiletries bag shimmered my mother's amethyst necklace. I had retrieved it from the living room floor after Richard had pitched it against the wall.

Obviously, I no longer looked to my mother as if she were some sort of angelic being. I didn't hate her, I supposed. As hard as I tried, I found it was difficult to sustain much hatred for someone I had never met. Yet that sting of rejection, the feelings of loss and abandonment, I imagined, would never go away.

Still, there was something about that stone that soothed me. Maybe it was the part of my mind that clung to the idea of that mystical version of her. The idea that there was someone out there in the ether who sent me waves of unconditional love through space and time. Maybe in my subconscious, that purple gem represented the fantasy version of the mother I had wanted. Not the one who had left. Whatever it was, when I slipped it in my pocket, I felt my tension begin to ease—just a little bit.

My first stop was the green room to give Richard his assignment. I hadn't revealed to him what his job would be. I wanted to think about it. I needed to use him strategically to infiltrate the staff and bring back useful information. As I knocked on the door, I fully expected having to rouse him. But much to my surprise, he was showered and shaved and ready to go. "Ready to report for duty, sir," he said with less sarcasm than his words implied.

"Richard, I want you to work on the grounds keeping crew. Just look for the warehouse on the north side of the complex with all the landscaping equipment. Report to Henry by nine o'clock. Tell him I sent you for training."

"*Grounds keeping?* You mean like *maintenance?*" Richard scoffed. "Are you serious?"

"No. Not like maintenance. You won't be scrubbing toilets. Listen, Richard, you said you wanted a job. We talked about this—"

"But *grounds keeping?*"

"Honestly, Richard, what other skills do you have?"

"You could have me working in the garage. C'mon, you know I'm good with cars. You know that's a better fit for me. I could be a mechanic.

Or even one of those hearse drivers. Just don't put me on no chain gang, sis."

"Yes. OK. I get that you want to work with cars. I'm sorry. But you need to remember why we're here." I softly shut the door and whispered, "We're trying to figure out what really happened to Uncle Clayton. And I need your help. Think of it as going on a secret mission."

"What sort of secret mission?" he asked, somewhat intrigued.

I rustled through my bag and produced a freshly drawn map of the grounds I had prepared the night before. "I want you to find out what they are working on here." I pointed to the desolate woods at the edge of the map. "Listen to anything they say about those woods. See if you can get assigned on a crew working out there. I have a suspicion that something fishy is going on in that pine forest."

"Like what?"

"I'm not sure just yet. Ned told me there's nothing but an old root cellar out there. But I'm not that trusting of Ned these days."

"So what if no one says anything about those woods? What if I can't get on a crew going out there?"

"That's where the *mission* part comes in. Break away and go investigate for yourself if you have to. Maybe you can find something I didn't. If it really is some type of cellar, see if you can find your way inside. See what's in there. Just report back to me as soon as you find out anything."

"Aye, aye captain," he said as he reopened the door.

"And, Richard," I stopped him before leaving the room. "Whatever you do, don't go here." I circled the marshes next to the pine forest with my finger. "It's a bog. And you *will* get stuck in it if you're not careful."

He nodded and shouted "later" as he took off down the hall.

"How do I look?" I asked Ned as I smiled uneasily at his office door.

"Very professional, Miss Lisa. It looks as if you are off to a great start."

"I don't know. I'm just so nervous," I confessed. "I have no clue how I'm supposed to do this."

"Oh no, no, no. You mustn't be nervous. Yes, you are quite young for such a position. But you're eighteen now. So it's perfectly legal. Besides, what we older folks don't let on is that we haven't the faintest idea what we're doing either. We just make things up as we go along." He chuckled and then winked. "Besides, if you need anything at all, you know right where to find me. And I'll be happy to help."

"Thanks so much, Ned. I'll be in Uncle Clayton's office if you need me."

"It's *your* office now, dear."

I climbed the narrow steps and sat in his chair. It took me a moment to figure out how to lower its height so I didn't feel as if I were a toddler in a highchair. I had just sat down. And already, being in that office, towering above the grounds so far away from the rest of the staff, I instantly felt isolated. And lonely. I was used to working with Ned—or the guests, running them back and forth between rooms, showing them caskets.

The oversize desk enveloped me. I couldn't even reach my arms halfway across. I stood and stretched to reach the stack of papers piled on the other side. I rifled through the invoices, revenue statements, and what looked to be some sort of monthly reports from the individual departments. I was used to handling the invoices at the gas station. And knew how to read a revenue statement. *Maybe I can actually do this.* In one of the drawers, I found a list of department heads along with their phone extensions.

It was then I had the idea to do something bold. Something drastic. Why not? After all, at that moment, it was my company. And as a reasonable head of any company enduring a scandal, I would need to make the changes necessary to ensure it wouldn't happen again. And how would I go about that? By changing our practices. The terrible things my mother instituted, and Uncle Clayton continued to perpetuate, needed to be undone. And who better to undo them than her own daughter?

I picked up the phone and dialed Henry in grounds keeping. "Henry here."

"Henry, this is Lisa Jacobs."

"Yes, Miss Jacobs? How can I help you?" he asked astutely. "Your brother, he has found his way here just fine. And I will personally train him."

"Good. Good. Please keep me updated on how he is working out. But, Henry, I have more important business to discuss with you at the moment."

"Certainly, ma'am. What is it?"

"It's about the bodies in the marshes. I need them cleaned out." There was silence for about thirty seconds. I wasn't sure what that meant, so I followed up with what I figured a no-nonsense boss would say: "Do you understand?"

"Yes, ma'am. I do," he said with a stumbling hesitation, which led me to believe he was surprised I even knew of the prisoner-dumping policy. "But I'll need some dragging hooks. And chains."

"Fine. Get whatever you need. I'll add it into your department's budget."

"What are we supposed to do with them after we drag them out?"

"Give them a proper grave site," I demanded.

"With all due respect, ma'am, I am the head of grounds keeping. And we don't get involved in burial affairs. The department that could help you would be grave digging. And besides that, how are we to know who they are? A lot of those corpses are in pretty bad shape. How would we ID them?"

"Can you fish them out or not?"

"Sure. Well, some of them anyway. Depending on how many chunks they're in."

"OK, so just fish out the fresh ones and throw the rotten ones back. I'll alert the morgue you'll be dropping bodies off for processing. That shouldn't be too much work for them since we're not accepting intakes yet. Maybe they can ID them based on their records? If they can, grave digging will take over from there. Does that sound OK?"

"Works for me."

Feeling pleased with myself, next I dialed up the crematorium. "Yes, this is Lisa Jacobs. From now on, fire up the furnaces every day if you have to. And no more mixing and matching ashes. Each corpse's remains must be burned separately. And then the ashes must be carefully labeled for accurate burial or placement in urns. Got it?"

"Yes," said Nathan, head of the crematorium, "But I may need more staff."

"You got it."

"Then the only problem is the morgue. They deliver corpses to us in batches, all at once. It's too difficult to keep track."

"Not anymore they don't," I promised. "We are no longer a corrupt institution. Spread the word. Tell it to your staff and everyone else. And if someone doesn't like it, tell them they'll need to find a job somewhere else because otherwise they'll be fired."

I leaned back in my chair feeling damn good. My first morning as CEO, and I had already made progress. I even giggled as a strange new feeling bubbled to the surface, a feeling I hadn't had the luxury of fully experiencing before: power. When I spoke, they really listened. And then, even more satisfying, they responded. I stood in front of the window and looked over the vast cemetery grounds. *I could really change this place for the better. I could make it my own.* I smiled as I watched a gray cat weave between the headstones, its tail happily darting into the air.

But the cat soon dashed out of view, scared off by none other than Ned. He had started down one of the walking paths. I watched as he made his way through the gravestones. The farther he got, the more he began to stumble, wobbling forward as if his shoes had already become uncomfortable. I hadn't known Ned to take midmorning walks before, much less walks in general. He was the type to work his day straight through. He'd even eat his lunch right at his desk.

Investigating was the sole reason I was back at Grand Hallow. And in my mind, Ned going for a midmorning walk qualified as suspicious — and worthy of investigation. I was compelled to see what he was up to. So as he dipped into the first gulley, I raced down the steps.

Briskly, I turned the corner to head to the main lobby — only to crash into someone coming around the corner from the opposite direction. Our bodies smacked together, and we gave each other a nice head-butt. I stepped back holding my head. "I'm so sorry. Are you OK?"

"Woah," said David, also holding his head. "Lucky I wasn't carrying a hot coffee." Dropping his hand from his face, he realized who I was. "Well, if it isn't Bette Davis."

"Very funny."

"Well, was I right? Or was I right? All I'm saying is, I just want it duly noted that I called it. I said you'd be the big boss running Grand Hallow. And here you are. Wow," he said, looking me up and down. "Wearing that pantsuit and with your hair pulled back like that, you look just like a younger version of her." I smoothed my hair self-consciously and tightened my ponytail, wondering if he'd have said that had he known I was in fact the daughter of the *real* "Bette Davis."

"Well *I* want it duly noted that I was right to be suspicious of your boss. Not only was he stealing corpses out of the morgue, I'm pretty sure he also murdered my father."

"Oh *that* has been duly noted," he assured me. "In fact, it's turned this place inside out. Have you taken a look around here lately? There were always more dead people than live ones. But this is ridiculous."

"We'll get back up and running soon," I promised. "I'm making some big changes."

"Yeah, I've heard you've got quite the iron fist."

"What's that supposed to mean?"

"Well I just got off the phone and was alerted we're soon to get a fresh shipment of rotten bodies to ID."

"Wow. That was fast."

"You speak. We jump."

"So my uncle put *you* in charge of the morgue after what happened with Norman—*happened*?"

"Would that be so awful?" he asked sarcastically. "Without Norman, there was chaos. Still is. But shortly after what happened with Norman—*happened*, your uncle promoted me to mortuary technician and switched me to day shifts. But no. I'm not in charge. No one is, really. All of us technicians and apprentices are in charge of ourselves now, I guess you could say. But I showed initiative, boss, and developed a scheduling system to keep us on track."

"Very impressive," I smirked. "David, I have to say I'm happy to see you're still here. I'm so glad you didn't get fired after helping me sneak out. I would've never forgiven myself."

"Well, even if you *had* gotten me fired, with your position now, you could've just hired me right back."

"Yeah, I guess I could've. So what exactly happened that night anyway?"

"We tried, and we got caught. Simple as that," he said without elaborating. "But it all worked out. Look. I got a promotion. And now, you're queen bee."

I dismissed his flippant flattery with an eye roll. "Hey, I have to ask. Do you know who prepped my uncle by any chance?"

"No. Like I said, without anyone overseeing the morgue, things are a bit—dysfunctional. It'd be hard to tell. But I can try to check into it if you want."

"When you get a chance," I said. "No hurry."

"Speaking of hurries. Where were you running off to when you about took me out?"

I pictured Ned scampering through the cemetery. *Damn. He's gotten away by now for sure.* "Just to the vending machine for some hot coffee," I replied with a wry smile. He then watched, perplexed, as instead of heading to the breakroom, I headed back where I came from. Myself scampering, back up to my office in the sky.

Chapter 27

Whispers in Skeleton City

"Did you check out the pine forest yet?" I asked Richard.

"No. Thanks to you, I've been pulling dead bodies out of a marsh all day. Damn if they're not ugly, but they smell fuckin' worse."

"But that's perfect."

"*Perfect?* Perfect for you maybe. I'm out there sweatin' my balls off in thousand-degree heat with stench like roadkill so strong I can barely breathe while you're sittin' up in an air-conditioned office behind a desk."

"It's perfect because the marsh is right next to the forest. Just sneak away. Or check it out on your lunch break."

"I'll try," he groaned reluctantly before shutting me out of his room.

I ran to the morgue and came back with a jar of VapoRub. "Here," I said, barging back in and handing it to him. "Dab a bit of this under your nose. For the smell." I shrugged before heading to my office.

I worked the morning scheduling meetings to take place over the following two weeks. The meetings would be with each of the department heads as well as the mortuary staff, who had no department head. On my agenda was outlining the new cremation policy as well as the immediate halt of prisoner dumping. I wanted to do it in person. It was crucial there were no misunderstandings.

And from them, I needed to understand how all the pieces of Grand Hallow worked together. For instance, who exactly was responsible for dumping the bodies in the marsh? Was it the grave digging department? The mortuary staff? Or another department? I needed to chart it all out. Figure out how everything flowed from intake to interment. Then I'd review the entire process and start making improvements.

But before I could get to work on my overhaul of Grand Hallow, there was a more pressing issue. Without Norman, the morgue structure would continue to be fractured. I needed to hire or appoint a new head mortician before we could even attempt to become fully operational again. So much to figure out! So much to do!

When I finished scheduling all the meetings, I took a stretch in front of the windows. And damn if I didn't catch Ned scurrying through the tombstones again! His new midmorning walking routine intrigued me enough to once again go barreling down the steps. Yet this time, I turned the corner with much more caution—before racing down the grand staircase and out the mammoth front doors.

By the time I rounded the main building, he was quite far down the path. But I could see his bald head bobbing in the distance. I followed behind, careful not to be seen. I was confident in my stealth tracking abilities, assuming Ned did not possess the supernatural sensory talents of the twins.

He had made it all the way out to Skeleton City. Things got a bit more difficult when he disappeared inside. I entered the maze of crypts, but couldn't see which way he went. I pursued him aimlessly, easily becoming lost among the aboveground corpse ovens. It wasn't until a slight breeze picked up that I was given some information: light whispers traveling over the roofs of the tombs. I warily followed them up the ridge. The voices came from a cluster of crypts below. At first, I couldn't make them out. But soon, without hearing exactly what he was saying, I picked up Ned's distinct drawl.

I stepped on the front stoop of one of the shorter crypts and shimmied my way onto its roof. The stone had already begun collecting the morning sun and was blazing hot as I lay on my stomach, attempting to slyly catch a view of just what was going on below. I could only see the top of Ned's head reflecting the sun. I couldn't see who was quietly whispering back to him. But as I inched myself closer to the edge, the picture became all too clear. Ned patted his sweltering head with a handkerchief as he listened intently—to two red-headed girls. As soon as I heard their signature giggles, I quickly scooted back and dropped from the roof as delicately as I could.

I couldn't believe it! Ned was sneaking away from work to talk to the ghost twins? Why were they appearing to Ned? Sure, random staffers may have caught glimpses of them playing in the cemetery. But I thought *I* was the only one who actually had interactions with them. Hell, they hadn't even made themselves known to their own father. So what were the three of them up to? I scurried away from Skeleton City. And to play it safe, I took a completely different route back to the campus.

There, I waited in my perch high above Grand Hallow, looking out over the panoramic view. About twenty minutes later, I watched as Ned emerged from the graves. I gave him time to get back to his office before I dialed his extension. "Ned, can I see you in my office please?" If I had uttered those words under any other circumstance, I would've felt super cool—and super important. But determining why Ned was having secret meetings with my dead, adolescent, wayward cousins was *not* a cool situation.

He appeared at the top of the stairs out of breath and lightly patting his chest. "Heavens me. I'm sure glad I'm not the one who has to climb those stairs every day. I just don't think I could do it," he said, panting as he made his way to the chair on the other side of the desk.

"I don't know. Seems to me you've been getting a lot of extra exercise lately." He tossed a look of confusion my way before I laid into him with, "Look, Ned, I'm going to ask you something. And please. I'm begging you. Don't lie to me"

"No, Miss Lisa," he said, still catching his breath, "I wouldn't think of lying to you," he promised, while beginning to fidget nervously. First with his tie. Then with his glasses.

"What have you been doing out in Skeleton City?"

"Skeleton City?"

I had forgotten that the nickname I had given to the vast cluster of crypts belonged only to me. "Out in the middle of the crypts," I clarified, "with Elizabeth and Imogene?"

The blood instantly drained from his face. His jaw went limp. He swallowed dryly. "Oh, Miss Lisa," he wailed, on the verge of breaking into tears, "I can't take it anymore. I'm so afraid—for you and me both."

"What are you afraid of, Ned?"

He turned away from me as if he couldn't bear to speak of it. "I'll tell you," he promised. "You're in charge of Grand Hallow now. So you should know everything. I don't care what happens to me anymore. I just can't keep doing this."

"Doing what? Ned! You need to calm down and tell me what's going on."

"I don't even know where to start."

"Start at the beginning. And tell me everything. When did you first meet the twins?"

"I first saw them a month or two after I came to Grand Hallow," he began. "We all did, from time to time. At first, they seemed harmless. Well, pretty harmless anyways. I'd say they seemed a bit spoiled. Mischievous. They would play pranks. Lead staff deep into the cemetery and get them lost. Games such as that. But other than those transgressions, nothing to be afraid of. I asked Clayton about them. And he acknowledged they were his daughters. But he warned me to never speak of them to anyone else. He told me for their own safety, they must be kept hidden. A secret. And he also said if they ever approached me to be sure to do exactly what they asked. Otherwise, there would be consequences. Well, I thought the whole affair was quite strange. But I didn't give it much thought as I didn't see them around much at all."

"Hold on a sec! You're telling me Uncle Clayton *knew* about them? When I told him I had seen them, he made me feel like I was going crazy. He told me they were dead."

"I don't know *what* they are, to tell you the truth. But I can assure you he knew of them. In fact, he spoke with them often. For being so young, they would give him things to do. Tasks, believe it or not. Instructions on how to run certain aspects of the organization. He seemed to be able to cope with this arrangement with very little discontent. That is, until we got word your father had been killed. It was then, at the twins' insistence, that you were to be brought here to Grand Hallow."

"You're saying it *wasn't* Uncle Clayton who wanted me here for the summer? Not Norman? It was the *twins?*"

Ned nodded. "That's right, Miss Lisa."

"But why?"

"At the time, I didn't have the answer to that. I was kept in the dark. All I knew was that it was very important that you come to Grand Hallow. But your uncle, he refused. It was the first time he dared protest the twins. But soon after, he came around to the idea."

"What changed his mind?"

"Oh, it was just awful," he winced. "The day before I was sent to pick you up, I was unlocking the showroom. Well before I knew it, from inside one of the coffins near the back, I heard something dreadful. Scratching and moaning noises. Oh, I nearly fainted, I'll tell you what. But when I finally worked up the nerve to see what the ruckus was and opened that coffin, there was your uncle trapped inside. Somehow, and I don't know how, those girls managed to get him inside. Good heavens, he was shut in that coffin overnight. Why, after that, he was never the same. And we both feared for our lives when it came to those girls."

So that finally explained why he was nervous and jittery, looking over his shoulder, when I had first arrived. He had just survived a night in a coffin and was forced against his will to summon me to Grand Hallow.

"And once you were here," he continued, "they told him to keep you on the grounds. Otherwise, he would be further punished. And they threatened that the second time, the punishment would be even more severe."

"That's why he was so angry I left in the hearse," I filled in. "That's why he locked me in my room."

Ned nodded. "Miss Lisa, he *wanted* to let you go. He really did. He didn't want to keep you at Grand Hallow. He never wanted you to have to come here in the first place. But you see, he didn't have a choice."

"But he *did* let me go. The week of my birthday. He let me leave."

"That's when it all came to a head, I'm afraid. He had called me into work early that morning. I had barely gotten to my office when he came in all riled up and out of sorts. Well, the twins must've told him something just awful that he didn't dare repeat. Oh dear, did he pace and fret about what to do. Finally, he decided we must get you out of Grand Hallow as soon as possible. Otherwise, you would be in terrible danger."

That was Monday. And by Wednesday, he was dead. Had the twins followed through with their threat? Was death his punishment for setting me free? Had he sacrificed himself so that I could escape—and survive? "He knew it," I declared. "He said he knew his days were numbered. The look in his eyes that morning we left. He knew it was coming. The question is, how did my uncle *really* die, Ned?"

"I haven't any idea," he reported solemnly, covering his mouth at the horror of it all.

"You didn't really find his body. Did you, Ned? You never even called an ambulance I take it?"

He nodded his head shamefully. "I didn't see his body until after it had been, shall I say, *fully aspirated.*"

"So he never went to the hospital. Which means his body never went to the coroner. No one even knows he's dead—or was murdered, for that matter."

"Unfortunately, that's right, Miss Lisa. They warned me I was not to report his death. I was instructed to just bury him in Grand Hallow as soon as I could. I was to hold a small funeral and keep it quiet. No one, except Grand Hallow employees, was to be alerted of his death."

"So that means no death certificate. How am I even the CEO without him officially declared dead?"

"Oh, but I saw a death certificate. In his file."

"How is that possible? It has to be a forgery."

"Yes," he agreed. "Created to circumvent the hospital and the coroner. All I know is, the paperwork, his trust, were handled by a Grand Hallow lawyer."

"So it's like he's just been—erased."

"Besides you and your brother, he has no other living relatives in the state. So it was quite easy for his death to slip between the cracks. Go unnoticed."

"You told me he died of a heart attack! You told me he was an organ donor. And that's why his insides looked like they had been sucked out through a straw! You could've told me the truth a lot sooner, Ned!"

"No, Miss Lisa, I couldn't. You see, after your uncle died . . . that's when the twins began approaching *me*. Well, I knew they had put poor Clayton in a coffin. And I knew he was terrified something awful just before his death. So what was I to do? I did only what I could. I did what they asked of me. Whoever questioned Clayton's death, I told them what I was supposed to say: that he had died of heart troubles. Lord knows it was wrong. But I just didn't know what else to do."

"So what now?" I asked. "The funeral is over. His body is buried. What could they possibly be calling you out to the crypts to discuss?" He shook his head and then turned away from me once more as if it was too wrenching to discuss. "Ned. You need to tell me," I demanded.

"They told me—they wanted you gone."

"*Gone?* That doesn't make any sense after they went through all the trouble of getting me here. Keeping me here. And now, with the death of Uncle Clayton, bringing me back to Grand Hallow once again."

"Oh no," his voice quivered. "They don't want you gone from Grand Hallow. They want you *gone*. Terminated. Deceased. And the worst part is—they expect *me* to do it."

I stood from my chair and braced myself as if the roof had just been torn off by a passing tornado and I needed to hang on for dear life. "They want *you* to *kill me*?" I asked, flabbergasted.

"Yes, Miss Lisa."

"And how do they expect you to do that?"

He nervously cleared his throat. "That's what they've been calling me out to the crypts to discuss. They tell me the most dreadful things. They—they've been giving me *ideas*," he revealed.

"*Ideas?* Like what?" I asked, horrified.

He pointed to the narrow stairs behind us. "One idea is to push you down those very stairs and make it look like an accident. Another is to hold you down. Sit on your chest and pour formaldehyde down your throat. Burn you alive in the crematorium. Lock you in one of the cooler drawers. Suffocate you in a body bag. Please, I beg of you. Don't make me repeat any more of their wicked ideas. They have a million of them. They told me all I have to do is pick just one. Carry it out. And when it's over, I'm to deliver your body to David."

"*David!* Why would the twins tell you to bring me to *David*— unless," my heart sank, "he's involved with them too?" I didn't want to believe it.

"I don't know how many others there are. It's hard to say for sure." He debated while anxiously tugging at his cuffs. "I only know my role, the instructions they give to me. Perhaps they have made themselves known to David. Perhaps they haven't. He *does* work in the morgue, don't forget. My bringing your body to him makes sense whether he's involved with the twins or not."

"Ned!" I said, flashing him a look of scorn. "You're not bringing my body *anywhere*."

"Oh. No, no. Of course not. Hypothetically speaking. Hypothetically," he repeated, embarrassed.

"So what did you say? When they were giving you all those ideas on how to murder me. What did you tell them you would do?"

"Dear God, forgive me. I told them—I would try. But I wasn't going to!" he quickly interjected. "You have to believe me," he said, throwing his hands in the air. "I've just been stalling. Not knowing what in the world to do. But they told me if I don't follow through with it soon, the same thing that happened to Clayton—will happen to me!"

I felt as if I were locked in a nightmare, about to go mad. "Why are they doing this!" I screamed.

"I was too afraid to ask that question," said Ned, answering my rhetorical outburst.

I began to pace as my mind raced. "Are they actually capable of all this?" I wondered aloud. "Using threats to control people? Orchestrating murders? As devious as they are, they're still just girls. Right?"

"Like I said, Miss Lisa, I don't know *what* they are."

"So then, Ned, let's find out."

Part VI
Chapter 28
Bumps in the Night

We waited until dark. With our flashlights firmly gripped, we scuttled our way across the campus to the storage barn, where the grave digging department kept its equipment. I scanned my beam over the multitude of tools hanging from hooks along the walls. I ended up choosing two shovels with sharp points and two square shovels.

Ned, however, had a different idea. From the back of the barn, two headlights blazed bright just before an engine roared to life. I was blinded by the lights as he drove the machine to the front of the barn. "Hop in, Miss Lisa," he instructed, parking it beside me. I dropped the shovels and climbed into the cab of what was some miniature version of a backhoe. I had seen them before, parked on the lawns and dotting the hills in the distance. They were painted green, to better blend in with the landscape, I assumed.

We wound up and down the paths of the east lawn. Honestly, we could've gotten there a lot faster. And been a heck of lot more discreet— on foot. If I was to believe Ned, and the jury was still out on that, there were two girls out there somewhere in the darkness conspiring to kill me. And there I was, riding in the loudest vehicle imaginable. And with my would-be assassin to boot. There was no way I should've felt as cozy as I did riding in that cab. But I couldn't help myself. However delusional, it was the first time in a long time I actually felt relaxed. Maybe it was the slow purr of the motor that soothed me. Or the peaceful night breeze. Whatever it was, I enjoyed my moonlit tour through the scenic hills of Grand Hallow.

Nearly a half hour had gone by before I had to ask, "Are you sure you know where we're going?"

"Sure do," he said and pointed ahead. "See that hill? They're on top of that."

As we approached, I began to recognize the hill in the dark distance. When we finally reached its crest, Ned jerked the machine off the pavement and barreled down a row between the headstones. I gripped the side handle as we careened close to the stones down the narrow path. "Don't worry. These gravediggers can fit into a lot tighter spots than this. Should be around here," he said, abruptly applying the brakes. The machine jerked to a halt. My scenic tour was over.

I jumped out and examined the markers. It took me a moment to gain my bearings in the darkness. But soon, I found it. There it was. The grave of my runaway mother, *Lynn Jacobs*. The last time I had stood on that hill, the grave and the jar of cherry-red blood set in front of its stone had effectively distracted me from the two smaller headstones before it. Those belonging to *Elizabeth Jacobs* and *Imogene Jacobs*.

I signaled to Ned, and he positioned the excavator between the two graves. He swiveled the cab and stretched forward the long arm until the scoop reached the base of Elizabeth's stone. Then, he forced its teeth into the earth. I stood next to it, shining the flashlight on the plot so Ned could see where to dig. He sure had the right idea. It was much easier holding a flashlight instead of trying to dig up six feet of dirt with some elbow grease and a couple of shovels. The powerful machine easily tore through the soil. He scooped up the piles of dirt and dumped them beside the grave. And when I heard the bucket scrape the top of the coffin, I waved my arms for him to stop.

Ned jumped out of the cab and examined the site he had expertly excavated. "Let's not open it yet," I instructed. "First, uncover Imogene's casket. Then we'll open them both. Together."

"Whatever you say, Miss Lisa."

When he finished with Imogene's grave, we brushed aside the loose dirt on the tops and sides of the coffins, just enough to grasp the lids. When we were ready for the unveiling, Ned stood in Elizabeth's grave. And I stood in Imogene's. As I unlatched the lid, a twinge of apprehension hit my stomach. And fear. Fear of the unknown finally becoming known. "On the count of three," I announced timidly as my arms began to shake. "One. Two. Three!"

In one brisk motion, I forced open the lid and shined my light into the coffin. First, I gasped, startled by the sight. And then, I was simply bewildered. Ned and I climbed out from the graves. We stood aboveground and crossed our beams to compare findings. Just like the twins, what we found was identical. Only they were not corpses. What we had unearthed were matching life-size stuffed sock monkeys, complete with oversize red lips and tassels made of red yarn at the top of their caps. Their black button eyes stared back at us vacantly, the pair seemingly uncaring that we had finally discovered their misfortune.

"Oh my heavens. What does this mean?"

"It means we're not dealing with ghosts. It means Elizabeth and Imogene—are real." That realization lingered in the air a moment as we stood above the faux grave sites. And in that time, my thoughts turned to Uncle Clayton. What had he believed? And what had he truly known about his own twin daughters? And what of the twins themselves? If they no longer lived in the cobblestone house, how were two *very real* girls surviving out in 578 acres of graves, swamps, and forests? As things went at Grand Hallow, I had found an answer but remained nonetheless perplexed.

Not having the patience for the ride back in the excavator, I started down the hillside. "It's a long way back," Ned called after me.

"It's OK. I've done it before. And I could use the walk. Go ahead and take the gravedigger back."

"No. No. I think it's better. Don't you? If we stick together?" he said, catching up to me. And so we left the hill on foot, not bothering to fill in the empty graves.

I felt bad. Although he didn't complain once, by the time we got back, Ned had produced a full-on limp. Still, he walked me to the door of the cottage house. "Are you sure you'll be all right?" he asked. "With us running at such a low capacity nowadays, I believe you'll be all alone out here tonight."

"I can handle myself," I assured him. "And remember, Richard is still on-site in the main building if I need anything."

"Ah, yes."

"Now go home and get some rest. We've both had a long day. Tomorrow, I start my interviews with the department heads. If the twins are trying to control any of them, I bet I'll get at least a couple of them to crack."

"If anyone can make them crack, it'd be you, Miss Lisa. Have a good night."

I tossed and turned, unable to get the button eyes of those damned monkeys out of my head. I'd fall asleep for a short while but waken easily at every bump and knock the stone house produced. It was sometime after 2:00 a.m. when I was awakened by creaks. I was eager to dismiss them as more harmless noises in a strange, new place. But it was the dramatic scraping that followed that caused me to jolt up and take notice. By this point, I was obviously no rookie when it came to Grand Hallow's after-dark disturbances. But what caused added terror was that this was occurring in the stone house, not the mortuary. It was an invasion. An ambush. And it was personal.

I clutched the knob. Ready to yell. Fight. Defend myself. But when I heard those distinctive giggles, I lost my moxie. Instead, fear kicked in. And I locked the door. The twins were in the house. And from the sounds of things, they were there to cause mayhem. Footsteps whizzed back and forth on the other side of the bedroom door. They were accompanied by laughter. Cupboards slamming. Furniture moving. Glass breaking. And then, there was a knock at the door. "C'mon, Dandelion. We know you're in there."

"Go away!" I shouted. "Get the hell out of here! Leave me alone!"

But my response only instigated them to escalate their urgent knocks to fist-pounding bangs. "Come! Out! And! Play! With! Us!" demanded Elizabeth, clearly relishing the torment she caused.

"Elizabeth has a new game," Imogene promised.

"I don't want to play any more of your games!" I screamed. "Now go! Please!"

Frantically, my eyes scanned the room for a weapon. In the corner sat a statue of a life-size ceramic cat with a long, exaggerated neck. I grabbed it by the base as if it were a bat. I took a deep breath, preparing to swing open the door and rush the pair. But suddenly, the pounding, the commotion—stopped. All was silent as I unlocked the door and slowly swung it open.

Cautiously, I emerged from the room with the statue over my head. The bookshelf in the living room had been turned over. The kitchen was trashed. Cupboards flung open. Plates and glasses smashed onto the tile floor. But there was no sign of the twins. *Where are you?* I stalked the rooms, clenching my weapon. Even though Ned and I had made the discovery that they were likely more earthbound than ethereal, they sure came and went like a couple of nasty poltergeists.

I found the front door ajar, so I shut and locked it. Then, I traded the cat statue for a broom and began sweeping up the broken glass in the kitchen. Yet as I swept, something caught my eye at the end of the hall.

The dresser I had used to block the twins' pink bedroom had been pushed to the side. And the door to the room was open, just a sliver. I gripped the broom as I headed down the hall. Was that where they were hiding? A glimpse of the dull pink carpeting made me feel instantly queasy. Slowly, I pushed open the door with the broom handle. "Are you in there?" I asked timidly before taking a reluctant step inside.

Their dolls and stuffed animals had been yanked off the shelves and were strewn about the room. Their giant dollhouse was demolished, stomped upon and smashed to smithereens. I took another few steps in and inadvertently stepped on the lopped-off head of one of the Play-Doh snowmen.

But what called my attention most—what struck immediate terror in my bones—were the child-size lumps beneath the covers of each bed. Was it some sort of trap? Elizabeth's new game? I stood at the head of one of the beds. I had to quickly summon my courage in order to grasp the corner of the Strawberry Shortcake sheet. And with a swift yank, the sheet and blanket atop it flew from the bed, revealing the soulless button eyes of a giant sock monkey. I yanked the covers off the other bed to reveal its twin.

The girls had brought their decoys back from the graves. To frighten. To intimidate. To let me know they knew what Ned and I had been up to. But I didn't scream. I didn't panic. Instead, I slowly backed out of the room and shut the door behind me. And for what was left of the rest of the night, I sat on the couch clutching the neck of the ceramic cat while monitoring the front door.

With the first rays of light, I got ready and dressed in a flash before heading over to the main complex. I wanted to catch Richard before he left for the bog. I didn't even know what I'd tell him so he'd understand. Where would I start? That our dead sisters/cousins were in fact alive? That it was they who killed both our father and our uncle—or perhaps used threats and manipulation to coerce others into committing the murders? However I explained it, he needed to be warned. If, God forbid, they were successful in taking me out, perhaps he'd be next.

I knocked on the door to the green room, and it opened by itself. At such an early hour, I was expecting to wake him. But Richard was not even there. *Where is he?* It was too early for him to report to work. And Richard was not one to squander sleep. Perhaps he had finally reached his breaking point? I supposed if he had, he had lasted longer than I had expected. And how could I have blamed him? Pulling bodies out of a bog for minimum wage was not exactly Richard's style. But no. That couldn't have been it. His bags were right there in the corner. I stood for a minute outside the locker room. After cracking open the door, I did not hear any water running. He wasn't in there either.

Puzzled, I headed to Ned's office. But he too was missing. Worry began to creep into my mind. Ned always arrived precisely at seven o'clock. And it was nearing seven thirty. I picked up his phone and dialed Henry. "Is Richard with you this morning?" I asked.

"Not yet. The crew's shift doesn't start for another hour."

"That's what I thought. Thanks."

As I hung up, I was startled by the sudden appearance of someone standing in the doorway. "Is this where I'm supposed to be?" asked the woman in the paisley dress. "I'm sorry. I know I'm a bit early. But I was supposed to meet with Ned Cummings about picking out a casket for my mother's funeral."

"Yes, of course," I said with a smile, hiding my anxiety as I fished through the drawer for his keys. "Ned isn't in yet. But let me take you to our showroom downstairs, where you can take a look at all of our available models."

I fumbled with the key ring before finally unlocking the door. The lights flickered before the sea of coffins came into full view. "Just take a look around and let me know if you have any questions."

I took a seat at the desk, trying to find the order forms as she perused the latest casket styles. I had just found one of the slips when the woman yelled from across the room. "Miss! Miss! Come here quickly!" I hurried to the back of the room. She stood with her mouth open, pointing to the

Solid Cherry Casket with Almond Velvet Interior, model number 8864, for $1,300.

"What is it?" I asked. But then I heard the muffled moans and the gentle tapping from inside the closed coffin. The woman began to hyperventilate. "It's OK," I promised her. "Why don't you wait outside?"

"What's going on!" she shrieked.

"Could be rats?" I shrugged before gently placing my hand on her shoulder and ushering her out of the room. "I'll be back with you in a minute."

Without any patience left for being terrorized, I swiftly returned to the coffin and lifted the lid as if I were ripping off a Band-Aid. "Holy shit!"

Tears streamed down his face as he moaned and whimpered. His hands had been bound. And his lips had been sewn shut with three stitches made of thick, black thread. Blood trickled down his chin from the puncture wounds. I rushed to find a pair of scissors on the desk. Then carefully, I cut his lips apart. "Oh, Miss Lisa . . . thank God . . . you found me," he gasped, his lips throbbing in pain, his voice hoarse and dry. "Elizabeth. Imogene. They know . . . that we know . . . their bodies are not . . . in those graves."

"I know, Ned. They paid me a visit last night too." He winced as I pulled the threads from his lips as gently as I could. "What happened?" I asked, helping him climb out from the coffin.

"I came back to my office last night. For my keys. And on my way out, I was grabbed from behind and shoved into the showroom. The twins, they were inside. Waiting for me. They forced me into the coffin. One held me down, while the other sewed shut my lips. Lord knows, I tried to fight them off. But I couldn't. They were just too strong. So strong. As the one girl, I believe it was Elizabeth, threaded the needle through my lips, she told me it was my punishment for talking to you about them. And sealing me in the coffin—that was punishment for digging up their graves. And now—now," he agonized, "they said if I don't 'take care of you' by tonight, I'll be dead before tomorrow."

Chapter 29

The Show Must Go On

"We have to find my brother and leave. Now! And then we have to get you to the hospital," I said to Ned, holed up in his office as he applied disinfectant ointment to his lips.

"Oh no, Miss Lisa, we cannot leave. Guests are arriving as we speak. In order to begin clearing out the backlog of delayed funerals, I booked three back-to-back this morning. We have two officiants and a pastor coming. We cannot simply turn them away. And we certainly cannot turn away those poor mourners. No, ma'am. As they say in show business—and in the funeral industry—*the show must go on*," he said, followed by a short, dry laugh.

Ned was something else. Even after his boss had been murdered and he himself had been accused of that murder, threatened, intimidated, and locked overnight in a casket with his lips sewn shut, he remained nothing if not consistent in his loyalty to Grand Hallow.

"OK. Fine," I relented. "But I'm shutting the rest of Grand Hallow down. We don't know who shoved you into the showroom with the twins. We don't know just how deep the twins' influence runs with the rest of the Grand Hallow staff. We can't be too careful."

"I'll second that."

"And after I shut it down, I'm calling the police," I added.

Ned gasped in protest. "But the twins forbid it!"

"The *twins* want you to kill me, Ned! What's going to happen when you don't offer up my corpse by the end of the night? Since we dug up those graves, I've been harassed. You were assaulted. And Richard is missing. It's time to end this!"

He nodded reluctantly in agreement. "But which station are you going to call? Grand Hallow doesn't have its own police department."

"Oh, I know just who to call," I said, picking up his phone.

"I can't believe you're calling," chastised Tina. "I told you after your uncle's funeral never to call me again, you traitor!"

"Tina! You can't be serious. I told you how sorry I was for missing the party."

"No, I'm not serious. But it wasn't just *any* party. It was *your* party. I had freakin' blow-up palm trees for Christ sake," she pouted. "And not only that, you've left me behind in Podunk Ruthsford while you're in Sleepy Hallow or wherever gettin' rich off dead people. You are totally lame. And you totally suck."

"I know I'm lame. I know I suck. Those palm trees *were* totally awesome. And believe me, I don't want to stay in *Sleepy Hallow* any longer than I have to. But Tina, I need you to get a hold of Sternhardt for me—one last time."

"Christ, Lisa. You'd think you'd have the Ruthsford PD on speed dial after playin' Russian roulette with that list of devil houses."

"I know. Like I said, I'm lame. But you seem to have Sternhardt wrapped around your finger these days. And it really needs to be him. He knows this case better than anyone. So will you convince him to take a ride out here? As soon as he can?"

"Oh God. You're panicking. I can hear it in your voice. What the hell is goin' on over there this time?"

"My uncle, he didn't have any heart attack. I know that for sure now. He was murdered. And if he was murdered, that means—"

"It *wasn't* the suicidal creep with the flapper hairdo who killed your dad?" she finished.

"I don't know. Maybe it was. Maybe it wasn't. All I know for sure is he wasn't the only one involved. There are others. Here, at Grand Hallow. So right now, me and Ned, we're stuck out here like a couple of sitting ducks."

"So get outta there! Leave right now!"

"I wish we could. But aside from the fact that about a hundred guests will be here any minute, Richard's missing," I said, my voice beginning to crack. "I can't find him anywhere."

"Got it," she said, grasping the seriousness of the situation. "I'll call Sternhardt right away."

I hung up the phone and took a deep breath, composing myself before turning to Ned. "OK. How do we get through this?"

"If you're sending all departments home, you'll have to take a break from your CEO duties and resume your old position."

"You mean coat check and wayfinding girl?"

"I'm afraid so," he affirmed.

As Ned hustled between the rooms making sure our guests had everything they needed, I manned the lobby. Like a robot with a smile, I took coats and passed out tickets with corresponding hanger numbers. An early fall chill had overtaken Grand Hallow. And with three overlapping funerals, the main coatroom quickly became filled. I could've used the two coat rooms on the other side of the lobby for the overflow. But since it was just me working the front, I jammed them in the best I could. Due to the frenzy, I haphazardly threw coats onto the racks behind me without any attention to order.

When the rush died down, I worked to better organize the coats according to their tag numbers. With coats suffocating me from all sides, it was claustrophobic. I could barely squeeze between the four racks that ran down the deep and narrow room. "What a mess," I groaned, rearranging hangers, drowning in a sea of cotton, wool, and leather. My only intention was to survive until Sternhardt could arrive. And there I was, stressing out over damned coats.

I was deep inside when I heard rustling on the opposite side of the room. I froze for a moment. But soon figured a coat must've simply fallen or shifted on its own. I continued sorting. But before long, I heard it again. Fabric brushing against fabric. And this time, it was followed by the scraping noise of hangers being slid across one of the racks. I peeled apart the coats nearest me to peer into the next aisle. But all I saw were more coats.

With my heart pounding, slowly I bent down to look beneath the coats. And on the other side of the room, near the rack against the wall, I saw a pair of legs. Dressed in white leggings and shiny black shoes, the legs cut through the row and took a step toward me. Without feeling the need to investigate further, I bolted for the door. But my escape was blocked by the second twin. Her back was to me. She leaned against the door with her head resting on her forearm.

"Now I'm going to count to five," she announced. "And then I'm gonna come find you. So you better hide real good. OK? Ready? One. Two."

I slowly stepped backward. There was nowhere to run. I was trapped.

"Three."

I dove into the sea of coats like a rabbit into a briar patch. And then I was as still as possible, cowering within the tightly packed coats, trying to steady my breathing.

"Four."

If she's about to leave the door, maybe I have a chance. Maybe I can run for it.

"Five!"

I waited a moment for her to step away from the door. And then I went for it. I leaped out of my hiding space. Only I didn't make it to the door. In fact, I didn't make it very far at all. As soon as I had made my move, from behind me, a coat came over my head. And with one strong yank, I was pulled to the ground in a flash.

Disoriented and gasping for air, I frantically tried to get back on my feet. But it was no use. I could feel them crawling all over me, laughing and biting me—hard. I screamed in agony as their teeth clamped down on my arms, legs, stomach. A piece of flesh was torn from my shoulder. I kicked and screamed until the coat finally came off my head. Imogene sat on my chest. A trickle of my blood dripped down the corner of her mouth.

"Why are you doing this!" I shouted to her. "What do you want from me!"

She grinned as she looked upon me. "Grand Hallow. We want Grand Hallow—all to ourselves."

"So that's what this is about? Me taking over Grand Hallow? Well guess what! I don't want it! You can have it! I will leave right now and never come back, and it will be all yours! Just tell me where my brother is. And I will leave tonight!"

Elizabeth stood from my legs. She grabbed a random hanger and threw the coat it was holding to the floor. She then knelt behind me and lifted the hanger high above her head. "Sorry," she said. "It's not going to be that easy."

I looked to Imogene pleadingly. I could've sworn I saw a glimmer of sympathy in her eyes before I closed my own, bracing myself for the blunt end of that hanger. But before it could happen, Imogene interrupted. "Look!" she cried excitedly. I opened my eyes to see her pointing to something on the floor to my left side. I glanced down to see the amethyst necklace. It must've fallen out of my pocket during the struggle. "Why did *she* get the amulet and not us? It's not fair!"

"Grab it!" hollered Elizabeth.

I quickly rolled it into my palm and closed my fist tight. "Give it to me!" screamed Imogene as she placed one hand around my neck and reached for the stone with the other.

"Move! So I can smash her head in!" ordered Elizabeth.

In the short moment Imogene released me so that her sister could have a good shot at my face, my arms were suddenly free. I took the opportunity to shove Imogene as hard as I could. I only wanted to get her off me. But what happened next was so far beyond my comprehension, it took me a moment to fully grasp that it was in fact real.

When I shoved her, she did not just fall away from me. Rather, she and the cluster of fallen coats nearest her shot straight into the air. The back of her skull slammed against the ceiling with a powerful force. And there she stayed, framed by the coats. Pinned. Screaming. Struggling to be released from gravity's bizarre reverse grip. "Let me down!" she wailed, terrified.

In the shock of it all, I managed to roll away from Elizabeth and stand on my wobbly legs. Yet in an instant, she charged me, fiercely striking my forehead with the hanger she wielded. Stunned, but with adrenaline blocking the pain, I struck back with my forearm across her shoulder. And Elizabeth flew backward through the center of the coatroom. She landed with such force, she collapsed one of the rods and was buried in a mound of coats.

I unclenched my fist and looked to the purple stone in my sweaty palm. Had it been the force behind the violent shoves? The force that continued to pin Imogene to the ceiling? If so, why hadn't it worked before? It was in my pocket the whole time I struggled with them on top of me. What was different? Besides that it was out of my pocket? Touching my skin?

The pile of coats in the center of the room began to surge. I quickly clasped the chain around my neck. I tucked the stone inside my shirt before rushing into the empty lobby. As I slammed the door behind me, I heard a scream followed by a loud thump. Imogene, it seemed, had finally been released from the ceiling.

Frantically, I made my way down the main corridor. "Ned!" I shouted. "Ned!" But it was no use. He was deep in the recesses of Grand Hallow. And with the funerals underway, I was essentially alone. At that moment, my pain receptors kicked in. I felt a large goose egg forming on my throbbing head as I climbed the grand staircase. Once I reached the balcony, I looked back to the lobby below—only to see the coatroom door was wide open. I scrambled up the narrow steps to my office, hoping to take refuge there until the crowds came back from the services. Yet just as I made it to the top of the stairs, Elizabeth stepped before the doorway.

"How'd you get up here? And so fast?" I wondered. She did not answer. She only eyed me like a snake ready to strike. "I don't want to hurt you," I warned her.

She stepped down to the first step, daring me to stand my ground. "You can't hurt me," she smirked. "And the only reason you have any strength at all is the amulet. Without it, you're just as weak as you were before."

"Was it your idea? To have Ned push me down these stairs?"

"Maybe," she smiled coyly. "But one thing my mother taught me: if you want something done right, you have to do it yourself." She dropped down another step. But I held my ground. My muscles tensed up. I was ready to fend her off. Only I was not prepared for what she did next.

In an instant, her legs left the floor. She flipped through the air and landed in a crouching position. Upside down. On the ceiling above the stairway. Her face obscured by her dangling red hair, she crawled forward down the slanted ceiling. She stopped just above my head. I was too stupefied to defend myself as she reached down and grabbed a fistful of her hair. She nearly lifted me off the steps by my scalp as I screamed wildly. With her other hand, she grabbed the chain around my neck. "It belongs to me!" she howled. She worked to pull the long chain out from my shirt—and the stone closer to her.

And just as the stone was about to be clutched by her grubby little fingers. Just as it dangled before my eyes—I reached up and grabbed it myself. As my fingers wrapped around it, I felt its warmth in my hand. And then, I yanked as hard as I could. The force jerked her from the ceiling. She fell on top of me. We clutched each other's hair as we tumbled, falling down the steps in turbulent somersaults. Somehow in the tumbling chaos, I managed to throw her off me, whipping her ahead and onto the final step.

I was shaken. Dizzy. There would be bruises. But I survived, still holding firmly onto the amethyst. I stood woozily over Elizabeth, who did not move. Her small body looked like a ragdoll that had been carelessly tossed to the floor. Her arms were twisted behind her back. Her legs were folded over her torso. And her neck was at such an odd angle. Warily, I bent down to feel for a pulse. But instead, I felt the sharp edge of a bone pressing out from her neck. It wasn't until blood began drooling from her mouth that I realized what I had done. I had killed her. I had actually killed Elizabeth. My cousin. My sister. She was a devil. But she was just a child.

Chapter 30

Truth or Dare

I trembled with panic. My God. There would be no explaining it. My head spun. What was I going to do? Who would believe that I had killed a child in self-defense? And shit! Sternhardt was on his way! Would he believe me? Never. Certainly not that she had crawled upon the ceiling and attacked me from overhead. Or that she had been plotting to kill me long before I had succeeded at killing her.

Could I sell the idea that it was an accident? That she had taken the tumble on her own? Maybe. I wasn't sure. Was her crumpled body at the bottom of the stairs indicative of a typical fall? Or would some expert, after examination, be able to determine that extra force was used?

I took a deep breath. *Wait a minute. Why am I in such a panic?* If she was supposed to be dead already, who was going to notice she was gone? There was already a gravestone with her name etched in it upon that distant hill on the east lawn. What could be easier? Ned and I could just bury her where she was supposed to have been all along. Instead of a giant sock monkey, the grave would finally hold the real Elizabeth Jacobs.

Voices from the first stream of visitors heading back to the lobby echoed from the floor below. I hurried to the morgue. I grabbed a gurney and a sheet. Luckily, thanks to the emergency closing, no one was on staff to see what I was up to. I piled her broken body upon the gurney and pushed it back to the morgue. At least there, it would be out of the way. It was perfect. Even with Sternhardt lurking about, what was one more body at Grand Hallow? I would store her in the cooler until Ned and I were able to bury her. And then that would be that. I wouldn't have to worry about Elizabeth again. Ever.

"I don't believe it!" he shouted as I reentered the morgue. Fuck! David. He stood at a slab in the middle of the prep room setting up his tray of tools. "You're turning into her more and more every day. Look. You're even wearing her necklace now." I looked to it dangling down my chest. Swiftly, I tucked the stone back into my shirt. "Where'd you get it?" he asked.

"It was a gift."

"A gift from who?"

"My uncle," I lied. "David, what are you doing here? Didn't you get my message? We're shut down for the day. Essential staff only."

"Are you saying I'm not essential?" he chuckled. "What do you have there?" he asked, pointing to the gurney I clutched, to the body beneath the sheet.

I couldn't let him see her body. It would look bad enough that I had killed a child. But based on what Ned had told me, revealing what I had done to Elizabeth could've been downright dangerous. If the twins *had* approached David, that meant he also might've been taking orders from them. Yet I just couldn't believe that David could've been under their influence. He was my friend. He had helped me break into Norman's office. Had helped me escape Grand Hallow, for crying out loud. There was no way he'd let the twins manipulate him. Still, I decided to play it cautious. "Just a new intake," I lied again.

"But last I heard, we're not accepting new intakes yet. Right?"

"Well this is a *special* intake. A personal exception. A young girl. So sad. Her parents called and asked if she could be buried in Grand Hallow's children cemetery. So I picked her up from the hospital myself."

"You took an intake through the lobby? In front of guests?"

"There's hardly anyone here today."

"No. Really," he pressed, unconvinced. "Who's under the sheet?"

"David." I stopped him, frustrated. "I need to ask you something. Have the twins come to you? Elizabeth and Imogene? You can tell me the truth. Are you working for them? I won't be upset. If you are, I know it's not your fault. I can help. Help you get out from under their control."

He laughed heartily. "I thought I already told you. I don't believe in ghosts."

"What if I told you they're *not* ghosts? What if I told you they're real?"

"Then I'd say you've finally lost your mind because I was at their funeral. They're dead."

Was he bluffing? I couldn't tell. David had such a wry way about him that it was difficult to tell which cards he held. Yet without his having to volunteer, one of his cards was about to be revealed on its own. Out of the corner of my eye, the color red suddenly entered my peripheral vision. I turned to see a slow, yet steady, stream of blood begin to make its way onto the main floor from behind the interior wall. He knew I had seen it. So there we stood, between the emerging flow of blood and Elizabeth's covered body—in a sort of morbid standoff. Our eyes locked. Neither of us moved a muscle.

"Where's that blood coming from?" I asked.

"Who's under the sheet?"

Slowly, I grabbed hold of the gurney and pulled it with me as I took two careful steps backward. I craned my neck, just a bit, to see behind the partition. And there they were. A cluster of barrels stacked three high. One of the barrels had a small hole in its bottom, supplying the growing stream of blood that gushed across the stark white floor. Had he mistakenly reused one of Norman's faulty barrels? Ironic if that was to be the mistake that finally revealed his hand.

"Why are there barrels filled with blood at the back of the morgue, David?"

Without averting his eyes from mine, he simply replied, "Our drainage system. It's broken."

"But last I heard, there was nothing wrong with the drainage system."

"There is now. It's all," he swallowed, "backed up."

"David, was it you who removed my uncle's organs? Are his body parts in one of those barrels? Did the twins make you do it?"

"Listen to what you're saying. You're letting this place get to you. I warned you. I've seen it happen before. It's like I told you about seeing ghosts. I get it. We're way out here. Isolated. You more so than anybody else. Jesus, you *live* here. Being around the dead all the time, it's not natural. It was bound to happen. Even to the best of us. We start to lose our minds. And especially after everything you've been through—"

I couldn't listen any longer. In a flash, I grabbed the scalpel from his tray. And before his reflexes even had a chance to kick in, I had already clutched his wrist and sliced open his forearm with the blade. I clamped my mouth over the laceration, slurping up his blood as fast as I could. I let it bathe my tongue. Cascade down my throat. Instantly, it began bringing me information.

"What the fuck!" he screamed as he tried to push me off him. But I was too strong. Only when I decided I had had enough did I let go. And then I collapsed to the floor, processing the bits and pieces as they came. They were scattered. Flashes. Yet clearer than ever before. More than just emotions. I saw visions. Perhaps it was due to the amount of blood I had ingested. Or because of its freshness. Or perhaps I was evolving, learning to hone my skill.

His red, rusted car. His room in his parents' basement. The love for some stupid video game. No! Focus.

OK. The Grand Hallow garage. I could smell grease and gasoline. Could see the hearses lined up. It was the night of my escape. What a strange sensation. Seeing myself as him. From his perspective. Watching me climb into the hearse. Drive through the bay door. As soon as the taillights reached the gate, he was off running. In the dark. Between tombstones. Out to Skeleton City. And aha! There they were. Just who I had been looking for inside his mind: the twins. He was reporting my escape to Shilling. It was *he* who had triggered the chain reaction. Panicking Uncle Clayton. Causing me to be locked inside the green room.

Then it faded. Beyond my control. Into something else. No. Wait. A concert. Some heavy metal band I had never heard of. Walking the boardwalk. At the beach. Looking at girls. Flirting. Stuck in a ditch. Buying a used Jeep. No! What else was I looking for? Concentrate.

OK. Inside the morgue. Elizabeth. Imogene. I could feel David's emotions. What they asked of him wasn't against his will. He was intrigued. Pleased. Willing. There was whispering of Norman's demise. And an offering. Talk of a trial. Promise of *mortuary technician?* Was this how he had truly earned his promotion?

As David, I then turned to see—Uncle Clayton on a slab. He wasn't dead. Not yet. *David—no!* I could feel the rush through his body and brain as, without remorse, without hesitation, he punctured the veins in Uncle Clayton's arms. Bleeding him out. Was this David's test? His trial? Uncle Clayton had been weakened, but was still conscious as David—*oh God*—sliced him open from stem to stern. While inhabiting the recordings deep inside his blood, there was no shutting my eyes. I was forced to watch as he gutted him alive. Carving out his organs as the twins watched in silence. Observing. And all the while, I felt the most inappropriate emotion coursing through him. I couldn't shake it. It enveloped me. I drowned in it: *glee.*

There was no disputing it. My travels through his soul had revealed the smoking gun. It was the second time I had been heartbroken after tasting the blood of a guy I really liked. He was a liar. And a traitor. He was a rat who worked for the twins. And he had done more for them than I had ever suspected. More than harvest organs of unwilling corpses. He might not have killed my father, but he *was* a killer.

It was *his* decision on how he would handle the twins' demands. Just as it was Uncle Clayton's, Ned's, Norman's—and whoever else they attempted to control. But David was no coerced victim. No, the difference with David, and it seemed with Norman before him, was the lack of struggle their plight had brought them. To the contrary, as told to me through his blood, through his emotions, David actually embraced their challenges. He rose to them. He was all too happy to participate in the murder and carnage.

Still half incapacitated on the floor, I looked up to David and promptly informed him, "You're fucking fired." I vowed then and there to rid Grand Hallow of all the twins' followers even if I had to taste every last one of the staff to suss them out. "Soon, you'll be in prison," I added.

But while I had been visiting the inside of his mind, uncovering his secrets by tasting his red and white blood cells, platelets, and plasma, he had uncovered the little secret I had been keeping as well. "Prison? What proof do you have I've done anything wrong? What? Some body parts in barrels? This is a morgue. There're body parts everywhere. But you— you've killed Elizabeth!" he roared over her undraped corpse.

He began pacing back and forth, chewing his nails. Based on his outburst, I didn't figure he anxiously paced over the loss of his job or even the possibility I'd turn him in. No, there was something else. "You have no idea what you've done," he warned. His angst built into a frenzy of aggression that terrified me. It was difficult, the need to retool in my mind exactly who David was while trying to erase who he had pretended to be.

Finally, he picked up his tray and let the tools clatter to the floor. "Oh, you're so dead. Right now, you're a bug flying straight for a windshield," he said before smashing the side of my head with the thick metal, knocking me into unconsciousness.

I woke in complete darkness. I forced my eyes open as wide as they would go, but it remained the deepest pitch black. It wasn't the gypsum mine. It wasn't the basement in Norman's house of blood and bones. This time, I knew I was blanketed by darkness in a much, much worse situation.

I was on my back in a tight space, barely more than the length of my body and no more than a foot above my head. It didn't take long to determine that I had been sealed in a coffin. And as if it couldn't get any worse, I had been pushed to one side of the confined space. This was because next to me, there was someone else. "Hello?" I asked, afraid, as I grabbed the person's leg. But he or she did not speak. Did not move. Did not breathe. It was my worst nightmare come to life. I was trapped in a coffin with a corpse.

I tried to listen outside the coffin for any clue of my whereabouts. But there were no sounds. It was completely quiet. Still. I could only hear my heart racing and my desperate breaths. *Maybe my magic necklace will give me the force I need to pound my way out?* I reached for the chain around my neck, but it had been removed. Of course it had. I began to panic, reaching all around the velvety interior that surrounded me. I pushed upon the lid as hard as I could. But it would not budge. I began pounding with my fists. "Hello! Let me out! Help!"

Just calm down. You're probably in the showroom. Someone will find you. Someone will let you out. Ned is out there. And Sternhardt is on his way. He's probably already here. And there's no way he's going to leave without finding you.

I tried to relax. And as I shifted into a more comfortable position, my cheek brushed against the body next to me. I felt prickly bristles. It was a man. I brought my hands to his face. He had a beard and thick mustache. Maybe there was something on him I could use? A light. A knife. God, even a stick of gum. Anything. I checked his pockets. Nothing. So I felt along his belt and then maneuvered my hand up his shirt. And that's when I felt it: a metal pin in the shape of a star. Unmistakably, it was a sheriff's badge. My heart leaped to my throat.

There was only one sheriff I knew of. And that sheriff was on his way to investigate a distress call coming from Grand Hallow.

And if Sternhardt had been killed, what of Ned? I didn't know how long I had been in that coffin. Perhaps his fate was the same as Sternhardt's. If that was true, with Richard missing, that meant no one would be looking for me. No one was coming. No one would find me, in time at least. Was this how I would die? Was I dead already? I couldn't be sure. I began pounding futilely in a claustrophobic frenzy. The air was getting thin. It was difficult to breathe. I was beginning to give up hope.

Chapter 31

Blood and Formaldehyde

The coffin shook and vibrated. I didn't know how long I was out before I awoke from the rattling. "Help!" I screamed. "I'm in here!" Soon, scraping noises took over the vibrations. And finally, a burst of twilight entered the coffin as the lid creaked open. As dim as it was, it might as well have been a thousand watts. It was the same to me. Light. Glorious light! As the fresh air rolled in, I gasped for more. Taking in as much as my lungs could hold.

With the lid fully opened and my eyes beginning to adjust, I realized I had been buried. In a grave. Six feet deep. It was a surreal sight, seeing Tina towering over the foot of my grave, furiously puffing on a cigarette. She looked so far away, as if she stood at the end of a long, dark, and narrow tunnel. The evening sky behind her was a dull, overcast gray. But I was happy to see it. I didn't think I'd ever see the sky again. Tina bent over to get a closer look. "Christ on a fuckin' cracker!" she screamed before taking another nervous drag. "You're alive!"

"Tina?" my dry voice croaked. "What're you doing here?"

"Ya didn't think I'd be sittin' at home after a call like that, did ya? Hey, is that—*Sternhardt* down there too?" she squinted.

"Yes," I said, finally able to positively identify him. "He didn't make it."

Ned stood in the pit beside the coffin. "Take it easy now, Miss Lisa. That's right. Nice and slow," he said as he grabbed my arm and helped me stand.

"How'd I get here?" I asked, disoriented. As I stood, a head rush came on so strong I nearly collapsed back into the coffin.

"It was that fucker," shouted Tina.

"David," Ned clarified.

"Yeah. *That* fucker. Anyways, we were lookin' all over for ya. And then out of the corner of my eye, I see this bulldozer thing movin' all the way out here. So we run all this way. Ned here about has a heart attack because he can't keep up and all. But finally, we get close enough to see this dude pushin' dirt over this grave. I gotta say. Even from far away, he looked kinda cute. Kinda nerdy. Kinda your type. But when Ned said he was from the morgue. And that he doesn't normally dig graves. *And* that there were supposed to be no burials goin' on. Well, we knew for sure he was up to no good."

"He killed my uncle," I warned. "I know that now."

"Shit!"

"Where is he now?" I asked in a panic.

"Oh, he took off runnin' for his life."

"What happened?"

"*This* happened," declared Tina. She produced her father's gun from her back pocket and struck a *Charlie's Angels* pose, holding it tight to her chest while jutting out her hip.

I let out a short snicker. Leave it to Tina to make me laugh after being buried alive. "You shot David?"

"Not exactly. I got a little—excited, I guess. So as we got closer to him, I pulled out my gun. Then I started screamin' and shoutin' at the fucker to freeze. Well, he didn't freeze. He took off runnin'. Damn. I would've started shootin' holes through the bastard if I knew for sure you were down there."

It took Ned a while to climb out of the grave. But once he rolled himself onto the surface, he and Tina helped pull me out. When I reached the surface, I realized we stood upon that familiar hill. I turned to the grave I had crawled out of—only to see that David had buried me beneath Elizabeth's tombstone. Fitting, I supposed, seeing as it was I who had taken her life.

"Poor Sternhardt," sighed Tina as we looked upon his body in the grave. "I can't believe it! I was just on the phone with him! I parked behind his squad car. He must've gotten here right before I did. And now look at him. What the hell?"

"David must've got him," I declared. "All I know is David coldcocked me. And then I woke up in a coffin next to Sternhardt's body."

"Goddamn. I gave him shit. But he did his best. He came out here as soon as I called. Ya know, he told me on the phone he knew somethin' was still up. That somethin' just wasn't right about your dad's case. Said he was never convinced the mortician was the killer. At least not convinced he did it on his own. That's why he never closed the case, even after that pasty maniac stabbed the shit outta himself. Guess ol' Sternhardt was right."

"Ladies," Ned interjected as he nervously scanned the radius of the hill, "we should probably get a move on. Upon this hill, I'm afraid we are quite—exposed."

Ned was right. I felt his anxiety too. The eyes of Grand Hallow were watching. Its ears were listening. We were vulnerable out in the wide open.

"So whatta we do now?" asked Tina. "Call more cops and have the fucker arrested?"

"What about your brother, Miss Lisa? Shouldn't we search the grounds for him?"

"Yes. We need to do both those things," I answered. "But before we search for Richard. Before we can call the cops, there's something we need to take care of first."

"You killed an eleven-year-old girl!" Tina hollered, shocked and bewildered as I scrambled around the morgue, looking for Elizabeth's body.

"I don't know if she was eleven exactly. Might've been ten. Or twelve. But yes. I killed her. Not on purpose, though! It was an accident. And she attacked me first," I tried to explain.

Tina stood hugging herself, tapping her foot on the morgue's tile while trying to process what I had done. "And this girl. She was your cousin? Or your sister? Whatever."

"Yes!" I shouted across the morgue while frantically searching one of the walk-in coolers.

"But I thought you said both those girls were dead?"

"I thought they were. Then I found out they weren't. But now one is. Look, I know it doesn't make any sense. But I can't explain it all right now. Will you both just help me look for her body? Please! Look, we can't call the police. Not until we find her—and get rid of the body. C'mon, where'd he put her?" I muttered under my breath as I began randomly opening the individual cooler drawers along the wall.

"Lisa, you're scaring me," said Tina. "Calm down. If it was an accident, it was an accident. The police will arrest that David dude. Not you. He tried to bury you alive! He killed your uncle for fuck sake!"

"You don't understand. I have no proof that David killed my uncle."

"How'd you find out then?"

"Because David told me he did. Sort of. In a way. I just know! The point is, he's not going to admit anything to the police. It'll be my word against his."

"OK. So you have no proof he killed your uncle. But he killed Sternhardt too! And we have proof of that. His damn body is out in that graveyard!"

"You're right. If he hasn't moved it, we have Sternhardt's body. But he has Elizabeth's. Don't you see? They cancel each other out. He knows I killed Elizabeth. And her body, he could use it against me if he wanted. That's why we have got to get rid of it!"

Ned needed no further convincing. He joined me in opening the drawers on the seemingly endless wall of built-in slabs. And that must've inspired Tina to do the same. She started on the far end of the wall. Ned in the middle. And I continued working my way from the corner nearest the stack of barrels.

Most of the cooler drawers were empty. Since the halt of intakes, the handful of corpses left had been there since Norman was in charge, still awaiting their postponed funeral dates. "If you find one, check to see if it's a red-headed girl," I instructed. We worked our way down the wall, systematically opening and closing drawers. If we found a body bag inside, we'd unzip it, just at the head, to see if it was Elizabeth.

We had checked at least a dozen a piece before Ned finally shouted, "My lord. Here she is!"

She was halfway between where Ned and I had started searching. Third drawer from the bottom. Ned fully extended the slab. And there she was. Elizabeth. She wasn't even in a body bag. She was just as I had left her. All twisted and crumpled, her red hair splayed across the slab. After David had knocked me out cold, I imagined Sternhardt had interrupted him. And in his haste, David must've simply shoved her in the drawer.

"Holy shit!" exclaimed Tina, examining her body. "What the hell did ya do to her? Beat her with a two-by-four until your arms cramped?"

"Believe me, I did nothing to her she didn't want to do to me. Now, what to do with her body?" I wondered.

"We gotta get Sternhardt outta that grave. Christ, the guy has family back in Ruthsford. At least I think he does? Let's throw her in it instead," offered Tina.

"No. That grave is too obvious now. That's what David would expect. Maybe if we dig a new grave site?" I suggested. "Somewhere random."

"He could be watching in the dark," countered Ned. "Then he'd know right where she is."

"You're right. How about in one of the forests?"

"Same problem, I'm afraid. It wouldn't take police long to find a grave in one of our small forests—if David tells them which one to search."

"The bog?"

"Grounds keeping is still running dragging hooks through it daily looking for corpses."

"Shit! What're we gonna do?"

"Oh my God!" shouted Tina, exasperated. "Why don't we just grind her up and stick her in one of those barrels!"

"No way. We are *not* like Norman—or David."

"I have an idea that might work, Miss Lisa. We could burn her," proposed Ned.

"Yes. The crematorium. That's it! Ned, I could just kiss you!"

"Um, gross. Please don't," Tina advised.

"Tina, since you have your gun, you could cover us while we move her to the crematorium."

She clamped both hands around its handle. "I'm ready," she declared.

"And then when it's done, we call the cops. Find Richard. And get the hell out of here."

"I'll support that," Ned agreed.

"OK. That's the plan. Let's be quick. And careful."

"Wait a second," Tina interjected. "How in the hell are we gonna find Richard in a place so big? I mean, there're like a million places to look. It'll take us forever, even if we split up."

"I don't know," I said honestly. "I haven't thought that far ahead. Let's just get this part over with. One thing's for sure, though, we are *not* splitting up." Tina nodded in agreement as I grabbed a gurney and wheeled it beneath Elizabeth's slab.

"Ned, can you get her down?"

"Sure can."

He grabbed Elizabeth's shoulder and hooked his other arm around one of her legs. But something strange happened as he transferred her to the gurney. Her eyelids began to twitch. And then to flutter. In my short time in the funeral industry, I had heard of bodies occasionally experiencing "residual" twitches. Muscle spasms after death. But I hadn't heard stories of eyes springing wide open, as in the case of Elizabeth Jacobs. And even more peculiar than her appearing to eyeball Ned, her face produced a frightening grimace. And her broken neck, it looked as if it were stretching forward—her jaws spreading apart. As he carefully placed her onto the gurney, I was unsure if I was merely projecting some form of consciousness on an unconscious cadaver.

My answer came in the next moment as I found myself shouting, "Ned! Watch out!" But I was too late. Elizabeth had clamped onto his arm. He let out a howl as she sunk her teeth deep into him, drawing blood. And when Tina became aware of what was happening, she easily eclipsed his scream with her own.

In the panic, I grabbed hold of Elizabeth and tugged on her shoulder. But her jaws wouldn't unclamp. I pulled as hard as I could, until I was finally able to rip her from Ned. And as they separated, she took a chunk of his flesh with her. He wailed in pain as I flung her off the gurney. Her gnarled body slapped to the tile.

All was still. But only for a moment, before Tina picked up right where she left off with another guttural scream. This time, she was reacting to Elizabeth's use of the arm and leg on the left side of her body to drag herself across the floor. She looked like a spider that had been stepped on and half-crushed, attempting to scurry away. Her head dragged behind her body, eyeing us as she chewed on Ned's torn flesh.

"What in the fuck is going on!" Tina yelled after her scream had been fully expelled from her lungs. I honestly didn't know. By the look on his terrorized face, neither did Ned. We huddled together as Elizabeth scampered away from us. Keeping a safe distance, we watched as she darted toward the stack of barrels and swiftly tucked herself behind them.

"I thought you said she was dead!" Tina frantically whispered.

"She was," I whispered back. "At least I thought so."

"So what now?"

I took a step forward. "Elizabeth?" I called to her in a light voice. "Are you OK?"

"She is *not* OK!" protested Tina. "She's all kinds of fucked up. Maybe she needs a doctor or something?"

"Ma'am, I don't think that's what she needs," said Ned, clutching his wounded arm.

From behind the barrels came a low growl. It sounded like a wounded animal warning us to stay away or risk becoming the victims of a vicious bite. Clearly getting the message, I took a step backward and rejoined the huddle.

Suddenly, Elizabeth's hand appeared, grasping the rim of one of the barrels. She pulled herself up its side. When her head came into view, it dangled grotesquely from her broken neck. Even so, she was able to skillfully climb the stack to the barrel on top. She clung to it while beginning to violently rock back and forth. The column of barrels teetered, threatening to collapse. And it appeared that was just what she wanted—as finally, the barrel she rode toppled. It smashed to the ground. The lid broke open, spilling chunks of innards, which floated on a river of blood across the floor. Thrown from the barrel, Elizabeth rode the spillage as if she were on some demented water ride. As she lay in the middle of the gruesome flood, she frantically reached for the chunks of spilled entrails, kidneys, livers, hearts. She crammed them in her mouth as fast as she could swallow.

"This isn't right," I said under my breath.

"Ya think?" Tina shot back as we each began taking cautious steps backward.

As we watched from the morgue's prep room, something began happening to Elizabeth. As she ate her morsels of diced organs, her bent leg appeared to straighten. She once again gained control of her twisted and paralyzed arm. And her broken neck bone seemed to fuse, allowing her head to sit straight upon her shoulders once more.

Slowly, she stood to face us, fully erect and in near perfect posture. She was covered in the blood she had rolled in. It dripped from her fingertips and from the edges of her skirt. It saturated her red hair, which was plastered to her face. A low gurgle came from her throat. She crossed her arms over her stomach. The stuttered moan that followed sent chills down my spine. Between the gurgles and moans, she spat up blood and bits of meat. When she finally recovered from her bouts of indigestion, a sneer of confidence took over her blood-smeared face. And then, she began taking steps toward us.

"Tina," I whispered as Elizabeth crossed into the prep room. "Get your gun ready."

"But I can't shoot an eleven-year-old girl. Can I?" she asked, nervously clutching her gun.

"She's no girl," I said. "Not an ordinary one, anyhow." Spotting Tina's gun, Elizabeth began marching toward her with fierceness in her eyes. "Shoot her!" I screamed as she got dangerously close. Tina apprehensively lifted her gun and aimed it at the advancing Elizabeth. She pulled the trigger and—nothing happened.

"It doesn't work!" she screamed in a panic.

"The safety!" shouted Ned. "Have you turned off the safety switch?"

"Where the hell's the safety switch!" screamed Tina as she cocked the gun to its side, searching. But it was too late. Elizabeth swiftly jumped onto her, tackling Tina to the ground. She mauled her like a rabid dog, biting and clawing while Tina fought, screaming at the top of her lungs.

Ned tried pulling Elizabeth off, but was quickly thrown to the floor. I ran to the counter. Near the sinks was a large glass jug. I grabbed it and rushed back to the pair. "Step back!" I yelled to Ned. And without giving it a second thought, I smashed the jug as hard as I could over Elizabeth's head. The thick glass shattered against her skull, releasing the liquid that spilled over her and Tina.

Both began gasping from the high concentration of fumes. It was enough of a distraction to drag Tina out from under her. Yet neither the blow to her head nor the fumes were enough to totally incapacitate Elizabeth. She struggled to regain her stance. But having seen her make a remarkable recovery from crumpled corpse to walking menace, I knew we hadn't much time.

"That was formaldehyde," said Ned, "and it's highly flammable. Do either of you have a light?"

Tina stood dazed. Coughing. Checking her wounds. I looked to Ned at a loss—until I remembered Tina's smoking habit. "Tina! Your cigarette lighter!" Shell-shocked, Tina was unresponsive. Yet eventually, the information found its way among her synapses. She searched through her pocket and produced the lighter. Yet she only stared at it in her palm with a puzzled look. So I grabbed it from her.

Elizabeth was still trying to shake off her own daze. She was on all fours with her head hung low. The formaldehyde's suffocating odor made my throat gag and my eyes water as I crouched next to her. I lit the lighter. My hand began to shake as I lowered it close to her. She snarled and then lunged at me with her open jaws. She swiped for the lighter, and the flame went out. I relit it quickly. And as she briefly turned from me, I held it to her long hair, soaked in blood and formaldehyde.

In an instant, her hair accepted the tiny flame. The flames spread to her head and face. And then quickly down her torso before engulfing her entire body. She sprang up, screaming. She twirled and jerked about the room in a frightening dance, zigzagging her way to the back door. And as she fumbled for its knob, her feet began to rise from the floor. The louder her screams, the more she seemed to lose her grip on gravity. Finally, she burst through the door. The three of us ran to see her floating and screaming through the cemetery. We stood outside watching the dreadful yet dazzling sight of Elizabeth, lit in flames, flying just over the tops of the gravestones. Howling into the night.

Something I took note of—she moved with purpose. She moved in a deliberate, straight line toward somewhere, something in the dark and vast cemetery. "We have to follow her," I announced. Seeing as she was a beacon lit in flames against the night sky, I didn't figure it would be that difficult. "Maybe we *don't* have to aimlessly search all of Grand Hallow. This is just a hunch. But maybe if we follow her, *she* will lead us straight to Richard."

"But, Miss Lisa. What about David? And Imogene?" asked Ned. "I'm willing to bet they're out there too. Somewhere between us—and wherever Elizabeth is headed."

"Imogene?" Tina questioned.

"Her twin sister. And she's just as bad," I warned. "I say we follow her, and—" I hesitated before saying it, but felt it needed to be said aloud. "And if anyone gets in our way, we kill them." Ned and Tina were silent for a moment, yet nodded slowly in agreement. "But Tina, you should stay here," I advised, looking at her bite wounds.

"Hell no," she replied, apparently recovered from her trauma. "I just found the safety switch on this damn gun."

Chapter 32

Follow the Flaming Light

We followed the flaming light. We ran up the hills. Down the gullies. Through the twisted paths. "C'mon Ned. Keep up!" chastised Tina.

"I'm running . . . as fast . . . as I can," Ned huffed behind us.

"Keep your eyes on Elizabeth," I instructed. "We can't let her out of our sight." We ran for what seemed like miles among the infinite graves of Grand Hallow. We followed the trajectory of the red flame that flew over the tombstones like a hot and angry meteorite.

"Who's that out there?" asked Tina. Far off to our right, we caught glimpses of a second figure in white, glowing dimly in the distance.

"I don't know. Just keep following that light. And be ready for anything."

The farther out the flaming light took us, the more evident it became that the path of the figure in white began to intersect with our own. It had a strange, etheric quality. It took steps, but its feet did not seem to make contact with the ground. Rather, it seemed to glide toward us with little effort. As the entity came closer, its features became more defined.

It wasn't very tall in stature. And it wore a white evening shawl draped over its shoulders. But it was not until it began furiously waving to us—not until I heard that giggle—did I know exactly who it was. "Lissssaaa," she called across the stretch of graves. "Come play with me."

"Imogene," Tina declared with unease. "Are we gonna set her on fire too?"

Elizabeth's flame flickered not that far ahead. "No. They've done this kind of thing to me before. It's a trick. She's just trying to distract us. Throw us off."

In my peripheral vision, I saw Imogene performing tricks atop gravestones, desperately trying to gain our attention. She'd balance on top of a headstone before easily leaping over two or three only to land safely atop another.

"I could shoot the little gremlin right now. Just give me the word," offered Tina.

"Just keep moving. Ned, are you doing OK?"

"I'm not . . . too far . . . behind, Miss Lisa," he panted.

Impressive as it was, Imogene's routine was not enough to convince us to change our course. Realizing she was failing to sway our direction, she began swiftly making her way toward us, all the while demonstrating her magical leaping and balancing act atop the stones. And just as she was about to cross our path, she plunged behind a headstone right before us. I clutched the scalpel I had slid in my pocket, trying to anticipate where she might pop up next. And in the next instant, she reappeared behind a different gravestone. This time to our left.

Tina and I kept our focus and continued running forward. But Ned, he ran off the path and into the rows of gravestones. I didn't know what possessed him to lunge his bulky frame straight toward her. But he ran at Imogene with his arms wide open as if he planned to tackle her. Only just as he got several feet before her, he suddenly disappeared. He fell forward. And the earth simply swallowed him whole.

In a panic, we backtracked, weaving between headstones to the spot where Ned had vanished. There, at the head of a freshly dug grave, stood Imogene. She giggled deviously with her hand covering her mouth.

As we approached the foot of the grave, we saw Ned stuck deep in the hole. Bewildered at his predicament, he slowly sat upon his knees. Just what I had been afraid of—Imogene had led one of us into a trap. As Ned looked up to us, I was horrified. Shards of glass had impaled his face. Blood gushed from the gashes. Suddenly realizing it himself, he brought his hands to his face and let out a whimper. He looked down to see broken glass had also pierced his chest and stomach. Small pinpricks of blood soon grew to large red splotches across his white dress shirt. "I'm so sorry, Miss Lisa," he apologized, pitifully calling from the bottom of the grave. "I was only trying to stop her from interfering."

"I know, Ned. You don't have to be sorry."

By the time I looked back to the situation aboveground, Tina had her gun drawn and pointed squarely at Imogene. "Please don't hurt me like you hurt Elizabeth," she begged.

"Should I shoot her?" whispered Tina.

"Yes," I answered emphatically. But Tina hesitated. Her hand trembled slightly with her finger on the trigger. "What're you waiting for?"

"I'll do it!" she promised. "But seeing her up close. I mean, she's wearin' a shawl for Christ sake. I know her sister's a creature feature. And I'm sure she is too. But she looks just like a normal girl."

"She's *not* normal. She lined that grave with broken glass. And then she lured Ned to fall inside!"

"Fuck!" shouted Tina, upset with herself. "You know what would help? If she attacked me. If she came at me like that other one—all fucked up and drippin' blood like Carrie at the prom. Then I'd know for sure. Then I'd have no problem puttin' a bullet in her skull. C'mon, Punky Brewster," she yelled to Imogene. "Come and get me!"

But Imogene's reaction to Tina's taunt was to let out a disorienting, ear-piercing scream. She then bent her knees and catapulted high into the air. Tina, finally shook enough to take action, shot at Imogene twice as she flew backward and landed behind a tall headstone. "Did I get her?" she asked, keeping aim at the headstone.

"I couldn't tell. Just keep your eyes peeled," I advised before turning back to Ned in the grave. "Let's get you out of there." I reached my hand down to him, but he did not bother reaching back. He only turned over his palms and shrugged. They too were embedded with tiny bits of glass.

"You won't be able to pull me out," he said, wincing as he removed a single shard. "Not even the two of you together. Now don't you worry about me. Oh, it'll take some time to extract this glass from my skin. And when I do, I'll manage to crawl out of here. But you and Miss Cashmere better run along now if you intend to catch up with Elizabeth."

I looked to the light flickering in the distance. He was right. "OK," I halfheartedly agreed. "But we're coming back for you as soon as we find Richard. And if you get out before then, let's meet back in the lobby."

"That sounds like a fine plan, Miss Lisa. Now go. Find your brother." Tina and I moved on without Ned. I was reluctant to leave him behind, yet determined to discover Elizabeth's final destination. As we passed the tall headstone Imogene had leaped behind, Tina kept her gun ready. But Imogene—had disappeared once again.

By the time we had come upon a small grove of trees lining either side of the path, Elizabeth's flame was beginning to dim. "We've got to hurry!" I panicked.

We charged forward side by side through the trees—until Tina suddenly brought her hands to the back of her head. "What's happening!" she screamed as she felt her hair begin to rise off her scalp.

I looked over to see Imogene's hands clamped onto locks of Tina's hair. She floated behind Tina in midair, holding onto her hair like a pair of reins. She let out a giggle before shouting, "I'm playing horses! Giddyap!" she commanded while firmly tugging on Tina's hair. Tina let out a bloodcurdling wail. She took off running with Imogene sailing in the air just behind her, laughing and howling in delight. Beyond terrorized, Tina shot three bullets over her head. I cowered from the blasts. When they were over, I spun around to assess the outcome. But suddenly, I was alone. Tina and Imogene were nowhere in sight.

"Tina!" I shouted into the night. But all was silent. I cautiously moved to the end of the grove. "Tina!"

"Lisa?" I heard her call back faintly. But I couldn't tell from where.

"Where are you!"

"Up here!" she shouted back.

I looked up into the branches of the half-dead giant oaks. In the murky night sky, the disorienting twists and turns of the mostly leafless branches made me dizzy. I couldn't see her at first. But then, in the last tree that lined the path, I saw a dim figure clinging precariously to the thin branches at the very top of the colossal tree. She desperately tried to find solid footing as the breeze caused the branches to sway. "How in the hell did you get up there?"

"That flyin' monkey! She grabbed me from under my goddamn armpits and dragged me up here!"

"Can you get down?"

"Well, I can't exactly jump without breakin' all my fuckin' bones. And I can barely see where to step. But I'll get down—eventually. Hey," she shouted down to me, "from up here, I can see where that flamin' witch is headed."

I looked to see the light emanating from Elizabeth go from a dim glow to completely extinguished. "Where?"

"She landed in those woods. Just over there," Tina said, pointing. Against the dark night sky, I could see the even darker trees of the forest just ahead. And instantly, I knew exactly where she had landed. *Of course. I should've known.* It was the pine forest next to the bog. The forest with the mysterious mound at its center. The mound with the pipes sticking out that Ned claimed belonged to an old root cellar. The place I had sent Richard to investigate.

I looked up to Tina helplessly. "You better get going if you want to catch her," she advised.

"We left Ned behind. I can't leave you now too."

"But you have to get to Richard. Here, I'll throw my gun down to you," she shouted. "That's just as good as having me there."

"No. It isn't. Look, I'll go. But keep your gun, OK? You never know when you'll need it around here."

"Something tells me you're gonna need it more than I will where you're goin'."

"Don't worry. I have my scalpel. Besides, the first time I killed Elizabeth, it was with my bare hands."

"Maybe that was the problem. She didn't *stay* dead, remember?"

"She will this time," I vowed. "You just worry about getting down in one piece. And when you get back on the ground, meet me in the center of that forest. OK?"

"OK. Fine. But if I'm keepin' this gun, the next time I see that monkey, I'm gonna shoot her right outta the sky," yelled Tina.

"Good!" I yelled back as I began making my way to the forest.

Part VII
Chapter 33
Devil Shit

I peered into its deep darkness. The clouds had begun to part. But the dim moonlight only penetrated the thick pines in random patches. As I entered the cluster of trees that made up the outer rim, it was not lost on me that I was likely falling into a trap. I wasn't that naive. Ned trapped in a freshly dug grave? Tina stuck in a tree like a helpless cat? No, Imogene had ended up being quite successful at her task: separating me from my friends.

I tried to be as stealthy as possible, tiptoeing through the forest. I successfully avoided the plentiful depressions filled with swamp water on my way to the clearing at the forest's center. And when I finally reached the clearing, I hid in the trees just outside. Without trees to filter the moonlight, the clearing was lit in a pale, eerie tone. I eyed the top of the mound for any activity. Seeing nothing out of the ordinary, I skirted the edge until I had a view of the ridge on the opposite side.

There, I noticed more equipment had been delivered to the site since I had last been there. More lumber. A wooden trailer bed filled with buckets and tools. And most conspicuously, a small tractor parked beside the cluster of boulders.

It appeared desolate. So, cautiously, I stepped out into the open. I was startled as an owl swooped across my path and then back into the trees. I approached the base of the ridge looking for any evidence of the twins—or Richard. Belongings of theirs. Disturbed pine needles on the forest floor. Anything. It was then that I heard movement on the mound above. A broken stick at first. Then a shuffle. Suddenly, a dark figure appeared. I stumbled back a few steps as it loomed over me. It was too tall to be one of the twins. "Richard? Is that you?" I asked before the figure boldly jumped off the ridge, landing directly before me.

"It was my mistake. Instead of burying you alive, I should've killed you like I did that cop. But there was something I liked about the idea of you trapped in that box. Suffering. Pounding away until your air ran out. You know what? It really turned me on."

I pulled the scalpel from my pocket and yanked off its sheath. I held it firmly in my grip, pointing the blade at him. "Stay the hell away from me, David!" He laughed at my modest weapon. From behind his back, he produced a large cleaver like the one I had seen Norman use to hack off limbs in his body factory. *Fuck! Why didn't I grab something like that?*

"I know exactly who you are now," I said, slowly backing away from him. "You're nothing more than a second-rate version of Norman, who was pretty pathetic to begin with. Taking orders from demonic girls. Supplying them with blood and guts. Killing for them. For what! For a chance to finally break free of your parents' basement? To afford a new set of wheels? Give me a break! You're nothing but a pawn. And what makes you even more pathetic is that you don't even realize it!"

"You know, when you first came to Grand Hallow, at the beginning of summer, I didn't even believe in Elizabeth and Imogene. I had no idea what Norman was up to afterhours. Remember when you asked what kind of guy likes to embalm corpses? And I told you I only did it for the money? I was telling the truth. But when the twins made themselves known to me, I soon realized that even though I'm the kind of guy who finds embalming corpses dull, I *do* like dismembering them. And thanks to the twins, I also realized I'm the kind of guy who likes *making* them too."

With that, he raised the cleaver over his head and rushed me. As he brought the blade down upon me, I dropped the scalpel and grabbed his wrist with both my hands. The force of the collision toppled us over. I pushed against his arm with all my might—until my muscles began to tremble. The tip of his blade dropped lower and lower over the base of my throat.

The look on his face communicated that same gleeful emotion I felt in his blood as I experienced his killing Uncle Clayton. I hated him. And I resented the fact that it was only because his physical strength was greater than mine that he would prevail. It wasn't fair. It wasn't right. If I had had the amethyst—or a bit of that power Elizabeth had demonstrated after eating the bits of diced organs—I could've easily overwhelmed him. Then, it would've been me who survived. It was dumb really, that life and death had to come down to such a primitive difference.

Yet something unexpected happened as I felt the blade begin to puncture my throat: an arm came from out of nowhere. It swung around David's neck. And in a split second, he was dragged away from me. His body flew off mine and was hauled across the forest floor before slamming against the bottom of the ridge. And there he sat. Dazed.

Suddenly, popping her head out from behind him—was Imogene. It was an odd sight, his larger frame sitting in her small lap as she restrained his neck in a lock. She flashed me a smile as she grabbed his hand that clutched the cleaver. Controlling him like a puppet, in one swift motion, she plunged the blade into his abdomen. "David," she said in a sweet, hushed voice, "we decided we don't need you anymore." She then used a sawing motion to bring the blade up through his torso as he groaned in agony.

As David gasped his last breaths, I quickly leaped to my feet, frightened of what she'd do next. Frantically, I scanned the ground for my scalpel. It was impossible to find on the forest floor. But Imogene barely seemed aware of my presence. Instead, she straddled David's corpse and began digging for morsels inside his abdomen. She pulled out a handful of his moist entrails and began immediately consuming them. Blood covered her hands, her lips, her chin. It stained her pretty white shawl. I watched mesmerized as she feasted over her fresh kill like a hungry cougar.

Yet Imogene's meal was soon interrupted by a banshee's battle cry—and a swift pummel to the head. Tina had entered the scene. And immediately upon witnessing the feasting Imogene, she had grabbed a two-by-four from the nearby stack of lumber. As Imogene began to sit upright, Tina, with a loud grunt, whacked her over the head a second time. Imogene began to cough. She spit up blood and pieces of David's insides as she crawled around the forest floor, discombobulated.

Tina dropped the board, trading it for her gun. Yet this time, she aimed with confidence at the weakened twin. "Now *this* was the sign I was lookin' for. This little devil piggin' out on blood and guts is exactly what I needed to fuckin' see," she declared just as she was about to pull the trigger.

"Tina—no!" I shouted as I rushed to her side and lowered her arms. "David, he was going to kill me. He had a knife to my throat. And Imogene, she saved me."

"Did she? Did she really?" Tina asked, about to go into hysterics. "Are ya sure she just wasn't hungry? Are ya sure she just didn't want to eat him? And who's to know she didn't plan on eatin' you next!"

"She might've been," I confessed, not believing I was actually asking for Imogene's absolution. "But I'm OK. And David's no longer a threat. If she comes anywhere near you, please, shoot her. Be my guest. Just not this second," I asked.

Imogene quickly recuperated from Tina's blows—at least enough to stand upon her knees. She scuttled that way, on her knees, in front of the ridge until she made it to the far end. And there, as if by some type of sorcery, she simply peeled back a layer of the earth. With a flick of her wrist, she opened the side of the hill and magically disappeared inside. "Did you see that!" I asked Tina.

"Yeah," she replied. "I saw it. Freakin' Devil shit. You shoulda let me shoot her." I rushed to examine the spot on the ridge where she had disappeared. "Are you crazy? Get away from there!" warned Tina.

But I ran my hands over the layer of soil, sticks, and dried pine needles that covered the ridge. And unexpectedly, without actually seeing it, I felt—a seam. I ran my hand along the edge of what was a cleverly woven, definitely handcrafted blind. It was made of all the natural material that surrounded it on the hill. And when I peeled back the layer, affixed by ropes at the top of the ridge, it revealed an old wooden door made of weathered barn planks.

"It's not Devil shit," I declared. "Look, it's a door." I yanked on the ropes, and the crafty camouflage fell to the ground.

"Holy shit. Where does it go?"

"Ned thinks there's an old root cellar beneath this hill. But something tells me there's more than vegetables calling it home now." I grasped the rusted handle.

"Lisa, don't even think about it. Don't you dare go through that door!"

"But this is why we're here. What if Richard's inside?"

"Well, we just can't go waltzin' in."

"OK. You're right." I thought a moment. "Your gun. It can slow them down. But if I could break Elizabeth's neck and she still survived, it's not going to be enough."

"Well it's better than nuthin'. What other ammo do ya have in mind? You hidin' a bazooka up your ass?"

"No, I do not have a bazooka up my ass. But we might have something better. Something to level the playing field." I stepped over to David's body. "Tina, I don't want you to watch this. Just turn your back. Look away, OK? And I'll tell you when I'm done."

"What the hell are you gonna do?" she asked apprehensively.

"Look, we're cousins. Sisters. Whether I like it or not, they're part of me. And in some ways. OK, in very few ways, I'm like them. You've seen what eating those body parts did for Elizabeth. They cured her. Gave her strength. And Imogene, floating around and lifting you into the trees. I've got to believe it was from the same thing. So just let me do this. I've got to at least try."

Tina understood what I was proposing. Yet she didn't look any less stunned by the idea. She didn't say a word as I knelt next to David's body as if I were a vulture that had sniffed out a leftover carcass. She only covered her mouth and turned away in anticipated disgust.

He was still warm as I slipped my hand inside. I fished around for something I could grab onto. But everything was so slippery. Each time I closed my fist, a slick tendril shot right out of my hand. It wasn't until I reached both hands inside that I was able to firmly grab hold of something. I worked hard to dislodge whatever it was. And when I finally ripped it from his torso, I didn't know whether it was a kidney, liver, spleen—or something else. It simply looked like a raw piece of meat marinated in blood.

I brought it to my mouth, trying not to think that what I was about to chew on was an actual human organ. I clamped down on it, using my side teeth to rip off a generous piece like a starving jackal. As I chewed, the first thing I noticed was that it was salty—and that it had the texture of a raw piece of fish. It wasn't exactly delicious. But it didn't make me nauseous either. In fact, it didn't taste so bad. Not bad at all.

And when I swallowed, and it hit my gut, I felt fulfilled—and instantly energized. It wasn't like normal food. It didn't feel like anything my body needed to process. It felt as though my body was able to accept it whole and use it whole. There was no need for digestion. It simply converted the meat into pure energy and strength. I took another bite. And then another, until the entire organ was gone. And after I swallowed the last bit, I reached straight inside David for a second helping. I pulled out a smaller organ shaped somewhat like a pear.

It was at that point I heard Tina vomiting profusely behind me. "Tina! I told you not to look," I scolded. Quickly, I devoured the pear-shaped morsel before turning to face her. Tina held her stomach with a look on her face as if she had just drunk a glass of sour milk. And as if totally grossing out my best friend wasn't mortifying enough, she stood watching me along with a very dismayed Ned. "Ned! I'm so glad you're OK!" I said as I leaped up to give him a hug.

But Ned, struggling to make sense of the sight he had stumbled upon, swiftly, yet politely, declined my embrace by holding up his hand. "Oh my." He motioned to the corners of his mouth and then pointed at mine. "There's blood. Ahem. Dripping from your lips."

Embarrassed, I wiped my bloodstained hands on my pants before using my shirt to clean my lips. "OK. Without context, I know what this looks like," I admitted, tossing a glance back to David's corpse. "But I only ate a few pieces—and just so I could compete with the twins," I explained in my defense. "What're you doing out here anyway, Ned?" I asked, as if I could casually shift the attention away from my cannibalism. I examined the dirt-smeared, swollen, and still-bleeding lacerations on his face and arms. "You're in no shape to be out in the woods."

"I wouldn't have felt right, leaving you girls out here alone. So after I managed to climb my way out of that grave, I headed in this direction—until I heard quite a scream coming from within these woods. I figured this would be the place."

"This is it," I confirmed. "We found the twins' hideout. It's here, inside one of those old root cellars you told me about."

Tina, still struggling with bouts of dry heaves, managed to ask, "So? What's it feel like?"

As I figured, escaping the subject of my newfound penchant for organ eating wasn't going to be that easy. The truth was, I felt the strongest I had ever felt. The effect of the steroids Richard took years before paled in comparison to the strength I sensed had been given to my muscles. And coursing through my veins was an energy that felt more powerful than adrenaline. Yet unlike adrenaline, I was able to consciously control its surge. It tingled just below the surface, as if I could summon its magic at a moment of my choosing. This overwhelming mix of reserved strength and energy made me feel as if I wore armor. More than confident, I was invincible. "It feels like—this could actually work," I finally answered.

"So whatta we do? Just storm inside?" she asked as we stood before the door.

I tried to temper the incredible way David's organs made me feel by applying some logic to the situation. I forced myself to consider that while the playing field may have been leveled—just a bit—I was still the rookie. "Probably not the best idea," I concluded.

"Yeah," agreed Tina. "We need a plan."

"Wait a minute," I said, looking to the nearby tractor and cluster of boulders. "Ned, do you think that tractor over there would be strong enough to roll one of those boulders?"

"If I could get it to start, I don't see why not." Stiff and in pain, he climbed up the tractor and into its seat. "The keys are in the ignition," he reported.

"So how about Tina and I ambush the cellar? See if we can find Richard. And while we're in there, you move the biggest one of those boulders right up to the door. And as soon as we come out—bam! You barricade the place in. That way, whatever's in there, whatever evil we leave behind—stays inside. For good." Ned and Tina exchanged glances as if they were silently determining my sanity. *"OK?"* I asked, fishing for whether or not they were with me.

"You got it, Miss Lisa," answered Ned as Tina followed suit with a steadfast nod.

"All right then. Ned, wait until we get inside to start the tractor," I commanded. "We don't need the girls getting suspicious. Tina, this is it. Are you ready?" I asked as we took our positions before the door.

She wiped her palms on her jeans before tightly gripping her pistol. "Shit yeah," she declared.

I held out my hand, ready to grab the knob. "On the count of three. One. Two—"

The door burst open. And there stood Imogene. She was dressed in a fresh floor-length nightgown with a rose petal border. "Don't shoot!" she said, holding up her hands. "It's just me, Imogene."

"But you're the one I *wanna* shoot, Smurfette," snarled Tina, struck by how oblivious she seemed to the fact that we *were* her enemy.

"I hafta invite you inside now," she announced. She remained firmly in the doorway, yet reached out her hand for me to join her.

Tina and I looked to each other, stunned. "Whatta we do now?" asked Tina.

"Go in," I shrugged.

Tina took a step forward. But Imogene swiftly reprimanded her. "No, silly! Not you. Only Lisa is allowed inside."

Tina, looking skeptical—and a bit trigger happy—would not budge from the door. I pulled her aside. "It's OK," I whispered. "Stick to the plan. This doesn't change a thing. In fact, this is better. Ned needs a lookout. We still don't know if the twins have gotten to any others—like they had gotten to David. Help Ned. Cover for him. Don't let anyone get in his way."

Tina took a reluctant step back as I accepted Imogene's hand. And then, I was whisked into her underground world.

Chapter 34

Insight and Power

We stood in a cramped foyer of sorts, lit by a lone, dim candle. I was not afraid. Energy surged through me with great force. It was as if I had the power of the amethyst with me. The only difference was the amethyst's power came from the outside in. And the power I possessed, from the organs I had eaten, flowed from the inside out.

Ned had been right. It was an old root cellar. But unlike what he had suspected, it hadn't collapsed or been filled in. Despite its obvious age, its structure remained quite well intact. Its low, arched ceiling was made of red, faded brick that transitioned to a mix of cobblestone and cement for its walls. Lining the walls was a series of old wooden shelves. Yet instead of vegetables, the shelves held a muddle of shoes and boots, bottles of cleaning supplies, and rolls of paper towel. A corner section of the shelving had been cut away. There stood a broom and several coats on hooks.

The door clicked shut behind us. And almost instantly, I heard the muffled purr of the tractor's engine. Ned had gotten it to start! Imogene, still clutching my hand, led me toward a thick, black curtain separating the entry area from the rest of the cellar. Tina may not have been invited inside. But as Imogene disappeared to the other side of the curtain, her scream penetrated the earth-covered walls. I jumped from the gunshot that followed. Disturbed, I instinctively reached behind me for the door. But Imogene tightened her grip, insistent on pulling me deeper inside

I took a deep, uneasy breath before passing through the curtain. And as the two halves parted, air from the main chamber rushed by my face. It carried with it a sweet, yet musky smell, like a dark and earthy patchouli. Burning on the top shelves were clusters of candles. They illuminated the red brick ceiling in dazzling balls of light. The light bounced off the ceiling, casting a subtle red hue throughout the room. Lining the shelves where there weren't candles were dozens of mason jars. The jars appeared almost decorative, meticulously placed with even spaces between them. Filled with blood and tiny bits of floating flesh, those closest to the candles glowed and flickered like deep crimson gaslight lanterns.

The room was shaped like a boat, bowed outward at its center and narrow at either end. Where the room was widest, small folding beds sat opposite each other. The lower shelves nearest the beds held clothing and blankets for each girl. Yet also neatly tucked beneath the shelves, lining the rest of the space along the walls, was a collection of the infamous plastic barrels from the morgue.

The cellar looked as if it was being renovated, which explained the equipment and tools outside. Two-by-fours framed out the skeletons of future, smaller rooms. Hardwood flooring covered half the space while the other half of the floor remained tightly compacted earth. Despite the dank atmosphere, it had little in common with the house Norman had seized and turned into his house of horrors. Sure, there were body parts in barrels lining the walls. And there were glowing jars of blood. But somehow, it was all made less unsettling. There were no piles of bodies in the corners. No decomposing corpses placed in macabre poses. No skeletons. It was discreet. Understated. And tidy.

Imogene marched me toward the rear of the room, where there was a platform built atop the floor. Made of wooden planks and lined in more black curtains, it resembled some type of makeshift stage or altar. I resisted her pull as I noticed that at the foot of this altar lay Elizabeth. "Don't worry," she whispered, "she won't attack you in here. Not now. She wouldn't dare." Her body was charred almost beyond recognition. Her red hair was gone. Her skin was melted, covered in black scorches and glistening red splotches. Her clothes were fused to her body.

Even though she had attempted to murder me in a variety of ways, I couldn't help but feel sorry for Elizabeth—lying there with her head on the platform, her breathing labored. But it was also curious. Why wasn't she feasting upon the organs that filled the barrels all around her? Surely their sustenance and reparative powers would've helped her once again, if not made her suffering more bearable.

Imogene unfolded an old wooden camping stool and placed it at the edge of the platform. She tapped the fabric seat, gesturing for me to sit down. "You're gonna love this," she promised excitedly, as if I were about to watch some spectacular stage show.

But I was confused. I didn't see anything on the empty platform. And after sitting there for a few minutes, I became irritated. Then furious. *What the hell am I doing in this cellar with these demented girls!* "What is all this! What the hell is going on!" I shouted. "What have you done with Richard!"

And then, as if to appease me, I could've sworn I saw some movement, a slight aberration against the curtains of black. I squinted in the dim light. Faintly, it appeared as if a portion of the dark fabric was fighting to become its own entity, gaining an ability to peel itself away and become individual. Slowly, before my eyes, it took shape. And when it finally won its fight to separate, it stepped forward to the front of the platform. The thing that had materialized and stood before me caused my heart to pump nothing but pure dread through my veins. It was the cloaked, hooded phantom. I swore it had been vanquished the night

Norman severed his jugular. But there it was. Back to torment me in the twins' secret cellar.

I attempted to stand on my trembling legs. Yet the mere sight of the creature effectively held me paralyzed in my seat. It made a gesture to Imogene, who then swiftly rushed away. As I sat captivated, it unwrapped a section of the black material it wore, revealing a thin, pale arm. Imogene promptly returned with an empty mason jar and handed it to the entity. It held the jar in one hand. And with the other, it produced a sharp dagger. The dagger's hilt was silver. And its blade looked as if it had been made from a polished black stone. Without so much as a flinch, the hooded demon cut into its own wrist. Thick, dark blood flowed into the jar. And when the jar was about a third full, it wrapped its spurting wrists tightly once again.

With its feet planted at the edge of the platform, it then leaned forward at such a steep angle, it was unnatural. It should've toppled over onto the dirt floor. But it did not lose its balance. Instead, like some type of circus acrobat, it stretched the considerable distance forward in order to offer me the jar.

Despite my fear. And despite the fact I wasn't under any illusion I actually had a choice, I accepted the jar willingly. It was not Norman. It clearly had been *this* creature that had left me jars of blood in Tina's basement—and at the house in Shilling. And when it had offered me that jar of blood at the house in Shilling, I regretted not tasting it right then and there. Regretted not knowing just what information the blood offering could've revealed.

And after the twins had stolen the Shilling jar from me, it was no doubt the phantom that had returned it to me, gifting me the remainder of the blood along with my mother's necklace.

So at that moment I knew, for better or worse, I needed to drink it down. It was the blood of the phantom itself. It held its secrets. And it was offering them directly to me. Finally, I would know the truth.

I cupped the jar with both hands and began drinking briskly. The blood quickly overpowered me. Its flavor was dark. Strong. Earthy. And by the time I set down the jar, I found the flimsy chair did not offer me enough support. It could no longer hold me. Gravity weighed me down. My head felt heavy. My body went limp. I slipped to the floor. I felt like liquid as my body pooled next to Elizabeth's. It was the strangest sensation. I stared into her burned face—until it seemed like some type of fading hallucination, until right before my eyes, she became distant.

It was at that point words came into my head that were not my own. And then my voice suddenly became hijacked. Involuntarily, I began reciting the following words aloud: *"Blood gives insight. Organs give power. Blood gives insight. Organs give power. Blood gives insight. Organs give power."* The words came to me in a mantra. Automatic. Rote. As if I were being forced to repeat a phrase in order to learn a new language. The phantom had plugged itself into my consciousness. And those words were like the initiating sequence.

Abruptly, the words stopped. And next, my brain was injected with a slew of images. The flashes were too fast, as if someone were clicking through a slideshow at the speed of light, like watching an entire life flash by in a matter of seconds. It was too much for my brain to handle. Dizzyingly incomprehensible. I pressed my palms against my temples, desperate for it to stop. Yet over time, the images began to slow. They became more focused. Concentrated. Until I saw a single moving image. It was of a younger version of my father. His face was more vibrant than I had ever seen it. He was trim. And had more hair. He strolled casually through a small cemetery on a summer afternoon. It felt so real. I just knew if I would've reached out to him, he'd have felt my presence riding the wind.

And overlaying this vision, this memory of my father, was a voice. Only this time, it wasn't my own. Like the images that came before it, it too was multilayered and incomprehensible. But soon, it became a singular, pervasive voice that began to synch with the vision. It was the voice of an astute woman.

"I had set my sights on Dale Jacobs, you see, when I had learned he was investing in a funeral home. Don't ask me how I had received that information.

I sense things, is all. Always have. What you must understand about me is that I have a gift in that I'm attracted to exactly what I need. Not particularly what I want. What I need, mind you. He was a budding entrepreneur interested in the funeral industry. And funeral homes happened to be a special interest of mine.

"Why, I didn't know anything of his brother at the time. Anything at all. True, I didn't think much of Dale. But I thought even less of his brother, Clayton, when it was revealed to me that he was to be brought on board as partner."

The image switched to one of a young Uncle Clayton. He was ushering mourners into what had to be one of the first funerals at Grand Hallow, when it consisted of just a single viewing room.

"At the time, it was Dale still running the show. So naturally, it was he with whom I'd start a family. And oh my, was that a mistake! Of course, as always, my instincts had led me to the right place. It was just the wrong man. Dale, it turned out he was a quitter. And I could never stand a quitter. Couldn't get along with Clayton, he complained. Was disrespectful of his decisions, he moaned. My lord. The two of them. Infants! So he gave it all up. Turned his back on his brother—and Grand Hallow. Started that lousy fueling station and repair business. Well, that right there defeated my entire purpose for being with him. I simply had to get back to that funeral home. That mortuary. Those bodies. And the reason for that, my dear, I think you know."

I sensed the cloaked demon kneeling next to me. It stroked my hair, understanding what its blood was doing to me.

"Let's just say I have an appetite. Oh what a ferocious appetite! And that appetite subsequently led me into the arms of Dale's brother, the stupendously incompetent Clayton. Not the brightest businessman. I really had no choice but to take over operations. But it was all for the good. You see, it just allowed me easier access to as much as I could eat and drink. And I can eat and drink a lot. And so could my two young daughters."

I saw Elizabeth and Imogene, barely six years old, running through the morgue. Playing among the corpses on the slabs. Using their hands to scoop out mashed organs from cereal bowls.

"*But soon, I became a liability in my own enterprise. Missing corpses. Body mutilations. Oh it all became just too much. Rumors among the staff began to swirl. About me and my girls being the source of such—barbarism. Well, I couldn't have that. I needed to distance myself from it. Keep my hands clean. I needed a way out. A way to disappear into the shadows. Yet still control from the shadows. Protect our food source.*"

"Emerald Bridge," I whispered without requiring the aid of any visuals.

"*Yes, that's right,*" she surprisingly confirmed inside my head. "*Well, it was just too fantastic. I demanded Clayton fake the funeral. And we were free. All I had to do was procure someone else to process the most succulent and powerful morsels from the freshest corpses.*"

"Norman."

"*An overzealous creature, indeed, yet eager to follow orders.*"

I shuddered as I saw Norman's face up close, grinning wildly as he gutted a fresh corpse. He worked merrily pulling out its insides, creating some meaty concoction for the family he served.

"*It all went swimmingly—for a while. Yet over time, I realized it just wasn't practical for us. Hiding inside that insipid stone cottage of a house. Staff would see us on occasion, through the windows. Or the girls playing in the cemetery after dusk. I quite relished scaring them out of their wits. But it became a temptation of fate, you understand. So we left Grand Hallow.*"

"And that's when you began living in abandoned houses."

"*We were free again. But with freedom came complications. It required Norman to deliver our sustenance. It also meant we needed to stay transient. Oh, we had our luck in that abandoned mansion in Ruthsford for quite some time before that outrageous couple with the tart daughter moved in. It was a fine lifestyle. Only it was not sustainable. A certain bothersome sheriff with little else to do began tracking our movements. Well, it was all I could do to stay ahead of his incessant persecution.*

"*That's why I had chosen Henry as the head of grounds keeping. Once again, my keen insights led me to him along with the plan that would bring us back to our rightful home, Grand Hallow. You see, I cannot be successful without my minions. And he was the proper choice to perform the discreet renovation of this cellar. I quite prefer our quarters out here among the forest creatures, living underground. Here, I can go unseen. Remove my coverings and move about. You'll find I am most at home in dank atmospheres, commingling with the rest of the snakes. Sssssssssssss."*

I felt her hot breath next to my ear. And immediately, I jerked up, snapping out of her spell.

Chapter 35

Beautiful Weed

She towered over me. Even though I had just felt her presence next to me, when I opened my eyes, she was still standing at the edge of the platform. No longer feeling the need to hide, she removed her hood. The juxtaposition of her golden hair against the dark fabric was striking. And when she revealed her face, it stole my breath. Compared to the old photos I had seen of her, she hadn't aged. Yet she didn't look exactly the same either. Branching up from the base of her neck was a network of red and blue veins. They covered her face, protruding strikingly from her skin.

Out from the corner of her mouth leaked a stream of thick blood. Instantly, the sight brought forth the image of blood leaking from her mouth Richard had told me about just before he thought she had died. Well, she wasn't dead. And that blood he had seen all those years ago, it wasn't from some brain aneurysm either. What she possessed was an affliction far, far worse. Swiftly, she used her finger to roll the spillage back into her mouth.

There she was. In the flesh. The woman who had abandoned me. Made me feel unwanted. Unloved. Had betrayed our family. How I wanted my emotions to be put on ice! Numbed! But I found I couldn't control my response to seeing her alive. It was the moment I had fantasized about a million times, the moment I had never thought could've actually been possible. Tears began streaming down my face. "I thought—I was sure you were dead."

"She can't die, silly," piped up Imogene. "Not anymore."

She was alive. But my fantasy had been defiled, come to life as the nightmare that stood before me. "Did you kill my dad?" I asked at once with a lump in my throat.

"You mean, you couldn't taste it in his blood?" she asked in the same voice that had just been inside my head. "I left a sample for you in that tart's basement. Ah well, you merely require more practice to hone your skills is all. But the answer is no. I didn't kill him. Well, not precisely. Oh, it was under my orders, to be sure. But I grew quite tired of getting my hands dirty long before then. It was Norman, in fact, who killed your father—if that's really important for you to know. And yes, we took his meat. And yes, we drank his blood. There was no sense letting it go to waste, was there? There, now you have it. Pity party can be over," she said, dusting off her hands.

"The more important factor to consider is that you were merely incubating before that point, before I set you free. The only purpose you've had your whole life was to simply make it to this moment. It had to be done. There were important outcomes from that killing, you understand. It was time. You were soon to be eighteen. I needed to get you out of that town. Away from that silly fueling station. Such a colossal waste of your time. And of your talents. It was time for you to take your rightful place at Grand Hallow. Clayton's run as figurehead had come to an end. He was far beyond his prime as it was. Even that mutt knew it. Our use for him was over."

"So your plan was to have me in charge of Grand Hallow so I could oversee supplying blood and organs to your secret hideout in the forest?"

"And partake, my dear. Partake!" she grinned, displaying blood-stained teeth. "You have no idea the power you possess. It's a gift. A special gift that only women of our bloodline can arouse. With the right ingredients and the proper nutrition, there's no limit to your potential."

"I don't get it," I said, maddened. "If you really wanted me to take over Grand Hallow, then why, from the moment I arrived here, was I tormented by Elizabeth and Imogene!"

"Ha! Ha! Ha!" she cackled. "My beautiful snakes! Jealousy, my dear. Natural predatory behavior. Territorial. That's all that was. They're young. But even they figured out that the one who controls the food ultimately controls the power. It made sense in so many ways why that must be you. But persist they did. So naturally, I told them to have at it. See if they could overtake you. Outsmart you. Turn my minions against you. I thought, *what a wonderful test.* You were simply on trial, my dear."

She stepped down from the altar and cupped my chin with her cold hand. She looked into my eyes with her solid black pupils. "Do you know why I call you *dandelion?*" I shook my head as it was in her grip. "Because you're a beautiful weed that always seems to find a way to choke everything else out!" She released my chin in a snap and placed her hand on Elizabeth's burned head. "I warned them if they weren't up to the task, there would be consequences for challenging my authority. And here you are. You found your way to me. And as I had suspected, they did not succeed."

"*Consequences?* What consequences?"

"Why that's entirely up to you, my dear. Starvation. Bloodletting. Destroy them if you so desire." She took off the necklace that had been tucked inside her cloak. She held it before me. The amethyst twinkled in the candlelight. "This amulet belongs to you," she said. "That is, if you accept and embrace your place in our family."

I was frightened by the feelings her proposal triggered within me. Terrified because I knew they were raw. Honest. I couldn't hide myself from myself. My God! How could I have been so torn? After witnessing, experiencing the murder and carnage that plagued their existence? After she had crucified my own father in order to summon me before her? I hated myself for it. But this offer, as foul as it made me feel, tempted me even more.

The first pervasive thought that flooded my mind was: I wanted that amulet—badly. Yet beyond that immediate craving, I thought of the insight I had experienced. The power I had possessed. And not only did I want more, I wanted to feel that way—all the time. Was she right? Was what she offered truly my destiny? Was it time to accept what was inherently in my blood?

They were exciting, these desires that coursed through me. Yet they also sent chills down my spine. To gain access to this power, to gain a sense of family once more, would I be able to leave behind the parts of myself that made me—*me*? Or was there a way to embrace this *gift*, as my mother called it, without the wickedness? Why did one have to come with the other?

When she had infused herself into the world of Grand Hallow, she had already made the first step of procuring the source of her power, fresh organs, that was humane and devoid of killing. So why then was she still a killer? I believed I had found that answer in her blood.

My mother was a self-described opportunist. And she was a natural predator. What her blood told me was that she couldn't help herself. She couldn't change. In fact, she relished the malicious. The evolution to gutting fresh corpses for their potent sustenance did not mean that *she* had evolved away from her need to kill. No, she didn't make that transition to end the suffering she had caused others. It was merely a tactic to ensure her survival. In fact, it was the suffering she savored just as much as the power she drew from the organs upon which she savagely gorged herself.

"I just have one request," I said finally. She nodded, allowing me to proceed. "Tell me which of these barrels Richard is inside of."

Her lips curled into a playful grin while Imogene revealed, "He isn't in one of the barrels. He came to us—fresh!"

"Fresh?"

"He simply showed up at our door," my mother explained. "Quite a gift. I told you, I have a way of attracting exactly what I need. And before me he came." She stepped to the back of the platform and yanked down the rear curtain to reveal the fate of my brother. There he was. Strung from the ceiling. His torso had been hollowed out. He hung like a gutted deer carcass. Beneath him was an old bathtub to collect the spillage.

I tried to hide my visceral reaction, maintain my composure. But my face must've given away my anguish. "There, there," she said. "Don't be so gloomy. He could never have tapped into what we have. His life, it had no true meaning. Take solace in that. He wasn't, shall I say, *enlightened* enough to help our operations. Why I couldn't have even used him as a minion. And yet he knew too much. He was in fact simply—a liability. A *delicious* liability. Donating his virile organs was the best purpose he could ever have served."

"Thank you for letting me know what happened to him," I said solemnly. I then accepted the necklace and placed it around my neck.

"Superb," she exclaimed, clasping her hands. "Now, I'm rather curious to see what you have come up with for their punishment. What will you do with them?" she asked in devilish delight. I turned away from the shell that was once Richard and looked upon the twins.

Imogene sat next to her suffering sister. The twins, I was them. They were me—if I had been raised by Lynn Jacobs. They were detached from the real world. Had no concept of it. Under our mother's dark wing, how could they? They consumed the organs of those they had never met as if they were anonymous cattle. Their life of hiding, controlling, deceiving others was all they knew. Elizabeth, I sensed, had been completely indoctrinated. But Imogene, I felt that maybe—just maybe—there was a small part of her childish soul that could be salvaged. A small part of her that perhaps had remained human. So when my mother asked what I would do with the twins, I responded in a way I felt was most fitting. Yet I also knew she would not be pleased.

For Elizabeth, who was being starved of the regenerative nourishment she needed, I grabbed a jar off one of the shelves. I chose the one with the meatiest bits and placed it before her.

For Imogene, I simply took her hand. And then, I turned my back on my mother. As fast as I could, I began pulling Imogene behind me— toward the front of the cellar. My strength and speed was such that as I towed her toward the door, she lifted off the ground behind me like a loose scarf blowing in the wind. With David's organs and the amethyst resting firmly against my chest, I felt unstoppable.

I realized quickly, however, my feeling of invincibility was only an illusion. I sensed a monster waking over my shoulder. I had betrayed her. I could feel her rage, the heat from her bulging eyes on the back of my neck. And just as we were about to break through to the other side of the black curtain, she pulled us back with a force so violent, my soul separated from my body. I crashed beneath the shelves and was wedged between two barrels. My vision was blurred as I slowly oozed back into myself. And when I could finally make her out, standing over me, she eyed me with such intensity I suspected her glare alone might kill me.

I tried to sit up but felt a cold hand reach from behind and clamp onto my forehead. It forced my head back to the dirt floor. My eyes scanned to my right and then to my left. It wasn't Imogene holding me down. She had landed behind our mother, attempting to stand with a wobble. Nor was it Elizabeth, who remained at the base of the altar, struggling, too weak to even unscrew the lid off the jar I had offered her.

I couldn't see it, but another hand suddenly gripped my throat. An invisible arm wrapped around my waist. And the weight of a full body straddled my chest. Together, they worked like a boa constrictor, forcing the air from my lungs and crushing my windpipe. I grabbed hold of the cold and bony flesh as it squeezed the life out of me. But it was no use. The disembodied predator was too strong.

Pinned and incapacitated, I looked to my mother. She bared her clenched teeth like an angry dog. The veins on her face pulsated with anger. The invisible arms and torso belonged to her. She projected them onto me—to snuff me out, her most wayward and disobedient daughter. I deserved it, I supposed, for foolishly trying to usurp her authority in her own lair.

I began to fade. Tiny pinpricks of darkness started taking over my vision. And after all went black, I could feel myself slipping into the ether, floating weightless in a dark netherworld. And then. Only then. Just as I had been forced to the very edge, just before the very moment I wouldn't have been able to find my way back, did she release her grip.

Desperately, I gasped for air. And as the oxygen entered my lungs and circulated its way to my brain, the darkness began to reverse. It was slowly replaced once more with the vision of her sneering face. I couldn't believe it. She had actually given me mercy. It was then I realized I had just completed my first lesson. She had taught me, quite effectively, that it would be futile to ever cross her again.

I watched Imogene stumble forward. I wondered if she even had the chance to realize my life had been spared before she executed a move much bolder than the one I had attempted. It was most unexpected when, from behind, she reached into our mother's cloak and produced the black stone dagger. She swung the blade high over her head. And in a swift and punishing move, plunged it into the base of our mother's skull.

Stunned, she turned to lay her eyes upon the second daughter who dared betray her that night. Imogene cowered as our mother reached for her. This time, with her own arms. But before she could wrap her hands around her neck, she began to stagger backward. And as she stumbled toward the altar, she opened her mouth as wide as it would go. The sound that came out was unlike anything I had ever heard. It was a low moan coupled with what sounded like a howling winter wind.

Imogene rushed to my side. She helped me stand as we watched what happened to our mother in disbelief. Her lips turned black. Her golden hair fell out in clumps. And the tufts of hair that remained turned gray before our eyes. Her face aged and shriveled. And as her skin sagged, it caused the red and blue veins to cluster together and overlap across her face.

"We have to go. *Now*, silly," Imogene whispered gravely, clutching my hand. I could feel her trembling as she tugged on my arm. But I was transfixed by the true face of my mother. There she was. An angry, snarling, wicked mess.

With the strength she had left, she managed to reach behind her head and extract the blade. Her feet lifted from the ground as she raised the dagger above her head. And then, with her black eyes fixed upon us, she began to sail across the room. I wasn't sure who pulled whom as we held hands, racing for the door, the sound of her bone-chilling moan just over our shoulders. But Imogene and I flew through that front curtain and slipped with precision like a pair of barn swallows through the half-jammed door.

Chapter 36

Morning Light

We tumbled out of the cellar and onto the pine needle floor. I wouldn't let go of Imogene's hand as I commanded Ned, out of breath, to seal the door at once. The tractor was running. The boulder was set. He took his foot from the clutch, and the massive rock jerked forward. It teetered—just for a moment. And in that moment, I saw the ravaged face of my mother peering at us through the crack in the door. And then, the huge rock crashed into place. It rested against the ridge, sealing the entirety of the opening.

I collapsed back onto the soft pine needles. It was impossible to know just what was going through my mother's wicked mind in the brief look we had exchanged. It sure seemed as though she had been set on catching us, ripping us to shreds—but couldn't. Yet part of me couldn't help think that even in her weakened state, she had let us escape. After all, she was going to spare my life after I had tried to steal Imogene from her. So I had to wonder if she was perhaps simply curious to see just how far we'd take our convictions before she'd once again have to demonstrate the consequences of defying her authority. Yet even if it *was* some sort of test, I knew she wouldn't have allowed herself to be so restrained—had she known Ned was on the other side of that door about to release a giant boulder.

"That's not Richard!" Tina panicked, standing over us. "You were supposed to come out of there with Richard! What're you doing with *her?*"

I let go of Imogene and stood to give Tina a hearty hug. "I was so worried about you," I said. "I heard a gunshot."

"Yeah." She pointed nonchalantly with her thumb over her shoulder. "That guy. He tried to clock Ned with a freakin' garden rake. So I shot 'im."

"The courageous Miss Cashmere," commended Ned as he stepped down from the tractor. "She saved my life."

I looked to the body on the ground near the boulders. "Henry," I declared. "Head of grounds keeping. It's a good thing you shot him."

"So no Richard?"

"No," I sighed. "He's dead."

"Fuck. What happened in there?"

"C'mon," I motioned and then climbed the ridge. Tina and Ned followed. We huddled around one of the ventilation pipes. "Do you hear that?" I asked. It sounded as if a cyclone had been unleashed underground. The pipe carried to us the sounds of my mother flying about the cellar, scratching at the walls, breaking glass jars—all the while moaning and howling at the top of her lungs. "*That's* the evil we trapped inside."

"What about the evil you took *outside*?" Tina asked.

We stepped to the ridge and looked upon Imogene. She had stayed below and was staring catatonically at the massive boulder trapping her mother and sister inside. I felt a sense of satisfaction knowing that, because of me, she stood on our side of that rock. When I had grabbed her hand and led her away from our mother, I showed her she had a chance at freedom. It had to be the spark that led to her brutal rebellion.

In that moment, she understood she had the possibility of a different kind of life. And where I had failed attempting to stand up to our mother, she had succeeded. "I know it sounds crazy. But I think I can help her."

"So what? We're like gonna hang out with her now? What're you two gonna stop for lunch together every time you pass some roadkill?" Tina asked in a sarcastic huff, folding her arms.

"Maybe," I shot back. "But by the time I'm done with her, she'll be rescuing kittens stuck in trees instead of sticking blondes up in them." I could see the corner of Tina's lips begin to curl before she burst into a laugh.

Ned called from the far side of the mound. He had his ear up to the second pipe. "Ladies, this doesn't sound good. No, not at all. It's getting louder," he reported.

We rushed to join him. Sure enough, the caterwauling had reached a new level of intensity. "It's Elizabeth," I surmised as I listened to the overlapping wails. "She must've eaten."

"Oh! My! God!" shouted Tina. "I am so sick of this bullshit!" She fumed as she marched to the base of the mound. She rummaged through the forest floor for a moment before hiking her way back up, balancing several large rocks in her arms. Angrily, she crammed the rocks down the pipe. Following Tina's lead, Ned and I also began hauling up rocks. We worked as a team until we had completely jammed both pipes.

And when the cellar was finally sealed as tight as a tomb, silencing the devils below, we stood atop its roof, catching our breath as we looked out over the forest. The first rays of morning sun began to light the tall structures of Grand Hallow in the distance. "What're you gonna do now?" asked Tina. "Reopen the station?"

My finger caressed the amethyst stone that dangled from my neck as I watched a lone bluebird enter the clearing. It cocked its head as if listening curiously for my answer. "No," I announced. "Ned and I have a lot to do before we'll be able to get Grand Hallow up and running again at full capacity. Right, Ned?"

"Yes, Miss Lisa. There're still funerals to plan for those left in the coolers. And we will certainly have to hire some new staff."

"Well then. We'd better get to work."

Stephen Stromp is also the author of *Where the Cats Will Not Follow* and *Cracking Grace*.

Books primarily rely on word of mouth to find their way to readers. The best way to help spread the word about books like *In the Graveyard Antemortem* is to leave a brief review on your favorite review site, such as <u>Amazon</u>.

Connect with Stephen Stromp
Join Email List: <u>eepurl.com/caHNZT</u>